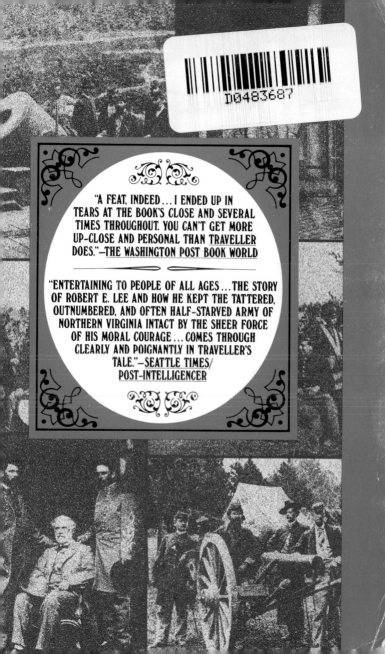

———————————————★———————————————

TRAVELLER
Richard Adams

———————————————★———————————————

ALSO BY RICHARD ADAMS

Watership Down
Shardik
The Plague Dogs
The Girl in a Swing
The Iron Wolf and Other Stories
Maia

TRAVEL
Voyage Through the Antarctic
(with R. M. Lockley)

PICTURE BOOKS IN VERSE
The Tyger Voyage
The Ship's Cat

NATURE
Nature Through the Seasons
Nature Day and Night
(both with Max Hooper)

Traveller

RICHARD ADAMS

A DELL BOOK

Published by
Dell Publishing
a division of
Bantam Doubleday Dell Publishing Group, Inc.
666 Fifth Avenue
New York, New York 10103

For information address Alfred A. Knopf, Inc., New York,
New York.

The trademark Dell ® is registered in the U.S. Patent and
Trademark Office.

ISBN: 0-440-20493-3

Reprinted by arrangement with Alfred A. Knopf, Inc.
Printed in the United States of America
Published simultaneously in Canada
December 1989

10 9 8 7 6 5 4 3 2 1

KRI

To my friends
Donald *and* Judy Lineback

πολλὰ δὲ πρόσθεν ξυγκαμών τε καὶ
ξυγκινδυνεύσας ᾿Αλεξάνδρω
ἀναβαινόμενός τε πρὸς μόνου
᾿Αλεξάνδρου, ὁ βουκεφάλας οὗτος ὅτι τους
ἄλλους πάντας ἀπηξιόυ ἀμβάτας καὶ
μεγέθει μέγας καὶ τῷ θυμῷ γενναῖος.
Arrian, *Anabasis*: V.xix

[This Bucephalus had, in the past, shared many a
hardship and many a danger with Alexander, and
had never been mounted by anyone else—for he
scorned all other riders; he was great in size and
noble in spirit.]

I dreamt last night that there was wind and rain.
I got up and looked out, but all was strange;
A muddy track across a wooded plain;
A distant tumult; angry cries, exchange
Of fire. And then, out of that dreadful night,
Appeared a scarecrow army, staggering,
Defiant, famished. In the quenched starlight
They marched on to their bitter reckoning.

Their sleepless, bloodshot eyes were turned to me.
Their flags hung black against the pelting sky.
Their jests and curses echoed whisperingly,
As though from long-lost years of sorrow— Why,
You're weeping! What, then? What more did
   you see?
A gray man on a gray horse rode by.

NOTES AND ACKNOWLEDGMENTS

Tom the Nipper and Baxter, the domestic cats of this story, were regarded as belonging to Mildred, Lee's youngest daughter, known in the family circle as "Life." Lee's son, Captain Robert E. Lee, Jr., in his *Recollections and Letters of General Robert E. Lee,* quotes a letter of the General to Mildred, dated December 21, 1866, in which he says, "Our feline companions are flourishing. Young Baxter . . . gives catlike evidence of future worth . . . and is strictly aristocratic in appearance and conduct. Tom, surnamed 'the Nipper,' from the manner in which he slaughters our enemies, the rats and the mice, is admired for his gravity and sobriety, as well as for his strict attention to the pursuits of his race." Captain Lee goes on to relate the story of the cat attracting attention by miaowing outside the house during a stormy night and then climbing up the crutch that the General held out of the window.

Traveller's evening chats with Tom Nipper are imagined as beginning in April, 1866, and continuing intermittently until October, 1870. In the story, most of these can be more or less dated from the daily events to which he refers. For example, we know that the mare Lucy Long was restored to the Lee ménage on December 21, 1866. Lee's riding holiday with Mildred, Traveller and Lucy Long (when the ferryman refused Lee's money) took place in late June, 1867; the whistling-back incident at the canal-boat landing happened in July of the same year, and so on.

Accounts of the injury to Lee's hands on August 31, 1862, vary in detail, but I have relied on that of

Colonel Walter H. Taylor, an eyewitness, in Chapter 8 of his *General Lee, 1861–1865.*

Anecdotes of Lee and Traveller are, of course, innumerable. The books I have most enjoyed are Douglas Southall Freeman's *R. E. Lee,* the above-mentioned book by Captain R. E. Lee, Jr., and Charles Bracelen Flood's *Lee: The Last Years.* Also of value are J. William Jones's *Personal Reminiscences,* Lee's own *Life and Letters* and Colonel A. L. Long's *Memoirs.*

In particular, I acknowledge with admiration and gratitude the invaluable instruction I have received from Lucy Rees's book *The Horse's Mind* and also from her personal advice on equine matters.

On Richmond's illness I had excellent guidance from Mr. G. H. Gilbert, M.R.C.V.S.

The authenticity of Traveller's Virginian idiom I owe almost entirely to Dr. Donald J. Lineback and to Dr. William L. Tazewell.

Friends who have given encouraging support and help include particularly my editor, Bob Gottlieb; and Barrett Clark, who found me scarce source books that I could not otherwise have obtained.

Finally, I am deeply grateful to my secretary, Mrs. Elizabeth Aydon, who not only typed the manuscript most accurately but corrected and checked it in detail with admirable perception and discernment.

PREFACE

by LUCY REES, author of *The Horse's Mind*

Robert E. Lee surrendered the Confederate Army of Northern Virginia to Ulysses S. Grant on April 9, 1865. On September 18th of that year, Lee, riding his horse Traveller, arrived in Lexington, Virginia, to take up the appointment of President of Washington College, which he had accepted at the invitation of the rector and trustees. From that time until Lee's death, in October, 1870, master and horse, living at Lexington, continued and, if anything, deepened the affectionate relationship they had developed during the war. Traveller died in June, 1871.

That the relationship between Lee and his horse was one of exceptional mutual trust and confidence is well documented. Lee himself wrote: "A poet . . . could . . . depict his worth and describe his endurance of toil, hunger, thirst, heat and cold, and the dangers and sufferings through which he passed. He could dilate upon his sagacity and affection and his invariable response to every wish of his rider. He might even imagine his thoughts through the long night-marches and days of battle through which he has passed."

What Traveller felt has not been chronicled before. How legitimate is the attempt to do so? Though his experiences were extraordinary and his stamina and intelligence well above average, Traveller must have shared the basic psychology common to all horses. His fears and pleasures, his eternal hopefulness, his striving to interpret events beyond his comprehension and his convinced misunderstandings will be as familiar as the smell of a horse to any rider. His peculiarly equine point of view, so accurately portrayed here, is as well supported by hard fact as the historical events that surrounded it.

What may not be so familiar is the complete faith that Traveller showed in Lee, and his ability, again well documented, to interpret Lee's slightest wishes without any apparent command or coercion. Traveller's descriptions of how it felt to him and of his lack of confidence in less sensitive hands are also deeply convincing.

I

Early spring, 1866. Lexington, Virginia: a small town in a rocky upland valley below the Blue Ridge Mountains. It is a lonely, remote place, difficult of access, the choice lying between a twenty-three-mile journey on a bad road from the railroad station at Goshen, and twelve hours by boat from Lynchburg along the James River and Kanawha Canal. A somewhat austere society—Presbyterian for the most part—its well-scrubbed, sober character reflected in the blue limestone streets running between red brick houses with stone facings, plain pillars and trim cedar hedges bordering brick-paved pathways. Although it is night now, the half-moonlight is enough to reveal the indigent and dilapidated appearance of the place—chipped paintwork, ill-pointed walls, sagging gates and broken fences. The town has no bank and hardly needs one. On the ridge above it rise the smashed and grimy walls of the Virginia Military Institute, raided by the Federals two years before.

The Washington College campus shares this general look of wear and tear. The violets are in bloom, certainly, and the leaves are already burgeoning on the trees—acacia, sweet maple, chestnut and sycamore. But there is an untended look to the lawns, the shrubs and the railings, suggesting not so much neglect as sheer shortage of money and hence of tools and human hands, black or white. The President's house, a handsome, two-storied building with sash windows and a flight of eight steps rising to a columned portico, is dark now—not a light showing—for the President encourages early nights and himself habitually goes to bed at ten. Here and there, a few students are crossing the campus on their way back to their rooms. Several look curiously mature for students; and so they are, being demobilized soldiers and, for lack of other clothes, still wearing patched and mended gray uniforms from which the insignia and badges of rank have been removed.

A black stableman, clapping his arms for warmth —for the air is somewhat chilly—makes his way across the yard behind the big house and, his day's chores done, enters his lamplit cabin and shuts the door for the night. A slim, quick-trotting young cat, intent upon rats, slinks along a wall and into the stable by way of a drain-hole. The stable is sound and snug —one of the best-repaired buildings on the place—and not a draft disturbs the straw-bedded stall where a powerful, nine-year-old gray gelding, of superb if veteran appearance, lies sleeping. He stirs.

The Blue men! The Blue men! They've got round behind us, they're in among those thick trees! The guns —the guns—I shall go mad! The ground's shaking! Run! Run! A horse that's afeared has to run, what else?

Pressure of Marse Robert's knees; steady hand smoothing my neck. "Easy, Traveller, easy! So, Colonel, what ought we to do?"

Horses plunging, screaming. That mare's been blowed to shreds. She ain't dead—she's squealing, struggling. "Steady, Traveller!" The smoke! I can't see! I can't see anything! Stand still! *Must* stand still! The Blue men are coming! No, it's the Yell! The Yell! Over there—in the trees! It's Cap-in-His-Eyes is coming!

Oh, I—my legs! This straw— Where am I? I'm in the stable! It was jest another of those dad-blamed dreams! No Blue men—not any more. No guns. I'm all a-sweat. I'd better stand up.

What's that? Who's that moving over there? Who are you? Oh, it's you, Tom Nipper, drat you! Come on out o' that there straw! Hunting rats? 'Say you're hunting rats on *my* 'count? Get along with you! It's on your own account. It's you that starts me on these durned dreams, comin' prowling in here jest when I've got to sleep, pushing up agin me in the straw 'cause you want to keep warm. That a rat you got there? Good fella! Well, I won't say you ain't a good cat. 'Fact, I heared Marse Robert say as much yesterday to your mistress. "That's a good cat you got there, Life," he said. "Makes a mighty good friend for Traveller, too."

Well, now, you settle down quiet. No, right there, where I can feel you. No more prowling around, giving me bad dreams. Tell me how you been getting along.

Yes, all right, I've heared that story 'bout you an' Marse Robert. Baxter told me. How you was miaowling round outside his bedroom in the rain, and he got up and opened the window, an' it was too high for you to jump in, so he held out one of the old lady's crutches and you climbed up it. Yeah, and he got wet doin' it, too. I'll say some of you cats have got 'nuff sass to jine the Texans! Fancy the likes of *you* getting Marse Robert out of bed and leaning out in the rain! And that Baxter! Hardly more'n a kitten, but 'fore long he'll be sassy as you. You're all the same: never been real hungry, never been on a march, never gone ary a mile in the dust, never smelt the smoke—never heared a gun, even.

Well, I guess it ain't your fault. Do you know, Tom, there was a time when *I'd* never heared a gun? Can you believe that? A time when I was a little foal, all head an' legs, alongside o' my dam? Well, and to begin with, I didn't even really know she *was* my dam.

The first thing I can remember—the first thing at all—
is pushing my nose into the dark shadow between her
legs, to get at the milk. All I knowed was I wanted the
milk, you see. But there was another mare in the field,
an' when I went and pushed up to her, 'course she
druv me off. That's how you larn who's your dam. To
begin with you jest want to push into the shadow
between anything up-an'-down. Why, I've even seed
a newborn foal push his nose into a deep crack in the
bark of a tree!

It was all milk and green grass in those days, and
larning to smell the difference between the kinds of
grasses an' plants there was to eat. We do jest about
hate anything bitter, you know, and soon as I started
grazing, I was larning to sniff out which was the bitter
plants and let 'em alone. I'd never have thought then
that there could be sech a thing as not getting 'nuff to
eat. 'Course, *you* don't eat grass, Tom, else you'd have a
long nose 'stead of a flat 'un. A horse can poke his
nose into the grass, you see, and still keep looking all
round at the same time. No horse is happy when he
can't see what's around him. You cats can trap a smell
up your nose and hold it, though, can't you, good as
any horse? I seed you opening your mouth and wrin-
kling up your face when you've smelt some strange
cat's piss along the fence out there.

'Course, it warn't long 'fore I had to larn some
manners in dealing with older horses. That was a big
field, where I was raised. In those days I thought it was
the whole world, with the split-rail fence all round it,
the shed at the top of the slope and the oak trees an'
the big pond down the bottom. There was a plenty of
horses there besides me and my dam—a good many of
'em born and raised there, like me. When you're a foal,
you've got to larn to respect your elders and behave
right. You've seed that puppy roll over in front of the
old dogs, haven't you? Well, when you're a foal you

don't roll over; you drop your ears an' stretch out your neck, and then you have to sort of draw back your lips and show your teeth while the older horse sniffs at you. Yeah, but as you grow up you soon stop that. I'd finished mouthing at older horses—oh, after my first year, I guess.

Of course, Tom, we grow up fast, you know. Faster'n a cat can imagine, I'm sure of that. You was a blind kitten, warn't you, crawling about for days in a basket? Why, the same day we're born we can stand up and walk, and follow along with our dams. Then there's the flies, of course. Don't take you long to larn to use your tail on them fellas. I've always wondered why there had to be flies in the world, but the way I figure it now, it's the Blue men turn into flies—you know, when they've finished bein' Blue men. Must be, 'cause there's always too many of 'em. Your first day, you start nibbling the grass; nibble a bit o' dung, too—that's important, else your stomach can't work, you know.

You cats don't really make friends, do you? I've noticed: most other cats—you jest can't see 'em off fast 'nuff. Now horses—horses *need* friends. Who's going to keep the flies off your face and out of your ears? Who's going to get your tangles out and clean you up? And you gotta do the same for him, 'course. Who's going to keep a lookout behind while you've got your head down, grazing? There was plenty of other foals in that big field, and as I began to stray away from my dam I soon got to racing and playing and pushing around. I had a few tussles—nothin' bad, though. But I soon larned where I stood, an' it was mighty high up. I could tell that much, jest from the way the men kind of seemed to be weighing me up while they was leaning over them rails and looking us over.

Back in those days we-all did jest about nothing all day. If only I'd 'a knowed! If only I'd 'a knowed!

Grazing, and jest loafing around. Standing head-to-tail with a friend, swishing the durned flies, stretching, yawning, scratching. I had a friend called Ruffian. Sorrel, he was. And years later, that night in the mud—that night in the mud when Marse Robert—well, never mind 'bout that for now. What else do I remember?

I remember the woods along the top end of the field, how the leaves came out in the spring, dogwood and redbud; and over the fence, in the wood, there'd be little white lilies; and down in the pond there was a pink, fluffy kind of a flower used to grow in clumps in the shallow water. I tried eating it once, but it warn't no use. That's how you find things out—try everything. 'Quisitive, Tom. A good foal's got to be 'quisitive. Why, I can remember a young filly—Moonlight, her name was—no older'n me, actually teaching herself to drink. Wouldn't never think you had to larn *that*, would you? First she stuck her nose right in deep an' ended up spluttering a noseful. Then she tried nibbling the water, as if it was grass. 'Took her—oh, a day or two—to larn to drop her ears and pull her nostrils back, the proper way.

We used to larn most things by playing, of course, same as you cats do. Sure, I've seed you and young Baxter playing around in the yard, jumping on the leaves and chasing each other an' all the rest of it. First of all I used to play with my dam—Flora, she was called—nibbling her tail, bumping her around. She took it all easy—well, she knowed I'd soon be off to play with the other foals, kicking around, pulling faces and swishing tails. You've gotta larn to get on with other horses, else you end up worse'n Richmond. Well, I ain't told you 'bout Richmond, Tom, have I? I will, sometime.

It was all through playing that I larned not to be afraid of men. 'Course, the men fed us in the cold weather, and combed us down, and took the older horses out to ride and all that. Men need horses same's they need dogs and cats. Without horses they couldn't get around. Without dogs they couldn't have cows or sheep, and I guess they'd all be robbing each other, too, with no dogs to bark for 'em. Without you cats the rats'd have every durned thing—oats, bran—the lot.

How did we play, did you say? My golly, I never realized then—well, 'course I didn't—the luck it was for me to be raised and trained the way I was! Since then I've seed that many young horses beaten and ill-treated—spirits broken, tempers spoiled—all on 'count o' what some men call training. They figure they've got to show the horse who's master—whips, spurs, hard words—until he's been driven jest about mad. And then they'll turn around an' say he's natcherly vicious! The Army—the Army was full of it; Marse Robert hisself was forever telling men not to whip their horses. But once a horse has been spoiled it's jest about too late, you see. There's no listening no more, no signals, no watching out either way.

Jim coming to play—well, I don't recollect 'zackly when he started, but I s'pose it might have been the summer after I was born—that or the next; I don't rightly recall. I know it was after they cut me between the legs, but I don't remember much about that neither; not after all this time. I can recall being throwed and held down. That was bad, and it hurt some, but anyhow it healed up quick.

The men used to lean over the fence, chatting an' lazing around, easy; they'd chew tobacco an' watch us foals playing together. The way I figure it now, they was sizing up a whole lot that way: which of us was timid, which was lazy, or 'quisitive, or heading to turn out steady—all that sort o' thing. 'Course, in them days it never crossed my mind.

I remember, one day, there was six or seven of us herded off into another big field next to the one we'd growed up in. There we was, all larking around, high-tailing, playing follow-the-leader, bumping each other and all the rest of it—having a high old time. An' then all of a sudden there was this young fella—Jim, they called him—I came to know later he was the boss's son —he jest came right on into the field an' sat hisself down on a log. I was kinda leery; I was wondering what he reckoned to do, but he never did nothing at all—not all the afternoon. He jest sat there, an' 'bout sunset he went off again. Next day it was the same; and the next. Sometimes he was sitting a-chewing to-bacco, and sometimes he was jest whittling away at a stick with his knife, or tossing bits of bread to the sparrows an' the juncos. 'Seemed to have jest about as much time for doing nothing as a horse.

In the end I got kinda 'quisitive 'bout him—you know, wondering why he was there. So I quit playing with the others and wandered over to him. He never took no notice. Finally I went right up to him and smelt him over. He never moved: jest raised one of his arms, after a bit, real slow, and began stroking me. He treated me like another horse would—you know, scratching my back, sniffing his nose along my mane an' all the rest—'ceptin' he was talking all the time, kinda quiet an' friendly—I could tell from the sound of his voice. He scratched my rump, too, and that's something all foals like a lot.

"Jeff," he kept saying. "Howdy, Jeff. Good boy, Jeff." He cut some apples up into pieces an' I ate them out of the flat of his hand. They was sweet—the sweetest things I'd ever tasted; they was real good. After that, whenever he came into the field I nearly always used to come up to him straightaway. But if I didn't, he jest sat down anyway. After a while I'd stand still and let him pick up my hind feet, run his fingers through my tail—anything. Sometimes he'd take his hat to the flies, flip them out of my eyes. 'Didn't seem to startle me none, the way he did it.

What about the play, you asked, Tom. Gosh sakes, that young Jim fella, it really used to tickle me, the games we got up to! I jest never knowed what we'd be doin' next. We'd get up to all sorts of tricks; like, he'd walk along in front and I'd come along behind him with a loose rope round my neck. One day we was taking a walk down the lane when all of a sudden this dad-burn rabbit run right acrost under my nose! I rar'd back an' jerked my head away. I would've run, too, but Jim jest stood there and kept talking quiet. "Jest a rabbit, Jeff. No call to be scairt of an old rabbit. Easy—easy—" All that sort o' thing, you know.

He never let the two of us get dull. It was always something new. Would you believe it, one day he brung along an old banjo and played it to me? First time I'd ever heared one, o' course. Heared plenty since. The soldiers—well, never mind that for now. Another day he laid down a big white sheet of cloth and called me to walk over it to get my apple. I warn't scared! 'Nother time it was six poles laid across pegs in the ground; he'd call me over to him and I had to be careful 'bout not knocking none of 'em off. Tricky, that was. Made me feel real clever. 'Nother day he came down to the field with a basket and put the handle in my mouth, for me to carry. We walked up to the big house, me still carrying that durned basket. There was a woman working in the yard. "Here's my Jeff, ma'am," says Jim. "He's brung back your basket." She laughed fit to bust. "You rascal!" she says to me, and then she give me a piece of sugar.

One time, though, when I was feeling a bit short-tempered with the flies, I turned my head and nipped Jim's shoulder—yeah, hard, too. He was on to me sharp as thorns! He cussed me out something terrible!

He spoke to me real angry, and then he jest walked away, like he didn't want to have no more to do with a horse like that. I felt bad. I never wanted to hear him speak to me like that again. I gave over nipping right then. That was all he did—it was all he had to do. Since then I've often seed horses whipped for less.

Well, Tom, I guess you won't want to be hearing 'bout lunges and bits and saddles and harness and all the rest of it. What's sech things to a cat? But you're a friend, all the same. You're company: I like company. A horse needs company. That young Jim, he was real good company. I can see now that's what he was aiming at. He wanted to make me feel like a smart horse, and he wanted to make me like going along with him and feel we was a-working together. And I did, too. 'Took him a long time; but bless you, what's time to a horse? In the end, when he rode me out in the lanes I really used to enjoy myself. You wouldn't understand —no cat would—but I used to feel prop'ly interested in whatever we was doing—*included in*, you might say. I felt I was doing what a horse ought to be doing.

Sharp tonight, 'tain't it? Touch of frost outside, you reckon? Aw, you don't know what cold is. Now when the Blue men crossed the river on their boat-bridges and we was stood a-waiting for 'em in the snow—now *that* was cold! 'Fore you was born, Tom; but never mind. We're warm, plenty to eat. And never a gun—never again. Think about that! Nothing but friends all round. Tell you what let's do. Let's go to sleep.

II

DURN IT, Tom, now the spring's coming on, the dad-blamed mice seem to be getting worse and worse. 'Tain't your fault, though, an' it ain't Baxter's. Without you I wouldn't get an hour's sleep. I 'spect the varmints'd be chewin' my hooves off. 'Spoil twice as much as they steal, too. Well, now you've got yourselves here—right cats, right time, right place—I'll keep quiet while you jest go on and carry out orders at discretion.

That's a good hour's work. Quite a pile, Colonel. Damn' Blue mice, I guess: real mean. 'Reckon you can rest a while. Why don't you jump up here in the manger and settle down in the hay? What's that? My breath makes you feel wet? All right, I'll breathe the other way.

Spring's a good time, ain't it? I was out grazing on the lawn this morning. Marse Robert, he was jest as busy as ever. Well, of course a commander's bound to be busier than most. Like our old stallion in the big field when I was a foal. His name was Monarch an' he sure was one. He looked after us young 'uns jest about like a sheepdog. All the same, when it came to someone having their own way, he'd give in to the mares nearly every time. Yeah, he'd be real obliging with them. Like he felt he didn't have to be the boss—jest the one who sort of kept us up together. Monarch used to play with the colts an' even the young foals, so all us young 'uns got to know him well. These days, when I go through the town with Marse Robert and he reins in and talks to anyone, even the kids, it always puts me in mind of old Monarch.

I really enjoy grazing alongside Marse Robert when he's working in the garden. And he sure has done a mighty lot o' work since we come here in the fall! He's laid out that there vegetable garden, paved the paths, planted the fruit trees—why, I've even seed him knocking in nails—setting this here stable to rights with his own hands! I figure he likes working like that, jest the same as he enjoys our riding out together in the afternoons. He enjoys playing that he's not the commander at all. Well, sometimes I like playing I'm jest an ordinary old horse. I often get to feeling that if someone pulls one more hair outa my tail 'cause I'm Traveller, I'll kick him from here to the canal. Marse Robert wouldn't like that, though. You gotta act grand: kinda quiet, like you know jest who you are. Why, the other day the town folks was going to take that there horse thief out of jail an' string him up, or so I heared. Marse Robert wouldn't let them, though. He jest put a stop to it in his quiet way. 'Didn't see it myself, but that's what the jailer's horse in town was telling me a day or two back, when we was hitched together outside the courthouse.

'Course, it's only now and then Marse Robert has time for digging an' hammering nails and all that. He's too busy talking—giving orders, running the country and seeing after all them young fellas. Not that they're all of them that young. Some of 'em I can remember when they was soldiers in the Army. Why, there was one came into the garden only yesterday, with a pile of books and papers under his arm, began talking to Marse Robert. I 'member him plain as plain from when the Army was crossing that big river up north.

He was one of Jine-the-Cavalry's fellas. A horse can often recall a man from where he's seed him, Tom, you know—same as you'd 'member someone from what they'd given you to eat, I reckon.

Well, I got some of that myself this morning, too. People—they're always bringing Marse Robert presents, you know. Not surprising, I s'pose—a country's commander is the commander, after all, and a champion's a champion—with horses, anyway. He gets the best, I know that much, even though I don't understand the most of what Marse Robert has to do since we stopped killing Blue men. He was planting a fruit bush and jest throwing me a few words every now and then, the way he does, when up the path comes this old lady carrying a bowl with a cloth over, and says him howdy. 'Course, Marse Robert's always mighty agreeable to ladies—jest like old Monarch was with the mares—and he puts down his spade and rubs the dirt off his hands, and they gets to smiling and talking away. And what it come down to was, she'd brung him a honeycomb.

Marse Robert thanks her as if she'd brung him a passel of Blue prisoners and their guns. "And of course Traveller must have a piece," he says then. "Traveller mustn't go without a piece." And with that he outs with his knife and slices off a lump as big as his thumb and holds it out to me. I licked his hand clean. Not that I was s'prised, of course. There's the two of us, you see. Always has been. But I'll jest remember that old lady if I see her again.

What I was telling you the other night, about the big field and Jim and the games we used to get up to—that set me to thinking. After Jim figured he was as good as through training me, the bossman, Andy—that was Jim's father—he used to take me out and ride me hisself lots of times. After Jim, Andy felt very quiet and steady. I liked Jim 'cause he was a lot of fun and 'cause I could feel it kind of roused him up when we was out together. 'Made me feel daring. Andy—well, he didn't make you feel that way—not feisty, like Jim did. He made you feel quiet-like—like being out of the wind in the lee of a shed. Other horses felt it, too. Andy made a horse feel safe and protected, like he was kind of guiding him—escorting him. You could feel all that experience seeping out of him like sweat. I liked the smell of him. I liked his hands and I liked his voice. 'Course, horses get to feel a whole lot about their riders, Tom. You see, that's why a horse—a no-fool horse—often behaves differently with one rider from what he does with another. If the man has slow, calm movements, it kind of makes the horse calm, you see. If the man's a bit frisky in his ways, it often makes the horse frisky; and if a man's afeared, it makes his horse afeared. But usually—ain't it queer?—the men don't realize nothing about that. Leastways, I've always figured they don't. It never seems to strike them that it's the way *they* are that makes the horse act the way *he* does. I've always been a bit nervous, myself—sort of jumpy and lively, you might say—and if I hadn't fetched up with Marse Robert, as understands everything, 'sakes only knows what might've become of me. The way I figure it now, I growed up that way 'cause Jim was that way hisself—sort of like wind in the grass, you might say.

It was Andy and Jim, both of them together, took me and some other horses to the big fair in town. Right up till then, that was the scariest thing I'd ever knowed. 'Hadn't 'a been for old Andy, 'reckon I'd 'a run away. The bits of bright-colored trash lying about everywhere, you wondered what they were—the crowds of people, the shouting and the noise—there was a band of music playing. 'Course, you ain't never heared a band, Tom, have you? Neither had I then—

the smell of so many strange horses—some of them
real sassy, too—and the smells of tromped grass and
smoke and strange animals, like—well, pigs, for instance, that I'd never smelt before. I've often thought,
you know, that it's funny horses take to men and
want to go along with 'em, 'cause all the things men
want horses to do, horses by nature mostly want to do
jest the opposite. A horse natcherly don't want nothing on his back. And he don't want nothing moving
about behind him where he can't see it. When anything startles him, the first thing he wants to do is to
run away. He don't like anything interfering with his
feet. He don't want to be shut up inside nowhere—not
even out of the rain or the snow. I was lucky, 'cause
Andy and young Jim, you see, they knowed all that,
and brung me up according. Since then, I've seed men
who reckon they're horsemen and seem to think 'bout
nothing 'cept spoiling a horse's nature.

When you first go to a place like this here fair,
with all the crowds and noise and strangers, you feel
jest like a length of wire strung tight between two
posts. I 'member, at one of these here gates on the way
in, I went rigid, and there was a big man behind, leading another horse, and he started cussing. Andy turned
round and cussed back, and 'course that made me
worse'n ever. I nearly pulled my halter off. Still, Andy
calmed me down and in the end we got to where we
was s'posed to be.

I don't remember all that well jest what we was
s'posed to do—not after all this time. But seems as
how I must 'a done something good at that there fair,
though I'll be whupped if I know what 'twas. Anyway, I finally had to be led out in front of all the folks,
and some boss fella stuck colored ribbons on me, and
Andy and Jim, they got some sort of ribbons, too. I'll
tell you what I do remember. You know I told you how

Jim was always up for games and funning? Well, after all this ribboning and messing around, he got up on my back again. There was a big kind of place all made of gray cloth and ropes and pegs—that was jest how it seemed to me at the time, you know. 'Course, it was a tent, and a big one; since then I seed as many as there's leaves on a tree, though not that big. And there was all these fellas going in and out, glasses in their hands, and all bawling and singing. I looked at it an' I could smell that smell—bottles and glasses—made me jumpy—I was pawing about—the smell seemed to get into my feet—but Jim, he jest dug in his heels and clicks his tongue and all these fellas crowding in, and he says, "Go on, Jeff, go on," and—would you believe it?—I went right on inside that tent—all the smell and the boots and the crushed grass—and then everything went kinda quiet, 'cause they was all a-staring. And Jim reined me in by this long table with the white cloth on it and speaks to this fella behind it, who gave him a glass; and I jest stood there, reins slack on my neck and this tromped grass under my hooves. In the end, I dropped my head and sniffed it for a nibble, but it warn't no good—tromped foul, you see. And Jim, he jest sat there on my back in all the tobacco smoke, drinking up his glass; and then we walked out again. Old Andy was outside, an' he was real mad. "You gone crazy?" he says to Jim. "Never in the world, sir," says Jim, jest keeping me still, and me pawing my forehooves about a little. We was teasing, Tom, you see. "I knowed he was a good horse, sir," he says. "I jest wanted to know he trusted me 'nuff to do anything I asked him."

I don't mind telling you, I was real glad to get out o' that fair. Jim rode me home, two hours by moonlight. It was lucky Andy's mare, Ruby, knowed the way, 'cause I figure she was the only one that did, that night. The men were sure 'nuff happy 'bout whatever we'd done. They warn't none too particular where we was going.

Durn it, I 'spect I've got a shoe coming loose! Hear that clink? Tom? Hear that clink? Oh! Now would you ever? They've both gone sound asleep in the hay!

III

I WAS right 'bout that shoe, Tom. 'Didn't take Marse Robert two shakes of a blue fly's tail to spot it. He was 'way off the other side o' the lawn, talking to some young fella, when all of a sudden he stops and stands looking at me, and I could tell he was waiting to see me move again. Then he whistled, the way he does when he wants me to come, and soon as I was standing right beside him, he picks up my hooves and looks at 'em one by one. Then he strokes my neck and scratches my ears. "You and me's going to the blacksmith, Traveller," he says. "Right this afternoon, too. But you can take it easy, 'cause I'll stay right with you till he's done."

Oh, I do hate that there blacksmith's! Mind you, the smith—Mr. Senseney, they call him—he's a good 'nuff fella; good at his job. But it's the fire, and the way they blow it up, kind o' roaring, and then all the hammering; and 'course it's indoors, not much light, and people coming behind you where you can't see. It's too much like the guns, and being back in those dad-burn woods at night with the Blue men around. I was hopping about, and Mr. Senseney, I reckon he mighta said a whole piece only for Marse Robert being there, holding my bridle. He was talking to Mr. Senseney, and I figure he was telling him to be patient on account of I was nervous after all the guns and the fighting. Anyway, it's finished now.

'Smell my hooves, Tom, can you, where they been singed? What's that? You wouldn't like to have hooves? Couldn't wash with 'em? Well, I guess they warn't meant for washing. Not for scratching, neither. Horses have got the lightest, strongest feet of any animal in the world, so old Monarch told me once't. Stand up to anything, go for miles. "You jest look after your hooves," he said, "and they'll look after you." Never knowed a horse yet that warn't extra careful to look after his feet. Anything that threatens a horse's feet threatens his life, 'cause the horse that can't run's a dead 'un. I don't like putting my feet down on anything I can't see it's straight-up. I don't like streams, I don't like marsh, I don't like them pontoon boat-bridges rocking round and booming under my feet; I don't like treading on anything that might crumble or move. What's that you say? A big animal like me, jest thinking how he can run away? A cat can climb a tree, Tom. A cat can scratch, too. We can't.

I was telling you, warn't I, 'bout the fair and 'bout how Jim rode me into the drinking tent? It was nearly next spring after we got home from the fair that all the horses round the place—pretty well all—began to smell that things was somehow changing. There was something exciting the men—getting 'em roused up, like stallions get. They didn't fight, though. In fact, they seemed to be getting on better'n usual. Whatever 'twas, it was exciting them morning, noon and night. I believe us horses could tell it better'n they could theirselves. They smelt different, and they kind of acted different; they talked different, they walked about different. There was a sorta unrest all over the place, and they all talked and shouted more'n usual. 'Nother thing we noticed, they all seemed to have taken to shotguns. 'Course, I'd heared guns round the place be-

fore, now and then—fella shooting a rabbit, maybe, or
a quail—and I warn't afraid of a gun going off at a
distance, though sometimes it'd make me startle and
gallop round a bit. But now there seemed to be guns
out all the time, and the men kept taking 'em to pieces
and cleaning 'em and showing 'em to each other and
talking 'bout 'em.

I 'member one mornin' I'd been out—Andy was
riding me—and we was coming back up the lane and
into the big yard in front of the house. Before we ever
got in the gate, I could see the yard was full of people.
The men was all standing in a knot and most of the
women had come out of the house, too; and some of
the black folks, they was stood over to one side. There
was a quiet-looking sort of a horse—a cob—between
the shafts of an open cart. He was a stranger. I'd never
seed him before. He was hitched by the reins to the
rails, and there was a man—quite an old man—in gray
clothes and a white shirt, smelling very clean, all soap
and no sweat—standing up on the back of this here
cart and hollering away at our people. They *liked* him
—you could tell that—even though he was talking as
if he was real mad. He kept waving his arms, and now
and then he'd shout an' go *thump! bang!* with his fist on
the cart. And every so often, when he stopped as if
he'd asked them something, our folks started in cheering and shouting "Yes! Yes! By golly we will!" and all
sech things as that—much as I could understand, anyways.

At first I thought he must have brung something
to sell—we used to get folks like that sometimes—
what they call peddlers, you know, Tom—and I figured old Andy'd soon be sending him 'bout his business pretty sharp. But he didn't. No, he got down off
my back and hitched me to the rails right 'longside
this horse of the stranger's, and then he jest stood and
listened like the rest.

I tried to make out from this old horse in the shafts what it was all about. Apparently he'd brung the man from town, and it seemed they'd been going quite a ways round the country, him talking like this everywhere they fetched up.

"He's telling them to fight," says this horse.

"Fight?" I said. "Fight who?"

"I'll be durned if I know," says the horse. "But that's the way I reckon it. They've all got to go somewhere or other to fight, that's what he keeps saying. But what beats me is, 'parently they all *want* to. You can tell they want to, can't you? Jest look at 'em. They're all right in 'greement with him."

After a while the man got through speechifying, and they all cheered even louder, and Andy and Jim and the ladies took him off with them into the big house. The way they was acting, they was going to treat him real sociable. The men was talking, too, among theirselves. I could understand some of it—mostly by the way they was behaving more'n anything else.

"Durn it!" says one. "I'm going!" Another man was kind of dancing 'bout the yard, singing "*Jine* up! *Jine* up!" and slapping the others on their backs. After a time they told one of the black fellas to lead me away and unsaddle me, so I never seed what happened when the old town man left.

Soon after that, there commenced a kind of a bustle 'bout the place. It was like when we was going off to the fair the summer before, only this time a whole lot more was going on. First off, a lot of our horses was sold—more'n I'd ever seed go at one time before. Usually, horses was sold in ones or twos, often to fellas who came regular. I'd got to know some of them by sight.

But nows all sorts of strangers seemed to be coming from all over, and they warn't particular 'bout the horses they bought, neither. They didn't lean on the rails and take their time and talk and then try three or four horses and maybe go up to the house with Andy and Jim. No, none o' that. They seemed in a hurry. They'd buy a horse, any horse, 'fore they was all gone. My friend Ruffian went among the first lot. He'd growed up good-looking an' easygoing, and a fella who'd come in a buggy with his wife and a young lad —his son, I s'pose—bought him in no time at all. They'd brung a harness with 'em, and the young lad saddled Ruffian up right away and rode him off down the lane behind the buggy. *He* had a gun with him, too —he had it slung acrost his back. Another man wanted to buy Flora, my dam, but Andy wouldn't sell her. I s'pose he figured she was too valuable—wanted to keep her for breeding. Before the redbud was out that spring, we was down to fewer horses and mares on the place than I'd ever knowed.

"You'll be going now for sure, Jeff," old Monarch used to say to me every time another stranger came. "You're young—fourth summer, ain't you?—and one of the best geldings on the place. You're sure to go."

"Go where?" I asked.

"To this here War," he answered. "That's where they're all a-going."

"Where is the War?" I said. "I never heared tell of it. What kind of a place is it?"

"Well, I don't jest rightly know," said Monarch, "but by all I can make out, it's some place they're all set on going to, so it must be real good." What the town cob told me had got around, you see.

"Is it far to the War?" I asked.

"I don't know," said Monarch again, "and I don't even know if it's a town or a farm or what, but it's a special place they're all crazy to go to, and they need horses to go there."

I felt excited. I couldn't wait to be off to this here

War, wherever it was. It was the restlessness and activity in the air round the whole place: all the coming and going, and the strangers, and the feeling of everything being different—something you couldn't smell or see that had changed everything and was more important than anything else. I felt life'd gotten dull in the field and the stable. I had a stable by then, you see, and I often used to feel bored in there—lack of company. One time I even got to biting my crib for something to do, 'cause nowadays Jim seemed busy from morning till night—too busy to play with me. I figured wherever this here War was, where they was all going, it'd be a whole lot different there. Better'n one day same's another and Jim an' Andy having no time to ride me.

What made everything still duller was that as summer wore on, the weather turned real nasty—no kind of weather at all. It rained near 'bout every day—morning to night, very often—and there was too much wind. That kind of thing interferes with a horse's way of life, you see, Tom. To stay in good condition we need to eat pretty steady, but you can't settle down to grazing if it keeps raining and blowing on and off all the time. You want to get out of the wind, and if you let yourself get wet through, you start shivering with cold. Sometimes there was thunder with it—building up, you know, close and oppressive—made me jumpy and restless. I recollect one day, when I was in my stable, Jim came in to look me over and see how I was getting on, and while he was stroking me an' talking to me, my back jest started to crackle and spark, you'd 'a thought 'twas a fire in the grass.

It was a few days after that when still another young stranger came riding in, looking to buy a horse. Weather was fine for once't, and old Monarch and me and one or two others was out in the field next to the stables. This young man was riding a young brown mare. I liked the look of her. She was excited with coming to a strange place, full of strange horses; you could see that from the way she was acting—pricked-up ears, arched neck and her tail up high. Andy and Jim had come out, real respectful, to meet the young fella, and as he dismounted and hitched her up she let out a nice, friendly sort of neigh to us. I warn't far off, so I answered her and jest strolled over to make acquaintance. She was groomed real pretty, her coat jest shining, and anyone could tell she was used to being understood by her man and being prop'ly ridden. She was wearing a new saddle, girth and stirrups, all real smart and smellin' of saddle soap.

The young man was smart, too. He was about the same age and build as Jim, and I 'member thinking they looked like the same tree, one in summer and one in winter. Jim, you see, he used to wear a high-crowned hat with a big brim and a colored band round; and he'd have a red-and-blue handkerchief loose round his neck and a bright-colored shirt. This other fella had a low gray cap with a peak in front, and all his clothes was gray, too, with shiny yellow buttons—metal, they was. His belt and boots was shiny, too—as smart as the mare's tack.

'Course, I know now that I was looking at a gray soldier—one of *our* soldiers—no different from thousands I was going to see later, 'ceptin' he looked so smart. But I'd never seed ary a soldier then, gray or blue, and that morning he seemed strange.

There was nothing strange about his ways, though. You could tell at once that he knowed horses almost like Jim and Andy did. As I came up to put my nose agin his mare's and have a chat with her, he showed right away that he liked the looks of me.

"That sure looks a good 'un," he says to Andy, and he began stroking my nose and talking to me. I could tell from his mare, as much as from him, that he was all right. Andy answered something about me not jest suiting everybody, but that I was one of the good 'uns he'd kept back for men who'd know how to use 'em right. And then Jim said, "D'you want to try him, Captain Broun?" So they saddled me up and this Captain Broun rode me round the field and up the lane a piece.

Now, you know, Tom, it's not everyone likes riding me, as I've come to larn over the years. It takes a durned good man to ride me, and I've no use for any other sort. I've got a lot of go in me, and I jest can't abide hanging around. I *will* walk, mind you, if a man really wants it and insists, but I always keep it fast and springy. What I really like, though, is a sort of a short, high trot—what they call a buck-trot—and that always seems to go hard on a rider unless he's got a real good seat. Why, I've kept up that kind of a trot for thirty mile or more before now, and jest *refused* to walk. I've always reckoned a good horse has to put a proper value on hisself, or no one else will.

Well, this Captain Broun, I trotted him up and down quite a ways, and then Andy took Monarch out with us for a few miles. After a while, though, I lit out —left 'em behind, and came back to meet them when Captain Broun turned me around. I'd put a lot of energy into that ride, 'cause the way I figured it, if I *was* going to this War place, wherever it was, I didn't want to go with a man who couldn't live up to me and go along with me doing things *my* way. But this Captain Broun, pretty soon I could tell that though he warn't nothing like the top-notchers Andy and Jim was, all the same he liked an energetic horse and he liked my style.

"He'll be good," he said to Andy, patting my neck as we walked over the field and back to his own mare. (She'd been let graze, but she came up to him of her own accord—a good sign, I figured.) "What's his name?"

"Jeff Davis," says Andy, grinning.

"Then I guess he's *got* to be a winner," says Captain Broun, laughing back. He got off, took my bridle, stroked my nose and blowed into it.

"Howdy, Jeff!" he says. "I'm Joe. Joe, see?" He talked to me some more—real friendly—and then one of the black folks, a groom called Zeb, took me away to unsaddle.

"He's bought you right 'nuff," says Monarch later on, when we was side by side in our stalls and Zeb was cleaning the mud off us.

"How do y'know that?" I asked.

"I know the way they go 'bout it," he said. "They sort of spit, and clap their hands, and then there's some small, round, shining thing, and sometimes they stand and drink right where they are. Yeah, you'll be off—and, Jeff, I must say I'll be sorry to see you go. As good a four-year-old as ever I 'member to have seed. You'll do well—'long as you stay in the right hands. 'Dare say you're heading for a nice, safe, peaceful life, same as I've had."

After that I was jest waiting for this Joe to come in and take me away. 'Fact, I was waiting all day, but he didn't come. He didn't come the next day neither, and when we went out of stables I could tell the mare was gone. I s'posed he'd come back, or maybe send a black fella to collect me, but as the days went by and nothing happened it jest slipped my mind and I went on loafing around as usual—as best I could for the rain, that is.

'Bout then Jim disappeared right off the place altogether. 'Course, he'd been gone before sometimes, a day or two here, a day or two there—buying and selling, I guess; but now he was gone the way we began to wonder if he was ever coming back. This bothered me 'cause, as I've told you, he'd been there all my life and I'd always thought of him as my man. 'Long as he was round, I could stand for him to be too busy to have time to play with me, but to have him real gone was jest to know how close, really, we'd always been. Made me fret—same as I'd fretted after Ruffian went. Zeb understood all right. "Aw, Jeff," he says one day when he was rubbing me down. "Horses is like black folks—ain't got no say-so. Forever sayin' good-bye. But Marse Jim, he comin' back—he comin' back sure."

I didn't feel so sure. What men say to horses is mostly jest what they reckon they'd like, you know, or what they can't say to anyone else. Even Marse Robert's no different there.

And then, one wet afternoon in the first of the fall, Jim *did* come back! I was in my stable; I heared his voice outside and I started to whinnying and stamping all I could. He opened the half-door, he was laughing up a storm, and he came striding in and slapped me on the withers. Then he gave me half an apple and began making a real fuss 'bout me.

"Hi, there, Jeff!" he keeps saying. "You ready? 'Cause you're off, boy, you're off to the War!"

What I hadn't reckoned on was he'd turned his-self into a soldier, like Captain Joe. All his clothes was that same kinda gray, butternut color, and they didn't smell like any clothes I was used to. It made me sniff over his jacket and his sleeve. 'Course, he jest stood and laughed, all friendly-like. 'Twas the same old Jim —he made me sure 'nuff of that, playing some of our old tricks, making me stand still while he shouted "Boo!" in my ear, and all that. He'd brung me a new horse blanket, too, real smart, and he started in then and there trying it, folding it and getting it comfort-able on my back. Then he give me a bit of an extra grooming hisself, and all the time he was jest quietly singing away between his teeth, "War-war-war, War-war-war."

Now during these days while I was standing round the stable and waiting, Tom, I'd come to have quite an idea in my own head of what this here War place was gonna be like. First off, it must be a mighty fine place, a whole lot finer'n where we was living now. That stood to reason—why else would the men be so all-fired hankering to go there? I kinda visioned it as a real big house o' red bricks—I'd seed one or two when we was coming and going to the fairs, you know —and it was going to have a big stone doorway in the middle and stone steps going up from the lawn out front. Green shutters on the windows. Tall chimneys. A nice, friendly touch of wood smoke in the air, trees round 'bout the house, and all the leaves red in the fall, maple and beech and sechlike. Fine evenings, the black folks'd be singing and dancing bit of a ways off, back o' the big house—near the stables, maybe, where I could hear 'em for company, evenings. The sun'd shine and the grass in the big meadows'd be jest right. Trees to scratch on, good spots for horses to dung in their proper ways—'cause that's important to us, Tom, you know; stallions, mares, geldings, we've all got our ways and places and got to do it right. Hay and oats. Warm in winter, not too hot in summer but plenty of shade when 'twas. Breezes at dawn and dusk so's you're a bit lively and playful. I could believe 'most anything 'bout it, but I jest couldn't believe there'd be no flies; that'd be asking altogether too much, but maybe they'd be fewer. 'Course, the men and the horses'd be the best of company. I knowed I was a good horse, and they must be picking the good horses to go to the War.

'Bout Jim an' Joe, I jest couldn't figure it out. Would they both be there? Maybe Joe would take Andy's place, 'cause Andy warn't going. I knowed that. All summer I'd noticed that only young fellas went; the ones left now was the older men, an' black folks like Zeb. Well, at the War they'd have their own black folks, o' course, born and raised there.

Next morning, Jim and me was off, all in the rain: first yellow leaves blowing down from the trees, wind tugging at the long grass in the big field and the rain-drops dripping steady off the fence rails. Jest about everyone came out to see us go. I felt real proud. I arched my neck, tossed my head, held my tail up and nuzzled Andy's shoulder. What I couldn't really make a guess at was whether it would be far to the War—a short road or a long 'un. I still don't know the answer to that, Tom, 'cause o' course, as I'm gonna tell you, we never got there. We never did.

IV

BEEN RIDING out to that there Rockbridge today, Tom, to see the old lady. Marse Robert brung her right up to me, too, in that rolling chair of her'n, and she stroked my nose and talked to me a piece. Too bad she can't walk. She's been at Rockbridge a while now, you know, and we ride over pretty reg'lar.

It's real nice in summer—'bout 'leven mile of road an' plenty of shade, sun through the leaves, creek winding in and out through the rocks down below. Maybe stop for a mouthful of grass now and then. Lotsa hills, too, and that's what I like. Y'see, me and Marse Robert, we don't need all that much in the way of signals from me and orders from him. I don't think 'bout him on my back no more'n I think 'bout the shoes on my feet. He's jest natcherly there and he don't aim to go holding me in. I can't abide holding in; I'm a big horse—big man, big horse—I mean big in our spirits, Tom; an' if I ain't ridden hard I get real fretful, like a dog chained in a barrel—'ceptin' I don't howl none. When we get to a hill, I aim to have what Marse Robert calls a breather—we jest light out and go galloping hard up them long hills. 'Makes you feel real good to beat 'em—feel 'em falling away under your hooves, trees going by, dust a-kicking up. S'afternoon, when we was galloping lickety-split, we overtook two

fellas riding along, easy-like, gentlemen who live here
and help Marse Robert with his commanding. So he
pulls me up and gives a howdy to 'em. "I thought a
little run would be good for Traveller," he says. One
of their horses blows out of his nose at me,
"Hrrrrmph," friendly-like, 'much as to say "A little
run, hunh?" I'd like to see *him* try a full gallop up that
there hill. Guess he'd soon be hollering 'nuff.

Early fall, 1861. A bleak, rolling, precipitous wilderness, disclosing itself in glimpses between drifting rain
clouds, stretching northward into an infinity of mist
and wooded solitude: the Allegheny Mountains of
western Virginia. Between the cliffs and chasms, the
desolate uplands are covered not only with virgin forest but also, in many places, with thick undergrowths
of laurel, so dense and interlocked as to be almost im-
penetrable. These are now heavy with water, millions
of gallons of rain held in suspension among the
branches and foliage, so that anyone trying to push
through even a few yards is instantly soaked to the
skin. Daily, for weeks past, it has rained; it is still
raining. The more open uplands are quagmires in
which advancing men sink suddenly to their knees,
cursing and calling for help. Every small creek cours-
ing down these westward-facing slopes has covered its
rocks, burst its banks. Many are impassable; turbid
brown torrents, chattering and growling. From time to
time the bleak wind, which stirs but never disperses
the low clouds, creeps lower to swirl the mists hanging
in the chasms, veiling and half-revealing the sheer
drops, intensifying their naturally sinister aspect.

In this fastness, a terrain where any kind of coor-
dinated movement has become virtually impossible,
where both motion and immobility are alike misery,
where the few dirt tracks are morasses and a man
without a compass can become lost and disoriented
within minutes, two tiny armies—each numbering
fewer than ten thousand—are engaged upon an almost

mutual sequence of blunders, dissensions and suffering that for want of a better term must still be called a campaign. It is to neither's advantage to move. The side attempting an attack will be defeated; or else, not improbably, never succeed in reaching the enemy at all, as has already happened at Cheat Mountain, in the wilds between Monterey and Huttonsville.

This place of torment is made of rain. Men breathe the rain, sleep in it, are soaked in it, die in it. Tentless and shelterless, the young farmhands, counter clerks and smallholders' sons who comprise the disjointed Confederate forces opposed to Cox and Rosecrans stand, sit or lie shivering in the chill air, their original fervor of enlistment leaking away through sodden, rotting boots. A large proportion have gone sick with scurvy, dysentery, pneumonia. A plague of measles has swept through the camps.

The local people evince no friendliness. The army might as well be in enemy country. Their doings, their every movement are reported to the Federals. General Garnett has been killed in action. Generals Floyd and Wise have been on bad terms, refusing to cooperate with each other, though both have been equally resentful of the command of General Robert E. Lee, appointed by President Davis to reconcile their differences and reorganize the army—such as it is. General Wise has been relieved of his command.

As the approach of winter makes itself daily more evident, General Lee, who has with difficulty withdrawn southward from Cheat Mountain down the Greenbrier valley, has all he can do even to get food through to the soldiers and horses. The enemy, on Great Sewell Mountain, are in sight, but upon them, as upon the Southerners, the mountains and the weather have clamped an immobility like that of a dream. Troops and horses live only from day to day, drenched, suffering, irresolute and down at heart.

Well, like I was telling you, Tom, we come along in the rain: quite a piece, and past that there town

where I went to the fair. I seed plenty of chaps in gray
clothes like Jim's: one bunch was all marching along
together in the rain, and every one of 'em carrying
guns. Some of 'em called out and waved as we went
by, and Jim waved back. Raining? It was raining like a
cow pissing on a flat rock!

Well, o' course, I didn't know where in heck we
was going, nor how far. But pretty soon after that, we
turned onto a dirt road and started up into the mountains. You better believe it, Tom, when I tell you that
I'd never seed anything like that sort of country before. I wondered where on earth we'd come to—yeah,
and where we'd be finishing up, too. Made me real
jumpy—I was startling at jest about everything. It was
all strange. A lot of the time there was trees all round,
close together, and the red and yellow fall leaves still
on 'em so thick you couldn't see more'n a few yards
any which way. They warn't big old trees like the ones
back home by the pond, neither. They was little, thin,
spindly things, all a-crowding close to each other—
what they call a mountain wilderness. The track was
like bran mash, too, an' deep, so's I was going in over
my fetlocks and afraid for my hooves every time one
of 'em turned on a rock I couldn't see. And on top o'
that, time and again a gray soldier would step out suddenly from the trees, asking who we was or had Jim
got any tobacco or sechlike. I went along 'cause I
trusted Jim. And even at that I was fidgeting; I
wouldn't have done it for no other rider. It was a
durned sight worse'n the drink tent at the fair, 'cause
the men—all of 'em—was in a bad mood—troubled
with a feeling of jitters and gloominess.

Evening time, we fetched up somewheres we was
'parently s'posed to be. But there was no house, no
fields, no stables, no black folks around—jest a nasty,
wet clearing in them hills, a patch no different from
any other. There was a whole passel of gray soldiers,

all looking 'bout as cheerful as treed coons. They was keeping fires going—best as they could in the rain—and trying to get dry. They all looked mighty down in the mouth—thin, pinched faces, lot of 'em shivering and fixing to be sick, so I figured. And my ears! Didn't the whole place smell bad? I'd smelt nary place like that, not in my whole life.

They had a few horses—not many; jest tethered among the trees. They was half-starved—ribs showing, most of 'em. I nickered to 'em, but hardly a one nickered back. They was all feeling too lowdown. Well, I thought, I b'lieve I'm jest going to take agin this place, more'n any place I ever seed. I jest hope we'll light out tomorrow and get to the War.

Jim, he got off my back an' spoke very respectful to some man who seemed to be the boss. This man stroked my nose and I could tell he was praising me, but then he shook his head and said something to Jim 'bout how they was in a bad way and there was precious little for the horses to eat; he'd have to make out best he could.

All the same, Jim did manage to find me some hay, and some oats, too. Goodness only knows how he did it—'cepting I've larned since then that a good soldier's like a good cat: he's gotta be a good thief, too. You should jest 'a knowed General Red Shirt's Sergeant Tucker, Tom. Still, never mind 'bout him for now. All through those next days, like I say, somehow or other Jim always found some way to keep me fed. Even if it warn't 'nuff, I didn't never starve. He kept me well groomed, too, and he slept right 'longside o' me, so no one could steal my blanket.

But we didn't keep on. I couldn't make it out. We moved about in them dad-burn mountains until I got to knowing miles of the place and hating it more an' more every day. 'Fact, I'd jest as soon stop thinking 'bout it. I'll jest tell you one thing, Tom, that I recall;

one thing. It was early afternoon, and Jim and me was floundering along one of them mashed mountain roads, when we met a double team of horses hitched up to a cart that hadn't no more on it but a load of hay. And the axles of that there wagon was scraping and leveling the bed of the road; it was hub-deep in mud, and the poor devils of horses was heaving away at it step by step. 'Course, they was bogged down, too. I've never forgot it.

Jim and me used to get around lots. The way I see it now, looking back, I was the best horse in that outfit and the only one that warn't next thing to exhausted, so they figured to use me and Jim for taking messages and keeping in touch with the other outfits, and so on. This here warn't a horse outfit, you see—not cavalry. They was foot soldiers, and they jest had a few horses with 'em. 'Course, I didn't know none of that then. Now I'm what they call a veteran, I've larned a whole lot more 'bout armies. All I knowed then was that I was hungry and a long ways from home and it was a mighty bad place.

Now one morning me an' Jim, we was out in the rain, riding up a right steep stretch of mountain in the open. Jim had let me have my head and I was cracking on the pace—much as you could on that sorta ground —when we seed a little group of riders coming towards us, going t'other way. We'd have had to pass them, but before it come to that Jim reined me in, pulled me over into the bushes one side and waited, very polite, to let them have the best of it. There was only two-three of them, but it was this one man I noticed particular.

He noticed me, too. He reined in his horse and came up to us where we was stood. And that's right where he found hisself in a peck o' trouble, on account of this horse of his had what you might call strong peculiarities. For a start, he didn't like me—I knowed that at once. He'd put on a stiff neck, a long nose and a real tight mouth, and his ears was laid back as though he'd be at me if he could. And then all of a sudden he let out a squeal; and he would have reared, too, only his man—who evidently knowed what he was like—was holding him in real firm. He pulled away, but the man pulled him back and spoke to him and got him quiet. Watching him, I got a notion that this man knowed everything about horses, and I wondered what the heck he could be doing with sech a troublesome one.

Anyways, he got off, and give the horse to one of his mates, who led it off a ways, and at this Jim got off, too, stood up straight and touched his hat real smart. "Good morning, my man," says the other fella. "Good morning, General," answers Jim. "That's a fine horse you got there," says the General. "Where's he from?" "Blue Sulphur Springs in Greenbrier, sir," answers Jim.

Well, then the two of 'em got to talking, a whole lot more'n I could understand, and while they was at it I natcherly took a look at this stranger and set in to sizing him up. First off, he was an old man, older'n any other soldier I'd seed yet. I figured he was older'n Andy back home. He didn't have no beard—no, Tom, not then he didn't—jest a gray mustache. He was very quiet and sure of hisself, as if he was used to being the boss, but used to people liking him, too. Evidently he didn't aim to go shouting or finding fault, or making trouble for ordinary fellas like Jim. I found myself liking his style.

He was dressed in gray, like all the other soldiers, and he was wearing a big black hat with a broad brim to it. After a while he took my bridle and began talking to me.

Now during this time on the mountain, I'd got pretty well used to strangers doing that. I was a horse

folks noticed, you see. Mostly I jest waited till they'd
finished. But this man was different. I don't rightly
know jest how to put it, but it seemed like he *was* a
horse hisself. I felt he understood me through and
through, and knowed everything I had to tell him. He
knowed I was homesick and bewildered, and strung-
up with being in a strange place and not knowing
what the heck was s'posed to be happening on this
durned mountain. He knowed I got along well with
Jim and he knowed I didn't like his own horse. He was
as good as telling me *he* didn't like him neither—figured he was a troublesome fella. I thought, I wish *I*
was his horse; I'd do for him better'n that pest over
there. And jest as I'd got to thinking that way, he nodded to Jim, put his foot in the stirrup, mounted me and
off we went along the track.

   We hadn't gone twenty yards 'fore all the uneasiness was gone out of me. I hadn't even realized, till
then, how tight-up I'd been all along, ever since we'd
come to that there mountain. How could you relax
and respond to your rider when you was wet through
an' hungry all the time, in a strange place where the
ground was a bog and you had no idea what was going
to happen next? But this man on my back, he *knowed*
all this, and he was as good as telling me to take it
easy, 'cause he had everything in hand. I understood
then that he must be the boss of the whole place.
Whatever we was doing there, he was the one setting
it up.

   Every signal from me, this man seemed to understand it. Jest the feel of his hands and the tone of his
voice made you want to give him your best. I began to
feel kind of—well, merry and alert—I'd forgotten
what it felt like—and I broke into my buck-trot. The
man liked this—I could feel he did. Somehow or other,
I was cheering him up. Poor fella, I thought, he hasn't

ridden a decent horse for months, and he's sure been missing it. I'll show him!

We didn't gallop, though. Soon's I lit out, he turned me back. But the way he did it, it was like he was apologizing. "I know you'd like to gallop," his hands and knees was saying. "I'd like it, too, only right now we don't have the time. But it's sure been a pleasure meeting you."

We came back to the others. He hadn't changed jest that morning for me; he'd changed my life, even if I never seed him again. I hadn't knowed there could be a horseman like that—a horseman who knowed what you was feeling nigh on 'fore you felt it yourself. Sure, Jim was a good horseman, but this man—well, like I said, he was a horse who'd somehow been turned into a man. Leastways, he spoke horse language. You remember, Tom, I told you how when Andy first rode me I could feel his reliability and experience? Well, what was pouring out of this man, jest like water into a trough, was fellow-feeling for me and for every animal in the world. Come to think of it, now that I'm telling you 'bout that first meeting of ours, maybe I don't really blame you so much for that business of miaowling in the rain and climbing up the crutch. Jest come natcherl, I 'spect.

Well, the General got off my back, patted my neck and gave me a heap of praise.

"Good horse, General?" says the black-haired young man who's holding his own for him.

"Yes, indeed," says the General, and then he turned to Jim an' talked some more. The way I figured it, he was asking Jim whether he could have me for his own horse, and of course Jim was saying no he couldn't, though it was all very friendly. But then I thought—best as I could understand it—Jim was saying maybe he could fix it up. I lost track of the talk;

but somehow, as the General and his 'uns rode away, I got a hunch I hadn't seed the last of him. He didn't know it—Jim didn't know it—but I *did*.

The next day I got another surprise. Jim rode me right down through the woods to a camp of soldiers where we'd never been before. This was a horse outfit —any number of horses—but that warn't the surprise. The surprise was that the first man I seed was Captain Joe, the soldier who'd come to the meadow back home and tried me out. So that was it! He *had* bought me, and now the time had come for Jim to turn me over to Joe.

'Fore he went away, Jim more or less cried on my neck. He went off without looking back, like he couldn't bear to. I never seed him again from that day to this. Like Zeb said, horses are forever parting. At the time, though, I didn't feel it like I should have, because Captain Joe began making sech a fuss over me. I was hungry as could be, and first thing off he gave me a real good feed—'bout the best I'd had since we come to the mountain. After that he jest natcherly couldn't resist showing me off to a whole passel of his friends. I spent that night on the picket lines with the other horses. It was nice to be back in a crowd of company again, even though every durned horse was wishing he was somewheres else. I remember there was a mare called Daffodil, an' she told me she'd been up and down this mountain country for somethin' like five months and felt ready to lie down and die on it.

During the rest of the time we spent on the mountain, I was ridden every day, sometimes by Captain Joe and sometimes by another fella—his brother, I reckon, 'cause they was so much alike in their ways, as well as to smell and to look at. But although they was a couple of real nice fellas, and looked after me best as they could in that place and that weather, somehow I jest couldn't settle down with 'em in the kind of way that ought to be between a horse and his master. It was partly the hard conditions, of course, and partly jest wanting to be back home, but the real thing was that every time a bunch of us horses was rode out to have a look round the mountain—which seemed to be our job—we'd often as not meet the General riding around. Even if he seed us some ways off, and we wouldn't natcherly have met, he'd still ride acrost to speak to Joe—or to his brother—whichever one was a-riding me.

"Ah, there's my colt," he'd say, keeping his own horse up tight. "How's my colt making out?"

"Oh, jest fine, General, sir," they'd answer. "Best horse in the Army, that's for sure."

One day the General rode me again—not far; half a mile, maybe—and this time it left me with the feeling that I'd never be really happy again, on account of I didn't belong to him. Well, when you've had a taste —even if it's only a taste—of what's perfect, it's hard, ain't it, to settle for anything less? I jest had to keep telling myself that I mustn't go a-pining an' getting a lot of ideas 'bove my way of life. The General had jest taken a fancy to me for a while, and that was all there was to it.

Only, somehow, it didn't altogether feel that way. I mean, it didn't feel like it was a passing notion to him, any more'n it was to me. For one thing, his own horse was so terrible. His name was Richmond, and the best I can say for Richmond is that sometime or other he must have been treated real bad. He hated most other horses, and any time there was other horses round he was liable to set up this dad-blamed squealing. Goodness knows why. It was enough to throw everyone into confusion, and yet the General never beat him, never cussed at him—jest kept on bringing him firmly to order. I hated to be near Richmond. He warn't fit to be a bossman's horse. Plain truth was, he did the General no credit. People liable to start thinking, Well, what you a General for and you can't get yourself a better horse'n that? Maybe you ain't a very good General, neither.

He had another horse, called Brown-Roan. Brown-Roan was better. But bless you, he'd no real spirit! Poor fella, he hadn't any courage in him—anyone could tell that. He was fit to do what he was told, but that was about all he was fit for. You see, Tom, a real horse ain't there jest to do what he's told. A real horse has got to be *part* of his man—to *want* to be part of his man. Once't they begin to fit together 'zackly, the man ought to be free to forget 'bout managing the horse all the time and get on with whatever he has to do. The horse jest *knows* what the man wants. There's hundreds of little ways a horse can tell. And there's hundreds of ways the man can tell 'bout the horse, too, without really taking his mind off of what else he's doing. But it's got to be the right man and the right horse.

Now the General knowed all that, and he knowed I was the right horse and Brown-Roan warn't. Only Brown-Roan *didn't* know it, you see, because he'd never larned more'n half of what there is to know, and he reckoned it was all there was.

What it come down to was that the General would have liked me for his own, and by the time we was done on that mountain he'd made that pretty plain. For one thing, he never used my name. "How's my colt?" he used to say. "Nasty weather for the horses. Ain't got no saddle sores, I hope? Do you figure, Captain, maybe that girth might be a little tight?" And so on. And one day he said, "Look after my colt, because I'm going to need him later on."

Durned cat's gone to sleep again. Can't blame

him. 'Don't mean no harm. How much can you 'spect a cat to understand, anyways? Take a rest in your dry straw, old soldier, you've seed many worse nights. Leastways, I know when I'm well off.

V

Tom, do you figure I've got the mumps? Do you happen to know what the mumps might be? Well, neither do I, 'ceptin' I guess it must be some kind of a sickness. I ain't aiming to go sick, and I don't reckon it's likely, not if I didn't go sick with being three years and more in the Army. I'm s'prised Marse Robert would even let the idea come into his head.

No, Tom, he cert'nly *did* let it come into his head. It was this way. S'afternoon we started out on our ride as usual, and we was jest heading out of town along one of the quiet back streets, when we come up with two little girls was riding up and down on an old horse —jest passing the time, you know. I've seed them round afore now—and the horse, too. They belong to one of them fellas that helps Marse Robert with his commanding the country and speechifying and all the rest of it. Marse Robert pulls me up and offs with his hat to these little girls, and then he said if they liked to come 'long with us, he'd show 'em a real fine ride.

'Course, they was both as pleased as two foals loose in a meadow. I'll be starved if I was, though. I'd been reckoning the two of us was all set to light out on one of our twenty-milers in the country. 'Stead, here's me dawdling 'longside this old nag—his name's Frisky; can you beat that?—like a couple of baggage-train mules with double loads on. I guess I must have showed how I felt, 'cause after a bit this old Frisky sort o' huffles to me, " 'Tain't my fault, Mr. Traveller, sir." 'Course, I treated him friendly; Marse Robert wouldn't 'spect anything else. But I couldn't help wondering what folks was going to think—me an' this poor old Frisky keeping company together in town, where there was plenty of other horses round to see us.

Anyways, I jest kept myself in step with Frisky best as I could, and we-all went out of town beyond the fairground. Well, it's real fine out that way, Tom, you know; the whole outlook kind of opens up towards the mountains. And of course the little girls was delighted—jest about set 'em up for the afternoon. Marse Robert and me rode around with 'em a goodish while. One of them had her face all tied up in a cloth, and Marse Robert says to her, "I hope you won't give Traveller the mumps. Whatever shall we do if Traveller gets the mumps?" 'Fore we was done, we took 'em home. Coming through town, I felt I jest had to put the best face on it I could, so I stepped out the same as if we was reviewing a big parade. When we got to their home, Marse Robert, he lifted 'em both down and kissed them good-bye. "Oh, General Lee," they said, "we'll never forget this afternoon!" Me neither, Tom, me neither. And I still don't know what the mumps are, 'cepting I ain't got 'em.

But I was telling you, warn't I, 'bout that mountain in the rain? We quit at the end of the fall, and a good job, too, 'fore every man and beast died of the weather. I know now, 'course, that we was s'posed to be looking for Blue men, but I never seed none all the time we was there, and in them days I shouldn't have knowed 'em if I had. I 'spect they was afraid to try attacking us and we didn't figure on attacking them, on account of it was nigh on to impossible for horse or man to move in the wet.

Somehow I never really settled down with Joe and his brother. They was good 'nuff masters and looked after me very well, but it warn't like me and Jim had been—no real fun, no games. I still felt homesick. And I don't think Joe's brother, the major, ever really 'preciated my buck-trot. It seems to come awful hard to some riders, and he hadn't been the one who tried me out and bought me. But there was another thing on top o' that. I couldn't get the recollection of the General out of my mind—the feel of his hands and knees. Whenever either of the brothers rode me, I always used to find myself thinking, I've knowed better'n this; I jest wish that there General would come back. The weather was bad, too, where we was—the winter'd come on, you see—and all of us horses spent a lot of time in stables. I felt all bottled up, and once't or twice't I found myself biting my crib again, out of sheer boredom. Some of the other horses was the same. There was one called Bandit, I remember, who got to weaving. That's when a horse stands with his legs apart, you know, Tom, and keeps shifting his weight from side to side. 'May do that for hours. That sort of thing's catching, too. One horse gets to doing it and then the others take it up.

Another thing I didn't like was that Joe changed my name. My name was Jeff; Jim had always called me Jeff. That's a nice, sharp-sounding name a horse can recognize, and I liked it. But Captain Joe, he took to calling me "Greenbrier." I jest couldn't answer to it the same way. I was still homesick for Jim and the big field at home, and when Joe called me Greenbrier, I used to think, Durn it, they've even taken away my name! All the same, I could have been a sight worse off. I know that now.

Anyway, it didn't last long. We was soon off again, and this was the first time I'd ever been on a railroad. You'll never see a railroad, Tom, and I don't figure I can give you much idea of it. Horses and men —all of 'em—have to get into sort of stables on iron wheels, like big carts with roofs on, and then these carts go 'long on their own. It's all done with noise and smoke and shaking about, but it's a nasty, dirty smoke, not like the wood smoke here. The shaking makes you afeared of losing your feet and falling, and the smell in itself's 'nuff to upset a horse. The whole thing's scary—all the rumblin' and banging, and then maybe the whole shebang stops suddenly and pitches you one way or t'other. One horse gets to panicking and then maybe it spreads. I don't like railroads, but you can get used to 'em, like everything else.

We went a long way on this railroad—hundreds of miles, I figure. It was only jest Captain Joe had come —not his brother. It must have taken quite a while— longer'n I thought—because when we fin'lly got off, 'twarn't winter. It was real warm and the air smelt beautiful—all green leaves and flowers. There was 'nother smell, too—something I'd never smelt before: a salty, muddy kind of a smell, like a lot of salty water. And a day or two later, when Joe and some of his men took us out along the country a piece, I seed that was 'zackly what it was. All along to one side of us there was this water in among the land: great fields of water, all moving up an' down, and smelling of salt and mud. And even the air, too, seemed to be sort of watery—all soft and thick. Slowed you down an' made it harder to breathe.

That was the strangest country I've ever seed. When we went out on them cavalry rides, as they call 'em, we was forever working along the banks o' creeks and picking our way acrost soft ground, marshes and mud, and every now and then we'd come out and see this great field of salt water rocking up and down. There was flowers everywhere—big, colored flowers with strong, sweet smells. The roses was bigger and smelt stronger'n any I'd ever seed back home, and there was lots of long, climbing plants, some of them with bright red fruit growing on them. Joe gave me some to eat; they was good—redder and softer'n apples, but tasting different.

And then one day, while we was riding nice and easy along the bank of a big river, we came round the corner of a grove of live oaks and there, not fifty yards ahead, was the General. He warn't riding Richmond; he was riding Brown-Roan, and seemed like he was looking around him, kinda getting to know the place. Soon as he seed him, Joe pushed his heels into my sides and clicked his tongue, and we went straight acrost. Joe saluted. When the General seed who 'twas, he smiled.

"Ah!" he said. "There's my colt! So you've brung my colt, Captain Broun, have you?"

I think I knowed right then—that very moment—that I was going to belong to the General. Somehow seemed like—well, my fate, I guess. I felt I wouldn't mind not getting to the War, if only he was to become my master. I felt sure, too, that he'd never really forgotten me since the day we first met on that mountain, an' he looked jest as I remembered him, 'ceptin' now he'd growed a white beard.

Well, Tom, I guess you ain't biting your tail and waiting to hear what happened next, 'cause you know he *did* become my master. It took a while, though. I went to the General for some-odd days and then I was taken back to Joe. But somehow that didn't worry me none, 'cause all the time the General was riding me I jest knowed I was meant to be his horse and that he felt the same and had no fault to find with me. The second time I was taken back to him, I knowed it was for keeps.

I s'posed that the General, seeing as he was a bossman, would have a real fine place where he lived.

But he didn't. And all along, for more'n three years, till we come here, he never did. 'Course now I know why. We had to fight to get it. But then it seemed strange that he lived in jest any old place, nothing at all to where Andy and Jim lived—or a lot of the folks we used to visit and he'd talk to 'em. The house where we lived in that warm country was jest an old, knock-down kind of a place, with a bit of a shed round the back for the horses. There warn't no fields or rails or none o' that. Still, we didn't need 'em, 'cause we was out and about pretty well all the time.

I got to know the people who lived with the General. There was the young dark-haired fella who'd been on the mountain—Major Taylor—and another called Colonel Long, and some more, too. But they only talked to the General and rode round with him. The most important people was two black fellas called Perry and Meredith. Perry had the real important things to do. He used to clean the General's boots and hand him his big gloves when he came out to ride me, and he'd bring him cups of coffee and things to eat and all the rest of it. Sometimes he'd actually scold the General—the others never did that—like he'd say, "Marse Robert, you jest got this here coat in sech a state as Ah never seed. Ah'm goin' to have a real job to get it right." Or he'd say, "You jest see you's back in time for dinner, Marse Robert—ain't no sense in lettin' it spoil." And Marse Robert'd say, "Very well, Perry," or, "Couldn't be helped, Perry," or some sech. The white fellas, Marse Taylor and the others, they mostly talked very respectful and did whatever the General said, riding here and there with him. It was really on account of Perry and Meredith that I got to thinking of the General as "Marse Robert." I wanted to feel I was as close to him as Perry was.

I soon got to know what we was to do, me and Marse Robert. It was everlasting riding around and making the gray soldiers dig big ditches. And my gracious, didn't they jest about have to dig? All up and down the land there was crowds and crowds of 'em, digging and sweating in that thick, watery heat, along by the creeks and sometimes near the salt water. And every day Marse Robert used to ride up and down to make sure they got on with it. He'd go for miles. Sometimes he'd ride Brown-Roan, but more often it'd be me. I'll tell you it was real hard work in that weather, but I never let up. I wanted to stay with Marse Robert more'n I wanted anything else, and I thought that if I showed any signs of being a quitter, maybe he'd start looking for a better horse.

What happened, though, was that as the weeks went by, me and Marse Robert gradually got 'bout as close together as a man and a horse can get. When we was riding alone, he often used to talk to me, and I got to feeling I was talking back to him. He made me feel that without me he wouldn't be able to do a durned thing. Like I said, he was really a kind of a horse hisself. However far we'd gone and however much he had to see to those digging men, he always used to see to me first. We'd get some place, and first off he'd get the saddle and bridle off me and make sure I had a drink and a nose bag or else somewhere to graze, and he'd see that I was in the shade—or at any rate that there *was* some shade where I could get to it if'n I wanted. He made me feel as important as Perry. He treated me like I was the most 'spensive thing he had in the world, and pretty soon I got to believing it myself. I lived up to it, you might say. He warn't much o' one for games and tricks, Marse Robert—not like Jim. But then, Tom, you see, he *warn't* Jim, so I warn't the same horse that Jim played with in the meadow and rode into the drinking tent. 'Guess it's hard to explain —'specially to a cat—but when a horse changes hands, his whole world changes. His feelings can change, his

habits can change. But that takes time. 'Course Marse
Robert, he knowed that, and in the middle of all the
digging work and pushing the soldiers, he always had
patience and time to help me change to his ways. He
never used a whip or a spur on me and he never lost
his temper or raised his voice. Jest the way he said
"No" was 'nuff to let me understand he wanted something different from whatever I was doing. F'rinstance,
he pretty near always let me stop to drink if'n I
wanted. But one day—I s'pose we must 'a been in a
hurry or something—we come to a creek, jest a piece
off to one side, and I was going to turn in there, but he
jest pulled the reins a little and said, "No, not now,"
and I jest natcherly found myself going on. And then
he patted my neck and said, "Sorry—won't be long."
Marse Robert had a heart that felt respect for every
living creature, and he knowed that in coming to him
I'd come to a strange world. He paid as much attention
to me, and seeing I felt easy in his world, as what he
did to the soldiers and their digging. I figure now he
knowed he was going to need me even more later on.

He had plenty of time for it, too, on these long,
lonely rides. Sometimes Marse Taylor or Marse Long
would come with us, but often we'd be by ourselves,
and that was when I could feel him putting all he had
into getting to know me. He'd watch for things I did
and get to know what they meant. And with all his
attention on me, I could put all my attention on him.
It's jest a matter of habits, Tom, you see. I larned his
habits and he larned mine.

It sounds crazy, I know, seeing as he's always had
to do with so many people, but Marse Robert's really a
kind of a lonely man. There's something—well, grave
and solitary deep down in him. I don't know who'd
know that after all this time if'n it's not me. Sort of
wishing to be simple and plain. I've knowed one or
two horses like that. Marse Robert's always been able

to make men trust him and be ready to fight for him or do anything he says—I've seed it over and over—and the men, they love him; but he's not really close friends with none of 'em, not like me and Ruffian used to be friends. Horses make special friends with other horses and stick to 'em, and if a horse's friend's taken away, he mopes and feels bad. Marse Robert's never had a friend like that—not a human friend. It's jest the plain truth that *I'm* his best friend. Now he's commanding the whole country, when he has to go away anywheres I jest know he's missing me all the time, 'cause I'm missing him. The whole time he's away he misses me. Marse Robert and me are more at home with each other'n with anyone else—horse or man.

It warn't the same for Brown-Roan. Brown-Roan was a decent little horse and always done his best. But he was nervous in his ways and things bothered him. Marse Robert was always good to him, same's he is to everyone—and me, I warn't jealous of that. I knowed I didn't have to be.

"Oh, the heat!" Brown-Roan used to groan whenever he was getting up, or Marse Robert was mounting him. "And these long rides! He asks sech a lot of a horse!" I always acted sympathetic, but the truth was he warn't really the horse for the job. Richmond warn't there that time—jest me and Brown-Roan.

The soldiers didn't like the digging. They used to grumble and cuss and say they didn't figure it was work for white men. Marse Robert and me had to keep after 'em from morning till night. Up and down we went, pushing 'em to get on with it. One day, Tom, believe it or not, we rode forty mile, nigh on to. When we finally stopped, I was real beat. Marse Robert, he got off, put his arms right round my neck and said, "Well done, boy, well done!" Some other officer who was with him says, "What a horse, General! What a traveller!"

Marse Robert kinda looks up real slow, as though this fella had said something real important. Then he nods his head two-three times and says, "Good name! We'll *call* him 'Traveller.'"

After that he never called me anything else. And do you know, Tom, I felt I'd jest stepped right into the skin of the real horse I was? I'd only jest *thought* I was Jeff Davis, because Jim and Andy had said so. Then Joe had taken away my name and given me one I didn't like. But now Marse Robert had found out my *right* name, and put it on me like he put on my saddle —he used to saddle me hisself lots of times, to make sure I was comfortable. Now I was comfortable with my name. I was me; I was what you might call a real, true part of Marse Robert and his outfit, and since then I've never been nothing 'cept Traveller.

During them warm days down south, we used to see hundreds of horses. Like I was saying, we often rode alone and Marse Robert would go into any stables where we fetched up, jest to look at the horses and make sure they was being prop'ly cared for. But he did it all so quiet and homey—none of this here "I'm the General: jest you stand up straight!" stuff— that a lot of the soldiers never even knowed who he was. One day he stopped to talk to two fellas driving a team of horses, but one of 'em was deaf, and as we was moving on, this deaf fella said to the other, real loud, "Who is that durned ol' fool? He's always a-pokin' round my horses as if he meant to steal one of 'em!"

★
VI

'SEEMS LIKE quite a while since you been in here to see me, Tom. You killed that many rats early on this summer, I s'pose you've no particular reason to come and sit in here nights. 'Met the goat, have you? That's Sandy. Marse Robert's put him in here for company, seeing as how Ajax is down in the other shed. And powerful good company he is, too. Sandy, this is Tom the Nipper, Marse Robert's commander of ratcatchers. He has the most refined manners of any cat I've met.

Y'know, one thing I like 'bout this here place is that even though we're pretty far on with summer now, the flies ain't all that bad. Why, I've knowed 'em worse this time of year when we was up north. But 'course, any Army draws flies—the crowds of men and horses natcherly breed 'em. It's different here. Well, for one thing it's cooler, an' 'tain't a lot o' horses, neither. S'afternoon, when me and Marse Robert was riding over to Rockbridge, he stopped off once't or twice't, like he gen'rally does, to talk with folks 'long the way. He's that friendly, they've all got to know him real well. He was talking to this old fella quite a spell—'bout his corn crop, I figure, from the way they was both looking at the plants. I was hitched to the gate an' hardly a fly come round. Jest had to twitch my skin and stamp some; that was 'nuff to fix 'em.

That was what set me to remembering 'bout the time I was telling you, Tom, when we was down south and doing all that digging round the creeks and swamps. Now down there it's skeeters pretty well round the year, but the time we was there was the best time of year for losing 'em, so this horse told me— nearest it ever gets to winter, he said. It was jest getting to early spring, and I was dreading what a full crop of skeeters would be like—worse'n flies, I 'spect —when one day we-all lit out and headed north on the railroad. I was a-feared it was back to the dad-burn mountain, but Marse Robert, I reckon he knowed I was worried, 'cause he came several times to have a word with me and make sure I was all right on the journey.

What we came to warn't the mountain, though. It was a city—the biggest city in the world. Leastways, I've never seed or heared tell of a bigger one. I can't really describe it, Tom. It's a thousand times bigger'n this here little town—lots more houses, more people, more noise. When we got off the railroad—why, it was like the whole world was a city—streets and streets, an' all full of horses and carts, crowds of people pushing up and down the sidewalks and everywhere men shouting to each other over the noise of wheels on the cobblestones. And that's not all, neither. There was them kind of long wagons with flat tops; carriages like, and full of men and women, with horses to pull 'em on rails, running up and down the streets. Don't they jest 'bout rattle and bang, too? I was being ridden by one of Marse Robert's soldiers, and I s'pect I was kinda hard to handle, 'cause I was feeling a mite nervous and skittish then. But Brown-Roan was a lot of help; he'd seed all o' this truck before, and his acting manageable made me feel quieter, too. 'Sides, there was plenty more horses round and they warn't letting things faze them one bit.

What really fazed me, when we got to Marse Robert's place in this here city, was there was that durned Richmond in the stable, his loose box right next to mine. I hadn't figured on meeting him ever again, not never; and there he was. When he seed me, he jest wrinkled his nose and laid his ears back. It was evidently jest as nasty a surprise for him as it was for me. What I know now is that Richmond knowed real well, even then, that Marse Robert found him a troublesome fella and was looking out for a better horse. He didn't know—but he was going to—that I was that better horse. Well, maybe he did know, for he never really troubled to make an enemy of Brown-Roan. It was me in particular he didn't like.

I didn't care for the stables in the city. There warn't 'nuff for a horse to do. 'Fact, there was nothing to do, 'cause of Marse Robert seemed to have quit riding. I couldn't make it out. 'Course, he used to come into the stable to look us over and talk to us, but it was jest only for a few minutes mostly, and then he always seemed to have something else uppermost in his mind. The stablemen used to take us out for exercise, and they'd ride us 'longside the big river, but I couldn't never really get to liking it, 'cause I knowed I warn't working for Marse Robert. And anyway, like I was telling you, Tom, 'far as I was concerned Marse Robert had become the center of things. He was my whole world. I know I was difficult once't or twice't. I couldn't relax, and there warn't one of the soldiers looking after us that I really took to. 'Sides, they kept a-changing, and that didn't help none neither. 'Nother thing that didn't help was the few times Marse Robert did take me out hisself, I could tell—a good horse can always tell, Tom, you know—that he was out o' sorts and discontented. Whatever 'twas he had to do in that city, he didn't like it. What it come down to was he was fretting and so was I.

'Twarn't really surprising, though, that I felt
strung up tight. You could feel the same thing all over
the city—in the men and women, I mean: the way
they stood, the way they moved and held theirselves,
the sound of their voices. They didn't know it, maybe,
but I felt it whenever I was out of my stable. I noticed
it most particular in the soldiers. The whole place was
filling up with more and more soldiers. They'd come
marching through the streets, sometimes, when we
was a-riding out—bands playing, and always a fella
out in front carrying one of these here colored cloths
on sticks. You see, they're real important, Tom—them
colored cloths on sticks. Soldiers can't be soldiers unless they've got one of 'em going on in front. What?
Oh, never mind why. I do know, mind you, but I can't
tell you, 'cause it's a military secret. They control the
weather, an' make sick men better an' a whole lot of
other things—never you mind. The cloth I particularly
got to know was red, with blue crisscross stripes and
sort of spiky white spots on, but each bunch of
soldiers had their own kind, you see. The noises the
bands made was different, too, but they had their fa-
vorites, and I got so's I could recognize the particular
sorta beat of some of them noises.

It was real spring—a perfect day, sunny and warm
—more'n a month after we'd come, when a big crowd
of soldiers—horse and foot—come marching into the
city. The fella who was riding me out turned back to
watch. The people on the sidewalks was all a-cheering
and a-waving their hats. It made them forget their
troubles and look real happy. The gardens was all full
of flowers, I 'member, and the women was running out
of their houses and giving the soldiers cakes and flowers as they marched 'long the street. After a bit you
could smell the flowers better'n what you could the
soldiers—and that's saying something. The soldiers
stuck the flowers in their caps, in their guns, round

their necks. I 'spect that was the best day of their lives, a lot of 'em.

Twice't, 'long 'bout that time, Marse Robert took me out hisself and rode me out of the city and down the river—some four mile, I guess. All I 'member 'bout it is men digging and working everywhere. Mud and high water, and Marse Robert calling out to 'em and urging 'em on. But that was when I first heared guns, Tom: the real big guns—the bangs! When they began, we was crossing the river flats. The noise—oh, you can't describe it! And the ground shook. To a horse, that's even more frightening than the noise. You never lose the fear of that. I was rarin' up and dancing about, and Marse Robert had his hands full to calm me down. What did finally calm me was the sight of one of Marse Robert's soldiers on Richmond. Richmond was really making trouble, an' I didn't nohow want to be like him. All the same, we warn't in a battle that day. I hadn't been in one yet, and I'd no idea what was going on. What I guess now is that the Blue men—I hadn't even seed any Blue men then—was trying to get up the river, but we stopped 'em with our banging away.

I'll tell you 'bout the next time I was in the bangs, Tom, 'cause that really was an important time—for Marse Robert and for me and for everybody.

It was early summer, only not so's you could tell it. The weather had turned real bad. It had been raining and raining for days. Marse Robert had been riding Brown-Roan mostly—Richmond once't or twice't. This particular morning, though, he rode me out of the city and we headed east. Marse Taylor was with us, I remember, and one or two more. That day was dull and cloudy, but no rain. I could hear some bangs, but they was a long ways off. The road was soft and muddy, and there was plenty of trees either side, and a wooden plank house or two in the clearings. What you'd call sheltered, really. Marse Robert seemed sort of dejected and restless. He rode along without a word, but I could feel he was on edge. I felt on edge, too. I reckon I knowed we was a-heading for trouble, but I didn't know 'zackly what sort.

We came to a bend in the road, and up ahead, in the scrubland, there was a whole passel of our soldiers, all in long lines stretching jest 'bout as far as you could see. They was on edge, too. Everybody was waiting for something. Marse Robert got off and began talking to another man I figured was a general like hisself. This other man was giving orders, and round where we was people kept a-coming and a-going. A long ways off there was everlasting bangs, but still nothing 'peared to happen. The soldiers didn't move. We must have stuck round there for the best part of three-four hours.

Then the other general called for his horse and rode away, and jest as he did, a man in ordinary clothes—not a soldier—came riding up to us. Marse Robert walked forward to meet him.

I liked the look of this other man's horse. As he came up, he nickered to me real friendly, and I nickered back. His man dismounts and hitches him 'long-side me.

"You're Traveller, ain't you?" this horse asks me straight off. "I've heared o' you. My name's Thunder. Is that General Lee, your man?"

"Sure," I says. "He's the boss round here."

"That's where you're wrong," says this other horse, but still very friendly. "*My* man's the boss. He's the President, and he's the boss of the whole shooting match. You stick around and you'll see for yourself."

"What's he doing here?" I says.

"There's going to be a battle," says Thunder. "A bad one, too, if'n I know anything 'bout it. I'm scairt. I only hope to goodness we get out of it all right."

"How do you know?" I says.

"Can't you hear the guns and the muskets?" he says, looking real nervous and rolling his eye. "Our fellas must be attacking the enemy right this minute."

So then Marse Robert and this here President mounts us again and we set off on the road. It was getting pretty late in the afternoon now and the sun was a-dropping down towards the top of the woods behind us. It had turned out a finer evening than what the day had been.

Suddenly, 'fore I knowed what was happening, there commenced an infernal row and all round us confusion sech as you never seed, Tom, and can't imagine. I could see whole lines of our gray soldiers going forward—or trying to—'mong the trees and scrub, shouting and yelling. Every second or so there'd be a great bang—smoke and flame—and some of 'em would fall down, screaming and cussing, over in the logs and the bushes. There was smoke everywhere, and that was the first time, Tom, that I smelt that smell —what they call battle smoke. Two fellas come limping back past us, one holding t'other up. You could see they was both hurt real bad. One was as good as blind, and the blood was streaming down his face. The other kept on kind o' crying, "Ah! Ah!" There was horsemen everywhere, galloping 'bout in the smoke and shouting to each other. No one could tell what they was meant to be doing.

Then I knowed that this other horse had been right: his man *was* the boss. He had to be, 'cause Marse Robert was jest sitting still and letting him take care of things. To tell the truth, Marse Robert had plenty of work keeping me quiet, 'cause I was all over the road. "Easy, Traveller, easy!" I wonder how often since then I've heared them same words? The other horse was calm as you like, and his man, this here President, he was giving orders, pointing up the road and shouting, and two soldiers on horses lit out like crazy the way we'd come, to see to whatever he'd said had got to be done.

It was getting on to twilight now, and more and more of our soldiers was streaming back out of the thickets. A whole lot of 'em was wounded and they all 'peared to be frightened. A man rode up and tried to tell the President to mind hisself and clear out o' there, but he jest shook him off and kept on a-giving out his orders.

I'd become hysterical near 'bouts, and it was only Marse Robert's voice and hands that kept me from charging away through the soldiers, jest knocking 'em over. And then, all of a sudden, Marse Robert grabbed the President's arm and pointed up the road. Two men was carrying a stretcher and shouting to the soldiers to get out o' the way. They came right up to us. Laying on the stretcher was the other general—the man Marse Robert had been talking to when we first got there. Anyone could see he was shot to blazes—hurt real bad. He was groaning with pain and his gray uniform was all soaked in blood. The President bent down and spoke to him and so did Marse Robert, but he could hardly say a word. You could tell they was both real upset to see him that way. They hadn't expected nothing like that. "Why, durn it!" says the President's horse to me. "General Johnston! Now that's terrible bad! Anything can happen now."

They carried the general away. The banging gradually died down and our own soldiers, in little groups, came back acrost the road and throwed theirselves down every which way among the trees. They was beat to a frazzle—jest plumb wore out. But I figure the enemy must have been beat, too, 'cause they didn't show. After a while, all I could hear in the near dark was voices giving orders and wounded men crying and cussing.

Then another man—'nother general—come up

out of the trees and commenced to talking and explaining things to the President and Marse Robert. All I understood of this was that finally the President told this man to make the soldiers stay where they was for the night. Then him and Marse Robert turned us back the way we'd come, and off we went—that's to say, best we could.

The road was all tromped to deep mush; it was bad going. We went through crowds of soldiers in the dark, and other horses pulling ambulances full of wounded men. I could smell blood everywhere—men and horses, too—but I warn't afraid now the bangs had stopped. I figured we was going home.

All along the road, Marse Robert and the President was talking, talking together—'bout the battle having gone so bad, I guess, and 'bout this here General Johnston being hurt so terrible. But after a while, there was a long silence 'tween them. And then at last the President says, "General Lee, I want you to take over command of the Army. You start tomorrow." Well, that's jest how I recall it, Tom, y'know. And I remember what his horse said to me, too. He said, "I sure hope you enjoy yourself."

June 1, 1862. The plight of the Confederacy is desperate. Despite all diplomatic efforts, not one of the European powers has acknowledged the independence of the South: they are waiting upon the event. The withholding of cotton exports has proved an ineffective blunder, for there is a glut of cotton on the world market, and now the Confederacy has lost incoming funds that might have bought the arms so urgently needed. The Federal naval blockade is beginning to bite. In the West, the war has gone badly. New Orleans is lost and so is the whole state of Missouri.

Worst of all, General McClellan, having landed a Federal army of more than 90,000 men on the southeastern tip of the Virginia Peninsula lying be-

tween the York and the James Rivers, has advanced
sixty miles to the very outskirts of Richmond. Despite
a brilliant diversionary campaign by Stonewall Jackson in the Shenandoah Valley, the Confederate capital
seems about to fall to McClellan. Two days ago, the
Confederate army defending the city, commanded by
General Joseph E. Johnston, launched a counterattack
upon McClellan—the so-called battle of Seven Pines.
Yesterday General Robert E. Lee, chafing and frus-
trated in his anomalous post as "conductor of military
operations under the direction of the President," himself rode out of Richmond to view what he could of
the battlefield. Arrived there, he was shortly joined by
none other than President Davis. Under Federal fire, as
darkness fell the two saw the mismanaged Confederate attack peter out into a drawn battle, in which General Johnston himself was seriously wounded.

General Lee, now aged fifty-five, has been appointed by the President to the command of the army.
His reputation is not particularly high, and little enthusiasm attends the announcement. Lee is regarded
by Johnston's lieutenants as a nonentity and the nearest thing to a mere staff officer. Richmond newspapers
disparage him. Since last August he has conducted a
small and unsuccessful campaign in western Virginia,
and then spent four months of the winter strengthen-
ing the coastal defenses of South Carolina. Now, at no
notice at all, the fate of Richmond itself has been laid
upon his shoulders.

What use is a general in the field without a steady
and reliable horse? About as much use as a shepherd
without a dog.

That day—that day I was telling you 'bout, Tom
—that's what they call "coming under fire." That was
the first day I ever come under fire. I was scairt out o'
my wits—dancing 'bout all over the place—and I don't
reckon that there President's horse was no better, neither. Sometimes it seems like I've reg'lar lived under

fire from that day to this. I mean, if it's not bangs right now, then it's *going* to be bangs, or else it *has* been bangs an' you're still shaking. And if it's not that, why then you can go to sleep and jest *dream* 'bout bangs instead. Only there's been no bangs now—no more ground shaking—for a long time—oh, two summers. Marse Robert, he put a stop to the bangs, you see, in the end. Well, I'll tell you all 'bout that some other time. For now, I'll— Hey, stop batting my tail around, and jest listen, will ya? I've had 'nuff folks messing with my tail.

Where was I? Oh, yeah: first thing that happened after that day was we-all moved out of the city. I was right glad 'bout that. As I told you, I'd never liked living in the city—no grass, lots of smoke in the air and Marse Robert 'parently too busy to ride. But now that was all going to change. Marse Robert hisself rode me out to this here farm place, a mile or so out of town, on the same road where we'd talked to the President. We lived there best part of a month, I figure. The house was very plain and trim, jest like t'other used to be when we was down south. When we got there, I remember, Perry and Meredith and the other fella—a white fella, Bryan he was called—they was all bustling round, getting the place ready and talking to the farm lady—Miss Dabbs, they called her. Us three horses was given a nice stable, warm an' dry. There was a plenty of other horses around, 'course, but the General's horses had their own stable.

It needed to be warm an' dry, too. My ears and tail, didn't it rain 'bout then? You never seed nothing like it. Rained like it was never going to stop. My chief recollection of them days at old Miss Dabbs's is the everlasting rain. You'd 'a drowned for sure. Do you know, Tom, I more'n once seed horses mired knee-deep? True.

The funny thing was Marse Robert, he seemed

real pleased. More it rained, better he liked it. "Aha, Traveller," he says to me one day, jest as we was setting out in a real downpour, "this'll keep 'em quiet! Couldn't be better, could it?" My oats! I thought; I don't see how it could be much worse. Still, if it pleased Marse Robert, that was all right with me; he must have his reasons. 'Nother day, Marse Taylor looks up at the sky and says to him, "Strikes me, sir, Little Mac's going to need his mac today," and then they both bust out laughing like to split. They was real happy. Blest if I was.

And nor was the soldiers. You should have heared 'em swearing and cussing. 'Cause Marse Robert, he had 'em on the same as before—digging! All in the rain—I can see 'em still—the long, long lines of men, soaking wet, cussing up a storm and the shovels shining in the rain and the pits half-full of water, plop-plop-plop as fast they was dug.

"Hey, Gin'ral!" A fella calls out to Marse Robert one day, real sassy, "Hey, Gin'ral! We-all didn't jine up to do nigger work! We-all jined up to fight!"

"We've got to protect Richmond first, my man," answers Marse Robert. "Then we'll fight, sure 'nuff."

I didn't rightly know what he meant, or why we had to protect Richmond. Of all the cussed, ornery horses I ever met, Richmond was jest about the worst. I really got to hate him, and he took care I did, too. I don't know what had been done to him when he was a colt, but that horse hated jest 'bout everybody and everything. He was a big bay stallion, and one way or 'nother he was never tired of saying so. He was full of hisself, Richmond was. "You ball-less gray brute," he said to me one day, "do you reckon Marse Robert's going to get any use out o' *you*? Why, he only took you to do your master a favor." He'd never use my right name, neither. He always called me Greenbrier, jest 'cause he knowed I didn't like it. "Oh, here comes

Greenbrier," he'd say to Brown-Roan when I come in streaming wet from a long day on the trenches with Marse Robert. "*He* wouldn't know what to do with a mare if he had a field-full to choose from!" He hated all other horses, and if he had to go near any he didn't know, he'd commence to squealing. As time went on, he got to know sure 'nuff that Marse Robert preferred me to hisself, and that made him still madder. I never used to answer him back; I didn't have to, after all. I'd jest toss my head and eat my hay.

Brown-Roan was another matter. I liked Brown-Roan. He was what's knowed as "a nice, quiet horse." He never did no one any harm in his life. Trouble was the poor fella was jest *too* quiet. He hadn't got the keep-going or the spunk you needed to be one of Marse Robert's horses. There's awful big demands on a general's horse, Tom, you see; it's not like reg'lar work. You might go thirty mile in a day, and then, jest when you figure you're going into stable, the general suddenly needs another five mile or more out of you. You've got to *love* your man to be up to that—you've got to feel what *he* feels. You've got to be *part* of your man. Poor Brown-Roan was never that.

"Oh, I wish I'd 'a never jined up with Marse Robert," he says to me one evening when he'd come in soaked through. "I warn't made for this!"

"Why," I says to him—one of our soldiers was rubbing him down at the time—"you've got to look at it different. You couldn't have a better horseman for a master. And you're a general's horse. That ought to make you mighty proud."

"I know it makes me tired," says he, stamping his nearside rear hoof. "I believe I've strained a muscle." He was forever believing he'd strained a muscle.

You couldn't dislike Brown-Roan. He was always pleasant in his temper, and he was no quitter, neither. 'Best he could, he gave what he had, but he jest hadn't got 'nuff; the shame was no one—not even Marse Robert—found out in time. I only wish they had.

But Marse Robert was terrible busy in them days! He had a whole lot on his mind. I haven't given you no idea, Tom. Very often we'd be out all day, up and down them gun pits and trenches, and mostly in the rain. Even Marse Taylor told him one day that he figured he'd surely done 'nuff, and he'd wear hisself out. "I can't ask those men to stand anything I won't stand myself," he answered. "How can I expect them to keep working in that rain if'n they don't see me out there with 'em?"

Sure 'nuff, pretty soon I could see the soldiers was getting more chipper, and the reason was they was trustful of Marse Robert. He was forever praising them and telling them their work was the best he'd ever seed. He made 'em dig like they was to bury a pack of horses, but he'd always remember to put in a joke or a good word. After a bit the grumbling stopped, and when we come round it'd be "Howdy, General!" or "Come and have a look at this, General!" Now and then someone'd say, "How's your horse to-day, General?" And he'd say, "Fine—couldn't want for a better." 'Course, for all I know he may have said that when he was on Richmond, too. Some of them fellas couldn't tell a dad-burn horse from a bucket. They was only young boys for the most part, you know, Tom—lot of 'em younger'n the boys you can see round here now.

As the days went by, I gradually got to know most of the people who came to see the General. There was one afternoon in particular comes back to me now. It jest happened to be hot and sunny for a change, and I was hitched to the rails in front of the house when a young fella comes riding up on a real fine brown horse. Now this young fella, he was what you might call a sight to see. First of all, he'd strike anyone as an uncommon robust and vigorous kind of a man. He warn't tall out o' the ordinary, but he was powerful and broad-shouldered, and there was a kinda go and dash 'bout him, so's you felt he'd be ready to jump his horse over the house if'n anyone dared him to. The way he was turned out, smart warn't no word for it. He had gold spurs on his boots. His hat was sorta looped up with a gold-colored brooch and there was a great, floating black plume stuck in it. His jacket was covered with gold braid and all the buttons was bright gold, too. His gloves, which looked new, came up to his elbows and he had a yellow silk sash tied round his waist. On 'count of the day being hot, he'd throwed back his cape, and you could see it was all lined with some sorta very fine, shining-smooth stuff, bright scarlet. Although he had a huge, curling mustache and a big brown beard—biggest I ever seed, I reckon—the way he was acting he'd put anyone in mind not so much of a general as of some young fella riding out for a whole load of fun. I 'member there was some red roses stuck in his horse's headstall, and as he come riding up he was a-singin'— jest out of high spirits, so I figured.

As for his horse, he made me feel like I was some kinda small-time cob. And I'm telling you, Tom, I've never been in the habit of calling other horses real fine. That's what's knowed as self-respect. But this here horse, he had a very quiet, superior kind of a manner, like he knowed everyone knowed he was so good there was no need even to be mentioning it. All his movements was very refined and confident, an' he'd been groomed so he shone glossy all over. But his appearance warn't the end of it—not by a long piece. I sorta got an uncomfortable notion that he might jest be able to give me a considerable run over twenty mile. Anyone could see he had quality from his nose to his hooves.

I nickered to him and he nickered back. Nothing quarrelsome; nothing wrong there. His master dismounted, hitched him 'longside and took a good look at me.

Jest then Perry come out of the house, toting a bucket of garbage.

"Hey!" calls out the young fella, putting his hand on my nose. "What horse is this?"

"Dat's Traveller, General, sah," answers Perry. "General Lee's horse."

"Howdy there, Traveller!" says he. "Why, you look too good to stand fretting on a rail. If you want to have a good time, jine the cavalry! Jine the cavalry!"

He'd plainly taken a liking to me, and I found myself feeling the same way 'bout him. I even felt that if Marse Robert hadn't 'a been my master, maybe it wouldn't be so bad belonging to this young fella. For one thing, you could tell at a glance that he was a natchral-born horseman like no one else in the world. He was the only other man 'sides Marse Robert who ever made me feel that he *was* a kind of horse hisself. The way he looked me over, I figured he understood every last thing 'bout me. And yet it didn't make me fidgety or nervous, on account of it was a sympathetic sort of understanding.

Jest then Marse Robert came out of the house hisself. The young fella saluted him and then they shook hands and walked away together, talking. Marse Robert 'peared to regard him as an old friend.

"Who's your master?" I asked the brown horse.

Now you gotta know, Tom, that ever since I jined up with Marse Robert, I'd got into the habit of considering myself as good as any other horse, and better'n most; an' they mostly went along with this and acted according. But now I found myself being looked at by this horse—well, sort of judicious-like, as you might say.

"You don't know?" he says at length, and then he don't say no more, so in the end I had to say, "No, I don't."

"That's General Jeb Stuart," he says, "commanding the cavalry in this here Army."

This made me feel so small I almost mouthed at him, like I was a colt again. I began to explain that Marse Robert and me hadn't been all that long in command. That was all right, though; this horse—Skylark, he told me he was called—had all the good manners of someone that knows his own worth.

"Glad to know you, Traveller," he says. "Dare say you'll be seeing a good deal of us—that's to say, when we're around. There's quite a passel of us belonging to General Stuart—Star of the East's a particular friend of mine. And 'sides him, there's Lady Margaret and Lily of the Valley. Only, we spend a lot of our time riding round behind the Blue men, you know, finding things out."

"The Blue men?" I says. "Who are they?"

Even that didn't shake him out of his manners. "Why, the enemy," he says.

I didn't even rightly know what *that* meant, Tom, any more'n you do. But before he could go on, Marse Robert and "Jine-the-Cavalry" came back, and Marse Robert called out to two soldiers to lead us over into the shade and give Skylark a feed. We fetched up in different places, so that was all I seed of him that time. But he was right. We *did* come to see a lot of each other, and I got to know Jine-the-Cavalry very well, too.

I had my own names for the people Marse Robert seed the most of: it come easier. For one thing, as far as I could make out they was mostly called General Hill. Well, leastways, two of 'em was. Don't ask me why. How can we understand half the crazy things men do? Anyways, I came to think of them two Hills as "Red

Shirt" and "the Little General." I say I had my own names; like one of 'em, General Pickett—a youngish fella—I called "Ringlets," on account of his long, scented hair—but there was one that all the soldiers called the same's I did, an' that was "Old Pete"—General Longstreet. I never entirely liked Old Pete. Hard to say 'zackly why, but somehow I got the notion that he didn't really respect Marse Robert or like the idea of Marse Robert being his boss. 'Course, I couldn't understand a lot of their talk, but very often, as we went along, I could tell jest from the sound of their voices that he was argufying with Marse Robert and kinda telling him what he ought to do. And Marse Robert, Tom, you see, he was always so kind and gentlemanly to everybody, he never could bring hisself to tell this here Pete to go and jump in the ditch, like he oughta. I knowed Marse Robert jest couldn't do that to save his life, but quite often I used to feel like kicking Old Pete myself. Jest the sound of his voice worried me. Still, he was a soldier sure 'nuff, and a lot braver under fire'n what I was, as I found out later on. But in them days I'm speaking of now, I didn't know what we was in for n'more'n if I'd been old Miss Dabbs's cat.

I knowed there was something in the wind, though. Us horses are always sensitive to any kind of uneasiness or tenseness, Tom, you know, and that time I could feel the stress kinda building up all over, day by day. One day, 'stead of 'tending to the digging, Marse Robert and Colonel Long—Ginger, his horse was called; nice fella—rode us out five or six mile north and acrost a bit of a river. Marse Robert and me stopped on a slope t'other side of this here river, and he held up a pair of bottles to his eyes. What? No, 'course I don't understand why. But he was forever holding up them bottles.

"Now, Colonel Long," he says, pointing out over

the country, "how can we *get* at those people? What ought we to do?"

I wonder how many times I've heared Marse Robert say that since. I come to know jest rightly what it meant—trouble, always. When he said that to someone, like it might be Jine-the-Cavalry or Red Shirt or Colonel Long, he didn't really want them to answer him back. Sometimes they did and sometimes they didn't. It was a kind of game with Marse Robert. He already knowed what he was going to do. Colonel Long knowed that, so he didn't say nothing.

The two of 'em rode round a while, Marse Robert sometimes talking and pointing, and then again holding them bottles up to his eyes. The reason it puzzled me was that there was no soldiers digging—no one there at all 'cepting him and Marse Long.

When we got back to old Miss Dabbs's, first person we seed outside was Old Pete. "Ah, General Longstreet," says Marse Robert; and him and Old Pete got to talking right there in the yard. Marse Robert was scratching in the dust with a stick, and pointing here and there. They was at it a long time.

Over the next few days lots of people came and went—Red Shirt, the Little General—yeah, and the President, too. And somehow I got the idea they was all in some kind of secret together. I couldn't bottom it out; and you see, there warn't no other horse I could ask. I'd never ask Richmond nothing, and all Brown-Roan knowed was that he didn't like the mounting feeling of strain. Well, neither did I—and yet, Tom, do you know? I felt, too, that I didn't want to be left out of it, whatever it was.

One afternoon, not long after that ride acrost the river, I was grazing in the meadow, right 'longside the yard outside the house. I knowed Marse Robert was inside, and I couldn't help wondering what he could be a-doing all that time. You see, Tom, we'd growed

that close I sometimes used to feel a mite jealous and
grudging on days when he was a long time indoors
and we warn't together. It was fine weather for a
change, and suddenly I seed the dust of horsemen
quite a ways off. Turned out there was two of 'em,
riding up to the house. First thing, I could see the
horses was all tuckered out. They was sweating, frothing at their bits and panting. I didn't envy them.
Wherever they'd come from, they'd come far and
they'd come fast. One of the men dismounted very
slow and stiff, and gave his horse to the other. Then he
walked up to the door, and Perry came and spoke with
him a piece. Then he came back and jest leant over
agin the fence, with his head dropped down on his
chest and his cap pulled right down over his eyes like
he didn't want no one to know who he was. I could
smell his sweat from where I was standing. And that
was the first time I ever seed Cap-in-His-Eyes—General Stonewall Jackson, to give him his right name.

T'other man who'd come in with him had taken
the horses round to the stable yard back o' the house,
and so there was no one around 'cepting me and this
man leaning hard on the fence, with his head down on
his chest. He was covered with dust, and the sweat
had made long streaks on his face. I figured he must be
some soldier who'd been sent to deliver a message. But
what struck me most 'bout him, jest at that moment,
was the way he seemed perfectly content to do nothing at all. I mean, Tom, you know what men are like,
don't you? 'Cepting when they're asleep, they're very
seldom doing nothing at all. Either they're talking, or
they're eating or drinking, or mending this or cleaning
that. This man jest simply stayed put, like now he'd
got his journey over he warn't aiming to do nothing
else. He put me in mind of a tree; that's to say, he
'peared like he was doing all he had to do jest standing
there and nothing was going to shift him. And yet

somehow he made me feel he was friendly. I sorta sidled along the fence till I was close up to him, and at that he looked round and spoke to me and stroked my nose, but all the time 'twas plain he was a-thinking 'bout something else. He was a tall, gaunt, awkward-looking kind of a fella, and his clothes worn all any-how. I wondered why he didn't go and ask for some-thin' to eat and drink. I remember, too, that as I went back to grazing, he suddenly throwed both his hands up in the air. 'Looked real strange. I couldn't make him out at all.

Jest then who should come riding up the road but the Little General, and when he seed Cap-in-His-Eyes leaning on the fence, he called out to him like he was real s'prised. "Why, Jackson," he says, "what the devil are you doing here?" "Ah, Hill!" answers the other fella. And then the Little General got down and shook hands jest like Cap-in-His-Eyes was his oldest friend. As they stood there talking together, I realized that this awkward-looking soldier must be another general, and a pretty important one, too. Well, actually I only reckoned this a bit later on, 'cause what happened then was they both went in the house together, and soon after, Red Shirt and Old Pete turned up. So then I knowed that all these here generals must 'a come to hear what Marse Robert had got to say to 'em. They stayed a long time, too, 'cause they hadn't come out by sunset, when I was taken back to stables. I felt Marse Robert had left me real flat, that time.

Well, 'course I don't recollect everything, Tom, not day by day. What I recall next is maybe two-three days later, and Marse Robert riding me out at early morning through great crowds of soldiers and guns and wagons on the road, till we stopped at another farm, up top a long slope. Beyond us, the road went down the other side to a river—'cepting the bridge was all smashed—and from there back up to a little village

—if'n you could call it a village; a few houses, that's all. It was clear, open ground—more'n a mile, I'd say—nice and green after the rain, and some trees down beside the river. It all looked real peaceful.

We stayed there most of the day, and the President came, riding Thunder, and a whole lot of other important-looking people, some of 'em soldiers and some not. Mid-afternoon, when I was reckoning it must be 'bout time we was going home, all of a sudden I got the shock of my life. It was so durned unexpected. The bangs began, over on t'other side of the river. It was fighting, like that other evening by the road in the woods. The whole valley, all round, was full of firing, echoing up and down. Everywhere bugles was blowing, men getting on their horses. The soldiers—hundreds of 'em—who'd been lying down beside the road in the sunshine, all jumped up and got into lines. People was calling out orders, harness jingling, hooves thudding, messengers dashing here and there—you never seed such a commotion all in a minute. Far off, over the river, there was big guns firing, and I could see that there battle-smoke. Pretty soon I could smell it, too.

What was happening was our soldiers was attacking, and that was the first time, Tom, that I actually seed the Blue men. There was crowds of 'em on t'other side of the river, and all round that little village place —only they was all running away and our fellas was coming on acrost the fields, and shooting as they came.

Anyways, that was how it looked like to begin with. But pretty soon the smoke seemed to cover everything. I reckoned it must have got to real bad fighting, and our men might likely be in as much trouble as the Blue men.

That there President's horse, Thunder, was hitched nearabouts. "What's going on?" I asked him.

"What are they doing?" I hadn't been expecting none of it, you see.

"Killing each other," he said. "Best they can, I mean."

"Killing each other?" I says to him. "For goodness' sake, why they doing that?"

He kinda looked me over for a bit without answering. At last he said, "You really the General's horse? You're real green, ain't you? Killing each other? That's what men do. You didn't know?"

"But why?" I said.

"Oh, for gosh sakes!" he snorted through his nose. "You might's well ask me why the sun goes acrost the sky. It's what they do, like flies bite. They always have and they always will."

I thought 'bout this, best as I could for all the noise and confusion. And it struck me that Jim and Andy and all the fellas back home hadn't gone in for killing each other. So there must be some sort of between-whiles now and then.

"Don't they sometimes stop?" I said. "Like flies in winter?"

"That's so," he answered. "But if'n I've understood it rightly, they won't stop for good until either the Blue men or our men quit and say they've had 'nuff. And that's a long time off, I reckon. You can forget it. Flies don't stop biting, do they?"

I was going to ask him some more, but jest then the President's man came up and took Thunder away. Next thing I knowed, the Little General was on his horse, too, and line after line of our soldiers was going down to the river. They throwed down some planks and got acrost, even without no bridge, and pretty soon I seed the President go acrost on his horse.

Then Marse Robert called for me, and we went down and over the river, too, and straight up the road on t'other side—straight up to that little village place.

And when we got there—oh, my! It was lots worse'n I can tell you, Tom. 'Course, I seed plenty worse since, but that was the first time. There was dead men—dead horses, too—laying round everywhere, and worse'n that was the wounded and the dying, all crying and hollering out something terrible. And all the time the bangs kept on, right in 'mongst where we was. Suddenly there'd be a kinda howling noise in the air, coming closer, and then a great, bright flash and a bang that knocked all the sense out o' you. There was horses squealing and men running away and crawling under anything they could find—fences, bushes—anything. I couldn't see a lot for the smoke. I do remember a loose horse come charging down out of the smoke, straight towards us. He jest missed me. One of the flying stirrup irons hit me acrost the withers as he went by. Once't I actually had to step over two dead men on the ground. Oh, I seed things I couldn't tell you, Tom.

There warn't no Blue men left in the village—only dead 'uns. We'd chased 'em all out. But after a bit I realized what was happening. Them bangs can go an awful long way through the air, y'see. They can go as far as right acrost this town—further'n that, too. The Blue men had run off—retreated, as they call it—a mile or so to a lot of trees out t'other side of the village, and that's where the bangs was coming from. Some of our fellas had gone out to get 'em there, too.

In the middle of all this ruckus, Marse Robert was sitting on my back jest as quiet and steady as if we was out watching the men a-digging. I could feel his pulse perfectly regular, and his breathing real easy—which was more'n mine was. After a bit I reckoned I understood. The way I figured it at that time, nothing could hurt Marse Robert. The bangs couldn't hit him, and he knowed this. I reckoned that's why the President had made him head of the Army. And if I was his horse, then maybe I couldn't be hurt neither. Well, I mean, I *hoped* this more'n I really believed it. I'd jest gone rigid—I couldn't move my mouth or my jaw or my neck, and my hindquarters felt like they was made of wood and didn't belong to me at all.

Then I realized that Marse Robert knowed jest how I was feeling. In the middle of all this, he was finding the time to reassure me. He kept talking to me, quiet and steady-like, and every now and then he'd lean forward and stroke my face or my neck. He wanted me to try'n relax, to trust him and believe that the two of us was on top of all this. I knowed *he* was, but I warn't so sure 'bout me.

Jest then a horse come a-tearing out 'tween two of the shacks. His ears was laid back and his eyes was rolling all white. Anybody'd know he was terrified—bolting. The man on his back was terrified, too. He couldn't stop his horse, and he was leaning right over its neck, which of course didn't help him none. They'd frightened each other to pieces, that was what it come to. I'd no sooner seed them than they was gone, but I could hear the man shouting still—he was making 'nuff noise to frighten a whole pack of horses.

Reckon I don't want to be a horse like that, I thought. A fine sight that'd be—the General's horse bolting off with him. I tried to stand entirely still, but I jest couldn't help pawing the ground some. What really fixed me was that there was no alarm or excitement at all in what Marse Robert was doing or saying. If I'd 'a been stone-deaf, and able to go by nothing 'cept the feel of his hands and knees, I wouldn't have knowed when there was a bang and when there warn't.

Not far off, standing in all the wreckage, I could see the President and a whole crowd of other fellas—they warn't soldiers—'long with him. Marse Robert kept looking acrost to them, and after a bit he rode me over to where they was.

"Mr. President," says he, real chilly-like, "who is this army of people and what are they doing here?" (Bang! Bang!)

The President, he looked real taken aback.

"Er—well—er, General," he says. "It's not *my* Army."

"Well, it cert'nly ain't *mine*," answers Marse Robert, "and this is no place for it."

And do you know, Tom, at that the President jest touched his hat and took the whole crowd off down the hill? I nickered after Thunder—I couldn't help it— "*Who* did you say was boss of this whole durned outfit?" He didn't answer me back, neither.

We stayed where we was, and the guns from beyond the village, out by the trees, they went on until well after sunset and for quite a while after that, even in the dark. Marse Robert kept right on a-riding up and down; we went everywhere. We went and talked to Old Pete, and then to Red Shirt and to the Little General. Everyone struck me as being in pretty low spirits. 'Far as I could understand it, we'd been 'specting to beat the Blue men all hollow and drive 'em off, but we hadn't managed to do it. We'd only druv 'em out of the village, and they was still fighting out by the creek 'mong the trees. And top o' that, a whole lot of our fellas had been shot—more'n what theirs had. That was what it come down to.

It was getting on to the middle of the night when Marse Robert rode me back acrost the river, and up to the farm on the hill. When he got down, Tom, he stood by my head a while and petted me. "That's my brave Traveller," he says. "Well done! Well done, Traveller; you're the greatest horse in the world! Thank you!"

I was jest a-shaking all over, and when I got in to

stable I couldn't even have told you whether Richmond said anything spiteful or not. If he did, I didn't hear it. I had a drink and a feed and went to sleep as tired as I'd ary been in my whole life.

VII

I T WAS a short night—real short. It was jest coming on daylight when all three of us was saddled up and led out into the farmyard. There warn't a cloud in the sky, but jest a purple rim to the horizon; it was going to be a real scorching day. Marse Robert came out and Perry gave him his hat and his gloves, as usual. He jest hesitated a moment, and then he spoke to Marse Taylor, mounted Brown-Roan and rode out into the lane. Two soldiers followed behind, riding me and Richmond, and there was the usual little bunch of Marse Robert's officers.

We went back acrost the river and out t'other side of that little village; and there we waited, with Marse Robert watching the crowds of soldiers going forward. There was still bangs, and a few bullets, too, like the day before, but pretty soon it seemed like the Blue men was gone out o' the trees, and Marse Robert jined up with Old Pete and rode down into the bottom and acrost the creek. There was dead fellas—ours and the enemy's, too—laying around everywhere, but I never took no notice—didn't shy—jest went right on through 'em. Once't or twice't it seemed like Brown-Roan was kinda fumbling in his tracks, and coming over the bridge I seed him falter and jib at the hollow noise of his own hooves on the planks. Marse Robert jest spoke to him, gentle-like, coaxed him up t'other side, and we went up through the brush. It was pretty thick, and there was big ditches and barricades of felled trees that the Blue men must 'a made while they was holding the line of that creek. There was a mill, I remember, jest 'bout there, but 'course it was all smashed to pieces—jest a lot o' rubble. Marse Robert kept pulling up to talk to the soldiers, and every time he did, I seed Brown-Roan sort of peering round and hesitating. His mouth was very tight and he kept bobbing his head and then jerking it back, like he felt uneasy. 'Course, I thought, he hasn't come under fire before, poor fella. I sure hoped for his sake he'd be all right, on account of I liked him. Anyways, Marse Robert didn't seem bothered, so I jest turned back to watching where I put my own hooves down in all that mess.

Soon after, Marse Robert left us behind and rode off somewhere or other on his own account, with Major Taylor. He was always doing that on the field of battle. You never knowed where he'd be going next. Me and Richmond was taken on down the lane, closer to the few bangs that was still a-comin' over. After maybe two mile we turned off and went down to a biggish house in a grove of trees 'bove the river. I remember there was bonfires—piles of stuff—boots, boxes of food, all sorts of things—all a-burning. I reckoned the Blue men must have set them afire before they skedaddled, so our fellas wouldn't get 'em.

We had a feed, but they wouldn't put us out to grass—on 'count o' the bangs, I reckon. We stood around in the front courtyard. I tried to act friendly to Richmond—it's my nature, Tom—but he warn't having none of that. Once't, when I moved up close, he tried to kick out at me, so after that I jest let him be. After a while Marse Robert came back on Brown-Roan, and then Old Pete an' Red Shirt arrived and they all went in the house—to get to consulting 'bout the fighting, I reckon.

And that was when I got a chance to listen to Brown-Roan. There warn't a lot of shade around by this time of day, and it was sweltering hot. We was all given a drink and picketed together in what little shade there was.

Brown-Roan was shaking all over and sweating real bad.

"What's the matter?" I asked. "Is it the bangs? You don't have to be scairt of the bangs when you're with Marse Robert. They can't hurt him, you know."

He didn't answer right away—jest sorta dropped his head and swung it from side to side. At last he said, "Traveller, what'll I do? I'm going blind!"

"Never in the world!" I told him. " 'Course you're not going blind!"

I laid my head 'longside his neck and nibbled and groomed him, friendly-like, and he switched his tail acrost my withers.

"I am!" he says. "It kinda comes and goes, but more'n once't or twice't this morning I couldn't rightly see at all—only this sorta swirling gray, like clouds moving, and the real things coming and going in between."

"Can you see all right now?" I asked.

"More or less," he answered, "but not so clear as I used to. I've felt it coming on before, but never so bad as today."

"I'd try to forget 'bout it if I was you," I said. "Have a rest and cool down—it'll pass."

"He's scairt!" snorted Richmond. "The dad-burn—"

"Oh, hush up!" I told him. "Ain't we all scairt, for goodness' sake?"

Brown-Roan didn't say no more—jest dropped his head and swished the flies. It was quiet in the

shade—real sultry—but you could still hear the bangs,
every minute or so, coming from a distance.

Then, suddenly, there come the crackling noise of
muskets—a whole passel of it—what us soldiers call
"furious fire," Tom, y'know. Marse Robert and the
rest came out in a hurry, and he jest grabbed Brown-
Roan's bridle and galloped off up the lane. Richmond
and me was brought on behind.

After maybe a mile—it was pretty thick country,
all trees and brush—we came to another steep creek
and another smashed-up millhouse. There was some
of the Blue men—yeah, I seed 'em, up t'other side—
but they was soon gone, and we went acrost and up
into open fields—corn and grain, all tromped down.
And now the bullets began a-flying all round. They
really do scare you, Tom, you know. They come past
—zip! zip!—and you don't hear 'em come till they've
gone, and every now and then there's a kind of a
"y-ooow" noise when one of 'em bounces off of a stone.
I seed some of our officers pointing and asking Marse
Robert to go back out of the way, but 'course he
didn't. He was riding round 'mong the soldiers, cheering 'em up and telling 'em to go on and fight those
people—he always used to call the Blue men "those
people"—for all they was worth.

Well, soon after that we come up near to where
the Blue men had fixed theirselves—the place where
they meant to stick and fight us. We was on a sort of a
road by now—the air all full of dust—and the Blue
men's lines was way off to the right.

Oh, Tom, you never seed sech a terrible place in
all your life! I've often dreamed 'bout it since. I reckon
now that maybe of all the dreadful places where our
fellas fought the Blue men, that was the very worst. It
began with a whole passel of trees and bushes, mighty
thick. Then a little ways off they all went sloping
down out of sight, steep, and I could smell there was a

creek down there, and a nasty, marshy one at that—
real wide and muddy. T'other side went up jest as
steep, and this was where the Blue men had got to—
you could see 'em—they was stood waiting for us,
guns and all.

Oh, beans an' clover, I thought, even Marse
Robert'll never go sending soldiers down there! Then I
thought of what that horse had said: "That's what
men do—kill each other." And jest then there come a
flash and a bang, real close—my soldier jumped in the
saddle—and I thought, That General Johnston that
was wounded so bad—did *he* have a horse? I wonder
what happened to it.

Marse Robert called for General Hill, and pretty
soon Red Shirt rode up to him and began talking and
pointing down towards the creek. All the while he was
a-talking, Marse Robert kept nodding his head. I
couldn't believe it. I felt as though everything that had
gone before had been quiet and homey compared to
this.

Our side of the creek was some fields, right in
front of where our fellas—thousands of 'em—was all
strung out in long lines; and acrost them fields they
went, Tom, like they was a-walking down the street,
and the enemy firing right in among 'em all the time. I
was thinking, Men are crazy! They're all crazy! Leastways, much as I could think at all. We was drenched in
noise and uproar like over your ears in water.

They went out of sight, over the edge and down
towards the creek, and a moment later there came sech
a crash of guns as I've never heared since—no, not in
no fight we was ever in later. Our fellas had gone
straight down into that.

It was blazing hot by now, and the battle smoke
was a-laying so thick that even without the trees you
couldn't 'a seed anything. But when I heared those
bangs and felt the ground shake like I never had be-

fore—well, it was all jest one entire bang, really—I knowed our fellas must be done for.

And so they was. Jest a few came back up out of that creek, running and stumbling and crawling, and some of them was wounded so bad they needn't have bothered. Well, I thought, I reckon now everyone'll have done 'nuff killing for one day. Even Marse Robert'll have had 'nuff now.

I jest recollect one thing an' another, y'know, out of that bad afternoon. I remember Cap-in-His-Eyes, all covered in dust and sucking a lemon, riding up to talk to Marse Robert on what looked to me like a dirty little scrap of a horse. That was the first time I ever seed Little Sorrel—him as later on I got to respect more'n any horse I've ever knowed. "Ah, General Jackson," says Marse Robert, "I'm very glad to see you. I'd hoped to be with you before." He said a lot more, but you couldn't hear for the row.

It was jest at that moment that Brown-Roan stumbled again and nearly fell down. Marse Robert dismounted, and waved acrost towards us for another horse. 'Twas Richmond was taken to him, not me. The soldier led Brown-Roan back to where I was stood waiting, and he came 'longside of me and stopped.

"It's worse'n ever, Traveller," says Brown-Roan, shivering. "I can't see—I can't see a thing!"

I knowed now what it must have been. I've seed it happen two-three times since then. He'd been scared blind with the bangs and the ground shaking. That happens, sometimes, you know. It can happen to horses and it can even happen to men. A horse won't quit, but it's jest like his sight or his legs or something was 'bliged to quit on his account. I've even seed a horse drop dead and nary a mark on him.

"Take it easy," I says. "Take it easy. It'll pass, you'll see."

It didn't get much chance to pass, though, because

jest then, as Cap-in-His-Eyes rode off, the bangs and
bullets growed even worse. One of our men, standing
near me, was hit in the shoulder and fell down a-crying. Marse Robert rode a little ways off, and waved for
me and my soldier to follow him.

It was evening now. We-all rode along the road a
piece, through all the confusion, with the sun sinking
behind us. I could see Marse Robert was having some
trouble with Richmond, but he was able to hold him
more or less steady while he gave out orders. By this
time I was feeling pretty shook up myself, and kinda
losing my grip on things in all the noise, when I seed a
really fine-looking young man—a tall, kinda loose-
jointed fella, with a long sort of a face and a yellowish
beard—ride up to Marse Robert and salute him.

"General Hood!" says Marse Robert, and with
that there come another bang that blowed a great
cloud of dust all over us, so you couldn't see or think.
When it cleared, neither Marse Robert nor this General Hood had moved a hair; they was still sat a-talking. Marse Robert was pointing acrost at the trees
down in the bottom.

"This must be done," he said. "Can you break the
line?"

"I'll try," answers the big young fella. He had a
strong, powerful voice and sounded very confident.

Marse Robert was jest backing Richmond away
when he stopped and lifted his hat. Then he said
something I didn't catch—sounded like "Good-bye to
you." I reckoned he s'posed he'd never see this here
general again.

And that was the very first time, Tom, that I ever
seed General Hood and his Texans. Oh, we was a
rough, tough Army sure 'nuff, but I'm here to tell you
there warn't a tougher bunch in the whole outfit than
them Texans. I larned that later—yeah, larned it over
and over. But they never—no, they never went

through worse nor druv the Blue men harder'n what they did on that dreadful evening. Marse Robert never forgot it—I know that. Always, after that, it was like the Texans was the fellas he relied on most of all to beat the Blue men when we was in a tight spot.

I'd figured out that it couldn't be done—pushing those people out of t'other side of that swamp; it jest couldn't be done. But them Texans did it. 'Course, where we was, you couldn't see what was happening down the bottom, 'ceptin' there was an awful lot o' heavy firing and smoke. And then, jest as the sun was dropping behind the woods, by golly! there was those people all a-scrambling out and running away, and the Texans after 'em, and all the rest of our fellas strung out—oh, a mile acrost, I reckon—yelling and chasing after 'em for all they was worth! I couldn't see no more, on account of it had got too dark. I jest knowed a fearful lot of soldiers, both sides, must 'a been shot and wounded, 'cause you could hear 'em all crying and calling out in the dark.

But we didn't stick around that swamp. We-all went back to the big house among the trees, and there we had a feed and was stabled up for the night. Brown-Roan was led in after me, and I seed the poor fella walk right into the doorpost and fetch up trembling and turning his head from side to side.

"Are you there, Traveller?"

I nickered acrost to him. It was meant to be reassuring, but I was feeling pretty shook up myself.

He sort of fell into his stall and only jest seemed to keep on his feet. I could hear his hooves clattering on the bricks.

"Blind, Traveller, I'm blind!"

Jest then Marse Robert came in, and the groom—nice young lad, name of Dave—told him something was wrong with Brown-Roan. Marse Robert went over and stroked his nose, talked to him a few mo-

ments and passed his hand acrost his eyes once't or
twice't. Then he says to Dave, "I'm sorry, I can't spare
the time now. One of you had better find some farmer
or sechlike round here to take the horse. Both the others I shall need at first light tomorrow."

"Very good, sir," says Dave. "Will two be 'nuff?"

Marse Robert only nodded. Then, jest as he went
out, he smiled and said, " 'Long as we've got Traveller."

That was the last night I ever seed poor ol'
Brown-Roan, because we was up and off first thing in
the morning. He was well out of it. I guess they put
him on one of the farms round 'bout, and maybe his
blindness passed off. I missed him; he was the nearest
thing I had to a friend in them days, but I never larned
n'more 'bout where he might 'a fetched up. Like Zeb
said, horses are forever saying good-bye.

There was hardly light in the sky when Marse
Robert rode me back to the battlefield. It seemed
strange: everything was that quiet—not a Blue man
anywheres, only jest the dead 'uns. It was quiet all
that day and pretty quiet the next, too. Jest big bangs
—very big—far off, and great clouds of dust in the
sky. It was the Blue men, blowing up their own things
and running away for all they was worth. What I
mostly remember is the terrible hot sun, and the choking dust along the roads full of our soldiers, and the
clouds of flies and skeeters in them woods and
swamps. Everywhere was broken carts and burning
haystacks and barns; yeah, and laying round there was
bay'nets and guns and belts—all sorts o' things—'coutrements as the Blue men had throwed away when
they was skedaddling. You never seed sech a mess.
And on through it all we went, soldiers and horses and
wagons, and Marse Robert and me forever riding here
and there 'mong the woods and clearings and acrost
the little bits o' fields. It was all that mixed-up, you'd

wonder the Army didn't run itself astray. It's my belief that's what happened, 'cause no one rightly knowed where they was meant to be heading for.

What I mostly recollect, Tom, is the way we was all so short of sleep. That was the very middle of summer, and I guess Marse Robert figured we had to be after those people every hour of daylight there was. A lot of them last days of the fighting I was as good as beat—sleeping on my feet—but I was jiggered if I was going to give up, long's Marse Robert wanted to keep a-moving. It was him that kept me going. I couldn't 'a done it for nobody else.

One evening, when it seemed jest like we'd been up and down in the heat forever, I was feeling like I was going to cave in right that very moment. I pulled up and stood panting, head hanging down, jest like an old donkey under two grain sacks. And then, Tom, if'n you can follow me, I realized that although I *thought* I'd stopped on my own 'count, the fact was Marse Robert, he'd reined me in. We always understood each other through and through, you see, and he'd knowed I was beat before I knowed it myself. We was like that, him and me, I could sense what he wanted without him having to give me no signal like another rider would, and 'course that made his life a lot easier, considering all he'd got to think about from morning till night. But that there was the first time I got to know it worked both ways.

It was almost dark, and we jest happened to be some little ways off from the nearest soldiers. Marse Robert dismounted, patted my neck and spoke to me real soft. "Easy, Traveller, easy! Been a long day. Soon be done now. We'll both rest a spell, you and me together." And with that he hitched me to the branch of a tree, sat down under it hisself and closed his eyes.

We didn't get long, though. We'd only been resting there for jest a few minutes in the dusk when all of a sudden up comes an officer on his horse, all in a sweat and a hurry.

"'Come on, old man!" calls out this officer to Marse Robert. "I need that there tree for a hospital. There's wounded men I got to look after. Out of the way, now!"

Marse Robert told him, near as I could understand, that he'd be leaving right away, soon's the wounded came, but he figured till then there was room for both of 'em.

I thought the officer was going to bust, but afore he could start in yelling at Marse Robert, up rides Major Taylor, dismounts and salutes.

"I'm sorry to disturb you, General Lee, sir," he says, "but I have a dispatch here from General Hill."

I reckon that there hospital officer didn't know which way to turn. He went red from the neck up. Then he began stammering something 'bout he was real sorry, he hadn't recognized Marse Robert in the bad light.

"It's no matter, Doctor," says Marse Robert, smiling. "There's plenty o' room for both of us."

Soon after, I let him know I was ready to go on, and we rode back to headquarters with Major Taylor.

I can't recall whether it was next morning, but anyways it was very early some morning soon after, we rode down to a little railroad station jest as the sun was coming up. Usual weather, all calm and nary a cloud. There was several officers with Marse Robert, but he told 'em to stop and wait for him; and then him and me, we went on a ways with nobody else but young Dave riding Richmond. I could see somebody was coming the other way to meet us. Whoever he was, he'd done like Marse Robert and left a bunch of his own people behind to wait. He was sitting up very stiff in the saddle. I recognized the horse before I recognized the man. It was that scrubby little horse I'd

seed the afternoon of the big battle at the creek. That
same moment Marse Robert, he dismounted, gave my
bridle to Dave and went forward to meet Cap-in-His-
Eyes, who'd dismounted too. Well, Tom, you better
believe that them last few days I'd seed a plenty of
wore-out and dusty-looking soldiers, but I never in
my life seed nothing to come nigh Cap-in-His-Eyes
that early morning. He looked like he was half-starved
and hadn't slept for days. I 'spect he hadn't, too. I
could see the skin stretched tight acrost all the bones
of his face. He was covered in dust from his boots to
his head—hair, beard, face, clothes jest one heap o'
gray-white dust; and his buttons, too. And that dirty
little peaked cap was pulled even lower down over his
eyes—'fact, the peak was down so low you couldn't
see his eyes at all.

Little Sorrel, he went trotting back on his own to
the officers that was waiting, and Dave followed, leading me beside Richmond. Well, that was when I got
another turn, Tom—one I winded 'fore I actually seed
it. Laying right beside the road was dead fellas—our
poor fellas—rows and rows all laid out the same,
hands acrost their chests, and their eyes staring up to
the sky. It had rained in the night, and they was all
bleached white and streaked with the rain. Lots, their
foreheads was marked with trickles of dried blood
from the bullets. And there was other soldiers—living
ones—going up and down and peering 'mong 'em—
trying to recognize their friends, I reckon.

I seed Cap-in-His-Eyes look jest a moment towards them rows of dead men; then he turned away as
if he'd something better to do. I was stood right beside
Little Sorrel. I nuzzled his neck and passed him the
time of day. I could tell right off that for all he looked
like a midget, him and his Stonewall Jackson felt the
same way 'bout each other as me and Marse Robert.
He told me they'd been up north, a-going for days on

end—hardly a wink o' sleep—never stopped. He said Cap-in-His-Eyes had gone night and day, beating the Blue men to kingdom come, one bunch after t'other. Then they'd come straight here to jine us. He felt fit to drop, he said, but he was durned if he was quitting. He said Cap-in-His-Eyes was the greatest master in the world.

Well, I could tell, from the way Marse Robert and Cap-in-His-Eyes was talking together, that he was the general Marse Robert must respect and trust maybe most of all. For a start, Cap-in-His-Eyes was doing the talking and Marse Robert was doing the listening. Cap-in-His-Eyes was talking kind of quick and excited, and he kept pushing the toe of his boot around in the dust of the road and then looking up at Marse Robert. Then all of a sudden he stamped his boot down hard. "We've got him!" he says, and with that he waved his hand for Little Sorrel.

"I'll see you again, Traveller," says Little Sorrel as he started forward. "Don't forget me! Today's going to work out bad—I don't know 'zactly how—but don't worry, you'll be all right."

Right till then I'd felt the equal of any horse I'd met, 'ceptin' maybe for Skylark. But somehow Little Sorrel was different. 'Fact, I ain't bottomed it out yet. Cap-in-His-Eyes must 'a been a real smart judge o' horses, 'cause most men would have jest walked past Little Sorrel and not reckoned him worth a handful o' damp hay. It took another horse, really, to catch on to the real spirit that was in him. But there was something else, too—something strange 'bout Sorrel; I could sense it. He was the sorta horse that gets hunches 'bout what's going to happen. I've knowed maybe two-three like that in my time—very few. I even did it myself once't—only jest the once't. But I've never knowed any horse that could feel things coming on like Sorrel could. I figure maybe that kind of horse can sense what's in his master's fate that the master don't know hisself. To do that, you gotta be real close to your man.

I don't recall jest what we did after Cap-in-His-Eyes and his 'uns had rode off. But I sure remember something that happened that afternoon, 'cause it scairt me real bad; bad as I'd been scairt any time them last few days o' fighting. 'Twas 'bout the middle of the day, and so hot the ground was a-rippling acrost my eyes. It was all forest and underbrush we was in, and they was dancing in the heat. There was guns started firing up 'way ahead, and soon as he heared them, Marse Robert rode me forward through the trees. We came to a little clearing 'mong some pines, and there was Old Pete, riding Hero, and the President on Thunder. Thunder was pawing round in the dirt an' didn't look happy at all.

Right off, 'fore Marse Robert could say a word, the President speaks up. "Why, General Lee," he says, "what are you a-doing here? It's too dangerous, and you the boss of this here Army."

"Well," says Marse Robert, very civil, "I'm trying to find out something 'bout those people," he says, "and what they're up to. But come to that," he says, "what do you reckon *you're* a-doing here, and you s'posed to be *my* boss and everybody else's?"

Me and Thunder looks at each other.

"Oh," says the President, very airy-like, "I'm a-doing jest the same as *you're* a-doing," he says—like what he meant was "If you figure on sending me away a second time, you've made a mistake." So then they gets to talking, and jest then the Blue men, 'way down through the trees, opens up with their guns and the bangs started in a-bursting all round us. They was busting this side and that side—there was horses squealing and shying and bucking all over the clearing —and them two, Marse Robert and the President, jest a-sitting there like they was waiting for the mail cart. I'll say that for Thunder: he never moved a hoof.

"Here's General Hill," says the President, peering into the smoke. And with that up comes Red Shirt, full gallop. "Gentlemen!" he shouts through all the noise, "this is no place for either of you! *I'm* in command here, and I order you both to the rear!"

So then the President kinda grins, making a joke of it, and says they'll go, and the two of 'em rides off jest a little ways. But Red Shirt warn't having none of that—he follows 'em. "Didn't I tell you to get to the rear?" he yells. " 'Nother one o' them bangs and we'll be clean out of bosses forever!"

So then Marse Robert and the President, they both went back outen the way. I don't know 'bout Thunder, but I've never been so glad of anything in my life. That night Dave found two bleeding scratches acrost my withers. I hadn't felt 'em at the time. That's often the way, you know, Tom.

Well, jest 'bout then Marse Robert changed horses and I can't say I was all that sorry. He set off on Richmond, and he hadn't been gone more'n a little while when the bangs got even louder, and more of 'em. Well, I thought, Richmond's welcome to 'em; I reckon I done plenty for one day. I had a drink from a little creek and waited with Dave in the shade. You couldn't see a thing that was going on round there; it was all woodland and brush, creeks and swamp.

There was terrible fighting all the rest of that afternoon and evening, but I hardly seed none of it—jest waited, and kept listening to the bangs; and they went right on into the darkness. Goodness knows where we spent that night. I only know it was out in the open and we was picketed. Marse Robert and Richmond came back to headquarters in the dark, and I could see right away that Marse Robert was in a real bad humor. He had a hot temper, you know, Tom, in them days. I could often feel it, but nearly always he kept it close-reined, and he never took it out on me—not once't. That night he was in real low spirits. I figure we hadn't killed as many Blue men as he'd been a-hoping for. He was gloomy and out of sorts. He didn't even have a word for me, the way he usually did.

Still, I had something else to think about that night. Richmond came in sweating, and it warn't long before I realized he was one sick horse. Well, I hadn't been feeling none too good myself, so I could tell what the trouble was. It's what they call colic, Tom, you know, and horses are liable to get it when they're living the way we was. Horses, y'see—we-all got a terrible big gut—bigger'n any other animal, I guess—and there's a lot can go wrong with it. If'n you're a horse, you gotta keep your gut full and you got to dung reg'lar. A horse that gets his gut blocked can find hisself in real bad trouble. Overwork—unwholesome food—irregular feeding; yeah, and shock, too—they can all go to the gut. And that there wind-sucking some horses do—that's no durned good neither.

I've told you, haven't I, that Richmond was a jumpy, nervy kind of a horse—a squealer and a bad-tempered sort? 'Course, we'd all been under a lot of strain, and Richmond had been under fire's much as I had. He was a wind-sucker, all right, but 'sides that he always used to pitch into his feed like he reckoned he was never going to get another. Well, that afternoon—the afternoon I got the splinters acrost my withers—Marse Robert and Richmond, they come under some real bad fire, so he told me that night. It 'pears Marse Robert actually rode out through our lines, right out in front, 'cause he wanted to see for hisself what the Blue men was up to. Richmond hadn't 'zackly cared for that, and I don't know as I blame him. Anyways, when he got back that night he was shaking all over—shocked by the bangs as much as anything. By golly!

He even *smelt* o' the battle smoke—and then he set to
and bolted his feed fast as he could.

"You'll do yourself a mischief," I says to him.
"Ease up!"

"Oh, go jump in the creek, Greenbrier!" says
Richmond. "You think you can tell me anything? Jest
hush up! I was carrying a man when you was sucking
your dam."

That warn't true, of course, but I jest let him be.
There was 'nuff to worry 'bout without quarreling
with *him*. He bolted his feed, and it was a poor feed we
both had that night. The bran was sour. I let young
Dave know plain 'nuff I didn't jest 'zackly relish it,
and he come and looked it over. Then he emptied out
my nose bag and fetched some more. 'Warn't his fault,
I guess. When you're on campaign, you see, Tom,
things is apt to get kind o' wrong side up, and we'd
been going so hard we was in what they call short
supply. 'Sides, like I said, it was dark—jest lanterns.
Anyways, it was too late for Richmond—he'd eat it all
and wanted more.

'Fore first light next morning I heared him
a-stamping round, and every now and then he'd pass
wind something terrible. He was in pain all right. The
way he was carrying on, I reckon his gut must 'a been
blocked. I asked him how he was feeling, but all I got
for my trouble was more cussing. Young Dave was up
well before first light—the sentry woke him—and it
didn't take him long to see Richmond was a sick horse.
'Course, as far as I was concerned, that meant jest one
thing. I was saddled up for Marse Robert; it was my
turn, anyway.

It was a terrible bad battle that day—worse'n I
can tell you, Tom. The Blue men had got 'emselves up
atop a big green hill, all open and plain, and our fellas
was stuck down in the woods and swamps at the bottom. It was nothing but guns, guns all that day. The

Blue men had more guns'n we did, and they was firing down the open hillside. I was lucky, 'cause for some reason Marse Robert didn't go acting crazy the way he'd done the day before. Early afternoon, him and Old Pete rode out a ways to one side o' that hill, looking round, I reckon, for the best chance of an attack. But then he came back again. Well, 'tell the truth, Tom, I figure that day no one knowed what they was a-doing at all—it was having no sleep for days, as much as anything else—and even Marse Robert wasn't jest rightly hisself. I could tell from how he felt on my back and the way he was acting and speaking. He wanted to drive the Blue men off'n that there hill like he'd druv them out of the swamp with the Texans, but he didn't rightly know how to go 'bout it. And in fact it never got done. When it came dark, our Army was still down to the bottom of that hill, 'ceptin' for a whole chance of our poor fellas laying dead and wounded on the open slope.

I never heared the wounded cry worse'n they did that night.

Headquarters had been set up at a house a ways back, and that was where I found Richmond that night, in the stable. He'd plainly been took worse and worse all day, and now there warn't no doubt he was very bad off. He was sweating real hard, breathing fast and blowing. Even from where I was, I could tell his pulse was too quick. He kept a-walking round and round his box, and every so often he'd throw hisself down and roll about real wild. Then he'd get up and stretch as if he wanted to pass water, but he couldn't do it. Every time the pain came on, he'd kick at his belly.

I figured young Dave had been with him all day, but there'd been no help to be had on 'count of the battle. Marse Robert and me, we'd been riding through the bivouacs long after dark, Marse Robert

talking to this general and that 'un. We was still out
when Jine-the-Cavalry rode up to talk to Marse Robert and find out what he wanted him to do. And when
we got back to headquarters, Tom, 'twas all Marse
Robert could do jest to get off'n my back, he was that
tired, and Dave had no chance at all to talk to him
'bout Richmond.

Getting on towards the middle of the night, a fog
come up and covered everything. You could feel it
creeping and thickening all around the stable, round
the house and out over the fields beyond, thick as
blankets. You could hear the sentries coughing, and
cussing to each other, up and down outside. I wondered whether it'd be laying high as the hill, soaking
into the dead and wounded, the dead horses laid stiff
alongside the guns they'd dragged up there. After a
while the air in the stable turned kind of moist and
cloudy, and all you could see outside was jest thick
gray.

I couldn't sleep. It got hard, in that air, to draw
your breath, and Richmond was forever shambling
round and round his box, crouching down, getting up
again and panting. Somehow I could sense that our
soldiers was down at heart. You could tell from the
tread of the sentries and the heavy kind of way they
was a-speaking and acting. We'd thought we was going to drive the Blue men off of that hill, and we
hadn't—and what was worse, there was a passel of our
fellas laying out there dead as flies.

First light, when it come at last, was thin and
gray, sort of filtering through a damp mist wet as rain.
I'd been 'specting Dave to saddle me up for Marse
Robert, but nothing happened—nothing at all. It
seemed a long time 'fore finally Dave and two-three
other soldiers came in. I thought they'd have 'tended
to Richmond, but 'stead of that they started putting
dry litter in the empty stalls. That was a fair-sized

stable, and best I could make out they was getting it ready for more horses. After they'd been working a while, Dave broke off to have a look at Richmond. He spoke to the other soldiers, and then he went away and came back with some sort of warm drink he'd made up for him. I could smell it from where I was stood. It had a kind of heady, herb-like smell. I guess there was some drug in it. Richmond drank some, but 'far as I could see he didn't drink it all, and I could tell Dave was flustered and felt he couldn't give Richmond all of his time.

By now the rain was jest streaming down. The yard outside was like a duckpond, and in one part of the roof, where there was a fair old hole, the water was pouring through like a creek a-running. Every man who came into the stable was drenched and cussing, and dripping all over the floor.

All of a sudden a soldier comes in leading Little Sorrel. He was put into the box next to mine. He was wetter'n a frog in a ditch, and they began rubbing him down. I asked him what was going on. He told me Cap-in-His-Eyes had ridden him over from his outfit to talk to Marse Robert.

"The Blue men have all gone off the hill," he said. "Vamoosed in the night. Stonewall's crazy to get after 'em and blow 'em to bits, but with this durned rain it's jest about impossible to move. You oughta see it, Traveller. Everything this side of the hill's turning into a lake miles wide, and all the wounded fellas crawling 'bout 'mong the dead 'uns, crying for the ambulances to come and pick 'em up. Our soldiers are trying to get fires going to dry theirselves out and dry their muskets."

"Where's Cap-in-His-Eyes now?" I asked.

"Inside," says Sorrel, "talking to Marse Robert. 'Far as I can make out, Marse Robert's none too pleased with him. That day I last seed you—day before yesterday—it seems he let the Blue men get away when he oughta've been pitching into 'em. I knowed how it would be. I told you, didn't I, that it'd work out bad—remember? He was so tired he jest couldn't think no more. I seed him actually falling asleep with the food between his teeth."

Jest then Hero—Old Pete's horse—was led in, and the rain a-pouring off'n him in streams. He told us that him and Old Pete had been riding all over the place, everywhere there was fighting the day before, checking things out.

"Even Old Pete's had 'nuff for a while," says Hero. "They's bodies laying everywhere—the Blue men and our fellas all mixed up together. I don't know who won—everyone seems shook up and real down-hearted but one thing—the Blue men's gone, that's for sure."

Hero warn't in the stable long. They'd hardly had a chance to rub him down when we heared Old Pete outside, callin' for him. When Hero warn't brung out quick 'nuff, he started in a-cussing real savage.

"I figure this is all the fighting there's likely to be," says Sorrel. "For a good while, anyways."

"How d'you know?" I asked.

"There's nowhere left for the Blue men to go," he answered. "But we ain't able to fight 'em no more. We're dead beat ourselves, and anyway they've got too many guns. Some of them guns yesterday was the heaviest I've ever heared."

"So what do you think'll happen?" I asked him.

"They'll go away," he said, "and leave us be—for now, that is."

The next horse that come in was Thunder, so I knowed without asking that the President must have come to see Marse Robert, too.

"What's the matter with Richmond?" asked Thunder at once. Richmond had been pretty quiet for a while, but now he was blowing again, tossing his head and walking his stall.

I said I reckoned it was his gut, and told Thunder 'bout the sour bran.

"He'll die," said Thunder, watching him. "Gut's blocked. I seed it afore now."

We stood around in the foggy air, stamping hooves and listening to the noise of the rain on the roof. Presently Dave came in to see what more he could do for Richmond, but by this time Richmond was in spasms and didn't even 'pear to feel it when he hit his head agin the wall in his tossing and turning.

It was early afternoon when Thunder was taken out for the President. I heared his hooves splashing out of the yard, and as they died away Marse Robert come in, a-talking to Dave. They went straight over to Richmond's box. When he seed Marse Robert, Richmond quieted down and let Marse Robert run his hand over him. The pain seemed to have left him and he began drinking from his water-trough.

"How long has he been like this?" says Marse Robert to Dave.

Before Dave could reply, Richmond staggered and set his four legs wide apart. 'Seemed like he was trying to stand, but then he give a quick lurch forward and fell over on his knees. He commenced to get up, but fell again. He was jerking and shaking all over, teeth bare, frothing at the mouth. It didn't go on very long, though: he went over on one side, kicked out, shuddered from head to foot and went still. I knowed he was dead.

Marse Robert dropped on one knee and felt his heart. Young Dave, beside him, was near'bouts to crying.

"What a shame!" says Marse Robert, running his hand over Richmond's body with the rain a-dripping off all down his sleeve. "What a shame! Died o' the colic. No fault of yours, my boy—these things happen in war. We have to bear them like everything else. Some of you lads better set to and bury the poor beast. He was an awkward fella, but so are we all, I guess. He always did best as he could. I'm sorry to see him go."

He waited a few moments. Then he turned away, came into my box and began stroking my nose and talking to me. "That jest leaves you and me now, Traveller," he says. "Jest the two of us. But I reckon you're all I'm going to be needing from now on. You and me, we'll make out jest fine."

"Is that right, sir," asks Dave, "the enemy's gone?"

"Yes, they're gone all right," answers Marse Robert. 'Peared like he was leaving, but then he spoke to me again, very low in my ear. "Oh, Traveller," he said, "by rights they should have been destroyed! They should have been *destroyed*!"

VIII

AUGUST 19, 1862. It is now seven weeks since General Lee, in the remarkable campaign known as the Seven Days, drove General McClellan's army back from the eastern outskirts of Richmond, by one engagement after another forcing them into retreat through the marshy, wooded country bordering the Chickahominy and finally into ignominious refuge under the protection of Federal gunboats along the northern shore of the James River. Had it not been for faulty staffwork and uncertain coordination of the conglomerate and as yet inexperienced Army of Northern Virginia, the Federals might well have been reduced to surrender. As matters stand, the hitherto unregarded General Lee has won the adulation of every officer and man under his command and the respect and confidence of the entire Confederacy. Now—so is the common feeling throughout the South—there is every prospect of such a victory as will bring about recognition by the European powers and a negotiated peace acknowledging independence.

Yet the cost in casualties, to a nation with less than half the manpower of its enemy, has been fearful. During the Seven Days' campaign, the flower of the South has perished. In particular the loss of junior officers—the fulcrum of any army and the reservoir of future senior command—has been grave. Such losses cannot be made good and the Confederacy cannot afford their continuance. As with material resources, so

with manpower; already, with courage and determination still high, the South has begun to feel the pinch.

General Lee is in no position to follow up or ex-
ploit his brilliant victory. He is like a man swimming
against the sea. As fast as he breasts the waves, they
close again. McClellan has evacuated his army to the
area of Fredericksburg. The Federal forces so skillfully
defeated by Stonewall Jackson in his Valley campaign
of June have been reorganized under the command of
General Pope on the upper Rappahannock. Here they
have been joined by reinforcements under General
Burnside.

There has been no time for the full period of rest,
refit and reinforcement that General Lee would have
wished for his men. The weaker side cannot afford to
wait. He must take the offensive—if possible, threaten
Washington, for Richmond is never so safe as when its
defenders are absent. If General Pope—a bombastic
and truculent character, regarded by Lee with con-
tempt—is to be suppressed, it must be quickly, before
McClellan's army can join him. Piecemeal and se-
cretly, the Army of Northern Virginia has been trans-
ported from Richmond to the area of Gordonsville in
the Piedmont, near the eastern foot of the Blue Ridge.
Until two days ago Pope was known to be lying some
twenty miles to the north, beyond the Rapidan. Now,
however, there is news that he has taken alarm and
begun a retreat northward towards the Rappahannock.
General Lee, accompanied by his subordinate General
Longstreet, has ridden to the top of Clark's Mountain
to see for himself.

Gets cold these midwinter nights, Tom, don't it? Been
pretty cold today, particular late afternoon. It's fine in
here, though. I guess you got to've been out cold
nights in the open 'fore you can really 'preciate a
warm stable like this 'un. That's it—rake round the
straw close up agin me and settle yourself in comfortable.

What's that? A new horse? You seed a new mare come with Marse Robert's son today? Tom, that was no new mare. My shoes and ears, give me the shock of my life! For a moment I thought I seed a ghost! That's Lucy Long, Tom—her as first soldiered with me four year ago and more. No, well, 'course you wouldn't know. Soon's ever I seed her coming round the corner with young Marse Rob, I recognized the blaze on her forehead and her white hind legs. 'Made me start all over, but then she nickered to me, jest like she used to, so I knowed it was Lucy all right. I 'membered her at once—that light brown color and the square build of her. Well, so I ought, after all we was through together.

'Course, there was a time once't when I didn't like Lucy. 'Twarn't no fault of her'n. I was jest plain mean, that was what it come down to: jealousy—that, and knowing well 'nuff why Marse Robert had felt 'bliged to get her. Yeah, well, I'll tell you all 'bout it sometime. But you couldn't dislike Lucy for long. For one thing, she's a shade older'n me, with real nice manners. Quiet kinda horse—no bad habits at all. Not half the trouble I can be. We got the same fast walk, but Lucy never cared for a trot. She liked an easy pace and a short canter. I got to admit she was what Marse Robert needed at the time. And it was all my fault—all my fault! Worst thing I ever done in my life. I hate to think of it even now.

Jine-the-Cavalry got her for Marse Robert, you know. 'Far's I can remember, I think Ajax must have come 'bout the same time. He came from somewhere down near Andy's, I believe. Ajax never suited Marse Robert, though—too tall. Well, he *is* kinda big and awkward, Tom, don't you reckon? And not all that much vigor, neither. Got him a reg'lar easy life, hasn't it? Warn't many bangs for Ajax—he never come much under fire, and he's sure comfortable 'nuff here.

What was it I was going to tell you, though? Oh, 'bout when me and Hero was up on Clark's Mountain, they calls it. It was a fine, clear morning in late summer—pretty hot day coming on. I knowed something was fixing to happen, jest from the general feel of the whole place. The mood of the soldiers—all strung up, y'know.

This was a different kinda country; we'd come up on the railroad, and it was—oh, yeah, a month and more'n a month—after the Blue men had run away off the hill in the fog and our headquarters had gone back to ol' Miss Dabbs's. No more swamps; jest nice, clear streams. Open country; no underbrush and hardly no forests—not as I seed. The roads was pretty good, too —more certain for my hooves. It was all long, low ridges, with fields of standing grass and crops, and here and there a high hill. The real mountains was far off. You could see 'em black agin the evening sky.

Well, that morning—getting on for mid-morning, 'twas—I was cropping some fresh grass, nice and easy, in the meadow near a farm where Marse Robert had set up headquarters, when up comes Old Pete and Hero. I was glad to see Hero, 'cause to tell you the truth I was still missing Brown-Roan, though 'course there was plenty of other horses round headquarters. Marse Robert and Old Pete, they got to talking together, leaning on the rail by the meadow; but I knowed they wouldn't be long, 'cause Old Pete had left Hero's saddle on. Sure 'nuff, the two of 'em, and Marse Taylor and a few more, we-all set off for a nice ride. We must'a gone maybe six or seven mile when we come to this here Clark's Mountain, and up we went on the open grass. Some of our soldiers was round, and they saluted Marse Robert. When we got to the top, out came everybody's two bottles up to their eyes. I was used to that by now.

"What're we all a-doing, d'you figure?" I asked Hero.

"Looking for Blue men, 'course," he says. "What else?"

Now you gotta know, Tom, that ever since that morning when Richmond died, I'd s'posed we was through with the Blue men. Don't ask me why I'd thought that, with soldiers and tents and guns all around, but I had. Well, 'cause I'd wanted to, I reckon. Y'see, Marse Robert had told Dave that the Blue men was gone right 'nuff, and I'd s'posed that meant for good. But Hero, he knowed better. When he told me that, I had a horrible sinking feeling in my gut. Again? I thought. Bangs, battles, horses squealing and bullets smacking up the dust? I was going to ask him how he knowed, but then I reckoned that wouldn't look right for Marse Robert's horse. So I jest turned my head and looked out over the country from up top there.

You could see a long ways. Jest below us, at the foot of the hill, was a real pretty river, all open, shining and glittering in the sunshine. Beyond that, on our left, ran a railroad, but I couldn't see no smoke, and no trains. And then, far off, after a bit I could make out some of them cloths on sticks fluttering in the distance, and white things moving.

"See?" says Hero. "See their wagons out there? They're retreating. They've got wind of us. Keep watching them camps down yonder."

Hero always understood so much more'n me— well, in them days he did—that I jest waited, puzzling. Everything seemed real quiet in the midday sun. The generals sat watching. I dropped my head for a mouthful or two of grass. Marse Robert, he didn't make no objection, so I jest went on browsing. Other horses began to do the same. I wished there was some water around.

The wagons vanished into the far distance; and

then, nearer, but still a long ways off, beyond the river, I seed the camps. They was all alive with little clouds of dust—Blue men on the march. Like Hero said, they was going away from us, and as they met up into columns the clouds of dust jined together in long trails. They drifted away in the bright haze of the afternoon sun. They got thinner and thinner and finally disappeared. Still no one spoke.

At last Marse Robert said to Old Pete something 'bout he'd never thought they'd turn their backs on us so soon. We-all went down off'n the hill, an' I had the drink I'd been wanting. Marse Robert never overlooked things like that, no matter how much he had on his mind. Well, like I said, it was always him and me, Tom, y'see.

Next thing I remember is very late that same night—almost morning. The moon was waning—jest a little light, but 'nuff for us. Our Army was fording that river I'd seed from the top of the hill; I could see the hill behind us, agin the night sky.

We was going after the Blue men—I knowed that. I remember how I come a-splashing up the far bank, and Marse Robert reined me in and waited to watch the men go past—boots and boots, and muskets a-sticking up every which way, and the cloths on sticks going by, and the fellas a-laughing and joking like they was sure of theirselves. Yes, they was in good spirits, rightly—blamed if'n I knowed why.

Myself, I was feeling bad. What Hero'd told me had sunk in and given me a shock. I didn't want no more battles—I hadn't reckoned on that. Jest thinking 'bout what I remembered made me feel bad 'nuff. Maybe the Blue men would keep on running away, I thought. Yeah, and maybe they wouldn't. I knowed the bangs couldn't hurt Marse Robert, but if you'd ever heared jest one bang, Tom, you'd know how I felt all the same. The bangs had driven Brown-Roan blind,

and they'd as good as killed Richmond. I felt sure o'
that. Without the bangs he wouldn't have got that
there colic or whatever 'twas as finished him off.

Our headquarters was advancing along with Cap-
in-His-Eyes an' his 'uns, but we didn't go far that day
—maybe twelve mile—'fore we pitched tents for the
night by the railroad we'd seed from the high hill the
day before. We spent the next two-three days working
along, on and off the bank of a pretty big river—bigger'n the one we'd crossed in the dark. There was no
fighting—none that I seed, anyways—but bangs in the
distance all day; and that was 'nuff to scare me,
though I did all I could to keep Marse Robert from
seeing anything was the matter.

I'll tell you one thing, Tom, as I remember jest
'bout that time. We was a-marching near the bank of
that river, along a pretty good road, when all of a sudden we come round a bend and there was a man's
body hanging from the branch of a tree, right 'side the
road. The bend was so sharp that I 'most ran agin it,
and I nearly shied. "Easy, Traveller, easy!" But I figured that jest then even Marse Robert warn't all that
easy. I felt him start in the saddle. Then he calls out to
some man 'side the road there. "What's this, Sergeant?" he says.

"Spy, sir," answers the fella, saluting. "Executed
by court-martial this morning, sir."

The man's head was covered and his hands was
roped behind him. He warn't dressed like a soldier—
jest ordinary—but his boots was gone—well, with our
Army boots never stayed long on dead bodies, you
know, Tom. There was jest 'nuff wind to swing him
gentle-like. Marse Robert nodded to the sergeant and
we rode on. But a ways further we stopped off—us
and Marse Taylor and Cap-in-His-Eyes and a few
more—and back down the road I could see the man

hanging there, while company after company rounded
the bend and come up agin him jest like we had.

It rained torrents that night, and I recollect, next
day, all the creeks and ditches boiling brown and chattering bubbles. Still no fighting, jest bangs all day long
and nothin' to be seed. Come night-time, an officer
rode up to headquarters on a sweating horse pretty
near done up. After they'd fed and watered the horse
and rubbed him down, he was picketed 'longside me
and Little Sorrel. He told us how him and his man had
been sent back by General Stuart, who was playin'
hell with the Blue men, he said, miles away acrost the
river. 'Peared Jine-the-Cavalry and his fellas had been
trying to burn a railroad bridge behind the Blue men,
but the heavy rain had put an end to that. This horse,
Rollo, kept on talking mighty big 'bout how fine it was
to be out behind the Blue men with Jine-the-Cavalry.
He said it was the greatest life in the world for a horse,
and then he was laying it on that Skylark was a personal friend o' his, and the real reason his man had
been sent back twenty-five mile to Marse Robert was
'cause he hisself was reckoned to be jest about the best
horse in the whole durned outfit.

"Any officer would 'a done," he said, "but not
any horse."

At last he really got to me with all this carrying-
on, and I said I 'lowed how it was jest 'bout time to go
to sleep.

"You're scairt, ain't you?" says Rollo. There still
come a bang every now and again, 'way off in the
dark, and he tosses his head to show what he meant.

"What reason you got to say that?" I answers
him.

"You smell like it, anyways," he says. "You smell
like a real headquarters horse—"

"I'll go further'n you any day," I says, "and *all*
day, too, come to that."

"No one's talking 'bout going further," says Rollo. "It's a battle I'm a-talking 'bout—"

Jest at that moment Little Sorrel, kinda slow and meditating-like, as if he hardly knowed what was in his own mind, says, "Any—horse—that wants a battle's a plain fool—'cause Marse Robert hisself don't want a battle right now." He stopped. Then, after a few moments, he added, "But he's going to get one, jest the same."

"What in the world you talking 'bout?" asks Rollo, raising one of his forelegs and lifting his tail.

I don't say he warn't a good horse, Tom, but he was like a lot of them there cavalry horses, you know —setting out to be a hell-raiser and a wildcat. There's more to soldiering 'n that, even if'n I didn't know it yet.

"Marse Robert ain't *looking* for a battle," says Sorrel again. "But—soon—a long ways from here—" And then he stopped again, like he'd never said nothing at all, and laid down on the straw.

"Well, what?" asks Rollo, kinda contemptuous-like.

Sorrel seemed like he was half-asleep. His eyes was closed. "Men marching. Marching hard and far. Smoke burning, up to the sky. Soldiers—soldiers throwing stones at the Blue men—no bullets left. Jest another hour, men—must hold on another hour— Marse Robert's coming—"

And then, Tom, dad burn my hooves, he went right off to sleep and even Rollo couldn't get no more out'n him! It stopped Rollo's carrying-on a sight better'n anything I could have said. There was something —well, almost scary 'bout it, like it had been some other horse talking all the time—some other horse that warn't there.

'Twas midday next morning 'fore the bangs began again—ours an' theirs together, it sounded—but I still

didn't see nothing, 'cause Marse Robert had moved
headquarters back a mile or two to a little village.
Early that afternoon I was standing round in a patch of
shade when one of the sentries nearby points and says
to his mate, "Look yonder. Ain't that General Jackson
a-coming?"

Sure 'nuff, Cap-in-His-Eyes come riding up and
goes straight into the house to talk to Marse Robert.
They took Sorrel and hitched him 'longside o' me.

First thing Sorrel said was he was glad we'd got
rid of Rollo. Then, after we'd stood and swished each
other's flies a while (it was real hot), he said, "I won't
be seeing you again, Traveller. Not until the battle. Me
and my general, we're in for a real long haul."

"How do you know?" I said. "If'n I've understood
it rightly, Marse Robert's only jest now telling Cap-in-
His-Eyes what we's going to do."

"Well, I *do* know," he said. "I jest do. A good
horse always knows what's back of his man's mind.
Often knows it better'n the man hisself. I mean, he
can feel what's *in* the man. That's why I hadn't got no
time for that there Rollo—he knowed nothing. The
reason you're scairt, Traveller—oh, yes, you are—is
that Marse Robert's scairt, too. Oh, he ain't afeared for
his own skin—I don't mean that. He's afeared for the
Army, on account of he can't rightly make up his
mind what we-all ought to be fixing to do. And 'cord-
ingly, being a good horse, *you're* scairt."

"But Cap-in-His-Eyes—" I began.

"Cap-in-His-Eyes—that's different. He's *determined* to have a battle," says Sorrel. "That's how I
know there's gonna be one. You should jest 'a been
with us in the Valley. You still got plenty to larn, Traveller, but one of these days you'll be same as me—
you'll find you jest do know things. All you need is
experience."

"I don't want that sort of experience," I said.

"Who does?" says Sorrel. "What you goin' to do 'bout it?"

I was still chewing on that when Cap-in-His-Eyes come out with two or three of his officers, and him and Sorrel was off and gone.

We stayed put right where we was, in the village. Best as I remember, 'twarn't till evening the next day that Jine-the-Cavalry rode up. This time he hadn't got Skylark—it was Star of the East, but the two of us hardly got no talk, 'cause they didn't stop long, neither. I remember Marse Robert come out of the house with Jine-the-Cavalry, and they stayed around talking a while, till finally Jine-the-Cavalry saluted and rode off. Marse Robert always had a special liking for Jine-the-Cavalry, you know, Tom—like he was his own son, I reckon.

But let me go right on telling you what happened to *me*, 'cause the way things turned out, the next few days was pretty near the most important in my life—a kind of turning point, you might say.

'Twas all bang! bang! for another couple of days, and still no real fighting; only, I was feeling more and more jittery on 'count of what Sorrel had said. But then we-all set off to marching, and that night I plumb forgot 'bout being jittery, on account of we fetched up at a real fine house—long avenue of trees—darkies singing and dancing—all the air smelling o' gardenia and white jasmine—a fine gentleman meeting Marse Robert, saying him howdy and taking off his hat— clean, warm stables and a hot bran mash for every horse in headquarters—why, for a time I really got to wondering whether this mightn't be that there War that Jim said we was going off to. 'Course, I knowed better'n that, but I liked pretending 'twas, 'cause it made me forget for a while 'bout the battle. Marse Robert, Old Pete and Marse Taylor and the others, they was all feeding and sleeping up at the big house, you see, Tom. So that was where we-all stayed that night. We was off real early in the morning, but everyone was up to see us go.

Marching, Tom; marching in the cool of the early morning, in summertime, 'fore it gets to be a real hot day. Mockingbirds singing, maybe one of them orioles, maybe a flicker or two, red-wing blackbirds in the trees; dew still shining on the grass; the soldiers singing behind you; hooves falling steady on a good, firm road, easy going, other horses all round—that's the life for a horse, for what I'd call a *valued* horse. I often think back to them early morning marches, but I remember that one 'specially, 'count of what happened in the middle of all my high spirits.

We was up at the front of the column—'fact, we was well ahead of it—Marse Robert, Major Taylor, Major Talcott and some more. That was jest fine, 'cause there's no dust, Tom, you see, when you're out like that in front of the line o' march. You can look out in front of you, breathing the air fresh and easy, and take an interest in whatever there is to be seed—people running to their gates to watch you go by, kids cheering and all the rest of it. Best part of soldiering.

I remember the place we'd got to real well. Up ahead I could see a little town we was coming to, beyond a turn in the road. One side was open woodland; t'other was a nice, neat timber house, all freshly whitewashed—looked good in the sunshine—an' a tolerable big patch of corn with all the cobs smellin' ripe. A mockingbird was singing up in a birch tree— oh, it was all jest as pretty and peaceful as it is right here in summer. And then, suddenly, in a cloud o' dust, round the bend ahead come one of our fellas, driving his horse for all he was worth. You couldn't tell which of them was in more of a lather, the horse or the man.

"The Blue men! The Blue men!" he was shouting,

and pointing up the road behind him. "Cavalry! They're right here!"

Well, there was jest the few of us, Tom, you see— what's knowed as the staff—not 'nuff to fight at all. Marse Robert calls out to the fella as he pulls up, "How far off are those people?" But 'fore he could answer, there they come, riding round the bend after him, a whole passel of Blue men, and they sure 'nuff looked like they meant business.

I'd never been so close to the Blue men before. One of their horses neighed to ours; I can hear it now. There's a lot of difference in neighing, Tom, you see. I mean, whether it's friends or strangers. This was a neigh to strangers—"Who the heck are you?"—and you could tell it was a stallion, 'cause he put in a kind of extra grunt at the end. As they come still closer, Major Talcott's horse answered him, sorta noncommittal.

"Go back, General Lee, go back!" shouts one of our officers. It was the first time I'd ever heared that, but I can tell you it warn't to be the last.

Marse Robert reined me in, looking up the road at the Blue men. They was so close I could see their eyes moving and smell their sweat. "Steady, Traveller!" But jest the same, he turned me around. And as he did so the whole staff—the majors, the couriers, everyone— formed a line acrost the road.

"Go back, General Lee! We'll hold 'em! Only go back!"

The Blue men pulled up. I figure they was wondering how many of us there was. I seed one of 'em ride acrost to another, and they started talking together and pointing at us. And then, all of a sudden, like they didn't care for the look of us, and even before Marse Robert had had time to get going—I could tell from the whole feel of him that he didn't care for the notion—they'd turned their horses round without firing a shot and ridden back the way they'd come.

Nobody, horse nor man, really had time to be scairt or reckon how much danger we was in. That's the kinda thing that only hits you afterwards, Tom, you see. I reckon most of our horses didn't even know jest what had happened. But I did. So it don't have to be a battle, I was thinking. The Blue men can appear any time, jest when you're on the road, and maybe shoot you down like a rabbit. Yeah, even when you're the General's horse. It didn't make me feel no better, I can tell you, 'bout the job we was doing. I recollected, too, what Sorrel had said 'bout Marse Robert not wanting a battle but getting one jest the same. To be honest, I wished I warn't in the Army.

That warn't the only thing that happened that morning, neither. We'd gone back closer to the head of the column, of course, and we was jogging along the road, kinda getting over the shock—well, I mean, Tom, jest s'pose me and Marse Robert had a' been taken prisoner by the Blue men!—when we come up with two-three ladies—*real* ladies; you could smell their rosewater and their gloves and all the rest—a-sitting outside a house by the road and looking at their nice, shiny carriage. It had polished silver fittings, lilac cushions, darky coachman in a top hat—the whole shebang. Well, near the whole shebang. The only thing missing was the horses. They'd gone, and the carriage was right square acrost the road, with the ends of the shafts down on the grass one side. Two of the ladies was a-crying, handkerchiefs up to their eyes.

'Course, Marse Robert rides up to them at once—you know how he always likes the ladies—and offs with his hat. And what it come down to was that the Blue men—them same Blue men, I reckon—had held the ladies up and taken their two horses. 'Course, they'd 'a been good 'uns, Tom, you see. This old lady said she'd come out with her daughters in the carriage on purpose to see Marse Robert go by and to say howdy.

"Well, I guess she's done that," mutters Major Talcott's horse to me while Marse Robert was telling her how sorry he was. That was Joker—he was jest right for a soldier; later on, when we was starving, he could still find some fun in 'most anything. But I'd been shook up bad already that morning and I didn't feel the same way. I was thinking 'bout them two fine horses, jest taking it easy along the road and likely thinking 'bout getting back to stables, when along comes the Blue men. So now they could look forward to bangs and exhaustion and cold nights and wind and rain and more bangs, until the bang that tore 'em to pieces, like all those artillery horses on the green hill the time Richmond died.

But I reckon I was the only one thinking that way. When we stopped off that night, camping in the open, you could tell the whole Army was in good spirits, and Marse Robert along with 'em. He took me for a little walk through the camp, the way he liked to when we was on the march, to talk to the soldiers and let them talk to him. Me, I helped out by nuzzling up and letting the men stroke me. By this time, you see, Tom, any man in the Army would 'a given Marse Robert the shirt off'n his back if he'd 'a wanted it. I 'spect no other general's ever had his men with him like Marse Robert. We was going here and there among the campfires, the fellas cooking or maybe picking the lice off'n each other, and calling out "Hey, there, General!" or "When we going to get at 'em, General?" Marse Robert was jest the same with everyone, quiet and friendly. He never dressed up, you know, Tom. He jest looked like any of our officers, 'cepting Perry and Meredith always kept his clothes and his boots real clean and tidy. I remember—yeah, it was that very same night, while we was finishing that little tour round the camp—one of the brigadiers—I don't recall rightly which one 'twas—asks him why he didn't dress like a general. "Oh," says Marse Robert, "I don't care to. I figure colonel's 'bout as high as I ought to have gotten—or maybe a cavalry brigade." He meant it, too. Well, that's all changed now right 'nuff, ain't it?

Next day, though—oh, Tom, that was a hard march! The heat and the dust on the road was 'nuff to drive you mad, horse or man. Marse Robert stopped several times to see different regiments go by, and it was like they was groping through a fog. Men had old scarves, pieces of sacking, rags—anything they could find—tied over their mouths and noses to try and keep the dust out. It got in your eyes and your ears. It got down your throat. It was 'nuff to blind and choke you. And the heat—everyone was sweating; and nothing to drink all day. They warn't gray men; they was *white* men—white with dust from head to foot, 'cepting where the sweat ran down. I seed men tear off their jackets and fall down by the roadside, coughing up spittle that was like gumbo, jest thick with dust. Pretty soon the Army was jest a-stumbling 'long, and seemed like Marse Robert hadn't the heart to push 'em faster. Maybe he *couldn't*. There's a limit to everything. But we kept on marching till the middle of the night, and when Marse Robert rode back along the column I seed crowds of soldiers that'd jest laid down and gone to sleep where they was halted—no fires, no food, nothing. I seed a boy that must 'a carried one of the cloths on sticks all day—it was an honor to do that, you know. He'd jest rolled hisself up in the cloth and gone to sleep so sound the sergeant couldn't wake him. "Let him be," says Marse Robert. "He's done his duty. No one can do more."

Well, I told you, Tom, didn't I, that I was uneasy
and fretful in myself? And it was going to get a lot
worse. Next morning we started going up into the
hills. Everyone was glad to get up higher, into cooler
air. It was mid-afternoon, and we'd come over the top
and started to come down when I first heared firing
ahead of us. It was coming out'n a kinda narrow,
rocky place, very steep. That's what we call a defile,
you know. I guess the rocks and the narrowness made
the noise worse. There was guns firing as well as muskets, and the first roar made me like to jump acrost the
road. I warn't the only horse, neither; one or two actu
ally bolted. 'Course, I knowed at once't there must be
Blue men down there. Well, I reckon so—that defile,
with rocks all round, was a natural place for 'em, same
as the swampy creek had been. But somehow we had
to get through it, y'see.

Marse Robert pulled me round and we lit off
straight to the top of a hill one side of the road. The
deafening fire was still coming up from below. Marse
Robert dismounted and gave my reins to the soldier
that was with us. By this time, you know, Tom, I was
beginning to understand more of what went on and
what was likely to happen. On the top of that hill I
felt the two of us was really taking a risk. The Blue
men must be able to see us, and any moment there'd
come a bang would tear me to bits, like I'd seed happen to other horses. But Marse Robert, he jest kept
a-looking out nice and steady and taking his time—
you'd 'a reckoned he was on a picnic. I'll tell you, I
was more'n glad when we come down off'n that hill.
Marse Robert couldn't have been much worried 'bout
the defile, though. He jest gave out some orders and
then we-all went off to another fine house for the
night. It was mighty strange, Tom, you know, this
dodging 'bout between horrible danger and what
you'd call the lap of luxury. Y'see, I hadn't larnt yet

that when you're a soldier you don't look ahead. You take whatever comes, and if it's good for the moment, then the moment's good 'nuff. But I kept thinking ahead, and for me that spoiled everything. Yet next morning the Blue men was gone—no one knowed why—and we-all jest went on down through the defile.

We'd gone 'long a little ways, and I was jest thinking that soon the heat and dust was going to be every bit as bad as before, when I smelt horses in the trees off to one side of the road. I remembered the enemy cavalry two days before, and I felt sure they must have come back—more of 'em this time—'nuff to pitch into us. Y'see, Tom, the state I'd got myself in, every durned thing that happened seemed like 'nother sharp stone on a bad road. The flies and the dust and the hot sun was all part of a bad place, and the place was bad 'cause it was dangerous. It must be hard for you to realize how defenseless a horse is. Come right down to it, we're more defenseless'n cats. No one wants to take *you* into a battle, and anyways there's a lot less of you to offer a target, ain't there? I did a little dance, bucking acrost the road, and Joker had to rear back to get out'n my way. "Found a bees' nest?" he snorts, but I was too busy getting myself under orders to answer him back. Any man but Marse Robert would have gotten impatient, I reckon.

But they was *our* horses, as I could have smelt plain 'nuff if I'd had any sense. 'Sides, they was carrying the red-and-blue cloth on a stick, though until they come close you could hardly see it for the dust. In front was Jine-the-Cavalry hisself, and this time he was riding Skylark. They come up to us straight off, and Jine-the-Cavalry commenced to talking to Marse Robert.

Skylark, as I've told you, was one of them high-bred horses that's able to hide everything behind a

bunch of polished manners. Those he certainly had.
As we went 'long side by side, he asked me how I was
getting on and whether we'd had a hard march and
had the dust been this bad all along and had I met his
friend Rollo the courier and a whole pile of politeness
of that sort. After a while I asked him whether he
knowed where we was a-going and what was likely to
happen. I should have explained, Tom, that all the
morning, while we'd been marching, there'd been on-
and-off sounds of guns from far ahead, and I asked
'bout them, too.

Skylark said it was Cap-in-His-Eyes' guns we
was hearing. He said the cavalry had come straight
from Cap-in-His-Eyes, who was being attacked by the
Blue men jest a few miles off.

"A battle?" I asked, trying not to show how I felt.

"I'm not sure," answers Skylark, kind of casual.
I'd 'a felt better if he'd said he *was* sure, one way or the
other. "How I understand it, we may disengage and go
round behind the Blue men again. What's called maneuver, you know," he added, like he was talking to a
foal.

I was jest going to ask some more when the whole
column, as far as I could see ahead for the dust, pulled
up and halted. This 'peared to be so that Jine-the-
Cavalry could take his horsemen acrost the road and
away on the other side.

"Ah, we're going to cover the flank," says Skylark. "Good luck, Traveller! See you later on today, I
'spect." And with that he and Jine-the-Cavalry was
off up the road.

The whole day became more and more like some
kind of disagreeable, troublesome dream. I kept blowing out dust and breathing in more that other horses
had blowed out. Whenever it was possible, Marse
Robert took us off'n the road, but that was only now
and again, 'cause of all the brush and trees alongside.

Anyways, the flies followed wherever we was and
there was no standing head-to-tail to get rid of the
critters. The horses was getting jumpy with each other
—"Can't you keep outa my dad-burn way?" "D'you
want the whole durned road?" and all that kind o'
talk. I'd have given my mane for a drink, but I could
tell that the way things was now, Marse Robert was in
a real hurry to get everyone forward. "Close up, men!
Close up!" he kept saying wherever we went, up and
down the column. "Keep moving!" But I could tell it
was jest like Sorrel had said: Marse Robert was really
uncertain in hisself and wondering what to do. I reckoned he was figuring he couldn't decide till we'd
caught up with Cap-in-His-Eyes.

We come through a town and jined another road. I
guess 'twas getting on to midday when Marse Robert
took us off'n to one side and up a little hill, where we
stopped. You could see the whole Army separating out
for miles acrost the country—what they call deploying, Tom, you know—that's what they do when
they're fixing for to fight. There was tromping and
shouting everywhere, and teams of horses a-dragging
guns up and down the slopes every which way. Marse
Robert dismounted and sat down on a tree stump, and
good old Dave come up and led me away to a little
creek for a drink. The water was thick and muddy
with all the horses—yeah, and the men, too—who'd
drunk from it, but I'd 'a drunk harness oil then, I'll tell
you. Then our guns started up real close by—'nuff to
worry any horse—and me and the others was brung
back to wait. You see, Tom, when there's a battle any
horse at headquarters is likely to be sent on an errand
any moment. If'n he's blowed to bits, that's jest too
bad.

All the men round Marse Robert was real edgy,
and the horses caught the feeling, like they always do.
Jest a ways off to one side was a regiment a-singing, all

solemn-like, and some of 'em was kneeling down on the ground with their eyes shut and their hands together. I often used to see our soldiers doing this, but I never could make out jest rightly why they did it. I reckon maybe 'twas like horses stamping. Horses'll pick a spot in the open for stamping, you know, Tom, and stamp it flat and bare in less'n a month. It does something for you, does stamping. So does rolling, of course; we have favorite rolling places, same as you choose trees and posts to clean your claws on.

All I recollect 'bout the rest of the day is the guns making a racket and the generals a-coming and going all afternoon. Cap-in-His-Eyes came, but I didn't get the chance to talk to Sorrel. Finally, Marse Robert called for me and rode out over the battlefield. But when we came back no one 'peared any better agreed 'bout what to do. All I could tell was that there must be a terrible battle going on somewhere else, where Cap-in-His-Eyes had come from, 'cause the guns never stopped. It was jest one long roar. I wondered when it was going to be our turn. But still nothing happened. It was getting pretty dark when the young Texas general—him as Marse Robert had told to fight his way acrost the swampy creek—come up to headquarters. Whatever he had to say to Marse Robert, I figured, from the way he kept shaking his head, it warn't much good.

There was nowhere for us to go that night. We jest went back a ways, to a little wooden hut. All us horses was picketed out in the open.

Well, 'twas next afternoon when our battle really began. Every regiment round us seemed to be going forward into the attack. You couldn't see nothing for the smoke nor hear nothing for the noise. I seed Old Pete and Hero galloping 'long our lines, urging the men on. An awful lot of 'em went down, but 'didn't seem to make no difference to the rest. Everything was all confused. Marse Robert rode me forward and it scared me stiff. There was bullets zipping past and shells a-bursting all round us, but we might jest as well have been back home for all the notice Marse Robert took of 'em. I believe he'd have ridden straight on into the Blue men—I could see 'em plain, lines of 'em, all firing—if Old Pete hadn't stopped him. But for all Old Pete could say, Marse Robert wouldn't go back, and finally Old Pete leaned over and took my bridle so we-all could get in under cover of some low-lying ground. Even then Marse Robert wouldn't stay there long. As the sun was setting, he rode me up and down them open ridges until I reckoned we must be as far forward as any soldier in the Army. I still don't know why nothing hit us. The ground was covered with dead and wounded men—ours and theirs. You could smell the blood and shit reg'lar filling the air. Marse Robert kept pulling up to talk to one soldier and 'nother. They was all a-busting now with a kind of crazy excitement. We'd beaten the Blue men and druv 'em off. Well, we always did, Tom, you know—always. But I jest felt wore out and ready to drop.

That night we was still out in the open. Dave and some o' the other soldiers lit a fire and kept it going, bringing in brush and branches. I was trembling—jest a-shaking all over. I ate my feed—sech as it was—but I couldn't sleep for the coming and going, and the continual noise and disturbance. 'Sides, it commenced to rain—it got pretty cold—and that kept up all night and on into the next morning, with a sharp wind a-nipping at us.

There was any amount of mud—bad going; and I warn't the only horse was hungry. Marse Robert had covered hisself all over in some sort of rubber stuff for to keep off the rain, and this bothered me 'cause he didn't smell like hisself—not like what I was used to. We rode out early, along with Cap-in-His-Eyes and

Sorrel. Sorrel told me they'd had terrible fighting for two days past—jest as he'd said they would—and he was expecting more soon. We was both shivering with the wind and rain, though we felt a bit warmer as we got going. I reckoned we was looking for the Blue men, and it might easily be as bad as the day before.

We went acrost a river that was so high it seemed likely to carry the bridge away any moment, and pretty soon we come under fire again—bullets, too, not just the big guns. A bullet jest whizzed past my ear I felt the wind of it. When we'd come back, Marse Robert took some time telling Old Pete and Cap-in-His-Eyes what he wanted 'em to do. Then we-all went forward again—everyone in headquarters. I 'member we come down a track into some thick woods, and Marse Robert pulled me up while he spoke to a soldier who was taking the boots off'n a dead Blue man. Oh, our fellas was forever doin' that, you know, Tom. Anything that was worth taking off'n a dead man, our fellas'd take it, 'cause we was always short of everything. But this time, for some reason, Marse Robert spoke sharply to the man—told him he shouldn't be there. The man didn't know 'twas Marse Robert and he sassed him back pretty strong. Marse Robert jest laughed and rode on. He never let on who he was, but then that was jest like him.

Now this is the bad part, Tom, and I'd only tell it to you. Even Lucy don't know this. I never told her, nor yet Ajax neither. And I don't want you telling that there Baxter, nor any other cat on the place, d'ye see? Mind what I say, now. Well, 'twas later on that same day, in the rain. We was still in the woods—quite a lot of men and horses. All the officers had dismounted, near'bouts to a great high kind of a bank—part of a railroad. There was all sorts of people crowded round me and Marse Robert, and he was stood there jest loosely a-holding my bridle while he talked to 'em. All

of a sudden I seed a whole passel of Blue men come
a-swarming over that bank and running towards us.
They was prisoners, and they was running on 'count
of being afraid of the bullets flying round up there.
But how the heck was I to know that? There was a
plenty of others 'sides me didn't realize the rights of it,
and a commotion commenced. Everyone was dashing
for their horses. Someone stumbled almost up agin
me, yelling right in my ear. It was 'nuff to startle any
horse, let alone a horse that had been through what I
had them last few days. Oh, I *say* that, Tom. I still say
it after all these years, but I feel mighty 'shamed. I
gave a real bad start. I didn't bolt, though—I *didn't*! I
guess I might have, but Marse Robert took a quick
step to grab my bridle with both hands—and then it
happened. He tripped in that durned rubber thing he
was wearing, and down he went on the ground. He
fell real heavy, Tom. He fell full length right beside
me, and he fell hard on his hands. Somebody caught
my bridle, though I'd already recovered myself. But
Marse Robert, he was hurt bad. Anyone could see
that. He lay there, where he was, until Major Taylor
holp him up. "It's nothing, Major. It's jest my hands,"
he says, biting his lip with the pain.

The Blue men, they was taken away by our
soldiers that was in charge of them. Some fella came
up and looked at Marse Robert's hands and shook his
head. Then they holp him up onto another horse—a
mare called Dewdrop, belonged to one of the orderlies
—and a soldier led her back to camp. Marse Robert
couldn't use his hands, not at all. The orderly rode me,
coming behind.

It was only later in the day that I realized jest how
bad Marse Robert's hands was hurt. They was all tied
up in bandages and splinters of wood—both of 'em.
He couldn't ride—not me nor any other horse. But the
Army still had to get on, hands or no hands, mud or

no mud. They got an ambulance wagon for Marse Robert to ride in. I was brung along behind, on a leading rein; nobody wanted to ride me, so it 'peared.

That was the very worst day of my life, Tom. I knowed I'd let Marse Robert down real bad. I was the one that had hurt him. Maybe—how could I tell?— with his hands that bad, he wouldn't be able to go on commanding the Army. And what was going to become of me then? Likely 'nuff Marse Robert wouldn't want me. He didn't come near me the rest of that day. Was that 'cause he was too busy, I wondered, or was he goin' to send me to the rear as soon as anyone had time to see to it? I didn't know, but I didn't reckon he'd be needin' a horse like me no more.

On top of everything else, the rain kept on all day —what you'd call relentless. Every horse was in mud up to the fetlocks or worse, and the wagons couldn't hardly move. Everyone was starving, and near 'nuff exhausted after the battle. Where were we-all a-going, and was I going, too? I don't like to think 'bout that time. The fear before had been bad 'nuff, but the feeling of bein' in disgrace was worse. No one said nothing; they jest acted like 'twas an unfortunate accident —the sort of thing that might have happened to any horse. But I couldn't see it that way. So I didn't sleep much that night, neither.

Next day there was a real bad thunderstorm. You couldn't tell which was guns and which was thunder. There was nothing for me to do but stand around in the rain and think my own thoughts. What was going to happen to me without Marse Robert? I'd come to be his horse in every way. I couldn't imagine life without him. Now, I s'posed, I'd be sold off to anyone who'd have me. I'd be lucky if it was someone half as good as Captain Broun.

A day or two later we was still marching 'long best as we could. No more fighting, but more'n 'nuff

mud to make any road bad going. But that warn't the
worst of it for me. One of them days, as I was standing
'bout at headquarters, up comes Jine-the-Cavalry, riding Skylark and leading a mare. And do you know
who that was, Tom? No? Well, it was Lucy Long.
Marse Robert come out to look at her, with his hands
still wrapped up.

"She looks fine, Stuart," says he.

"She'll be plenty quiet 'nuff for you, sir," says
Jine-the-Cavalry, stroking her nose. "She'll jest suit
you until you get your hands back."

So Marse Robert, he has her saddled up and rides
her up and down a piece. You could see she was quiet
'nuff for anyone—quiet 'nuff for a lady to ride. She
jined us that evening, but I warn't picketed near 'nuff
to speak to her. You can jest imagine how I felt. *All*
animals can get jealous—I know that—cats and dogs
as well as horses. I felt real lonely, on top of feeling
'shamed.

'Twas 'bout that time that Ajax arrived, too.
When I seed Ajax come in—some stranger was a-riding him—I felt plumb certain I was going to be sent
away. Only, Ajax—well, you know him, 'course—he's
big and powerful, ain't he? 'Twas plain 'nuff to me
that he was going to take my place as soon as Marse
Robert's hands was all right again.

But 'nother day or two went by and I was still at
headquarters. We'd come to a town, and at least it was
better to be out of the mud and in good, warm stables.
They was the stables of a gentleman's house where
Marse Robert was fixed up. There 'peared to be a
whole raft of people—soldiers and others, too—
a-coming and going, and I s'posed he'd forgotten 'bout
me, or else he was too busy to give any orders. Dave
used to take me out and ride me for exercise. I talked
some to Lucy when we had the chance. I had to admit
there was no harm in her. She was completely bewil-

dered by the Army and all the shouting and carrying-on of the soldiers. She'd never knowed nothing like that before. I couldn't help wondering how she'd take the guns; that's to say, if'n there *was* any more guns. You see, Tom, after every battle all us horses used to hope there wouldn't be no more guns.

Ajax struck me right off as a stolid, rather dull sort of fella. 'Twarn't so much that he didn't 'pear friendly as that he didn't seem capable of taking a lot of interest in anything much. Whatever come along, sun or storm, Ajax could take it—that was how I figured him out. No doubt, I thought, that would suit Marse Robert better'n a nervous, cowardly horse that had knocked him over and broke his hands. The only thing was, Ajax was sech a great big fella, a lot taller'n me, and I wondered whether that would altogether suit Marse Robert. Well, it wouldn't make no never-mind to me, I thought bitterly. Likely 'nuff I'd soon be pulling a wagon.

IX

EARLY SEPTEMBER, 1862. The Army of Northern Virginia, having seized the opportunity to win a brilliant victory near Manassas, no more than twenty-five miles west of Washington, the Federal capital, has once again been unable to reap any true reward. Torrential rain has denied all chance of effective pursuit. The blustering General Pope, though duly suppressed, has been able to withdraw his army to defensive works between Manassas and Washington, too strong for the Confederate force to assail. Indeed, the victory was won only in the nick of time, for now strong Federal reinforcements under General McClellan have united with General Pope. Yet the greatest hindrance has been sheer exhaustion. The Confederate army is consumed by fatigue, by disease, by hunger and lack of supplies. The men are in rags, many lacking even boots, let alone protection against the weather. Only their supreme *esprit de corps* and above all their unbounded confidence in General Lee have held them together under hardships as severe as few armies have undergone.

Whither shall they go now and what should they do? They cannot remain where they are—a little south of the Potomac, at Leesburg in Loudoun County. That would court disaster. General McClellan is coming. To go south would take them into country already stripped of provisions. To go westward would be to retreat, to admit failure. General Lee (who has a broken bone in one hand and the other painfully sprained), considering the situation at his headquarters at the home of Mr. Harrison at Leesburg, has determined on the bold step of crossing the Potomac and advancing into Maryland. Whatever the risk, the effect of this will be to draw the Federals away from their Washington defenses and relieve, during the harvest season, their threat to Virginia and to Richmond. There may even, perhaps, be a chance to harass the enemy further. At all events it will be possible to subsist off the country. The army must eat.

To cross the Potomac; to invade Maryland? There is reason to believe in strong sympathy in that state with the Confederate cause; sympathy controlled only by the power of the Federal government and ready to show itself, given the opportunity. The Army of Northern Virginia includes many Marylanders—volunteers. It is even conceivable that Maryland may join the Confederacy.

Northward, then, from Leesburg to White's Ford and across the Potomac—a state boundary indeed, 500 yards wide—the long, stumbling columns splashing and wading through the river, watched in the distance by the ever-present Federal cavalry. But is the Confederate army indeed victorious or fugitive? They cannot hope to take Washington: they cannot hope for gain from another pitched battle. At Manassas they have already lost 9000 dead and wounded. What, then, is their hope? As always, it is for recognition of the Confederacy by the European powers and that the Federals, discouraged by Southern valor, will decide that the price is too high, give up and negotiate a peace conceding independence.

But the army! Ah, the army that passes over that river! You can smell them coming. Many of the local people stare incredulously—and fearfully, too—at these stranger vagabonds, scarecrows such as they could never have imagined in rumor, fancy or tales. Look, there is a boy, Leighton Parks, who has watched them crossing. "They were the dirtiest men I ever saw, a most ragged, lean and hungry set of wolves. They were profane beyond belief. Many of them spoke a thick dialect that I could scarcely understand." The lank, rib-cage horses with their ragged riders; the filthy, unshaven, cadaverous foot soldiers, blistered feet showing through broken boots; the artillerymen fearful for their jolting, tilting guns, for the rickety axles and unsteady wheels of their caissons. Whither are you marching, soldiers, in your squalor, your tatters and your spirits that nothing can subdue? You are marching toward the zenith of the Confederate cause. Never again will the world watch so closely and weigh the odds on your victory. Never again will these men, these horses and above all this spirit and hope press onward against the Northern enemy. Or if they do, the enemy will have grown too strong.

Come on out, Tom Nipper! Come on out o' that there fur! No use saying you ain't in thar! I see your eyes sticking out, see your paws hanging down!

Aw, Tom, you needn't get that huffy, start walking off. It's only my old soldier's joke. We had all kinds of jokes in the Army, y'know. "Come on out o' that hat!" and so on. Fellas got to have something to laugh at in hard times. An' for gosh sakes, warn't them hard times, too?

I guess you must be feeling times are kinda hard for you, Tom, huh? With Miss Life staying away so long? She's been away two months and more now—ain't it?—and likely to be as long again, or maybe more. But bless you, that don't amount to hard times. She'll be back one of these here days, and that's more'n can be said for lots I've knowed, horse and man.

Did you hear how Lucy finished her journey here, when she came with young Marse Rob? I never seed her come, but Ajax did, and he told me. She was pulling a buggy, that's what! Yeah; Lucy, that's been in four big battles and been under fire with me! Pulling a buggy! She never told me herself—no fear! She jest told me that after she'd been sent to the rear, nearly three years ago, there was some mix-up and she got picked up by some ornery fella back there. She told me how young Marse Rob found her and brought her here, but she never said he druv her here from the railroad pulling a buggy. You wouldn't never see me pulling no buggy, that's for sure. I never been in shafts and I ain't reckoning on it. I don't figure Marse Robert would care for that, nohow.

Say, did you hear the callithumps the boys put on last night? You didn't? I could hear it from here. I seed a callithumps or two myself 'fore now, when Marse Robert's ridden me downtown to keep an eye open for trouble. The boys march downtown blowing trumpets and banging away on any old thing they can find—drums, trays, old cans—anything'll do, 'long as they make an infernal row. Put me in mind of old times, I declare it did. We had a band a-playing when we forded that there big river I was talking 'bout, but it would have taken more'n a band to put any heart in me jest then. Like I said, I figured me and Marse Robert was going to part.

Not that there was much show to the river crossing, Tom. Bless you, we warn't in no state to put on a show! Our fellas jest came up to the river and went wading acrost it. But when they came out the other side, they was all a-cheering, regiment after regiment. And there was one or two bands playing. I heared 'em.

Marse Robert was riding Lucy. Leastways, he was sitting in the saddle, but he couldn't use his hands on the reins. Dave was leading her, and Red Shirt was riding 'longside him an' keeping an eye on him to see nothin' went wrong. I was being led behind, with the rest of headquarters. When we-all came up to the ford, there was a whole lot of men—Red Shirt's men—

a-laying in the road, waiting to go in and wade acrost.
Red Shirt rides up to 'em and tells 'em to move out of
the way for General Lee.

Soon's he heared that, Marse Robert calls out,
"No, no, General Hill! Never mind that! Stay where
y'all are." And then he told Dave to lead Lucy round
the fellas, and we followed him over to t'other side.

'Tell you the truth, I don't recollect all that much
'bout the next two-three days, 'cepting that the roads
was hard—a lot harder'n I'd ever knowed or been used
to. There was any amount a-goin' on, but there was no
more marching—or very little—and none of the
soldiers at headquarters seemed to have time to do
more'n groom me. I got very little exercise. The way I
seed it, I was jest waiting around to be sent back acrost
the river. We was in a nice spot, a grove of oaks, pretty
close to where Old Pete was pitched. The trees smelt
good and fresh; it was shady and the weather warn't
too hot, so the grazing was good. I made friends with
one of our horses—Tempest, his name was. He reminded me, some ways, of Ruffian, him as was my
friend in the old days back at Andy's, when we used
to stand head-to-tail under the trees, groom each other
and swish the durned flies. I've always been proud of
my long, thick tail, y'know, and Marse Robert never
would have it cut short.

Now I come to look back on it, that was a real
good place, and I'd 'a been happy 'nuff and glad of the
break if only I hadn't been so durned miserable wondering when I was going to be sent away. Yeah, I'd
forgotten all 'bout Tempest. Wonder whatever become
of him? Horses forever saying good-bye.

Headquarters was jest a bunch of tents, like it
mostly was. Marse Robert didn't like to live in a
house, even if'n he sometimes spent a night in one
here and there, like I've been telling you. I could see
his tent from the picket lines, and often I'd see his

lamp burning away at night, and people a-coming and going, the light showing a long time after darkness had fallen.

One night a funny thing happened. I was jest rambling round where I was picketed, and either the peg up and pulled out or the rope come loose—I don't rightly know. Anyways, I found I was loose. I rambled round for a while, ate some grass in the moonlight and nickered to one or two other horses. Nary a sentry that I seed. And then, suddenly, I got the smell of Marse Robert, floating on the air from a little ways off. So I jest followed it, walking easy, and 'course I was going towards that lighted tent. When I got quite close up, I could hear Marse Robert's voice, so I reckoned there must be someone else with him—Old Pete, maybe, or another general. But I couldn't smell anyone else, or hear anyone answering Marse Robert. His voice was real low—near'bouts to whispering—and didn't sound 'zackly like he was talking to 'nother fella at all.

I went up to the tent and pushed my nose through the flap; and there was Marse Robert on his knees, with his hands together, same's them soldiers 'fore the battle, and he 'peared to be talking to hisself, like I've heared a groom do in stables sometimes. He had his back to me, and it took him a moment or two to realize I was there. When he did, he gave a little start, but then he got up straightaway and came out of the tent.

"Why, Traveller," he says, "come to look for me, have you? I should have come to look for you." Then he said some more I couldn't understand, but he was stroking my nose and speaking real kind and quiet all the time. I guess I must 'a been trailing my rope, 'cause I recall he led me back to the picket lines hisself, and I believe he'd have fastened me up with his own hands, only they was still bandaged up and splintered. He called a sentry, and I was picketed back in my place 'longside Lucy. Lucy never asked where'd I'd been nor nothing, but that was jest like her—she was never 'quisitive—and anyways she was so new to the Army that I reckon maybe she thought it was ordinary for headquarters horses to go wandering 'bout on the loose at night. So no one knowed, 'cepting for me and Marse Robert and the sentry.

I don't think it was the next day—maybe it was the day after—that Dave came down to the picket lines with my girth over his arm, and carrying my saddle. I thought he must have made a mistake and in a minute he'd go back for Lucy's, but he didn't. He saddled me up and 'fore I knowed what was happening I found myself up at the headquarters tents. There was Perry lecturing Marse Robert and giving him his hat and things, like he always did. He never gave him his big gloves, though. They put some kind of special gloves, made of sacking, over his bad hands. I was still wondering whether they'd made a mistake when Marse Robert spoke to me a moment and then got up into the saddle. He looked around, said something to Major Talcott and then, jest like he always did last thing before we started out in the mornings, he gave the order: "Strike the tent!" That meant that Bryan and Perry and the rest was to get packed up and moving.

Old Pete joined us directly. "You're back then, Traveller?" says Hero. " 'Reckoned you would be." I was still too much surprised to answer him, 'cepting for a friendly nicker. What was holding my attention was the change in the whole feel of Marse Robert. He warn't using his hands on the reins—well, not hardly at all. We was on a pretty smooth track to begin with and then we went out onto the road, so 'twarn't difficult for me to know where we was s'posed to be going. After a while, though, we came to some rough ground where the road was in bad repair, and I realized right away that Marse Robert couldn't use his hands to guide me. Dave rode up 'longside and took the bridle for a spell, and this worked well 'nuff—we warn't going no faster'n a walk. I didn't get no encouragement to break into my usual trot.

We hadn't gone more'n three-four mile—I remember the sun was right in our eyes as we went down the road—when I heared the guns in front of us. We was going straight toward them guns; they was up in the hills. And I knowed then—picking my way acrost that rough ground, with Dave's hand on my bridle—I knowed that I'd somehow changed. Not that I'd stopped being afeared—I'd always be afeared; no horse could help that—but I knowed I'd rather be with Marse Robert and do jest what he wanted me to do—I'd rather be with him than even save my life. I realized, too, that this was the way Skylark felt and Sorrel felt—only, they hadn't told me as much, 'cause it was something they couldn't.

Well, I'm not really explaining very well, Tom. I guess I'm not managing to make you understand that this was a mighty big change in me—bigger'n anything before or since. I'd thought before that I was Marse Robert's horse and real close to him, understanding jest what he wanted and all the rest. But I *hadn't* been—I was jest a good, strong horse that suited him better'n any other, and I'd thought that was all there was to it. Now I realized 'twarn't hardly a mouthful of it. The reason Marse Robert didn't 'pear to care 'bout the bangs was that he cared more for the Army—for our soldiers—than he did for his own life. I don't know whether I can put this to you jest rightly, Tom. I'll tell you something I remember. Once, when me and a couple of other horses was jest browsing round in some long grass, tearing it out in mouthfuls, you know, I came on a bird's nest in among the brush and undergrowth—one o' them flycatchers, maybe. The fledglings had hatched: the nest was full o' them.

And the mother bird went for me—she sure 'nuff did. She jest went for my nose and pecked me for fare-you-well, and a-chattering with rage all the time. She'd have done the same to you, Tom, or to anything else that threatened her young 'uns. She didn't care 'bout herself at all. 'Course I jest backed off and left her. I warn't aiming to hurt no nest.

Marse Robert needed me to feel 'bout the soldiers the way he felt hisself. And what it really come down to was I had to do jest what he wanted, 'cause I was the one critter in the whole Army closest to him—yeah, closer'n Perry, even if'n I didn't clean his boots. I knowed now that he'd never meant to send me away on account of I'd hurt his hands. That warn't why I'd changed—not the fear of bein' sent away. It was realizing that unless I could act like Marse Robert, I warn't his horse in the same way that Sorrel was Cap-in-His-Eyes' horse. And I'd been wrong: Marse Robert *could* be blowed to pieces, jest like anyone else. And if that happened, then I'd be blowed to pieces 'long with him, and that'd be better'n not being entirely his horse. It hadn't been like that before, but 'twas sure 'nuff like that now. I had either to go on or go back. I went on. You might say I gave myself up for dead. But I knowed then what I hadn't knowed before—that most of the Army had done that anyways.

All the same, Marse Robert and me didn't come under fire that day. Marse Robert was urging the soldiers on, telling 'em to keep moving through the dust and up towards the hills. In the afternoon, when we came close to the battle, he told Dave to pull me in to the side of the road, and we watched the men go by. I remember them Texans and their young General Hood. Marse Robert was talking to him real serious for some time, and when he finally rode off, all the Texans was a-cheering and yelling like crazy. I almost felt sorry for the Blue men they was fixing to fight. *I* wouldn't have cared to meet 'em, I'll tell you.

I could tell that Marse Robert was strung-up and anxious 'bout the battle, but his hands was so bad off that he didn't feel he could get forward and run it hisself, like he usually did. The firing went on until well after dark, and I knowed, from the way the horsemen who kept coming up to us was speaking to Marse Robert, that our fellas must be in a bad way and Marse Robert was worried.

Whatever else he had to worry 'bout, I thought, 'twarn't going to be me. Not no more.

We was on the march again in the dark. Everything I remember 'bout that night's confused. We crossed a creek and came to a little town. All I recollect 'bout the next day is the Blue men coming up, more and more of 'em in the distance. 'Peared like there was no end to 'em. All that evening they was coming up and deploying, and yet they didn't try to fight us; nor the next day, neither. I reckon they was scared, although they was so many. They didn't like the look of us. I didn't like the look of them, neither.

Cap-in-His-Eyes came riding Sorrel into camp and Old Pete and him was talking with Marse Robert and riding up and down the lines. I remember the guns firing. Sometimes Marse Robert rode me and sometimes he rode Lucy. I guess he wanted to get the feel of Lucy and get her accustomed to the guns. I remember him leading me through that little town by the bridle. It was full of our guns, and Marse Robert went here and there, talking to the gunners. There was nothing to eat—no hay, no oats, no nose bags going—and Lucy and me and the rest had to grab what grass we could get. Mighty poor stuff, too. Oh, and that evening it rained. 'Peared like it always rained when we was fixing to fight.

The fighting began before morning, in the dark. I

could hear the muskets from where we was stationed, up on a hill outside the town. But 'tell you the truth, Tom, I only recall things here and there out of that terrible day. 'Pears to me now that Marse Robert spent the whole time riding up and down, over the ridges, out of one valley and down into the next. I jest see things in my mind's eye, you know. I recollect Cap-in-His-Eyes a-sitting on Little Sorrel with one leg acrost the saddle, taking not the least notice of the shells a-bursting everywhere round him and eating peaches out'n a paper sack. I felt sure Sorrel would be killed—the fields and brush everywhere was filled with dead horses—I seed more dead horses and mules that day than I ever knowed was in our Army. Yet he warn't, nor Cap-in-His-Eyes warn't neither.

The Blue men—you should jest have seed 'em a-coming on! More Blue men than you'd think there was in the world. They kep' a-coming down through the woods like leaves blowing in the wind. I know Marse Robert hisself was wondering how it was going to turn out. I could tell that—though I don't think anyone else in the Army knowed it, horse nor man neither.

Now I recollect it, I'll tell you 'bout the pig, Tom! It's the pig that comes back to me now. It was quite early in the day, and 'far as I could make out things was going badly for us. There'd been a lot of firing—a big battle, by the sound of it—acrost the other side of the ridge from where we was, and thousands of our fellas had been sent over that way. Finally, Marse Robert must 'a figured he'd better go and see for hisself. So there we-all was, Marse Robert and Major Taylor and the rest of the staff, riding over the ridge towards the firing. Marse Robert had been speakin' to an officer we met 'bout bringing his guns forward, and then, jest as we was a-going on, we come upon this soldier all by hisself. He was a big black-bearded fella with a scar acrost his chin, I remember, and he was carrying the carcass of a pig. It was right acrost his shoulders and he was pretty well bent double under it, so he didn't see us until we'd got right up to him. It was plain 'nuff he must have shot it and taken it from some farm, and now he was heading back to camp, 'way from all the fighting. I don't reckon he'd been in the fighting at all. He was what we call a straggler, Tom, you know. A straggler's a fella who leaves the others, either on the march or in camp, and then lights out and looks after hisself best way he can. 'Course, them kind always made Marse Robert real angry, and now here was one of 'em carrying off a stolen pig, right before his very eyes!

Like I was saying, Tom, 'twas a bad time. I reckon every man we'd got had been sent to stop those people, and maybe even that warn't going to be 'nuff. So Marse Robert unloaded everything he was feeling onto this here fella. "Put him under arrest!" he shouted. "Stealing a pig—at a time like this, too! Take him to General Jackson! Tell him to have him shot!"

They took the man away. The pig was jest left laying on the ground. But later on, when we was riding back that way, it warn't there, so I reckon someone else must have finished off that bit of work after we'd gone.

It was later on that day that I seed something else I've never forgotten—something I still dream 'bout, Tom. The Blue men was still forever attacking us. Marse Robert had come back a mile or so to another part of the battlefield and he was talking to the other General Hill—the Little General, as I called him. They rode together all down the lines of the soldiers, and Marse Robert was encouraging them like he always did and telling 'em they was the greatest in the world and he knowed they was going to smash the Blue men all to pieces if they tried any more attacks. I hadn't

met the Little General's horse before. He was called
Chieftain, and he struck me as a real sensible sort—the
kind of horse I could easily take to if we'd happened
to be out in a field together.

"Does your man ever dismount?" he asked me as
we was going through a bit of a wood and the enemy
fire seemed to have slackened some.

I told him Marse Robert dismounted real often,
either to talk to soldiers or else to go forward to get to
places that'd be awkward for a horse; or jest to spare
me.

"My man hardly ever dismounts, wherever we
are," said Chieftain. "I guess it's 'cause he's sech a
small man. He feels he looks better on a horse and the
soldiers'll feel more respect for him. It's often bad and
risky, some of the places we go. We're often exposed,
and I get to feeling the Blue men are aiming straight at
us."

I told him I knowed how he felt, and I'd often felt
the same way myself. There warn't much more I could
say, seeing as how the whole place all round was covered with dead and wounded.

After a while Old Pete jined us, riding Hero as
usual. Old Pete had somehow or 'nother hurt his foot
a while before, and he was wearing a carpet slipper on
it. I recollect thinking we must have looked real
strange, three generals riding 'long, one with bandaged
hands and another with only one boot. Anyways, all
of us rode up towards a little hump in the ground, I
s'pose to catch a better sight of the Blue men and larn
what was a-going on. I seed then what Chieftain had
meant. Marse Robert took a look at the top of the
hump, where there was a few trees and no cover, and
then he nodded to Old Pete and dismounted. Old Pete
did the same, and me and Hero was held by Dave and
another soldier near the bottom of the hump. I
thought the Little General would dismount, too, but

'stead of that he rides straight up to the top. Old Pete calls out to him and says it was dangerous. If he was going to do that, he said, he'd better keep away from him and Marse Robert, 'cause they didn't favor getting shot. The Little General didn't take no notice, though. He jest kept right on a-looking out at the Blue men from where he was sitting.

All of a sudden Old Pete calls out "There's a shot!" or something o' the sort. The Little General turned in his saddle and looked like he was going to reply. But right then the shell came. You could hear the howl of it. It jest missed Marse Robert, who was standing close to the Little General and a-talking to him. It hit poor Chieftain. It clean cut off both his forelegs. Then it went whistling on down over the other side of the hump and I seed it burst in among a pack of our fellas.

Chieftain fell on his knees—he fell on the stumps of his legs—and buried his nose in the grass. He never made a sound—only struggled, kicking as best he could with his hind legs. The whole thing was horrible, 'cause Chieftain couldn't move and the Little General couldn't dismount—couldn't get his offside leg over the cantle of the saddle. In the end he managed to scramble off somehow or 'nother, and a soldier shot Chieftain through the head. We left him laying there.

It was a dreadful day of fighting, and it went on till nightfall. I seed men staggering out of the lines black as niggers and walking like they was drunk or crazy. Some of 'em as Marse Robert spoke to either couldn't hear him or couldn't answer. I seed an ambulance dragged by two mules, jolting along with the blood running out of it like water, Tom. As I looked, one of the mules fell dead in the shafts and nary a scratch on him. I seed men hollering and crying, too. 'Seed a man holding a dead soldier acrost his knees

and crying like a child. 'Seed men building a bank
out'n dead bodies, so they could lie behind it and go
on firing. I seed every dreadful thing you can imagine,
and the ground shook worse'n ever I'd knowed it. And
still the Blue men couldn't break through or lick us.
Hero told me later that Old Pete, riding round, had
come on one of our guns and all the gunners was dead.
So him and some of his staff fellas dismounted and got
to firing the gun theirselves. Old Pete always used to
go around with a cigar stuck in his mouth—never lit it.
Hero said he kep' chompin' on that cigar while he was
helping to fire this here gun.

I remember the Blue men a-coming on so's you
couldn't see the ground for 'em. But Marse Robert, he
never moves a muscle. He jest points away up the hill
and asks some officer to tell him who was them
soldiers coming acrost the top. He couldn't always
make things out so good as the younger fellas, you see.
The officer says they was ours, so we-all rode straight
off towards them. It was Red Shirt and a whole crowd
of his 'uns, come late to the battle. They piled straight
into those people—druv 'em right off. I reckon if they
hadn't come along when they did, we'd likely been
done for.

Soon after that it got dark. The Blue men had all
had 'nuff, or so it 'peared. Marse Robert rode back to
the headquarters tents on t'other side of that there
town. Lucy was with us; she was badly shook up. I
recollect another of the headquarters horses—Blacksmith, he was called—telling her she could relax,
'cause the fighting was over and done with and we
was sure to hightail it out that night. I don't think
Lucy really took it in, though. She was shaking from
mane to tail—hardly knowed where she was.

The generals come around, one by one, jest as
they left the field, to talk to Marse Robert: Cap-in-
His-Eyes, the Little General, Red Shirt, the Texas fella,

Jine-the-Cavalry—they was all there. Old Pete was the last to come. Marse Robert was walking here and there, a-talking to 'em. 'Far as I could make out, all of 'em was saying we was in a mighty bad way and we ought to retreat.

But we didn't retreat, Tom. I couldn't believe it when I seed Marse Robert telling the staff to post sentries and calling Perry and Meredith to get supper ready. Dave had somehow found some oats for me and Lucy, and we was jest standing by for nose bags when Marse Robert walked acrost and began petting us and talking to us.

"Well done, Lucy, well done!" he says, stroking her nose. Poor Lucy couldn't hardly stand on her feet, but she nuzzled him best she could. "Traveller," he says to me, "no other horse—no other horse at all— could do what you've done today. I'm real thankful for a horse like you. Tomorrow we'll see 'em licked to a frazzle!"

Tomorrow! I thought. We're going to stay here tomorrow? If'n the Blue men can still fight, I figure they'll walk straight through us like a stallion through a broken fence, Marse Robert or no Marse Robert. I was jest too wore out to worry, though. I couldn't even feel scairt. I jest lay down and slept.

But Marse Robert was right, same's he always was. At dawn he took Lucy out for a look-see but they come back right soon. Lucy said he'd been talking to Cap-in-His-Eyes 'bout attacking—yeah, attacking!— but 'far as she knowed nothing had come of it. And nothing happened all that day. 'Peared the Blue men had had 'nuff. And come the middle of that night we began to move—the whole Army. We came to the river—that same river we'd crossed afore, I reckon, but 'twarn't the same spot; had been, I'd 'a recognized it. Marse Robert reined me in on the bank and there we stayed, watching while the men and wagons went past us in the dark. As each general came up, he reported to Marse Robert, and Marse Robert had a good word for all of 'em.

I remember the horses—horse after horse—stopping to drink, and Marse Robert posting a fella to warn the men of a deep place—a place they wouldn't 'a knowed else. I can see the water splashing in the dim light. I can hear the wounded men a-crying in the ambulances as they pitched and jolted down into the water. We warn't the same Army that had crossed over that river before. That's how I felt that night. We'd lost a terrible number.

But we'd licked the Blue men! Oh, yeah, there was none of 'em round to try to bother us that night. They'd had a gutful. And I won't say I hadn't, neither. I remember the last commander finally coming up to report to Marse Robert. General Walker, 'twas—one of the Little General's fellas. He told Marse Robert there was no one left behind him. "Thank goodness!" says Marse Robert out loud, and down into the river we went. Old Pete was waiting on t'other side. 'Twas so dark I could smell the unlit cigar before I seed him. He had his men ready 'long the bank in case of trouble, but everything stayed quiet. Yeah, you bet.

X

NOVEMBER 20, 1862. General Lee, riding through a rising storm—the first of winter—has arrived at the little city of Fredericksburg, at the fall line of the Rappahannock. His decision to concentrate his army here to meet the Federal advance exemplifies yet again his remarkable ability to foresee and anticipate the intentions of the enemy.

During the past two months, since the savage battle of Sharpsburg and the return from Maryland across the Potomac, the Army of Northern Virginia has taken full advantage of the enemy's dilatory caution to rest, refit, reorganize and make up lost numbers. Although Lee's grand design to march to Harrisburg and threaten Washington from the Susquehanna was perforce abandoned as a result of sheer misfortune (McClellan's chance acquisition of a copy of a general order setting out Lee's dispositions and intentions), nevertheless the morale of his troops (most of whom felt little enthusiasm for the Maryland campaign, reckoning it to be nothing to do with the defense of their homeland) remains very high. Two months of fine fall weather have not only made easy their march back to the Rapidan, but also done much for the business of rest and re-equipment. At Sharpsburg, the army numbered fewer than 35,000. Now, thanks to recruitment and the rounding up of the large number of stragglers lacking enthusiasm for the Maryland campaign, it has increased to twice that size. There is,

however, a serious shortage of horses—a deficiency
that will continue until the end of the war.

During the mainly fine and sunny weather of late
September, of October and early November, General
Lee's strategy has been to avoid any further engagement with the enemy and await the arrival of his ally,
winter. Yet Richmond is still never so safe as when its
defenders are absent, and there is no retreat from the
Rapidan and Rappahannock. As the late October
leaves fall in windblown golden showers from the
birches, sycamores and maples of the Blue Ridge and
the Shenandoah, General McClellan, ever wary and
deliberate, crosses the Potomac and heads slowly
south, under vigilant observation by Stuart's cavalry.
A week into November and his army is at Warrenton,
a few miles north of the Rappahannock. Then follows
an unexpected pause, shortly explained by the news
that McClellan has been superseded by a newcomer,
General Ambrose Burnside. What will he make of the
Federal initiative, and how does he propose to set
about attacking Lee's army, which at Sharpsburg
showed itself able to daunt, if not defeat, more than
twice its numbers?

Studying reports of the enemy's movements and
weighing one factor with another, General Lee has
concluded that the Federal army will move southeast-
ward down the Rappahannock towards Fredericksburg.

For him personally this is a sad and difficult time.
His hands, badly damaged by the accident on August
31st, are still painful and of little use. Although he can
now dress himself with his left hand and sign his
name with his right, he is obliged to dictate all corre-
spondence, and for a horse he must rely for the most
part on the quiet, manageable mare Lucy Long. He has
received news of a bitter bereavement—the death
from illness of his beloved twenty-three-year-old
daughter, Annie. The hardship and strain of active
campaigning upon a man nearly fifty-six years old are
beginning to tell. Yet his greatest achievements still lie

ahead. Like leader, like army. "I never saw an army,"
wrote the visiting British General Sir Garnet Wolseley,
"composed of finer men, or one that looked more like
work."

Well, all the young fellas gone away for the rest of the
summer, Tom; guess Marse Robert's told 'em what
they got to do 'tween now and fall. They'll be mighty
busy, I 'spect, up and down on his affairs. As for me,
I'm taking it easy and cool in stables and out on the
lawn. This is the life, ain't it? Seems quite a while
since you and I was settled down together in the
straw. It's a good time of year for horses, and for cats,
too, I reckon. Sassafras leaves all green on the trees.
Did y'ever try sassafras? No, neither did I. No manner
of good—you can smell that.

I knowed you'd get a whole sight more chipper,
you and Baxter, soon as Miss Life come back. That's a
real nice girl—best out'n the three, I figure. This little
jaunt we've been on—Marse Robert and me and her
and Lucy—that was real good, all six days of it.
Mostly fine weather, good roads, no hurry, plenty to
eat, everyone mighty glad to see us—well, after all,
what would you expect? But everyone taking it easy—
no fuss, no bands, no folks crowding round Marse
Robert. Yeah, sure, Tom, if you like I'll tell you something 'bout it. Curl up, make yourself comfortable.

The four of us started out—I reckon it's been a
week now. It was real midsummer weather, warn't it?
Not too hot, not too dusty neither. No flies, no
soldiers, no wagons a-stirring up the dust: flowers
'longside the road, birds a-singing. I could have gone
forever, and so could Lucy. Once or twice on the hills
Marse Robert'd let me light out for a breather, and
when we got to the top he'd turn in the saddle and call
"Come along, Miss Lucy, Miss Lucy, Lucy Long!" It
was jest his fun, you know, Tom. Miss Life'd catch up

with us, face flushed, eyes bright; she was delighted to
be out on her own with Marse Robert. I felt jest like
we was a little headquarters on the march again. I
wisht Jine-the-Cavalry could 'a showed up. He always
had a way of showing up unexpectedly, you know.

It was lonely country we was riding through, and
I could tell Marse Robert was pleased as punch to be
out o' town and no business to 'tend to. As for me, I
was prancing round like a colt in a hayfield. When
Marse Robert stopped so's they could eat by the road,
the grass I nibbled was fresh and sweet as a meadow
in springtime. Aw, Tom, you cain't imagine what
that's like—a beautiful march like that—for an old
soldier like me that's slogged through heat and thirst
and flies, and dust so thick you couldn't see three
lengths ahead of you.

In the afternoon we come to a river. There was a
ferry to take folks acrost. And do you know who was
there, Tom—who was the ferryman, I mean? It was
the pig fella—yes, 'twas—the one Marse Robert had
caught stealing the pig in the middle of that there battle! So he hadn't been shot after all! Cap-in-His-Eyes
must 'a let him off—well, to get on and fight, I guess.
After all, Cap-in-His-Eyes must 'a realized Marse
Robert had lost his temper, and after all, what's the
use of shooting a fella when there's a passel o' soldiers
falling all round and those people a-coming on like
snow showers in midwinter? I knowed him all right—I
remembered him the moment I spied him—but Marse
Robert didn't. Natcherly, though, *he* knowed Marse
Robert, and he knowed me, too.

"You still got Traveller, then, General?" he says.
"There's a horse to go forever!"

Marse Robert said him howdy real friendly, and
they chatted for a while. Then he says Miss Life and
hisself was wishful to go acrost the river.

"I'll be mighty proud to take you over, General,"

says the fella, "but I ain't taking none of your money, not nohow."

Marse Robert, he outs with his money and tries to put it in the fella's hand, but the fella wouldn't have none o' that. Then he gets all teary-eyed and says, "I ain't taking no money from you, Marse Robert. I've followed you in many a battle. Never took no money for that, did we?"

He never said nothing 'bout the pig, though. No, no. In the end we went acrost on the ferry with the old soldier a-talking all the time. Did Marse Robert remember this and that and t'other thing? Natcherly, Marse Robert didn't want to show him no hurry-up, so we was a good while getting back on the road.

I remember something else that happened that afternoon, too. We was a-riding up through the mountains—there's mostly rough folks live up there, Tom, you know—and it was a real steep stretch o' road, and round a bend we come on a bunch of young 'uns playing catch-me-if-you-can. They was jest as dirty an' ragged as soldiers after a day's march. 'Course, like I've told you over and over, Marse Robert always stops to speak to young 'uns he meets 'long the roads; so he smiles at this lot and asks 'em if'n they'd ever tried washing their faces. They jest stared a moment or two and then scampered off real quick. Well, Marse Robert, he shrugs his shoulders, says a word to Miss Life and off we go. But we hadn't gone more'n two hundred yards round the bend, walking easy, when we come to a little cabin and out come all these young 'uns—clean aprons, faces washed, hair combed— you'd hardly knowed they was the same. "We know you're General Lee," says one of the little girls. And there they stood, all waving and calling out, "General Lee! God bless General Lee!"

Stables was good that night, at a big house up in a gap 'tween the hills. And then next day we-all rode up a mountain—what they call the Peaks of Otter, Tom, you know—real high up. There's two of 'em, side by side, and a big lake below—it's mighty pretty. I was half-expecting Old Pete to be waiting for us at the top, but there warn't no Pete, and no Blue men in the distance, neither. 'Course there wouldn't be—not no more. Lucy and me kept right on up through the woods, 'far's a horse could get. There was them little white lilies everywhere—reminded me of the woods beside the big field at Andy's, when I was a foal. Marse Robert and Miss Life left us hitched and climbed on—right up to the top, I reckon. When Marse Robert come back down, though, he seemed sad. He never said a word at all. Coming back down, I could feel he was real melancholy in his spirits. It's thinking of all our dead soldiers, Tom, you know. I reckon he never forgets 'em for long—the dead soldiers. Nor the dead horses, neither.

In the afternoon it come on to raining real heavy. We stopped off so Marse Robert and Miss Life could take shelter in another cabin where the hill folks live. I somehow felt the lady warn't what you'd call 'thusiastic 'bout our visit. We was muddy, and she didn't know it was Marse Robert, you see—leastways, not until we was jest fixing to leave. I think Miss Life must 'a told her while Marse Robert was gone to fetch me and Lucy out'n the shed. She seemed all a-flustered when we rode off—wondering what her husband would say when he come home, I reckon. She hadn't recognized General Lee!

We stopped off a couple of nights at one place and then another—friends o' Marse Robert's. Lucy and me was treated real good. I couldn't help remembering all the nights in the past when things hadn't been so good. It's a great thing, Tom, to feel that times are changed for the better—gives a real sense of satisfaction. The day we rode home I was feeling grand; so was Lucy. We did forty miles back yesterday, and I could have done a durned sight more, too.

Hush, Tom! Listen! Hear that? That gnawing? That's no mouse. That's a rat, if'n I'm any judge. Tom, that rat must be suppressed. Go and get a-holt of Baxter. He'd best make a flank movement outside, round behind the straw stack, and then you can move forward soon as he's distracted the rat's attention. That'll fix the varmint. Try to live off'n our supplies, would he?

Good work, Tom! Well done! Big 'un, ain't he? He made the mistake of coming on and walked right into you. It's not the first time I've seed it. The Blue men in the snow—that there little town in the snow! Marse Robert and the children in the mud! They was dirty right 'nuff, poor little critters. You want to hear 'bout it? Settle down, then. You can both chew up your rat whiles I tell you what happened.

It took a long time for Marse Robert's hands to recover from the hurt. The reason he rode me in the battle—even though I had to be led—and then back across the river was he figured I'd be steadier under fire than Lucy. You see, Tom, a horse has to have— what can you say?—he has to have *faith* in his man 'fore he can be brave hisself. Marse Robert knowed I had faith in him and I'd stand the guns, and that was what he valued, even though he couldn't use his own hands to guide me. Lucy, she was fine, 'long as there warn't too many guns.

I don't reckon she ever did larn entirely to trust Marse Robert under fire, and I don't know's how I altogether blame her. Lucy's a sensitive kind o' horse, you know. There's a durned sight of horses I've seed 'sides her that's showed theirselves mortally afeared of artillery fire. I've seed 'em lots o' times—where's the horse alive that's been under fire more'n me?—when the shells was flying low, close to their backs; they'd

squat down, a-shivering, till their bellies jest 'bout
touched the ground. Strange thing is, there's a power
of horses perfectly quiet in battle, jest so's their drivers
or riders are staying with 'em. Horses are best in battle
when they're mounted. 'Makes you feel a sight better
to have a steady, unexcited man on your back. I've
seed men that had to leave their horses—gunners, you
know, or wagon drivers—and when they come back
you'd hear the horses whinnying out loud to say how
pleased they was. I've seed wagon horses under fire
rubbing their heads agin their driver's shoulders.
Gives 'em reassurance, you see. They feel the bangs
can't hurt 'em as long as their own men are there.

Horses love each other, too. Well, I've told you
over and over, Tom, ain't I, how much horses depend
on friendship? I've seed more'n one horse whose mate
was killed go off into fits, neighing—terrified—gone
mad. I remember one of our headquarters wagon
horses—Martlet, he was called. His mate was knocked
over by a shell—jest laid low and deader'n mutton.
After that, poor Martlet jest refused to eat—he pined
away and died.

And then again I've knowed some horses seemed
to be thrilled rather'n terrified by the guns. Major
Talcott's horse, Joker, was like that. You couldn't help
admiring Joker. However tired he was, under fire he
was like a railroad engine on springs. Any man could
become a hero riding Joker—an orderly, a nigger—
anyone at all. Even wounds didn't worry him. In that
battle I've been telling you 'bout, Joker was wounded
two-three times. 'Didn't seem to make the least difference to him, and it warn't like he was stodgy, like
good old Ajax. Joker was a bright, sensible horse, who
knowed very well what was going on.

Anyway, it must have been—yeah, all of two
months after that battle, the time I'm going to tell you
'bout now. There'd been a few changes of horses in

headquarters—not many, though. We was a good bunch on the whole—got on well together. Even the mules warn't a bad crowd. Everyone was cheerful and most was feeling fresh as daisies—plenty to eat, not a lot of work, and our men in good spirits, too. The Army had marched back to camp by easy stages, and jest for once we'd been lucky with the weather. That was a nice, sunny fall. I remember the smell of the leaves and the little brown toadstools everywhere— mostly on branches and chunks of dead wood 'long the roads—and the spiders' webs shining on the hedges. Farriers was plenty busy: most of us was reshod. Needed it, too. Marse Robert was always mighty particular 'bout shoes. D'you know, Tom, I remember once in the middle of a real bad battle—shells dropping everywhere—we was getting ready to attack —and jest then along comes three-four mules pulling a wagon. "Some of them mules ain't got shoes," says Marse Robert. "Please see they're all shod right away."

Our Army was in pretty good shape by the time winter commenced to come on. Headquarters was in a pine thicket—nice, soft ground and very little mud as yet. All I had to do was daily exercise with Dave—not 'nuff for me, neither. Marse Robert used to take Lucy when he went round the camps. Sometimes, in the evenings, he'd take me a ways 'long the tracks here and there, and we'd stop and talk with the men off duty. Like as not we'd come on a crowd of 'em going in for that kneeling and singing and all the rest, an' then Marse Robert'd usually dismount and off with his hat and jine in. It pleased 'em heaps when he did that.

Well, there come a morning—a dark, stormy morning 'twas; the first of winter, I reckoned—when Marse Robert called for Lucy and soon's he was up in the saddle, he looks round like he always did, and orders, "Strike the tent!" Oh, thinks I, so we're moving at last, are we? Next moment it struck me: He's on Lucy! We're off on the march, and he's on *Lucy*! I felt real put out. Maybe his hands warn't right yet (and whose fault was that?), but jest the same I felt if he'd ridden me as a led horse in the battle and then through the big river, he could be riding me now. I began fidgeting and pawing round where Dave was holding me. "Don't worry, Traveller," says Joker as Major Talcott came up to jine us. "Didn't you know? They're keeping you for a Blue general they've took."

Next minute up comes—who d'you think, Tom? I'll tell you: it was young Marse Rob! He was a soldier then, and Marse Robert must 'a sent for him to come to headquarters. He saluted Marse Robert, they talked a few moments and next thing I knowed *he* was getting up on my back! What's more, he had his whole load of soldier's tackle strapped up with him—pack, blankets, the lot—so wherever we was going he was evidently reckoning on riding me all the way. He'd probably asked for me.

I'll give him a ride! I thought. He'll be sorry!

Well, the long and short of it was, Tom, that he couldn't ride me. I warn't aiming to throw him, 'course, nor he didn't fall off. But he jest didn't have the same control—the horsemanship—that Marse Robert had. Come right down to it, there's precious few can ride me comfortable. Well, I thought, I'll jest please myself and he can lump it. So I lit off, with everyone cheering and wishing him a nice ride.

We rode out of camp by ourselves. 'Parently we was to go on our own and not ride 'long of headquarters. Well, I hadn't had a lot of exercise for quite a few days past and I was feeling fretful. I reckon I real hammered young Marse Rob that day, Tom. I refused to walk one single durned step of the way. I went straight into my famous buck-trot, and I kept it up for thirty mile! I tell you, Marse Rob was real glad when that journey come to an end! I figure he could 'a walked the whole way and felt more comfortable. Add to all the rest, a real nasty storm come up, an' by the time we reached the little town beside the river— that's where we-all was bound for—it was jest pelting down as heavy as you please. Lots o' wind, too—not a leaf left on the trees.

I'd acted up like I did 'cause the terrible thought had come to me that *this* was how I was to be got rid of, after all. To be given to young Marse Rob! Thank goodness that turned out to be wrong! What happened was that, later on, Marse Rob was given one of Grace Darling's fillies for hisself. I'd only been lent to him for that one day—it was a long ride and I reckon Marse Robert figured it would still be too much for his hands.

One more thing 'bout that day: I'd forgot the dif- ference 'tween Marse Robert and every other rider you like. Well, you know yourself, Tom, that Marse Robert respects every living critter. He'd even respect that rat if'n he warn't no thief; and this feeling comes out in riding. It's real surprising how few horsemen ever bother to encourage a horse or give him praise. They jest stick to using hard words when he's done some- thing wrong. They never realize a horse likes praise and responds to it jest like he responds to being found fault with. A horse that feels his man's really his friend'll work hard for praise and take pleasure in de- serving it. I seed horses might's well be handcarts— you push 'em, they go—but that's not riding. Now Marse Robert—right from when we started together, he was always ready with a word of praise when you'd done what he wanted. That made you relax, Tom, you see. I've felt relaxed even under fire 'fore now, jest 'cause Marse Robert scratched my neck and praised me for doing nothing but standin' still.

Anyways, I was mighty glad to be ridden to head-quarters that night and handed over to Dave.

Now I'd best give you an idea of this place we come to that winter day, Tom, 'cause we was to do a lot there 'fore we was through. There was a mighty wide river—broader'n most I'd seed and no bridges neither, 'ceptin' for them the Blue men built later on. The town was on our side o' the river and it looked like a nice place, what I seed of it; neat, clean houses and a spire or two sticking up in the middle. But what I really noticed was the other side of the river. It was hilly—ground sloping up to the hills. And on them hills, Tom, was a whole power of Blue men. You could see their camps, see their fires, see 'em ridin' round and setting up their guns and wagons. For goodness' sake! I thought, no matter how many we kill there's always lots more. How're we going to get at 'em this time, though, without a bridge to cross?

Headquarters was jest the same—nothing you'd call grand. It was a ways out of town: a bunch of tents on the edge of a field, next to a patch of piney woods. There was plenty of timber for fires, and 'sides that, our soldiers rigged up pine branches to make shelters for the horses. We had blankets, 'course, but jest the same we was all feeling the cold. I remember some fella come 'long and give Marse Robert a whole mess of chickens as a present, so we had them cackling and squawking round for a while. Not long, though—they was soon eaten, all but one. That one went every-where with us best part of a year, on 'count of she laid eggs so good.

The first thing that happened, a day or two after we got there, was that all the townspeople had to leave their homes. I reckon they must 'a knowed the Blue men was going to fire on the town. That was a sad sight, Tom. I reckon you'd 'a been sorry to see it yourself, for there was cats, dogs, ponies—all manner

of critters mixed up in it; any critters at all as belonged
to the town folks. The worst was the bad weather.
That storm was still blowing—terrible wind and rain;
bitter cold—and everywhere deep in mud on 'count of
the soldiers an' all the wagons and horses. Marse Robert rode me as far as the edge of the town, where the
crowds was stumbling and trudging along. He kept
telling the people how sorry he was for all their troubles, and how much he hoped they'd be able to come
back soon. Some of 'em was able to leave by the railroad, but there was still a chance of 'em couldn't do
nothing but walk in the rain. You should jest 'a seed it,
Tom—old folks leaning on people's arms; a few lame
folks and blind folks; and women a-carrying babies in
their arms, with the young 'uns tagging along best
they could; and all the wind and the mud. There was
one or two carriages, but all the horses there was to
pull 'em was jest poor old nags that could hardly stag-
ger. Every horse worth a handful of bran was gone to
the guns or the wagons, you see.

Marse Robert—he was almost in tears to see the
folks suffering so. He give orders to the teamsters—all
our wagons and ambulances—to pick people up and
take 'em out of town easy. I seed our soldiers giving
their own food to the old folks and the young 'uns and
goodness knows they had none to spare. The mud was
so bad I had trouble myself—over the fetlocks and
deeper. Anyways, I don't believe a lot of them people
was headed anywhere special. They'd got nowheres to
go, 'cepting out of town. 'Had to camp in the woods
and fields. I 'spect some died.

Marse Robert and me, we was watching the folks
go by when 'long come a bunch of kids on their own,
getting by best they could. The biggest one yells out
"Hurrah for General Lee!" and they was all a-waving
to us. Marse Robert calls up the nearest cavalrymen—I
remember the wind blowing the horses' manes—and

tells 'em to pick up the young 'uns and carry 'em wherever they was going. "I never seed no finer folks," he says to Major Taylor. "They're an example to us all. Those people"—he points acrost the river— "those people should be 'shamed to cause sech suffering to women and children." "Yes, sir," says Major Taylor. It was 'bout all he could say, his teeth was a-chattering so with the cold.

Well, a few days after that, Tom, it began to snow. I recollect a bitter cold night with the snow driving hard in the dark. Like I said, our headquarters warn't in the town. We was downstream, 'longside a railroad at the foot of the hills 'bout a mile from the river, and most of us horses had been got into some old sheds. It was poor shelter—the walls had planks missing everywhere and the wind was driving the snow through in drifts. I was a-blowing and stamping to try and keep warm, when all of a sudden in comes Dave with a storm lantern, and another soldier leading Little Sorrel. I was surprised to see Sorrel, 'cause I hadn't seed Cap-in-His-Eyes nor any of his men since before that thirty-mile ride of mine with young Marse Rob.

Sorrel was rubbed down and given a bit of a feed. You could see he was as cold as the rest of us. After a while he looked round in a cloud of his own breath and recognized me.

"Howdy, Traveller," he said. "Is this the best they can do for headquarters horses?"

" 'Pears so," I said. "There's a lot of others in the open, I believe. Where's your man?"

"Stonewall's talking to Marse Robert," says Sorrel. "We rode ahead of our soldiers—to get some orders, I s'pose."

After a little he went on, "Our fellas are putting up with the cold better'n you'd figure. Well, they know it's to our advantage, after all."

"To our advantage?" I said. "How's that?"

"Why, the Blue men have got to attack us," said Sorrel, "*and* they've got to cross that river first. They're not going to find it easy in this weather."

And so it seemed, 'cause the days went by and still the Blue men stayed where they was on t'other side of the river. Marse Robert and me, we was out every day, getting things ready to give 'em a hot reception. Several mile of the railroad track was tore up and the wood come in useful for fires. Marse Robert spent a good deal of time up on the hills, a mile or so our side of the river, mostly saying where he wanted the guns put. In spite of the cold, our fellas was in fine spirits. There was a lot of snowball fighting and tobacco-spittin' contests, jest to pass the time. We certainly was a tough crowd. I seed plenty of men in the snow with no boots—'didn't 'pear to bother 'em none. But since the Blue men warn't in no hurry, we had time to get more boots and warm clothes up by the railroad. I remember going with Marse Robert to watch 'em being given out, right off'n the railroad cars.

And then, in the very middle of one night—a dark 'un, too—Marse Robert called for me to be saddled up, and off we went, stumbling through a thick mist. I remember Major Taylor and Major Talcott was with us, but I don't recall who else. I could hear muskets firing from the town ahead of us, but we didn't go down there. We went along a ways and then up a little hill, so that when it come light Marse Robert could see what was happening way out by the river.

Sorrel had been right, as usual. I'd s'posed those people, when they started, would come acrost in boats, but 'stead they was doing their best to build bridges by laying flat timber on top of boats, one behind t'other. This was what all the musket fire was about. We had fellas down in the town, Tom, you see, doing their best to stop 'em. After a while Marse Robert rode me down towards the town, but what with

the mist and the battle smoke, it was hard to see
'zackly what was going on, 'ceptin' that the Blue men
seemed to be in plenty of trouble from our fellas holed
up in the houses.

During the morning the haze lifted some, and
pretty soon the enemy's guns was firing into the town.
I could see 'em a-blazing away all along the hills on
t'other side of the river—jest one thick mass of smoke
and flame. The houses was still covered with mist, but
you could see the spires sticking up and the shells
bursting down there. I was hoping to goodness Marse
Robert wouldn't take it into his head to go right down
into the town. It was jest the sort o' thing he'd be
likely to do. The noise of the guns was as bad as I'd
ever heared, and pretty soon you could see that a lot
of the houses was on fire. Nothing come near us,
though, and after a time Marse Robert rode me back to
the hilltop.

It was afternoon 'fore the Blue men began crossing—in boats, after all; they couldn't finish no bridges.
The fighting went on all day. In the end they took the
town and finished building their boat-bridges, but not
before our fellas had given them a whole passel o'
trouble.

We stayed where we was all night; and I'll tell
you, Tom, *that* was cold. No one could sleep and the
horses was ridden every hour or so, jest to try to keep
'em warm. It was thick fog again the next morning;
plenty of gunfire from t'other side the river, but nothing more'n that—no Blue men moving out of the
town. It must 'a been nigh on to midday when Marse
Robert rode me off along the hills and we met Sorrel
and Cap-in-His-Eyes. There was another man with us:
one of Jine-the-Cavalry's officers—they called him
Bork or Pork or something. He was a huge great fella
—one of the biggest men I've ever seed—and all
dressed up, with a big horse to match. I'd come acrost

him before, 'cause he often used to bring messages to
Marse Robert from Jine-the-Cavalry. I always used to
call him "Vot-you-voz," from the funny way he had
of talking.

Vot-you-voz 'peared very excited. He kept pointing down towards the river, and after a while Marse
Robert and Cap-in-His-Eyes rode with him down the
hillside till we come to a barn. Then they dismounted
and left us with Dave and another soldier, while the
three of them went creeping real cautious downhill in
the fog.

Sorrel an' me—all the horses, in fact—we could
tell there must be a lot of Blue men nearby, this side of
the river. We could smell 'em through the fog and we
could hear 'em, too—the hollow noise of boots on
bridges and all the racket of hooves on planks, and
guns and wagons rumbling up. You could hear picks
and shovels going, too.

"There must be a powerful lot of 'em coming
acrost the river," says Sorrel. "All sorts—men, horses,
guns. Jest listen! What in the world d'you s'pose your
man and mine think they're up to?"

"I reckon they want to have a look at 'em close
up," I said. "Let's hope none o' the Blue men spot 'em.
I don't want to lose Marse Robert after all this."

"You won't," replied Sorrel. "It all feels safe 'nuff
to me. What I figure is, he jest wants to see whether
the most of 'em are crossing here or back in the town.
He wants to find out where their attack's coming
from."

Sorrel always knowed so much more 'bout
soldiering'n I did. I'd never have thought o' that, but
once't he'd said it I could see it was plain sense. After a
while the three of 'em come creeping back jest the way
they'd gone. As Marse Robert was mounting up, he
said to Cap-in-His-Eyes, real quiet, "I shall try to do

them all the damage in our power when they come on." Cap-in-His-Eyes jest nodded and we-all rode off.

It was even colder that night—the coldest night I've ever knowed in all my born days. I was wondering all night whether there mightn't be men—and horses, too—a-dying of the cold. There was no fires on our lines for fear of the Blue men ranging their guns on 'em. Good old Dave had somehow found me an extra blanket or I'd 'a come near dying myself. Cold's not really a question of courage, Tom, you see. A horse can bear only so much cold and no more. Our picket lines was real silent—not a nicker to be heared, only jest the blowing and stamping of hooves in the snow. The wind was terrible keen, and whichever way on you tried to stand, it only seemed worse. After what 'peared like about three days of darkness it died away, and with the first light of morning there come back the thick, freezing fog.

That *was* a thick fog, too—thicker'n anything you can imagine. You couldn't hardly see no distance at all and every sound—harness, hooves, men's voices—was muffled and soft. Marse Robert took me out onto the lines and 'cepting for the cussin' everywhere they was jest like ghost lines. The fellas was almost too cold to cuss, even. But a lot of 'em had lit fires, now that it was getting light—or next thing to light in the fog—and they was cooking. Marse Robert, he kept talking to 'em, cheering them up and telling them we was going to win a great victory. Everyone was slapping theirselves to keep warm, seeing to their guns and ammunition and getting into place. The Blue men must be doing the same, we knowed that. You couldn't see 'em 'way off in the mist, but you could hear 'em— their voices, their drums, their bugles. D'you know, Tom, I heared a band playing that morning, too? Jest plain's could be, a band coming up out of that thick mist 'tween us and the river.

Marse Robert and the rest of headquarters was
drawn up on that same little hill—Marse Robert's hill,
I called it—with the whole Army stretching away on
either side. All our guns was ready. There was two
extra big guns in position jest behind us, and some
smaller ones, too. I could imagine how much noise
they'd make when they began firing and I remember
thinking, Well, at least they'll make it warmer where
we are. All the usual headquarters comings and goings
began. Vot-you-voz come up—I s'pose with a report
from Jine-the-Cavalry—and then Old Pete come
a-riding out of the fog on Hero. We nuzzled each other's necks as our men saluted.

"Colder'n I've ever knowed," says I to Hero,
blowing hard.

Hero was seldom what you'd call talkative. "It'll
get a lot warmer soon."

Then all of a sudden up come Cap-in-His-Eyes on
a new horse—a stranger to me. My goodness, you
never seed sech a change in a man! I reckon I've given
you a pretty good idea, Tom, haven't I, of jest how
drab and kinda dingy Cap-in-His-Eyes looked in the
usual way? He'd never 'peared to anybody in the
Army as what you'd call a smart soldier. I can see him
now—stiff, gaunt figure, real sharp way of looking at
you; big, firm mouth, hardly ever smiled. Often
there'd be something loose 'bout him somewhere—a
bootstrap undone, maybe, or some buttons adrift—
something Marse Robert would have corrected sure
'nuff if he'd seed it on someone else. But this morning,
here he comes turned out almost smarter'n Jine-the-
Cavalry hisself. He was wearing a new coat with
bright buttons, gold braid all round his new black hat,
creases in his pants, shining boots and a fine, new
sword. And that horse, whoever he was—I wisht it
had been Sorrel—he was all got up in tackle picked
out in red and silver. You never seed sech a sight! As

Cap-in-His-Eyes dismounted, all the officers, from
Marse Robert downwards—well, they commenced to
laughing; but all the same, they told him he looked
jest fine. As for Cap-in-His-Eyes, he said that 'twarn't
none o' his doing at all. It had all been fixed by Jine-
the-Cavalry, he said. That explained everything, for as
I've told you, Tom, Jine-the-Cavalry was always
dressed up so fine hisself you'd think he was off to
dinner at some big house.

"You'll be afraid of getting them clothes dirty!"
shouts Old Pete. "You'll never get down to any work
today!" He waved his hand down the hill, towards the
Blue men in the fog. "What you going to do with
those people over there?" "Sir," answers Cap-in-His-
Eyes, "we will give 'em the *bayonet*!" Cap-in-His-Eyes
always loved talking 'bout bayonets.

Soon after that Marse Robert rode all along the
hills, together with Cap-in-His-Eyes, Vot-you-voz
and Jine-the-Cavalry. Our fellas was in high spirits,
and everywhere we went they was laughing, and
cheering Cap-in-His-Eyes. "Come on, General—come
on down out'n that hat! No use sayin' you ain't in
thar! See your legs a-hanging down!" I wonder how
often I've heared that joke, one way or t'other?

'Course, knowing Marse Robert, 'twarn't long
'fore we come under fire. He rode out a long ways
beyond our downstream flank, and by that time the
fog was jest starting in to lift. You could make out
there was a lot of Blue men out there. I began to hear
the bullets dropping, but this time I felt like I was a
new horse. I jest didn't care. I could feel Marse Robert's hands still warn't right, and I thought, I'll show
him! I'll show Skylark, too—him and his fancy ways!
When a bullet hit a rock and went whizzing off to one
side, it was Skylark who jumped—only a fraction, but
he *did*—and not me. I felt completely at one with

Marse Robert, ready to do whatever he wanted before he even gave me a signal.

We galloped back four mile to headquarters at Marse Robert's hill; the fellas was a-cheering us all the way. They knowed we was going to win and so did I. The fog was burning off now, and pretty soon the enemy's guns opened up—jest a few here and there. First you could see the spires sticking up out of the mist in the town and then the long line of the hills on t'other side of the river. Still we stood waiting around, and then suddenly there come a little wind and blowed away the last of the fog.

Oh, my, Tom! You never seed sech a sight in all your born days! All 'long below us, down on the flatland 'tween the hills and the river, there was the Blue men—thousands and thousands of 'em—I've never seed an Army like it! It stretched from the town on one side, all 'long our side of the river as far as you could see men, horses and guns. There come a kind of gasp from the fellas nearest to where we was, but Marse Robert, he never moved a muscle. I could feel him entirely still, where he was a-sitting on my back.

Then the Blue men began to advance to the attack. It was Red Shirt's fellas they started in on, 'way over beyond me. From where we was, we could see 'em plain as day. Red Shirt let 'em come on, right up the slope, real close, and then all his guns fired on 'em together. I don't remember 'zackly what happened after that, 'cause jest at that moment the big guns back of our hill began firing, too. They shook the ground, Tom, I'll tell you—and like to cut a hole right through your head from one side to t'other! And on top of that come the battle-smoke. I pranced here and there a little—I couldn't help it—and as I recovered myself I seed a teamster and his mules go dashing off to the rear.

The next thing I knowed there was masses of Blue

men pouring out of the town and coming straight up
the slope towards us. A little ways down below, on
my nearside, was a lane with a stone wall running all
'long in front of it. That lane was full of our fellas, and
they was taking 'vantage of that wall; yet that was
'zackly where the Blue men seemed to be fixing to get
to. The slope was steepest there, too. I jest couldn't
believe what I seed, but on they came.

Our guns didn't fire till they was near'bouts up to
the wall. Then they simply blowed 'em into screaming, yelling, running crowds. They warn't soldiers no
more! That was a terrible sight, Tom, but better'n if it
had been our own fellas.

All day long the enemy kept attacking us where
we stood tight on them hills. In the early afternoon
they tried again, over where Cap-in-His-Eyes was. It
looked bad for a while—we couldn't see 'zackly what
was going on. It was jest 'bout that time that one of
the enemy's shells buried itself in the ground right
under the parapet where we was. I felt the thud when
it hit, but it didn't explode. A minute or two later,
when Marse Robert and Old Pete and some others was
a-talking together, the big gun right next to us blowed
up. It bust all to bits—fragments a-flying every which
way—and yet nobody was hurt. Nobody at all! You
wouldn't believe it, would you?

Well, Tom, if'n I was to try to tell you and Baxter
everything that happened that day you'd fall asleep
even quicker'n what you *are* doing. The Blue men kept
on coming at us, but we kept on beating 'em back
every time. Now and then I'd hear our fellas raising
the Yell, and then I knowed we was on top. The
ground on the hillside below us was covered all over
with Blue men. I couldn't imagine how them that was
left could still keep a-coming on, but they did.

"Well, there's one good thing 'bout all this," mutters Joker to me, jest as he was fixing to set off on

some errand Marse Robert had given to Major Talcott. "I don't feel so durned cold now, do you?"

Actually, it warn't so much a matter of not feeling cold as of forgetting 'bout the cold. It stayed bitter cold all that day.

I don't reckon more'n a handful of the Blue men ever got close 'nuff to that wall of ours to have been able to throw a rock over it, even. In places, the dead was laying in great heaps, so's you couldn't even see the snow. I began to feel sorry for 'em—yes, I did. 'Twarn't really fighting, Tom, it was jest killing. I never felt half the fear I'd felt that day when the Little General's poor Chieftain had his legs blowed off. Of all the battles we ever fought, that was the easiest won.

It was dark—it had been dark for an hour or two —by the time the Blue men's last attack failed. Our gunners couldn't even see; I reckon they was jest shooting at the flashes from the enemy's muskets down the hill. At last all firing died away on both sides and it growed quiet, 'ceptin' for the crying of the wounded.

Now I'll tell you, Tom, 'bout something real strange that happened that night, after all the guns and the yelling had stopped—something the likes of which I've never seed before nor since. It began with a sort of shining, right away on the horizon, and that jest growed and growed. It was like looking at the freezing cold all a-glowing in the night. And then that glow turned into great, separate beams rising up into the sky from far off. They was moving all the time, too —flashing bright, sort of twisting and then disappearing and coming back again. It was 'nuff to frighten you —and nary a sound with it at all. Our soldiers was pointing up at the sky and calling out to one another. Some of 'em was getting down on their knees, like they used to back in camp. But Marse Robert 'parently

didn't like 'em doing that, not this time. Anyways, he
didn't jine in.

Him and me rode round a good ways, down to
that there sunken road our fellas had defended, and
back along the hills. We hadn't many dead at all. Everywhere we went the soldiers cheered him. The plain
truth was we'd whupped the Blue men again, and bad
this time.

'Course, it wouldn't have been like Marse Robert
not to make folks dig. All 'long the hills we'd been
holding there was men digging all night—hard work
in the frost. I guessed Marse Robert was expecting another attack next day, but he reckoned that if only we
was dug in, we could stop anything. Our fellas had so
much faith in Marse Robert, there warn't hardly no
grumbling—'spite of everyone being wore out with
the cold and the fighting all day.

Next morning the air was clear, and jest a little
warmer, though not much. Marse Robert rode 'long
the hills again, 'bout three mile, and him and Cap-in-
His-Eyes talked for a good long while. There was still
huge numbers of Blue men camped down below us,
but 'far as I could see they didn't want no fight. They
was busy burying the dead and bringing in the
wounded. And as it turned out nothing happened all
that day—hardly a gun fired, even.

That same night, soon as it got dark, a whole lot
of our fellas went creeping out to get theirselves boots
and warm clothes. You couldn't see a thing—the moon
was clouded over—but you could hear 'em crawling
and stumbling 'bout in the dark an' cussing up a
storm. The dead Blue men warn't all that far away
from us, you see—and every now and then there'd be
screaming and crying from some poor fella as warn't
dead, that felt his coat or his boots being pulled off'n
him.

Jest the same, all us horses was getting 'long easy

'nuff. The strain and tightness was far less—the stress had eased up considerable—and old Dave had somehow found a good feed both for me and Lucy. I had these two blankets, so I was as warm as any horse could expect to be that night.

Next day, 'far as I could make out, there 'peared to be some sort of agreement 'tween our fellas and the Blue men to stop fighting while things was cleaned up. It sure was needed, too. Marse Robert and me, we went down the hill to where our men was working at burying the dead and fetching in any wounded still left alive. In spite of the cold, I could smell that same nasty smell I'd gotten used to back in the summer. There was Blue men laying dead by the hundreds. Close up, they looked lots worse—all swollen up and puffy, lot of 'em turned black as niggers, with big, bulging eyes a-staring up at the sky. Yeah, and some with no heads, no legs, all tore to pieces, pools of blood frozen on the ground. You could see the holes where the bullets had gone in. I remembered what the President's horse had said to me before that battle I was in, back in the summer. "Killin' each other? That's what men do. You might as well ask why the sun goes crost the sky." Well, I thought, I guess I've come to take it for granted now. But I'm still durned if'n I can see why they do it. You wouldn't find horses or any other animals doing that to each other. I can't see no sense to it. All the same, my feeling mostly was 'bout Marse Robert and me, how we was still doing fine together—better'n any horse and man in the Army— so I jest settled for thinking he likely knowed more 'bout it than what I did. Anyway, I thought, seeing as how you ain't got much choice, you might's well be content with a good master. Yet I still wished, somehow, that Jim and me could have got to that there War he'd told me we was going to when we started out.

'Course, there was plenty of pulling off'n enemy

boots and stripping off'n coats and breeches and everything. I seed piles of Blue men left naked on the
ground, frozen stiff and all turned black. They didn't
get much burying, neither. In that hard ground the
fellas didn't want to dig no more'n they had to. I seed
a power of dead men shoveled under in heaps, hardly
covered at all, arms and legs left sticking out. Well,
arms and legs turn that stiff, Tom, you see, they won't
go under. Wherever there was a shed or an old barn,
they throwed 'em inside, jest to get 'em out of the
way.

That night was warmer, and it began to rain. Next
morning it was still raining, and the mist was so heavy
that no one could make out what the Blue men was up
to. But later on, when Marse Robert was out 'long the
railroad talking to Red Shirt and Cap-in-His-Eyes,
they told him that all the Blue men had snuck back
acrost the river in the night. Marse Robert couldn't
hardly believe it, but it turned out to be true. He was
disappointed, I could tell. He'd been hoping to do 'em
a lot more damage—kill a sight more, maybe even finish 'em off for good this time. He was kinda disheart-
ened all day. But me, Tom, I'll tell you, I was jest tickled we hadn't got to do no more fighting for a while.
Not till next time, I thought, and that's good 'nuff for
me. So you see, I was beginning to turn into some sort
of a soldier, after all. That's how us soldiers reckon
things: day to day, and a day alive's a good 'un.

Now why don't you take what's left of that rat
out of here, and let's get some sleep?

XI

H EY THERE, Tom! Did you hear 'bout my little adventure s'afternoon? It was sort of comical, in a way. Well, anyhow, it showed everyone that me and Marse Robert's jest 'bout as close as the bark is to the tree.

You know that young lady that's been visiting with Marse Robert's girls? Oh, you sat in her lap, did you? I wonder she let you. I guess that must 'a been jest out of politeness to Miss Life. Well, you won't be sitting there no more, 'cause this afternoon Marse Robert and me rode down to the canal-boat to see her on board for to go back home.

That was where this happened—down on the quay. Marse Robert dismounted and then, while he was a-talking to this young lady, he tied me up to a post. He was so taken up with his good manners, though, that he didn't do a proper job of it. Anyway, he gives the girl his arm onto the canal-boat and he keeps on a-talking. I was tossing my head some—the flies is awful bad down on the canal, you know—when all of a sudden I realized the reins had slipped and I was loose. I stepped back a ways, and jest then a young fella seed me and made a grab for the bridle. Well, that kind of upset me—reminded me, you know. The fella seemed all nervous and wound up—too snatchy—and I didn't like that. So I jest took off and lit out past him an' up the street. Then everything got worse. There seemed to be a whole passel of men and boys jumping out at me and chasing after me, all a-grabbing for the reins and shouting. 'Didn't none of 'em smell right to me, and the way they was carrying on was 'nuff to bother any horse. So I jest kept on going right up the street, and in no time I'd covered a lot of ground. I figured I'd go home by myself and get out of all that mess. I didn't feel answerable to that bunch; they'd got me to feeling real mean.

And jest then, Tom, all of a sudden, back behind me, I heared Marse Robert's voice. He was asking this crowd of folks would they kin'ly keep still and don't give me no more trouble—and 'course, seeing who he was, they did stop. Then, soon as things had quieted down some, he gives me our special, low whistle. That's a kind of a signal we have between us, him and me. It's jest for me, you know, Tom—'tain't for Lucy or Ajax or any other horse on the place. What it really says is "You're Traveller and I'm Marse Robert, remember? You can forget all the rest."

Well, soon's I heared that whistle, I remembered where we was. And I remembered all I'd done for Marse Robert and how he couldn't never have taken charge of anything at all without me. I'll confess I thought there might be a piece of sugar in it somewheres, too. Anyway, I jest turned and trotted back to him nice and easy-like. All the folks standing around was saying "Oh, my!" and "Did you ever?" But me and Marse Robert, we didn't have no truck with none o' them. We jest picked up right where we'd left off. I gave him a bit of a whinny as I came up and he patted me and praised me and then he hitched me up again. Some fella standing by says, "Well, I'd never have believed that, sir, if'n I hadn't 'a seed it myself!" All Marse Robert said was that he didn't see how any man could ride a horse for any length of time less'n a perfect understanding growed up between 'em.

I spent the evening grazing out on the lawn. There's one thing to be said for having been a soldier, Tom, you know: when you've been hungry—no use saying *you've* ever been hungry, 'cause you ain't, not really—it makes you 'preciate a nice, steady feed on good, fresh grass. That cold spell I was telling you 'bout—we was sure hungry then. Every horse in the Army was hungry. How can any horse work good when he's gone hungry for days? That cold spell, I seed plenty of artillery horses couldn't hardly pull the guns, a-slipping and sliding in the frozen mud. And it warn't scarcely no better for the men—there warn't much coming up on the railcars for horse nor man, neither. I remember riding down the whole length of the cars with Marse Robert one day, and he kept on saying, "Is that all? Is that all? Do they expect my soldiers to fight on that?"

'Course, very often the soldiers used to take matters into their own hands. Warn't no use to leave a pig or a sheep on the loose—not if you was a farmer. That'd be gone and not a whisker to show where. That's why I'm always saying, Tom, as you should 'a jined the Texans. Good cat's always a good thief, ain't he? You'd 'a been right at home. I remember Marse Robert, one evening, talking to that young general—the one that cleared the Blue men out o' the swamp. "General Hood," says he, "I ain't saying your men are thieves," says he. "All I'm saying is that when you Texans come round, the chickens have to roost mighty high."

'Course, as I've told you, Marse Robert believed in living real plain. I reckon he didn't want the men to think he lived any better'n what they did theirselves. But in headquarters we all figured that now and then he overdid it some—he often lived *worse*'n they did! I seed 'nuff to know that a good soldier's going to make hisself jest as comfortable as he can. But Marse Robert —well, now, Tom, I'll tell you a little story. One evening, when headquarters had spent a long day on the move, Marse Robert was seeing to the camps and looking out for any tricks the Blue men might be up to, and so he asked one of our officers—Colonel Long, 'twas—to find a place to camp for the night. 'Course, Colonel Long knowed Marse Robert wouldn't never go into a house—leastways, real seldom. He thought he ought to camp jest like the men. So the Colonel asked these here farm people if'n we-all could use the farmyard—not the house—and 'course they was delighted, seeing that it was the General. But Marse Robert, he wouldn't even have the farmyard! He told Colonel Long to find someplace else. So Colonel Long, he got mad at this—so his horse told me—and off he goes and chooses a field that was jest ram-jam full of the biggest stones you ever seed. They was so big and so thick there was scarcely no place to pitch the tents, let alone picket the horses. He figures he'd give Marse Robert a taste of what could be done to outsmart obstinate generals. But when Marse Robert gets there, he jest looks round at the stones and then he smiles and says, "Mighty fine! We won't be disturbing any farm folks here." You should jest 'a seed the Colonel's face!

Our headquarters was like most any other part of the camp, Tom. I wish you'd 'a been there; you'd have had some good hunting. There'd be a few pole tents, with their backs to a fence, maybe, in amongst rocky ground and near a stream of clean water. Three-four Army wagons drawn up any which way, and us horses, like as not, jest turned loose in the field to graze—if there *was* any grazing, that is. Some of our people used to sleep in the wagons or get under 'em. Perry and Meredith always did that—Bryan, too. They preferred it, I reckon. A lot of our stuff—tents and

wagons; horses, too—had been lifted off'n the Blue
men. When they first come, you could smell that, but
it soon wore off. Marse Taylor, Major Talcott and the
others, they slept two-three to each tent. They carried
very little stuff and neither did Marse Robert. I remember a lady come to visit our camp saying to Marse
Robert—she was feeding me some bread, that's why I
was by—"Why, General," she says, "this seems a
rocky, uncomfortable kind of a place for your camp."
"Yes, ma'am," says Marse Robert, smiling. "Colonel
Long has put me here in revenge for my refusing to go
to the farm." He seemed real delighted.

Did I ever tell you 'bout Jine-the-Cavalry and his
music fella Sweeny? This Sweeny, he was one of Jine-
the-Cavalry's men, and he was always kept round
'cause he could play music. He had a banjo, and he'd
sit there and make it go *pilly willy winky pinky pop*, sometimes for the whole evening, and the fellas'd all get to
singing, an' Jine-the-Cavalry'd fill up a big brown jug
and laugh and tell Sweeny to play some more. What
with the firelight dancing round, it was real cheerful
and pretty, and they'd all get to drinking and larking
up. I remember once Marse Robert come out of his
tent when all this here *plunka lunka lunka lunk* was going
on, and he peers down into the jug and then he says,
"Gentlemen, am I to thank General Stuart or the jug
for this fine music?" Then they all lifted up their pots
and cups and shouted, "Marse Robert! Marse Robert!"
"Gentlemen," he says, "this is a case of serious indis-
cipline! I shall postpone action until the morning,
when you will each receive a headache!" Well, it was
never dull, Tom, you know, when Jine-the-Cavalry
was around with that Sweeny fella a-plunking away
at night.

But jest the same, it was a hard winter, and in
spite of building shelters the men was cold, and hungry, too. What's that you said? Warn't it strange going

so many different places? No, it warn't, 'cause all them
places was really the same. Same rough old tents, same
people, same horses, same Marse Robert, same noises
and smells of the camp. And 'bove all, I knowed Marse
Robert would always *treat* me the same. Different
sounds and smells have different meanings, but as
long as each meaning stays the same, then a horse
knows where he is. Us horses like to feel settled, you
know, Tom, and know for sure what's wanted of us.
Then we can do our best without getting all scary and
strung-up. In the end I got almost to liking a rocky
field and poor grass. Anything else, and I'd be wondering why it had been changed and what was wrong. As
for cold, I don't so much mind a *dry* cold. But that
winter there was too much wind and too much rain.
Makes a horse nervy and irritable. Sure does.

That there hen I was telling you 'bout—the one
they didn't kill on 'count of she laid eggs so good—she
was a reg'lar part of camp, you know. 'Most every day
she laid an egg; and she had some sense, 'cause she
was jest 'nother one of us to get to larn Marse Robert
was fond of animals and birds. Do you know, every
day she always used to lay her egg right in Marse
Robert's tent and nowhere else? Under his bed, I
'member hearing Perry say. She became as much a soldier as any of us. The guns upset her—she couldn't lay
if'n the guns was firing. I remember once, when we
was told to get on the move, the wagons was all
loaded and everyone was ready, and then they
couldn't find that there hen! So we was held up. Everyone was looking for the durned hen—yeah, even
Marse Robert, he was hunting for her, too. In the end
Meredith come on her: she was a-sitting on a baggage
wagon and ready to go! Can you beat that?

Digging, digging, dirt a-flying and everyone waiting for an end to the winter. It put me in mind of that
time when we was down south, the year before. Only

difference was, now no one grumbled when Marse
Robert said they had to dig. Why, they thought so
much of him, they'd 'a jumped in the river if he'd 'a
said so! Food running short, horses often too starved to
pull the wagons, everyone bitter cold and a long, long
winter, but no one lost their faith in Marse Robert. I
knowed we was going to finish the Blue men in the
end, and he knowed it, too. I could hear it in his voice
and feel it in his hands. The way he talked to the men,
too; easy and kind. I recollect, f'rinstance, one day
when he was looking me over, he happened to see a
fella standin' round near the tent. "Come in, Captain,"
says Marse Robert. "Come in and take a seat."

"I'm no captain, General," says this man. "I'm jest
a private, sir."

"Come in, sir," says Marse Robert. "Take a seat.
You *ought* to be a captain, sir!"

I knowed Marse Robert so well—the whole feel
of him   that I was the first one, along towards the end
of that winter, to realize he was sick. One morning,
when he mounted me and rode out of camp in the
cold, I could feel his—well, his whole *balance* was
wrong. All of a sudden he reined me in, stopped and
gave a kind o' groan. The signals coming from him
was all of pain and discomfort. There was something
awkward 'bout the feel of his arms and the set of his
back. His pulse was wrong—I could feel the beat of his
blood was different. It made me nervous and jumpy.

"Come on, Traveller," he said at last, stroking my
neck. "We'll turn around."

Perry put him to bed—and if'n Perry said he had
to go to bed, even Marse Robert couldn't say no. But
the weather was that bad I guess even he figured he
was in the best place. Finally they moved him out of
camp altogether, somewheres where 'twas warm. So
maybe all of this here living like the men warn't sech a
good idea after all—not at his age. And I'll tell you

now, Tom—and if'n *I* don't know it, no one does—
he's never been entirely right since—not the beat of
his blood ain't, from that day to this. He's been an off-
an'-on sick man.

XII

EARLY SPRING, 1863. The unusually long, hard winter is at last drawing to an end. Since the beginning of February, General Burnside has been relieved of his command of the Army of the Potomac, to be succeeded by General Hooker, an ebullient character known as "Fighting Joe." The battle of Fredericksburg, fought on December 13, 1862, has proved a costly error on the part of Burnside, whose attempt to storm the Confederate defensive front resulted in total failure and a casualty list of 12,500 against Lee's 5,000.

The entire Union high command have now developed a certain feeling of inferiority to Lee as an adversary. "They are so skillful in strategy," confessed General Meade, after the Maryland campaign, of the Army of Northern Virginia. Yet in their apprehension the Federals are overestimating not Lee's personal ability—as to that they are accurate enough—but the sheer resources at his disposal. While the enlisted plowboys and clerks in his ranks are ready to follow him anywhere and to fight like tigers, his commissariat remains perhaps the most incapable in the history of modern warfare. His men are half-starved. His horses *are* starved, and he now suffers a crippling and endemic shortage of remounts that will continue throughout the next two years. To him, the battle of Fredericksburg has been a disappointment—no true victory—for he lacks all means to follow it up or to

pursue the Federals across the Rappahannock. Merely
to inflict heavy losses upon an enemy whose manpower resources are so great confers little advantage
beyond that of reputation. He cannot afford his own
casualties. His only course is to prepare and wait,
knowing that General Hooker is reorganizing the
Army of the Potomac for a fresh offensive. General
Stuart and his cavalry keep continual watch upon the
river for any sign of a Federal crossing in force.

Fifty miles away, in Richmond, the Confederate
government has shown unrealistic incompetence.
Congress spends its time in disputing niceties of political principle inappropriate to the situation of a country engaged in a desperate struggle for survival. No
adequate system has been devised for making good
the depletion of an army originally raised in the initial
fervor of voluntary enlistment. Conscription has been
adopted with reluctance. Meanwhile, inflation has
progressively reduced the value of the currency and
the economy has entered a spiraling decline. While
General Lee, rallying from a pericardial attack probably due in large part to hardship and stress, constructs
earthworks and looks out with grim realism upon the
falling Rappahannock and the enemy massing beyond
it, his political masters bicker in an ideological Cloud-
Cuckoo-land. As April draws to a close, Lee, with
some 57,000 men, faces General Hooker's army of
132,000, re-equipped and ready for renewed battle.

Scurvy has begun to appear. But so has the spring,
the young leaves burgeoning among miles of spindly
virgin forest and half-cleared, second-growth brush.
Colonel Northrop, the Confederate Commissary General, may be useless, but nature is not. Foraging parties
from the Confederate lines are sent out to gather sassafras buds, wild garlic, onions and the green haw-
thorn leaf buds that children call "bread-and-cheese."
Four ounces of bacon a day, ten pounds of rice per
hundred men every third day, dried fruit when available, no sugar whatever; in their loyalty to General Lee

(who eats as they eat) his men will endure on this, but
will they be able to march and fight on it?

Before daybreak on April 29th, the General, at his
headquarters south of Fredericksburg, is wakened by a
messenger from Stonewall Jackson. Union troops are
crossing the Rappahannock and concentrating below
the town. At noon General Stuart reports strong Federal forces fording the river thirty miles upstream. By
that evening they have crossed the Rapidan. General
Anderson is ordered to proceed at once to the road
junction at Chancellorsville, a lonely house in the wilderness ten miles west of Fredericksburg, to secure the
Confederate left, pending the advance of the greater
part of the Army of Northern Virginia. General Lee,
having discerned that Hooker's main attack is intended to come from upstream—from the west—has
decided to do the last thing that might be expected of
an army less than half the size of its enemy. He will
strike first.

We met some more little girls, Tom, when we was out
s'afternoon. I don't mind Marse Robert's being fond of
little girls, but when we stop and talk to 'em it certainly does a power to interrupt a good afternoon's run
in the country. At least this time it warn't that poor
old Frisky we met up with. It was a little girl Marse
Robert and me know well. Her name's Jennie. Her ma
sometimes brings her up here to tea, 'specially this
time of year when the weather's fine. Well, we was
trotting 'long nice and steady, jest somewhere on the
outskirts of town, when we come upon this here Jennie 'side the road. She had another little girl with her,
an even smaller one, and she was a-telling her to get
on home, 'cause she didn't want her following after
her. The smaller girl was a-sitting by the side of the
road, and you could see she warn't figuring on moving, neither.

When Jennie seed us, she ran up almost agin me, and Marse Robert had to pull me in pretty sharp.

"Oh, General Lee," she says, "won't you please make Fannie go home to Mother? I can't make her."

Marse Robert and me, we walked over to where Fannie was a-sitting, and he jest leaned over in the saddle and pulled her up onto his lap. I reckon that took care of all *her* objections. She was delighted to find herself a-sitting in front of Marse Robert; and Jennie, she got up as well. So we give 'em a ride for a block or two and seed 'em home. When we got there, their mother was on the porch, and 'course Marse Robert raises his hat and tells her what's happened.

"Good gracious!" she says to Jennie, "whatever do you think you're doing, giving General Lee so much trouble?"

"Well," says Jennie, "I couldn't make Fan go home, but I thought General Lee could do *anything*!"

I guess she was right there, Tom, too, as I'll tell you if you'll settle down and keep still. Oh, yeah, sure you can wash—that ain't no disturbance. 'Going to wash behind your ears? They always say that's a sign it's fixing to rain.

Now what was I telling you last night? I remember—'twas how the weather got warmer, warn't it, and how the Blue men came back over the river into the town? And how Cap-in-His-Eyes was crazy to attack 'em, but Marse Robert wouldn't 'low him. He figured that would be a waste, on 'count of that was what they wanted us to do. Them coming over into the town—that was what us soldiers call a stratagem, Tom, you see. 'Twas s'posed to deceive us. Only it didn't work. Marse Robert was a sight too smart for any o' that sorta hogwash. He waves his hand upriver, pointing.

"The main attack's coming from above," he says.

And then he tells Cap-in-His-Eyes he has to get all his
fellas up and away that very night.

I remember that night well. 'Twas full moonlight,
near'bouts bright as day. The Fat General's men went
first. He was one of Old Pete's commanders—General
McLaws. Myself, I always liked the Fat General, 'cause
he usually had a word and a pat for me, however busy
we was. He was real short and stout, dark and
swarthy, with a big black beard. And the way I sized
him up, he warn't one of our cleverest generals, but his
men thought the world of him and he was what you'd
call stubborn. In fact, I don't remember that him and
his fellas was ever once shifted by the Blue men.
Where they was put, there they stayed put. Marse
Robert had a lot of confidence in him.

When his fellas had marched off, Cap-in-His-
Eyes followed. Jest as they'd got under way, Jine-the-
Cavalry rode up and Vot-you-voz along with him, and
they evidently had a whole lot to tell Marse Robert—
stuff they'd found out 'bout the Blue men upriver, I
reckon. I was 'longside Skylark for a while, so I asked
him what was a-going on.

"Why," says Skylark, "there's a whole power of
the enemy upstream in the forest—horse, foot and
guns—this side of the river, too, and they're reckoning
on rolling us up."

"D'you figure they will?" I asked. Next moment I
felt real 'shamed. As a soldier I shouldn't 'a said any
sech thing, but it jest slipped out.

Skylark looks at me out'n the side of one eye.

"D'you ever hear the story," he says, "'bout the
vet who was going to give a big pill to a horse? He'd
got this pill in a tube, and he was countin' on blowing
it down the horse's throat. Well, he put one end in the
horse's mouth and he was all set to blow."

"What happened?" I asked, 'cause he'd stopped.

"The horse blowed first," said Skylark. "If you

want to have a good time, Traveller, jine the cavalry."
I was still thinking 'bout that when his master unhitched him and off they went.

By morning there come a thick fog—that place
seemed to specialize in fogs—but this time it favored
us, 'cause the Blue men down by the river, they
couldn't nohow tell what we was up to, you see.
Marse Robert and me spent the morning fixing the
guns, jest to give 'em a few surprises if'n they happened to try anything when the fog lifted. It warn't till
afternoon we set off upstream on the same road I came
down when I'd given Marse Rob sech a hard ride,
'time we arrived in the storm. It looked different now,
but you know, Tom, a lively horse that's interested in
his work can always recognize anywhere he's been before.

It warn't long 'fore I heared musketry. I figured it
must be Cap-in-His-Eyes and his fellas firing at the
Blue men, and I was right. But 'fore we reached him
we overtook Red Shirt's lot—the Light Division, as
they called 'em. Oh, Tom, you should 'a seed the way
them marching men was jest eating up the miles! They
warn't singing—jest marching 'long mighty quick,
thousands of feet beating down the dust of the road,
and their 'coutrements jingling as they went. Then
they halted a while, and as we rode past—Marse Robert and me and all the rest of headquarters—they
cheered him like you never heared in all your born
days. Marse Robert, he seemed—well—touched that
they was so glad to see him, and I remember him doing something he never done till then. He raised his
hat to 'em and held it over his head. All them fellas
jest went wild. They was shouting, "See that glorious
head! God bless it! God bless it!" When they started
up to marching again, Marse Robert halted the whole
of headquarters to stand and watch 'em go by.

'Twas some time after that when we come up

with Cap-in-His-Eyes. He was wearing the uniform
he'd had on for the battle in the snow. His fellas was
all strung out, firing into the woods, and best I could
see, the Blue men was falling back in front of 'em.
Marse Robert left him and rode off to have a bit of a
scout around, but I somehow felt he didn't like the
look of that there forest. I didn't blame him, neither.
You couldn't see no ways on 'count of the trees and all
the brush, and I reckoned that for us to try to go forward into that place, with the enemy already in there,
was the quickest way to get us all shot to bits. It reminded me of them little creeks and thickets where I'd
seed my first battles the summer before, 'cepting the
swamps was smaller.

'Twas twilight—well after sunset—when Marse
Robert rode back to Cap-in-His-Eyes. We caught up
with him at a crossroads in the forest, I remember, and
him and Marse Robert went over by some pine trees
and sat theirselves down on a log to talk.

Me and Sorrel, we was both hitched nearby. Sorrel seemed depressed, and after a while I asked him
what was wrong.

"That's jest it," he said. "I wish I knowed. Traveller, there's something badly wrong."

"You can't mean we're going to be beat?" I asked
him.

"No, 'tain't that," he answered. "'Tain't as bad as
that—and yet it's worse, too. I jest can't make it out
rightly, Traveller. You—what d'you think o' this here
how-d'ye-do?"

All I could see was our two masters talking together, Major Taylor's soldier grooming his horse and
Bryan and Perry getting supper ready; and that's what
I told him. But Sorrel didn't perk up none. 'Twarn't
like him to be gloomy, and I said so.

"Maybe it's jest this dad-blamed wilderness," he
said. "I never did like a lot of thick trees. Jest no telling

what's in among 'em. Might be our fellas, might be the enemy. Best to shoot first and ask afterwards. Yes!" he said suddenly. "Yes! That's what I can see now, Traveller! Men who shoot first and ask afterwards." He stopped. Then he said again, "Men who shoot first and ask afterwards. It's bad—*bad*!"

Later on, Marse Robert called Major Talcott and another officer and sent 'em off to see what the Blue men was getting up to. 'Peared like there was a whole lot of scheming a-going on, 'cause pretty soon after that, Jine-the-Cavalry came up and began talking real serious to Marse Robert and Cap-in-His-Eyes. ". . . a very *good* way round," I heared him say. Sorrel and me didn't get no chance to talk to Skylark, though. He was hitched a fair ways off.

There was no question of sleep that night. Officers kept coming and going all the time; I lost count how many. What I do remember is Marse Robert and Cap-in-His-Eyes a-walking through the trees towards me and Sorrel. When they come close-to, Marse Robert, he clenched his fist and said, "But how can we *get* at those people?" Oh, I've heared *that* before, I thought. If'n I'm any judge, there's going to be real trouble. I turned my head to look at Sorrel, but he seemed to be in a daze.

All of a sudden he says to me, "Do you remember me telling you how a good horse often knows some things his master don't know he knows?"

"I remember," I answers him back, "and I remember you saying all I needed was experience. I guess I've had some."

"They're both on edge," says Sorrel. "Both our men—strung-up. This forest is a bad place."

"It's going to be a sight worse for the Blue men soon," I says.

"That's your Marse Robert talking," says Sorrel. "What I mean is this is a dark, hit-or-miss kind of a place. There's something I can't see yet. Men shooting in the dark at—Traveller, something's wrong! There's something badly wrong!''

"'Tain't like you to say so,'' I answers him. He was jest a-trembling all over, and sweating in the cold.

Marse Robert and Cap-in-His-Eyes had stopped talking together. Cap-in-His-Eyes was smiling. He saluted and said something 'bout he'd have all his fellas ready to move. Then they both walked off.

Marse Robert, he didn't go far, though. He talked a while to some other man. Then he laid out his saddle blanket under a tree near the fire, covered hisself with his overcoat and went to sleep right there on the ground.

Later on, some officer came up and waked him. I recollect Marse Robert was teasing him and havin' a laugh on him. Then Cap-in-His-Eyes came back over to the fire, and this man that had been talking to Marse Robert 'long with him. They sat together on a cracker-barrel and talked, kind of disputing 'mong theirselves. I knowed right then there must be big trouble coming. I was afeared myself, and the whole place was full of disquiet—everyone on edge, even Dave. 'Twas 'nuff to unsettle every horse round there. I can see that dark place now—the fire of branches burning and crackling, the flames flickering low, Cap-in-His-Eyes putting questions to this man, stabbing with his finger, and the man answering him real quiet. Every now and then, somebody'd toss another branch on the fire.

After a while I dozed off on my feet. When I woke up, it seemed to have turned colder; the man was gone and Colonel Long was talking to Cap-in-His-Eyes while he drank some coffee. All of a sudden I heared a clatter. It was Cap-in-His-Eyes' sword had fallen over, where he'd left it leaning up agin a tree.

Colonel Long picked it up and gave it to him, and he fastened it on.

I seed Sorrel looking over to Cap-in-His-Eyes as he buckled the sword belt.

"Men shooting in the dark," he said again. "Then it all stops."

I asked him what he meant, but he didn't seem to know he'd said anything.

It was getting on to morning now, near as I could tell, and the camp was beginning to stir. Marse Robert woke. He came over and sat on the cracker-barrel beside Cap-in-His-Eyes. They began talking again and kept pointing this way and that.

At last Marse Robert stood up and put his hand on Cap-in-His-Eyes' shoulder. "Well," he said, "go on, then! Go on, General!"

At that Cap-in-His-Eyes called to his soldier to bring Sorrel. Neither of us said any more to each other. Cap-in-His-Eyes mounted and rode off. It was daylight now, good as. I was hoping for a bite to eat, but there warn't no more'n a drink and a mouthful or two of hay.

All the same, I did see Sorrel once more that morning. Marse Robert had moved headquarters a little ways, and me and him was a-standing 'side a dirt road leading off through the trees. Cap-in-His-Eyes' fellas come marching past, heading into the woods.

Cap-in-His-Eyes was riding at the back, and as he reached us he pulled Sorrel in, came up and spoke to Marse Robert—jest a few words. Us two horses was right up agin each other, and Sorrel nuzzled my neck.

"Good-bye, Traveller," he said. "You was born lucky. I can see green grass and daisies growing under your hooves right now."

Then they was off. The peak of the general's cap was right down over his eyes, jest the way I'd always thought of him; jest the way he'd looked that first day when he rode up to headquarters and stood leaning agin the fence all by hisself and spoke to me and stroked my nose. He could 'a been any one o' the soldiers.

I never seed Sorrel or Cap-in-His-Eyes again.

$\star$

XIII

THE REST of that morning was mighty quiet. I couldn't bottom it out, no way. You see, Tom, I figured that by this time I was getting to be an experienced soldier. I'd larned how things usually went from a horse's point of view—I mean, bein' strung out and bein' able to take it easy; times of danger and times of quiet. And what beat me was that though I could sense we warn't fixing to attack, I'd never knowed Marse Robert so edgy in all the time we'd been together. The whole feel of him was tense —his knees, his hands, his seat, the tone of his voice— even though I reckon I was the only one who could tell it. The Blue men warn't aiming to make no trouble on our front; I felt sure 'nuff of that—there warn't one o' them to be smelt or seed. And yet Marse Robert— well, all I can say is that if he'd had a tail, Tom, it would have been a-twitching like yours at a rathole.

We was waiting. We was waiting for something to happen—I knowed that much. But what was it? It warn't like that time in the snow when we was waiting for the enemy to come up from the town and the river. When there came the sound of a few guns in the forest, off'n the way where Cap-in-His-Eyes had gone, Marse Robert 'peared as near to shying as I'd ever knowed him do; and every time an officer rode up to headquarters, seemed like he couldn't wait to hear what he'd got to tell him. He'd listen hard and ask questions, and he kept tap-tapping one of his gloved hands agin his leg. But no one else could see—I was the only one who knowed. Now and then he'd be speaking jest to me. "Oh, Traveller," he said once't, real low, "only a little longer! Lord God, only a little longer!" He quite often used to call me "Lord God" when he was strung out and we was by ourselves. Maybe that was some other horse he'd had way back and he was a mite confused—I don't know.

Every now and then there'd be firing along our lines, close to where we was—mostly musketry, sometimes a gun. But 'twarn't that as had Marse Robert high strung. As the day went on, he kept looking up at the sun. He didn't want the daylight to end—I could tell that. Horsemen came and went, and Marse Robert talked to each one of them, but still nobody was telling him whatever 'twas he wanted to hear.

The sun was dropping—near 'nuff down into the trees—when all of a sudden, from far off, over the same way, there came a tremendous, deep sound of gunfire. I felt an instant change come over everyone in headquarters, from Marse Robert down to the soldiers. Major Taylor and Colonel Long was right beside Marse Robert, and they turned and looked at him without a word. Marse Robert spoke to them and pointed, saying something 'bout going forward to attack right away.

And so we did. Our soldiers, who'd been laying down under cover, got up and begun to advance, and our own guns commenced to firing. Marse Robert rode forward with the soldiers. You could see, up ahead, where the Blue men had cut down trees to fight behind. They was all lined up behind them, waiting for us.

All of a sudden I realized what we-all was a-doing. Cap-in-His-Eyes, that morning—he'd set out to

go right round behind the Blue men and catch them
where they warn't expecting him! Those must be *his*
guns we'd heared, a long ways off. That was what
Marse Robert had been waiting for all day. Now we-
all had to keep the Blue men in front of us busy, best
we could.

Marse Robert and me, we was right up in the battle. He kept on giving out orders, saying which outfits
he wanted to attack and all the rest of it. And attack
they did, Tom, yelling like a thousand stallions fighting! I'd come to know that Yell! I wish you could hear
it, jest once—it'd scare the fur right off'n your back! It
scared the Blue men all right. I couldn't see much,
'cause by now darkness was falling, but I knowed
there was fewer and fewer bullets dropping round us.
Not that Marse Robert ever took no notice o' *them*,
many or few; and like I told you, I'd larned not to—
well, near'bouts, anyways.

It was dark already when some of our soldiers
came up to Marse Robert and gave him a cloth on a
stick. It was one that had belonged to the Blue men—I
could tell that jest from the smell of it as they held it
up. Marse Robert, he says that's mighty fine, and
shakes hands with a bunch of 'em. He says he's
mighty proud to have sech soldiers fighting for him.

We stopped then—we was 'bliged to; it was too
dark to see no more. But the noise of that fighting in
the distance didn't stop. In fact, it growed louder. I
figured Cap-in-His-Eyes and his fellas must be fighting in the dark. After a while, I seed all the sky over
that way lit up. Oh, Tom, that was a sight! 'Twas like
a huge, long hedge of fire, way off on t'other side of
the forest, and it kept sort of swaying and spurting up
and down, and all shaking and full of the crashing of
the guns. The trees theirselves must 'a been on fire.
You could hear the muskets, too, crackling by the

thousand. And it went on half the night before it begun to die away.

I was real tired by this time—hungry, too, and short of sleep. But Marse Robert, he had to go on talking to the officers who kept on riding up to report, so I jest did my best—I reckoned if he could stick it, I could. But all that time he never forgot me. Every so often he'd stroke my neck and say, "Easy, Traveller! Good boy! Soon be time for a rest," or some sech; and I could tell jest by the tone of his voice that he was better pleased than he'd been all day. Things was turning out the way he'd meant 'em to.

At last, right into the night, he lay down to sleep there on the ground. So did I. I was tuckered out. Dave brung me a feed—a real, proper feed of oats; goodness knows where he'd found it—but I fell asleep 'fore I'd finished it. I remember the whippoorwills calling in the woods. Ever heared them? It's an eerie sort o' sound, ain't it? But it didn't bother me none that night.

I didn't sleep long, though. I don't know how much later 'twas, but anyways not long 'nuff, when I was woke by a horse being picketed 'longside me. As I turned over and sniffed at him, I realized I knowed him. He was a horse named Dancer, belonged to one of Cap-in-His-Eyes' staff officers, Captain Wilbourn. You could tell at once't that he was tired out and blowed.

"Howdy, Dancer," I says. "I thought you'd gone off yesterday."

"My man's ridden back to report to Marse Robert," he answered.

"What's happened?" I asked. "I heared the heck of a battle. You in that?"

"Sure was," he says. "We marched all day, and in the evening we came on a whole bunch o' the enemy. They was jest a-lounging round and cooking supper.

They'd no idea at all that we was there. Our fellas piled straight into them—they never had a chance. We was driving 'em through the woods like they was herds of durned cows. The guns was going forward right with us. You never seed nothing like it. It kept on into the dark—long after dark."

"I heared it," I said. "We've whupped 'em bad, then?"

"Best ever," said Dancer. "But—oh, Traveller—the general—"

"Cap-in-His-Eyes?" I said, real quick. "What 'bout him?" But 'twas like I knowed already.

"He's been hit," says Dancer. "Wounded something terrible. I reckon he—"

"What happened, for goodness' sake?" I asked.

"It was dark," said Dancer. "Jest a bit of a moon behind clouds, and we was all in among the trees. The fighting had near'bouts stopped, and the general and my man and quite a few more had gone forward, ahead of our lines, to have a look around and try to find out what the enemy was up to. Coming back, we was fired on—I reckon 'twas our own fellas got confused. The general's been hit real bad."

"You mean he'll die?" I asked.

"I don't know," said Dancer, "but I reckon maybe he will. He's done fighting for a long time, anyways."

"Sorrel—what about Sorrel?" I says.

"Sorrel and the general was close to me jest afore it happened," replies Dancer. "It was as if Sorrel'd been expecting it. We was right close to a turnpike in the woods. When the firing started—the first volley—there was a whole passel of the general's people hit and fell off their horses. 'Twas all confusion in the dark, but the general warn't hit that time. Sorrel galloped off like he was doing his best to get away out of it. But he'd gone hardly any ways at all, 'crost the turnpike, when there come another volley, and that

hit the general. You could see he was wounded real
bad. He still stuck on Sorrel's back, though. I seed a
branch hit him acrost the face—it tore off his cap and
knocked him right back'ards in the saddle, but he
didn't fall. He pulled hisself up, grabbed the bridle
again and turned Sorrel back towards us. He got him
into the turnpike, and that was where my man caught
up with them and grabbed the reins. There was horses
mad with fright running all ways. Some of 'em their
men had been shot and fallen off, others had jest gone
crazy and out of control. I seed four-five gallop off
towards the enemy's lines. The whole bunch of us was
jest shot or scairt to pieces, that was what it come to.
There was no one left around at all, 'ceptin' for my
man and one other. Then my man seed some stranger
fella sitting on a horse 'longside the road, and he told
him to go and see where the firing had come from. He
went off, but he never come back.

"The general was bleeding something terrible,
and he looked awful bad. I reckon he was in a lot of
pain. He couldn't dismount—he kind of fell forward
off'n Sorrel and my man caught him, but t'other officer
had to pull his feet out of the stirrups. They carried
him to the side of the road and laid him under a tree.
After a bit Red Shirt come up with his fellas. When he
seed what had happened, he was real shook. I seed
him kneel down and pull off the general's gloves, and
they was all full of blood. After a while two-three
fellas got him on his feet, but jest then the enemy's
guns commenced to firing and there was more confusion. The last I seed of the general, they was holding
him up either side and he was doing his best to walk
back all through the lines of Red Shirt's men as they
went forward to attack. But I figure he's a-going to die
sure 'nuff."

I could see Marse Robert walking up and down in
the light of the fire, talking to Dancer's man. You

could see he was shook up bad. Jest for once't he
'peared throwed completely off balance.

"Oh, Captain!" I heared him say. "General Jackson! General Jackson!"

I couldn't understand the rest, till all of a sudden
he bustèd out with "Those people must be pressed
today! They must be pressed *hard*!"

He pulls on his boots and someone called up the
rest of headquarters. I felt so tired I wondered if'n I
could make it, but somehow I did. Marse Robert had
jest spread out some food for Dancer's master—yeah,
Tom, he did that, right then, with his own hands—and
mounted me when another of Cap-in-His-Eyes' officers come up—one I knowed by sight. Marse Robert
listened to what he had to say, but he wouldn't let him
talk about Cap-in-His-Eyes. "I know 'bout General
Jackson," he said. "I don't want to hear any more."

The rest of that night was all coming and going,
and Marse Robert giving out his orders. All I understood was we had to attack the Blue men right where
they was, in the woods. Whatever had been the finish
of the business with Cap-in-His-Eyes, you could hear
the battle startin' up again over that way. And all
round us, as it growed light, our soldiers was advancing and our guns was firing. Pretty soon, I knowed we
must be driving the Blue men back, 'cause there was
their wounded and dead on the ground and we was
going right on past them.

And do you know, Tom, what Marse Robert was
a-doing while this here battle was going on? He was
sitting on my back, jest as nice as you please, talking
to some foreign fella—nothing to do with the fighting
or our people at all! I could tell this was some sort of
foreigner, on 'count of he had a funny way of talking
—something the same as Vot-you-voz. They was con-
versing jest as easy as if they'd been back home drink-

ing coffee on the stoop. As for me, I was near'bouts asleep on my hooves, 'spite of all the racket.

We went this way and that—a good mile or more through them woods. Near's I could tell, Marse Robert wanted to make sure our fellas and Cap-in-His-Eyes' lot was finally going to jine up together. I recollect seeing one of our wounded men a-laying there on the ground, waving his cap and shouting, "General Lee! General Lee!" Marse Robert pulled up an' said, "God bless you, my man!" I remember how we stopped off right where some of our guns was firing. The bangs— they shook me from head to hooves. Couldn't see straight, couldn't hear nothing else. Marse Robert, he was jest as calm as always, an' paying no never-mind at all to the enemy shells a-bursting round. I don't know why nothing hit us, but it didn't.

After a while we went forward with them guns. It was a pesky business our poor horses had of it, haul-ing 'em through the brush and in and out the soft ground, but after 'bout half a mile we come to a little bit of a hump rising atop the woods. There was a whole bunch of our guns had been dragged up there. They was jest a-blazing away, and 'far as I could tell in all the noise and smoke, the Blue men was good as cut to pieces and running off quick as they could. Every now and then I'd catch a sight of little groups of 'em, doing their best to keep in among the thickest parts of the trees. Their guns kept firing, though, and I seed a plenty of our poor horses go down. Our gunners, they was black from head to foot; and all the time there come a steady stream of wounded fellas back past us —some limping along, some leaning on others and some jest a-dragging theirselves over the ground. One man died almost under my hooves, and no one 'peared to have a moment even to pull him out the way.

By this time all the woods in front of this here hump we was on was a-burning. First one part would

catch fire and then another; then two parts'd jine together and go up in a great roar, high as the trees. You
couldn't tell that smoke from the battle-smoke of the
guns, nor you couldn't tell the Yell from the shouting
and screaming of the wounded trying to get out of the
fires. I recollect one of our men—jest a boy, really—
going on through the smoke, carrying one of our
cloths on sticks and calling out, "Come on! Come on,
y'all!" And when he went down, another young fella
grabbed the stick right out of his hand, and on they-
all went. I've been in a heap o' battles, Tom, but that's
one I'll never forget—standing as steady as I could on
that there hump and looking acrost the fighting and
the burning all around.

Pretty soon, though, Marse Robert was urging me
on—well, back towards where we'd started out from,
really, you see, 'cause now all our Army was back together and advancing in a line—if'n you could call it a
line, in that place where we was. There can't never
have been a mess like that since the world began.
There was dead horses, guns blowed up, wheels laying
around, limbers overturned, muskets and knapsacks
the Blue men had throwed away, blankets, caps, belts
—everything you can name. And the dead men—ours
an' theirs—was so thick I had to pick my way over 'em
like they was rocks. Some you couldn't scarcely tell
they'd ever been men. I went through it all jest like
Marse Robert signaled. That's what we call "battle-
hardened," Tom, you know.

At last we got to a kind of an open clearing, where
there was a house all afire. You could see where the
Blue men had dug up the ground for their trenches,
but now the place was full of our fellas. When they
seed me and Marse Robert, they went good as wild.
There was men crowding round us, trying to shake
Marse Robert's hand, grabbing at my bridle, cheering
—some of 'em crying, even. One fella laid his head

agin my neck and put his arm round it, shouting,
"Bless the General! Bless General Lee!" There was
thousands all round, yelling, "Marse Robert! Marse
Robert! Bless General Lee!" The soldiers was mostly in
rags, clothes all tore to shreds from the thickets, faces
streaked black, scratched and bleeding. There was
wounded fellas lifting up their hands to touch my legs,
touch the stirrups—anything.

Then three-four of our fellas come pushing up to
us with a whole passel of Blue men they'd taken prisoner. One of them calls out, "Surrendered, General!
They're surrendered!" Marse Robert jest nods and
salutes, and then he says they was to be taken away to
the rear and given some water. But I don't even know
if'n anyone could hear him, on 'count of the whole
place was that full o' shouting and yelling. We'd seed
some victories, but never one like this'n.

Even Marse Robert seemed sort of struck speech-
less. He sat where he was in the saddle—he couldn't
do nothing else; he'd been forced to a halt in the
crowd—and looked round him at his soldiers. Once't
or twice't he took the hands of the fellas nearest him.
He kept having to pull me in, else I'd have been treading the men down. I did my best to live up to it. I
picked up my hooves, arched my neck and tossed my
head, and tried all I could to act like a general's horse. I
jest wished Skylark had been around to see it.

In the middle of it all, I found myself wondering
where they'd taken poor Sorrel, and remembering
what he'd said 'bout a good horse often knowing
more'n what his man knowed. And then, all of a sudden, standing there in front of the burning house, up
to my fetlocks in the wreckage of the battle, I realized
there was something I knowed beyond doubt. I
knowed that in the end we *was* going to beat the enemy and there'd be an end to all the killing and the
guns and the fear of battle. We was going to make

them give up. I'd never thought 'bout this before, but I knowed it right 'nuff now. I knowed it jest like poor Sorrel had knowed—or half-knowed—'bout Cap-in-His-Eyes and the men shooting in the dark. I knowed where we was going and how we-all was going to finally come out.

By this time they'd put out part of the fire, and there was a piece of the house and some of the sheds where they'd put the wounded—our fellas and the enemy all together. Marse Robert dismounted and went to see them, like he always did after a battle. I was glad 'nuff jest to stand round and get a good, long drink. I felt real easy now. There was one thing 'bout that place, Tom, you know. The smoke kept down the dad-blame flies.

Later that afternoon, Marse Robert had a tent set up 'longside the road, and talked to the generals—Red Shirt, Jine-the-Cavalry and some more. He'd already ridden me a way through the woods to talk to the Fat General. Marse Robert evidently had some special job for the Fat General, 'cause I recollect how he saluted and went straight off to get his men together on the road. When we'd come back, I lay down on the ground right near that little tent and went to sleep as sound as though I'd been in stables.

Well, that was about it, Tom—our great victory. There was some more moving round, and I reckon the Fat General must 'a done some good fighting, 'cause I can recall Marse Robert riding up to him and telling him as much. But that's all I can remember, 'cause Marse Robert realized I was plumb wore out, and for the next two-three days he rode Lucy while I had a good rest. There was a vet come to look me over, but he couldn't find nothing wrong, 'ceptin' I was exhausted. Marse Robert found time, too, to come and talk to me. He brung the foreign fella with him. "Ah," he says to him, stroking my nose, "this is one of the bravest soldiers in my Army."

And do you know, Tom, that foreign fella, he actually captured some Blue men, too? Yes, he did, all on his own, and brung 'em back to headquarters! 'Parently he'd gone to look for something for his horse to eat, and near a farmhouse he come on these here Blue fellas. So he up and spoke to 'em real sharp—so his horse told me—'said there was a whole bunch of our cavalry coming along, and they'd best jest give theirselves up. And they was so scairt by everything that had happened that day they jest did what he told them. They was what we call demoralized, Tom, you see.

That reminds me of another thing I remember—'bout Jine-the-Cavalry's friend, Vot-you-voz. It was the night after the battle, and Marse Robert, he was a-setting by a little fire, all in among the thick trees. Vot-you-voz was with him, but whatever 'twas they had to be doing, the firelight was so dim they couldn't see to do it properly. So while Marse Robert was a-talking to someone else, Vot-you-voz slipped off and after a while he come back with a box of candles.

"Major," says Marse Robert, "I know where you went to get those. It was jest a few yards in front of the enemy lines, wasn't it?"

Vot-you-voz says yes, 'twas. "You acted wrongly," says Marse Robert, "to risk your life for that." And with that he looks at him real straight, to show he meant it.

I could see Vot-you-voz thinking that if it come down to risking lives, Marse Robert could get his nose out'n front of most people; but he never said so. He jest stayed quiet and lit one of the candles from the fire. But I didn't hear no more'n that, 'cause I fell fast asleep—yeah, even though the woods was full of the crying of wounded men and poor fellas calling out for water.

Two days later, I met Skylark again—Jine-the-Cavalry had ridden in to talk to Marse Robert—and he told me he knowed now that every single one of the Blue men had run back 'crost the river, 'ceptin' for the dead and wounded they'd left.

"I do hope everything went all right with you in the battle, Traveller?" says Skylark, like he was inquiring after my nose bag.

"Hadn't, I shouldn't be here," I answered.

"That's fine! You're not too tired, then?" he persisted. "Very little to eat jest now, ain't there? I hope you don't feel it too bad?"

If anyone'd been in three battles, one after t'other, Skylark's manners'd still have been 'nuff to make him feel small. Jest the same, he was a horse you couldn't dislike. The way *he* acted, anyone'd think he'd spent the last five days in a green meadow. He was hiding a limp, and I noticed that one of his ears had been nicked by a bullet—or by something, anyways.

Well, I guess now you sure are a well-washed cat, Tom. Why don't you hop up in the manger and go to sleep in the hay? Scares the mice away, that does—jest the smell of a cat.

XIV

H EY, THERE, Tom! For goodness' sakes, how long is it since we seed each other? 'Must be 'least two months! I seed you asleep on the brick wall s'afternoon when we come riding in, but I didn't figure on you larning so soon that we was back home. Well, 'course you'd know Marse Robert was back, so I guess you could reckon I was. I take it real kind you dropping in the first night I'm here. I hope you've been enjoying the summer weather while we've been away. Me, I'm glad to have it a mite cooler. 'Won't be long till fall now. I'm glad to be back. Mind you, stables have been real good everywhere we've been and we've had some great rides—best ever—but it's still good to be home. I reckon no one puts up a bran mash like good old Isaiah.

'Course, Isaiah was looking after things while we was gone, warn't he? There was Miss Agnes, and Miss Life and Mr. Custis came with us, and that young fella, Captain White, him that was in the Army 'long o' Marse Robert. General Pendleton's daughter come along, too. She's quite a friend of Miss Agnes, you know. Maybe they felt she could help with looking after the old lady. Well, the old lady's pretty well infirm now, Tom, you know. Can't hardly get out of that rolling chair of hers.

It was a real fine morning when we started out.

Marse Robert and me was riding, and Captain White
along with us. I like his mare. She's a real nice young
filly—good goer, too—name of Bluebird. We jest took
it nice and easy for a thirty-mile day—finished up at a
small town in the mountains; good stables. We met up
with the others there. They'd come by coaches and the
railroad, you see.

Now here's what I've got to tell you, Tom, and
this is really something. You know what? We set out
the next day, and when we started coming down out
of the mountains on t'other side, I suddenly realized
that I more or less knowed where I was! I hadn't
'zackly been over that particular chunk of road before,
but jest the same I knowed them mountains and that
there country—jest the smell of it! It was them same
wooded mountains where I'd first met up with Marse
Robert, years ago! Jest the smell of that durned ground
laurel brung it back to me, even though it warn't raining and the day was nice and sunny. 'Course, we was
traveling on a good road now—not a cloud in the sky,
plenty of food inside and a good night's sleep behind
me, but jest the same I couldn't help but recall something of that bad fall in the rain, with all the men sick
and the wagons axle-deep in the mud. If'n I'm any
judge, we warn't so far away from that very same
mountain, and we was back on the main pike to that
town where I took the prize and Jim rode me into the
tent. Made me feel jest like a colt again! But I was a
durn sight happier to feel Marse Robert on my back
than Captain Joe—yeah, or even Jim, even if'n he was
sech a nice young fella and trained me so well. I
thought of them days, and how far me and Marse
Robert had come since then. I can say this to *you*, Tom
—maybe you're the only one I *can* say it to: it's something to be not only Marse Robert's horse, but to
know that you're Marse Robert's horse 'cause you've

come through thick and thin with him and he never wanted another, never once't.

When we set off next morning, we very soon left the coach people behind, and it might have been—oh, maybe twenty mile to this here place we was heading to. We took it easy, you know—stopped for a bite round the middle of the day; and we got in and finished up pretty early on in the afternoon.

It was quite a place, Tom. Only a small town—oh, yeah, lots smaller'n here—but jest the same there was a power of people stopping at this one big house: old fellas like Marse Robert, 'long with their wives; lots of young ladies and gentlemen—all sorts—some of 'em had brung their own black folks along; and, 'course, a heap of horses, all in good stables round a fine, big yard. How I figured it, from the way they was all behaving and the high spirits they mostly seemed to be in, they'd all a-come together to have a high old time. So many horses and people, it was almost like being back in camp—'ceptin' for the girls: more girls'n men, near'bouts. And this sure warn't no camp. It was even grander and more showy'n them big houses where Marse Robert sometimes used to stay when we was on campaign.

The middle of this here place was a great, rambling building—real huge, Tom; I guess it'd need a hundred cats, a place like that—and it was all made of wood, painted white. They call it "The White," one of the horses there was telling me—and this was where most of the folks stayed, amusing theirselves. It had big white columns and long, wide porches—a bit like Marse Robert's house here, only lots bigger. And then a little ways off there was rows of cottages, and folks living in them, too. Marse Robert and the old lady had one of 'em, with a black girl to look after them. There was whole crowds of folks came to call on them—oh, every evening, near as I could make out. Of course,

Marse Robert always likes meeting different kinds of
folks and talking to them. What I came to conclude
after a day or two was that seeing who he is now,
nearly all them folks had come there 'specially to see
him and pay their respects. Well, it's only natchral,
ain't it?

Marse Robert soon began enjoying hisself. I could
tell that from the whole feel of him and the way he
was acting and talking. Whenever he came to my stable, he'd like as not have another man with him, or
maybe two, and he'd kind of introduce them to me.
"This here's Traveller," he'd say, and then they'd pat
me and ask him questions, and say had I really been
his one horse in all those battles, and so on. Sometimes
girls came, too. There was lots of sugar in it, and I ain't
never been too proud to take a piece of sugar, Tom,
you know, 'cause I remember all them times when
there warn't none. I felt Marse Robert was more at
ease with the girls than the fellas—I reckon 'cause
they warn't wanting to talk 'bout soldiering and fighting all the time. He's got 'nuff of that on his mind, you
know, without being made to talk 'bout it.

But I don't want you to think Marse Robert had
gone all that way jest to walk round among those folks
and say howdy and be treated like the commander.
No, sir. He'd come to get away and be alone with *me*—
more'n he can be here. Those summer days are long—
getting shorter already now, ain't they?—and most of
the time—mornings and afternoons, too—he'd spend
alone with me in the mountains. There's some real
wild, high, lonely mountains there, you know—
higher'n you can imagine, Tom—and in the mornings
we'd ride off and get up there for hours at a stretch—
maybe not see a soul, 'cepting now and then. You can't
imagine the enjoyment of jest trotting easy 'long those
tracks, under the sycamores and the white oaks all
green and shady, and never a signal needed from ei-

ther of us, 'cause each of us knows jest what t'other wants—well, we ain't separate, not really—and nary a thought of battle-smoke, and no soldiers a-sweating and a-cussing—jest living your life without having to think 'bout it none. I came to know them mountains for miles around. I got to know jest where the creeks was. I got to know the best patches of grass, and when we came to one I'd stop off and begin grazing and Marse Robert, he'd jest sit easy and look out acrost the ravines below and the valleys full of trees. Up there you could see for miles. We was both doing jest what we wanted, and we didn't want to be doing nothing else, neither. Marse Robert needs to be alone—alone with me, I mean. Well, for him that *is* alone. What he needs is solitude, and that's what them mountains have got. But without me he couldn't have it, you see.

He's often real sad in his thoughts, Tom, you know—and can you wonder? He's bound to be thinking of all them dead fellas. And the wounded, too—once't you've heared them cry you don't forget it, I'll tell you. I remember a horse I seed once when we was under fire. This horse had lost his lower jaw. Every breath he was blowing blood. That kind of thing you don't forget. But in the mountains—well, them mountains must 'a been there an awful long time. When I'd taken a good long breather—a gallop up one of them hill tracks—then I'd feel Marse Robert's heartsickness and bad memories all lifting like a mist and blowing away. It's important, Tom, you know, to do things without thinking 'bout 'em. That's the only way a horse and a man can really work together, but it takes a proper good man. There's too many men think horses was jest meant to be like plows or carts. Now Marse Robert, he'd really like to *be* a horse. "So, Traveller," he says out loud to me one day when we was in a rough place up in them mountains. "So, Traveller, what ought we to do?" 'Course, he had a pretty fair

idea hisself what we ought to do: it jest happened to
be the same's I had. When a horse and a man respect
each other, that's the way it works out.

Another day, we was jest getting ready to start
out from this White place when two girls got to telling
Marse Robert that they was going to climb the mountain back of the house. Well, you could tell that Marse
Robert, he didn't care for this notion. He figured it was
kind of a rough hike—too rough for a couple of girls.
All the same, he let them go off without saying nothing to 'em. But then, after they'd been gone a little
while, we set out to go up that there mountain ourselves, and I'm here to tell you, Tom, the going was
real steep. Well, pretty soon we came on the girls and
'course they was surprised to see us.

"Good afternoon," says Marse Robert, raising his
hat. "I jest had an idea you might be finding the going
a little hard," he says. "If you'll allow me, I'll come
some of the way with you." He invited first one of
them and then t'other to ride on me, but seein' as how
they declined, he jest led me by the bridle and we-all
walked up to the top and back down. 'Fore we was
done they was glad we had, too.

There was one other thing happened while we
was staying at The White. We was out riding one
morning, jest the two of us, through some of the hills
down lower. I remember a tree sparrow singing in the
brush, and a whole flock of killdeer a little way off,
feeding in an open field. Then, in the distance, I seed a
horseman riding towards us, and I reckoned I knowed
the horse without being able to recall 'zackly who he
was. And then suddenly, as they came closer, I
knowed who it was—it was Ruffian, the horse who'd
been my friend at Andy's, when we was colts together! I recognized that sorrel coloring and then,
'soon as we came close, I remembered the smell of him
—and where I'd seed him last.

He looked well cared for now. The man riding
him stopped for a chat with Marse Robert. When he
realized who it was, he began speaking real respectful,
but Marse Robert soon made him easy. He said they
warn't soldiers no more, and 'sides he was taking a
holiday. We-all rode along together and Ruffian told
me 'bout the bad time he'd had, serving with the guns.
I asked him whether he could remember me that time
on the night road—well, I ain't told you 'bout that yet,
Tom, though I will—but he couldn't recollect nothing
'bout it. I warn't altogether surprised. To tell you the
truth, I'd thought he was dying. But now here he was
on this dirt track, coat sleek and all a-shining, and him
jest as bobbish as a chipmunk in spring! "You owe that
to Marse Robert, you know," I said to him.

"Who's Marse Robert, Jeff?" he asked me. I
hadn't been called Jeff for years. It made me realize
what a long time had passed since them days in
Andy's meadow. There was jest too much to explain; I
left it.

"Oh, he's my man," I said. "A good 'un, too.
How's yours?"

"Fine!" said Ruffian. "He bought me out of the
artillery depot at the end of the war and looked after
me real well, till I was back to what I used to be. It's
funny, ain't it, that we should both come back to these
here parts? Do you live round here?"

"No," I answered. "I don't know how long we'll
be here, but our home's over a long way east."

"You don't know, then, that Andy's place ain't
more'n twenty, twenty-five mile from here?" he asks.

I'd never thought of it, Tom, you know, but now
he said that, I knowed it must be right. It felt that way.
I almost imagined I could smell the big meadow with
the pond at the bottom.

"I've been back there two-three times," said Ruffian, "when my man's had business there. Old Andy

recognized me straightaway. He never forgets a horse."

We talked on 'bout old times until we went our separate ways. I was hoping we'd meet again on some ride or other later on, and I believe we would have, too, if'n it hadn't 'a been for the way things turned out.

The very next day after that, Marse Robert was took sick. 'Course, you know, Tom, he was taken sick more'n once when we was on campaign, and I could tell that this was another go of the same thing. I was left fretting in stables for quite a while, though one of the black grooms took me out for a few miles' exercise every afternoon. I don't reckon he much 'preciated my buck-trot, though.

As soon as Marse Robert was on the mend, we-all shifted from this here White and went maybe ten mile to another place—pretty much the same sort. I guess he hoped the move would make him feel better, but what happened was that though he'd felt well 'nuff to ride me over there, he took a deal worse right away. "Oh, Traveller," he said to me jest as we was arriving, "I'm afraid I'm going to be took real bad this time." I could tell from the feel of him that he was right, too.

I didn't see him for days—half a month or more. I guess he was laid up in bed. 'Course, I knowed that one way or another he'd manage to see me again soon's he could. And that was what happened, as I've got good reason to recall.

It was like this. One morning I was led out of stables and round into the main courtyard of this big house. It was all fenced round, you know, with gates opposite the main doors. The first person I seed was Marse Robert, in his shirt and pants, looking pretty poorly and standing on what they call the piazza—the long porch with steps up to it. He gives me our whistle and calls, "Good boy, Traveller!" Jest at that moment,

into the courtyard come quite a little crowd of country
folk—mostly men—carrying baskets of plums and
berries and so on. Well, do you know, Tom, I recognized one of them fellas right off? The last time I'd
seed him, he was sighting a gun 'long a track in the
wilderness. But they was jest about all of 'em old
soldiers from our Army, and I reckon they was
near'bouts as ragged without uniforms as they had
been with 'em. Fact was, two of 'em *was* wearing old
uniforms, with the buttons cut off.

They all laid down their baskets and began cheering Marse Robert, right where they stood in the courtyard, and of course most of the ladies and gentlemen
came out to see what all the noise was about. I'll tell
you, the sound of that cheering took me back, Tom.
Only had to blink my eyes to see the Blue men running and hear the muskets! Marse Robert, he come
down the steps into the courtyard, sick as he was, and
shook hands with each one of 'em. There was plenty
wanted a word with me, too; they crowded round me,
stroked my neck and said all sorts o' fine things. When
they left, they insisted on giving all their fruit to
Marse Robert. Goodness knows what he did with it
all. I guess he must 'a told the folks who ran the place
to make their own best use of it, 'cause there was 'nuff
for near'bouts two companies of infantry.

What finally happened, when Marse Robert had
recovered, was that Mr. Custis took the ladies home
by coach, and us two followed in our own time. We
took it easy, only going a short ways every day, 'cause
Marse Robert was still pretty weak in hisself. Nor he
ain't right yet, Tom, you know. The first day we did
'bout thirty mile, but that left him so bad that we had
to stop off for four days. After that we went—well, I'd
guess 'bout ten mile a day for three days. The last
night, we stopped at that there Rockbridge place we
ride out to in the afternoons.

That should have been a real nice holiday altogether; and so 'twas, the first part. But you know, the truth is that Marse Robert's come back weaker'n he was when he set out with Captain White. *I* can tell, if'n nobody else can. When we arrived this afternoon, he had to be holpen up the steps to the door. Maybe a quiet fall at home'll be better for him than all that socializing at The White.

Me? Oh, I'm fine, Tom. Go forever! Come in tomorrow and I'll go on telling you what happened after that great victory in the woods, when we chased the enemy back acrost the river.

June, 1863: the third summer of the war. Whoever else in the South may have been dazzled, the splendor of his victory at Chancellorsville has not blinded General Lee to the true situation of the Confederacy and its increasingly desperate plight. In that battle, the Union lost fewer than 17,000 men, the Army of Northern Virginia over 13,000—a considerably higher proportion and more than it can afford of its total effectives. In particular, the death of Stonewall Jackson is a grave and irreparable loss, as well as a severe blow to General Lee's personal confidence and morale. The Confederacy is running out of every necessary resource—men, horses, food, clothes, boots, ammunition. The longer the war continues against so well-supplied an enemy, the surer becomes ultimate defeat. General Lee has, in effect, so advised the President in a formal letter, and recommended that every effort should be made to encourage the peace party in the North and to achieve a negotiated settlement, which may even now prove consistent with independence.

Meanwhile, what is the best use to be made of the declining though still formidable strength of the Army of Northern Virginia? The morale of the troops has never been higher, but the reorganization consequent upon the death of Jackson has inevitably resulted in a general lack of experience at corps, divisional and brigade command levels. "Our army would be invincible," Lee writes to General Hood of the Texan division, "if it could be properly organized and officered. There is the difficulty—proper commanders." He has to make the best selections he can from the officers available, and there is no time in which to train them. Action is imperative.

The one course that must not be taken is to wait passively south of the Rappahannock for General Hooker to recover and renew the offensive. Even his further defeat on that river would be of no substantial value, for the cost would be more lives and, as before, he would be able to escape behind it. Like McClellan in 1862, he must be induced by maneuver to move northward to some theatre of war nearer to Washington and further from Richmond. Bearing in mind the demoralized state of the Federals after their defeats at Fredericksburg and Chancellorsville, Lee is prepared, as the first step in a fresh campaign, to take the risk of moving his army westward up the Rappahannock. It is probable that Hooker will conform to the Confederate movement, with the result that his own offensive—if he is projecting one—will be forestalled.

Back, then, for a start—though warily and corps by corps—to Culpeper County. But then whither? Not again to northern Virginia, not to the plains of Manassas. Northern Virginia is stripped and bare; and besides, the enemy, if again defeated there, will—as Pope did—simply retire behind the prepared defenses near Washington. Yet there is a still stronger reason— the most compelling of all—for choosing to march elsewhere. The army is almost starving; and their own commissariat cannot feed them. To remain in existence at all, they must go where they can commandeer food and horse fodder. If the Potomac, then, is to be crossed a second time, it must be towards the plains of Pennsylvania, with the objects of maintaining the troops, drawing the enemy northwestward and thwarting his plans for the summer. And there, on those plains, perhaps, will recur the opportunity to win a great victory,

to march to the Susquehanna and, by bringing home
to the North the power and valor of the Army of
Northern Virginia, to effect the peace that will confer
independence upon the South.

The 2nd Corps, under the newly promoted Lieu-
tenant General Ewell, is the first to move northward,
followed by Longstreet and then by A. P. Hill. Such
opposition as the Federals offer en route is successfully
overcome. Ewell crosses the Potomac and presses on
into Pennsylvania. On June 25th, General Lee, riding
with Longstreet's corps, himself fords the river at Wil-
liamsport.

'Twarn't very long after our great victory in the
woods, Tom, as I was telling you 'bout, that Marse
Robert went back to our old headquarters downriver
of the little town. We stayed on there more'n half a
month. Lucy and me had the same old shed—the one
the snow had blowed into so bad the night Sorrel was
brought in late—but they'd patched it up and repaired
it, and anyways now summer had come we often
didn't spend nights in it. We was picketed in the open.
A horse always prefers to be in the open, you know,
even in the rain. If I'm out to grass and it starts blowing or raining, I'd always rather get behind a wall or a
good thick hedge than go into a shed. Leaves you free
to run if'n you have to, don't it? Marse Robert's always knowed this, of course, but it's surprising how
many men don't. They shut us up all the time and
then wonder why we get nervy. I don't really care for
a shed, 'ceptin' to get away from the flies in hot
weather. I've knowed horses their men thought was
bad-tempered or stupid by nature, but it was really on
'count of all the time they made them spend cooped
up inside. A good horse needs to get out plenty, like
we do here. We spent a lot of time in the open down
by that railroad track.

'Course, the generals kept a-coming to see Marse

Robert all the time. He didn't ride me a great deal during that month. He mostly took Lucy, the way he generally did when there warn't no fighting and he was jest out looking round. I was happy 'nuff to go for exercise with Dave along the hills. There was still lots of Blue men over t'other side of the river, but they evidently warn't aiming on coming acrost. They'd had 'nuff of that.

Little by little I come to realize that Cap-in-His-Eyes must be dead. He never came to the generals' meetings with Marse Robert. At first I reckoned this must be on 'count of the wound Dancer had told me about. He'd need time to get better, I thought. But what really brung it home to me, in the end, was Marse Robert hisself. He was a changed man, and I could feel it surer'n anyone else. Even his way of talking to me sounded different. For a time I thought it was 'cause he was wore out after the battle, but after a while I knowed it was more'n that. I remember one afternoon—he'd taken me out hisself for a ride round the gun positions—when he'd got off to fix my girth. There was no one around, and suddenly he gave a kind of sob and laid his head agin my neck. "Oh, Traveller," he said, "what's to become of us? I've lost my right arm!" All I knowed at the time was that something had made him wretched. I didn't know jest what—there was 'nuff things, after all—and I can't remember jest when I understood that it was Cap-in-His-Eyes he meant he'd lost. But by the time we broke up that headquarters by the railroad and Marse Robert finally said "Strike the tent!" I felt like I'd knowed it ever since the night I'd heared the news from Dancer in the firelight. Our best general was gone for good.

All the time we was marching upcountry—'long beside the mountains—I could feel Marse Robert was out of spirits, though whenever he was talking to the other generals he pretended he warn't. I remember, the

day before we crossed the big river again, he rode right
up the column from rear to front, stopping off whenever we came to anyone he wanted to speak with. We
rode beside General Ringlets for a while, and he was
full of high spirits and fight. He was always one for
show, was Ringlets. There was a man with him, an
officer he called "Eppa," and Marse Robert and this
here Eppa was riding 'long and talking together for a
goodish while. His horse, Sovereign, seemed in a sort
of a gloomy mood, and after a while I asked him
whether he was finding the flies troublesome or what.

"Flies are bad 'nuff," answers Sovereign, "but I
can tell my man figures we're in for a whole heap of
trouble. He's got a notion we may get beat, and if we
do, we'll have a job to get back all this way."

"Beat by the Blue men?" I said. "Us? When was
we ever? Anyways, wherever we're going there'll be
plenty of grass, for a change. Look at them poor old
mules over there—see their ribs sticking out? They
need to eat. I wouldn't wonder if'n we didn't finish
the Blue men for fare-you-well this time. Then maybe
you'll have a real rest and let yourself feel more cheerful."

"Well, Traveller," he says, "I s'pose you ought to
know. You must 'a seed a deal more'n I have."

The truth was, I felt I probably didn't know all
that much more'n he did. He looked a real old veteran,
but I reckoned 'twas my job to act cheerful, jest like
Marse Robert was doing. By the time we parted, I'd
got him into better spirits—better'n my own, really,
'cause I knowed Marse Robert jest couldn't help
thinking all the time how much better off we'd be if'n
only we had Cap-in-His-Eyes 'long with us.

The summer before when we'd crossed the big
river, 'twas by moonlight, and I hadn't really seed the
size of it. This time it was a wet morning—jest pouring
down rain and all the men and horses soaked through

before they got to wading at all. You could see the
whole length of the column splashing ahead, stretching out quite a ways even before it started going up
the bank on the far side. I remember watching one old
fella with a wagon and a pair of mules climbing down
to fix the drag on his wheel and then taking a-holt of
the bridles and backing down the slope into the water
as he led the mules in. There was a band a-playing on
the bank, and all the surface of the river, 'far's you
could see either way, was kind of speckled and glint-
ing under the rain. There was a little town on the further bank, all the roofs glistening, and the folks all out
of doors, never mind the rain, to watch us as we came
acrost.

Marse Robert and me, we crossed the river with
Old Pete and General Ringlets, us three horses splashing acrost side by side. Ringlets was riding a young
horse, a black gelding called Romeo. He hadn't been
long with the general and had almost no experience,
but he'd struck me as a good-natured sort of beast,
anxious to please his master and show he had as much
spunk as any horse in the Army. As we come up the
further bank, he jibbed and backed off for jest a moment before getting hisself pulled together. What had
startled him was a little crowd of ladies, all standing
together in the rain under a flock of umbrellas.
'Course, anything strange or unusual'll startle a young
horse, and I could guess that Romeo had never seed no
umbrellas till then—'specially bright green and blue
ones like these. Ringlets held him in as one of the
ladies stepped up and asked Marse Robert if'n he was
General Lee.

Marse Robert said he was. Then she went into a
whole long speech, introducing each o' the other ladies
and telling him they was all mighty glad to see him
and his Army come acrost the river. She said we was
saviors of freedom and a whole lot more that I

couldn't understand. Marse Robert listened to all this real polite, while the rain jest ran off'n us in streams and Romeo fidgeted from side to side. And then, if you please, when at last she'd done talking, this lady up with a big wreath of flowers, which she figured she was going to hang round *my* neck! A lot of horses would have shied, I reckon, when she suddenly lifted up this big, colored thing—for a moment I didn't know what 'twas—right in front of my nose, but I jest stood steady—well, maybe I tossed my head; I couldn't say—and waited. Marse Robert tells her he reckons she's mighty kind, but he don't think the flowers would look quite right, seeing as how we was soldiers on campaign.

Then these ladies started pressing Marse Robert that he really ought to accept the flowers; they was all on our side, they said. But Marse Robert, he stuck to it that there was jest no way a commanding general's horse could go around with a great wreath of flowers round his neck. I was glad, 'cause I felt the same. A fine fool I'd look, coming into the headquarters picket lines all covered over with red and blue flowers! I'd never hear the last o' that! In the end Marse Robert won. He accepted the flowers and said how much he 'preciated the ladies' kindness and all the trouble they'd took, and then he gave them to one of our soldiers to carry.

Jest the same, the ladies' welcome seemed to have lifted Marse Robert's spirits and cheered his mood. Headquarters had jest been set up, in a hickory grove a mile or so outside the town, when we had another visit—this time from a little boy I remembered to have come into camp and spoken to Marse Robert the summer before. Marse Robert made quite a fuss over this young man and had him sit down to eat with Major Taylor and General Red Shirt and hisself. Then Old Pete jined in, and said how would the boy like to be-

come a soldier and ride 'long with him and his fellas?
When me and Hero and the rest was led up for the
generals, Red Shirt told one of the soldiers to bring a
horse for the boy. I forget which of us 'twas, but anyways the boy was jest a little fella and he couldn't
mount him up. Marse Robert lifted him into the saddle and said by and by he'd be ready for the cavalry.
They was all full of jokes when we rode off to inspect
the camps.

Next morning, when we struck the tent and set
out on the march, it was still raining. We only had a
few miles to go to the next town. I remembered it from
the summer before, when Marse Robert had been riding round with his hands all bandaged up and a soldier
to lead me. That had been a real bad time for me, Tom,
as I've told you, and I didn't much relish seeing that
town again. But everyone was friendly and 'peared
glad to see us, and a lot o' people was cheering Marse
Robert and me as we rode through town.

Next thing was, another bunch of ladies come up
and regular surrounded us. One of them had a pair of
scissors, and it turned out that what she wanted was a
lock of Marse Robert's hair. Marse Robert, he says no,
he needed all the hair he'd got left, and why didn't she
have some of Ringlets', seeing as how he'd got more to
spare. But she didn't care for that notion. In the end
we-all jest told them good-day and rode on.

We went maybe twenty mile that afternoon, and
when we got to the next town Red Shirt come to meet
us; he must 'a gone ahead, I reckon, that same morning. "Ah, General Hill," says Marse Robert, riding up
to him, "I'm mighty glad to see you again, and your
fellas all in sech fine order." Marse Robert never
missed a chance of praising and encouraging. There
was another big hullabaloo, with folks gathering in
the square, but soon's he could Marse Robert took us
out of town and 'stablished headquarters near some

woods, 'longside a little stream. I remember what a
nice, quiet evening's grazing that was, with the sun
coming out after the rain and everything fresh and
green. Smelt real good. Me and Joker stood head to
tail, swished the flies and loafed around. Everything
'bout headquarters was jest like it always was on campaign: the tents, the baggage wagons and ambulances,
the old mules stamping round under the trees, couple
of red-and-blue cloths on sticks to show where we
was; messengers a-coming and a-going, Bryan and
Meredith getting everything ready for Marse Robert's
supper and Perry a-setting on a log and whistling
while he cleaned his boots. It was mighty peaceful. I
was expecting Skylark and Jine-the-Cavalry to ride up
any minute, or maybe Vot-you-voz. I hadn't seed
nothing of Jine-the-Cavalry for several days now, and
it seemed kind of queer, 'cause I'd come to understand,
from talking to Skylark, that Marse Robert relied on
him to tell him where the Blue men was and what
they was up to.

Still, if'n I didn't see Skylark or Star of the East or
any of their cavalry friends, I certainly seed some unusual horses come into the Army during them few
days. Looking back now, Tom, I can see we was getting jest about desperate for horses. We'd lost a lot in
the fighting, and others had wasted away to nothing
during the winter, and I guess there warn't 'nuff left
back home to replace them. Anyway, wherever we
went on this campaign, we took up horses—any
horses a-tall, whatever we could get. It was that evening or the next, while I was grazing and thinking
'bout nothing in particular, that I suddenly seed a little
group of our soldiers—artillerymen—coming down
the nearby track with three of the biggest horses I'd
ever seed in all my born days. They was huge. They
warn't jest cart horses, they was cart horses and then
some. I jest stood and stared at 'em. I'd never seed

nothing like 'em before, and I'm sure they'd never seed nor heared nor smelt nothing like our camp. They was acting real nervous, and 'cause they was so big the men was having some trouble with them. As I watched, one of them shied at the sun flashing on a tin bucket or some sech, and fairly dragged the two fellas who was leading him acrost the track and back.

"The three of 'em together's too much," says one of these soldiers. "Let's hitch this one here and come back for him when we've got t'other two to battery headquarters."

So then they hitched this huge great mountain of a horse to a rail not far from where I was, and went 'long with the others. The horse looked quiet 'nuff now, only fretting and upset, like he didn't know what was going to happen next. I felt sorry for him, so I gave him a neigh from where I was, and then I strolled acrost and gave him a nice, friendly nicker. He answered nervously, like he didn't know whether I was a friend or not.

"Jest come in?" I asked, sniffing him over. He smelt of hay and oats, mighty well fed. "Cheer up. It's not so bad once't you get used to it."

"Oh, dey joost take me avay," he said. "Dey take me avay! Master's angry, missus she's crying, very bad. Hardly finished de hay—"

"You come from a farm?" I asked.

"Yes, yes, alvays on de farm," he said. "Never been off de farm. Dose soldiers take me—master's very angry, says he'll be ruint."

Well, you know, Tom, I could see what he meant. I mean, if'n some fellas was to come in here now, and say they was requisitioning cats and took you away with 'em to some strange, noisy place, like nothing you'd ever seed or smelt, I reckon you'd be tolerable scairt, too. I tried to think how I could cheer him up.

"You pull heavy loads on the farm?" I asked.

"Oh, yes, yes," he answered. "All us Percherons pull, ve pull vagons, ve pull plows, ve pull big carts—pull any t'ing."

"Well, all you'll have to pull here'll be a gun," I said.

"Vot's a gun?" he asks, rolling his eyes white.

Jest then I seed the men a-coming back for him.

"Oh, it'll be nothing for the likes of you," I says. "A great big fella like you. You'd pull a hundred guns—you'll find it easy after the farm."

I didn't believe it, mind you. I was jest trying to cheer him up. In spite of his size, I couldn't help thinking he looked clumsy and flabby. If he'd never been off the farm where he was born, it was going to take him a long while to get used to the artillery—and the artillery horses, too. They was real mean, most of 'em. The life was 'nuff to make any horse mean—the noise and the danger and all the limbering and unlimbering in the smoke and dust. He'd soon thin down on that.

Come to think of it now, after all this time I don't know whether we ever really got much out of all the horses we took up in them parts. They was nearly all great clumsy Percherons, or else some as called theirselves Conestogas. They needed a big feed—more'n twice what our horses could live on—and yet they couldn't do half the work. And as for standing up to the hardship and exposure of campaigning—well, there jest warn't no comparison to us. They warn't made for it. Later on, when things got real bad, it was a shame to see how they suffered. I mean, can you imagine—well, of course, Tom, you've never seed a Percheron, but I was going to say can you imagine one of them Percherons being driven to dash off at full gallop with a gun? And what their daily ration with us was, was mostly dry broom sedge and maybe a quarter of a feed of weevily corn.

Still, we warn't forever taking horses and supplies

from the country folk. Marse Robert was always very
particular 'bout treating people right. "You jest remember, all of you," he said one day to a bunch of
soldiers he was talking to in camp, "you jest remember
that we only make war on armed men. The biggest
disgrace you can bring on the Army is harming anything that belongs to ordinary folk." And it was that
same day that he got down off my back, right there on
the road opposite a pasture, and put up some rails
with his own hands. One of our fellas had left 'em
down and the cattle could have strayed. He didn't
have no chance, though, when it come to pinching
hats. It was desperate hot jest then, Tom, you see, and
a lot of our fellas had no hats. So whenever we was
marching through crowds, usually one or two of 'em'd
snatch a man's hat off'n his head and run back into the
ranks faster'n a dog on a scent. 'Twarn't no use the
man complaining to an officer. No one could tell which
soldier had done it, and we warn't a-going to halt the
march nohow jest for that.

There was still no sign of Jine-the-Cavalry or any
of his 'uns, and after a day or so I realized that this
was worrying Marse Robert. "Where can General Stuart be?" I heared him say more'n once to Major Taylor.
I remembered how Skylark had told me that most of
their work was riding around behind the Blue men
and finding out what they was up to, and I couldn't
help wondering whether maybe they'd run into the
Blue men and got into a passel of trouble, or maybe
lost their way back. One thing was for sure, and that
was that Marse Robert was feeling the lack of them.
"What can we do without cavalry?" he said to Colonel
Long as we was riding out of camp one morning. "I've
never known this to happen before. It's like being
blind." Jest the same, I couldn't remember when I'd
seed our Army in better spirits; and better off, horse

an' man, than the time when we'd crossed the river the year before.

Headquarters only stayed three or four days at that place 'side the woods, though. I was hoping we'd be there longer, but when you're a soldier there's never no telling. It was a dark, stormy morning when we struck the tent and moved off, and Marse Robert seemed as gloomy as the sky. He kept asking different people 'bout General Stuart, but whatever he was told it certainly warn't nothing he wanted to hear. We finished up next afternoon at an old sawmill. All the sawmill folks seemed to have gone, so headquarters jest took it over for the night.

In the morning the weather was better, with a nice breeze. "You mark what I say, Traveller," said Joker as we was being saddled up. "We're going to hit on some Blue men before tonight."

"How can you tell?" I asked.

"Oh, jest a hunch," said Joker. "Wherever they are, they're not far off. Don't tell me we've come all this way not to find 'em."

Soon's he was in the saddle, Marse Robert called up Old Pete to ride with him. As we set off, I told Hero what Joker had said. Hero 'peared to be of the same mind. "The horses always know before the men," he said. "The enemy's near'bouts, sure 'nuff. Other side of these here mountains we're heading for, I reckon."

By the time we'd got to the mountains, the road had growed so thick and crowded with our soldiers on the march that Marse Robert and Old Pete took me and Hero on ahead, with the rest of headquarters following. We was well on the way up, and nicely out of all the dust and tromping, when suddenly Hero pricked up his ears.

"Didn't I say so?"

There was no mistaking what we could hear off a

ways. It was distant gunfire, coming from the direction in which we was headed. I could tell Marse Robert was wondering what it might mean. You see, Tom, when you're on campaign and you hear guns off out of sight, it may mean nothing much or it may be the start of a battle—there's no telling without you get news back by a horseman. But no horseman came, and Marse Robert was growing more and more impatient and uneasy.

"We're in the dark!" he said to Old Pete. "We're in the dark and that's the truth of it. We've been in the dark ever since we crossed the river."

We reached the top and looked down on t'other side, which was all steep ravines and gorges. The firing was louder now, and there was more of it, but still you couldn't rightly see what was happening.

"I'm going on ahead!" says Marse Robert to Old Pete, and with that he put me into a gallop and down the hill we went, leaving Old Pete to wait for his own soldiers to come up.

Pretty soon we came to a little town, and this was where we met up with Red Shirt. Red Shirt was a while talking with Marse Robert, but when I asked Champ, his horse, he told me they didn't know what the firing meant any more'n what we did. It was kind of rolling, hilly country we was in, and the sound of the guns came echoing from the other side of the hills. Red Shirt rode off to try to find out more, and when he was gone Marse Robert walked me forward a little ways, leaving the rest of headquarters a-waiting where they was. I could tell jest from the feel of his hands and the way he was sitting that he was worried.

"Oh, Traveller," he says, stroking my neck, but more like he was talking to hisself, really. "Oh, Traveller, what *can* have become of Stuart? We ought to have heared from him long before now."

Another general rode up to us—one of Red Shirt's

commanders—but I could tell he didn't know what was going on neither.

"If that's their whole Army," Marse Robert says to him, "we'll have to fight a battle *here*. But there's jest no telling."

They didn't talk much more. Marse Robert called up headquarters and we galloped on towards the sound of the firing. We could hear musketry now, as well as the guns, and I could see a long cloud of smoke on the horizon.

I don't exactly recollect, Tom, how long we kept going—several miles, that's for sure—but finally we left the hills behind and came out into more open country. And here we found whole crowds of our fellas, all spread out and waiting. I could see now that there was fighting going on up ahead, in the distance.

It was a hot afternoon. We waited there, Marse Robert and me, while he set about finding out what was going on. I could smell the crushed thyme in the grass, which was all tromped down, and there was any number of grasshoppers zipping away. It's funny, ain't it, how nothing disturbs them fellas? I remember dropping my nose for a bit of a browse round—Marse Robert never minded that—and I seed one sitting and rubbing his back legs together where I could almost have munched him up. He flew away—well, they good as fly, don't they?—when some officer planted one of our red-and-blue cloths on sticks right there, to show where Marse Robert had taken up his position.

It was plain that pretty soon the word began to get round that me and Marse Robert had arrived at this here battle. You see, Tom, when Marse Robert was running a battle, there was always horsemen coming and going to tell him what was happening and take his orders. I'd come to know a lot of the courier horses by now and mostly they came from Jine-the-Cavalry. Not this afternoon, though. These was Red Shirt's officers. Jine-the-Cavalry's outfit 'peared to have vanished off the face of the earth.

To begin with, 'far as I could make out, the Blue men was hard at it getting back out of our way; anyhow, their guns warn't firing like they'd been when Marse Robert and me first heared them up the mountain. But then they suddenly started up again, way over beyond the outskirts of the town, and a few minutes later one of Red Shirt's commanders come galloping up to Marse Robert. I knowed his horse, a chestnut called Trumpeter, so I asked him what was a-going on.

"We've got them beat all to a frazzle," says Trumpeter. "They've all run away into the town back there, but we're fixing to take that, too."

"Then what are their guns firing for," I asked, "over there on the sunset side?"

"It's the Bald General's fellas coming up," says Trumpeter. "They'll roll the Blue men up, after the licking they've jest had from us."

I could tell that Marse Robert had told Trumpeter's man to go back and order his 'uns to attack. Oh, Tom, you should 'a heared that Yell as they went forward! Marse Robert and me, we went forward jest behind them, and in less than an hour 'twas all over. We'd driven those people right out of the town and cut them up real bad. I remember how Marse Robert rode me downhill, over the creek at the bottom and up onto the ridge t'other side. We could see the town plain now, about half a mile below us, with two hills beyond it. The Blue men was all a-running off towards the hills—masses of 'em. Anyone could see they was licked, but there was still a few more up atop them hills.

Jest as I was wondering what we'd be doing next, up comes Old Pete on Hero. Old Pete took a long look at the town and the Blue men near the hills, and then he began talking almost afore Marse Robert had said a word. 'Course, I couldn't understand what he was saying to Marse Robert, but what I did know, Tom—and no horse could have mistaken this—was that he was laying down the law and more or less telling Marse Robert jest what he ought to do. He was saying what orders Marse Robert had best be giving and where our fellas had to go.

Marse Robert listened quietly—well, you know, Tom; you know yourself Marse Robert seldom lets anything upset him—and after a little he jest said something like if'n the Blue men was there, then we must attack them. But this didn't seem to suit Old Pete. He broke in and said a whole lot more, and I knowed Marse Robert was beginning to feel angry. I couldn't help wondering whether he'd tell Old Pete straight out that it warn't him that was commanding the Army. I reckon he might have, too, only jest then Colonel Long came up to report, and after him another officer I didn't know, whose horse told me they'd come from General Ewell—the Bald General—who'd got his 'uns already into the town.

Old Pete seemed to me to have turned real sulky. 'Far as I recollect, he hardly answered the next time Marse Robert spoke to him, and soon after that (it was getting on to evening now), he rode off—to get back to his men, he said, who was coming up by the same road we'd come by.

There was no more firing now from anywhere ahead, and Marse Robert and me set off down the hill for the town, 'long with Major Taylor and a few more. I remember how we went by a passel o' prisoners standing round the outskirts. Some of them recognized Marse Robert and pointed him out as we went by.

We pulled up at a house jest outside town. There was a little rose garden there, all in bloom, and a power of horses hitched to the rails. I could see the Bald General limping down the path to meet Marse

Robert as he dismounted—the Bald General had a wooden leg, Tom, you know; he'd lost a leg in the fighting—and some of his commanders 'long with him. The Cussing General—General Early—was one of them. I always thought of him that way, 'cause I don't believe he ever spoke without a-cussing, even when he was talking to Marse Robert.

All I can tell you, Tom, after all this time, is that I knowed at once't that the Bald General was feeling powerful jittery. You could tell that jest by looking at him. Whenever I smell evening roses now, it makes me recollect being hitched to that fence and seeing the Bald General and Marse Robert and the Cussing General and the rest walking off into a little kinda wooden house set among the roses and talking as they went.

The Bald General's horse was hitched right 'longside me. "What's the matter with your master?" I asked. "I thought your outfit had took the town and whupped the enemy?"

"They have," he answered, "but now, 'parently, my man don't know what to do next. They've all been trying to tell him, but he can't make up his mind. He's like that, you know. He's a good master to me and all his fellas like him, but it's always the same—he can't decide for hisself."

Well, the sun moved around and down into the west, the flies got less troublesome and the air began to cool, and still we-all stood there, blowing and stamping, while the generals talked in the rose garden. There was a fine red sunset and if'n you didn't know otherwise you'd have thought it was jest as nice and peaceful an evening as could be.

I kept looking at those two hills sticking up on the far side of the town. Hoof and tail!, I thought. What is there to be a-talking 'bout all this time? Even I can tell we ought to get on and take those hills afore the Blue men can dig in on 'em. I remembered how much care

Marse Robert had taken before the battle in the snow,
when him and me was riding round and fixing our
guns where they'd be able to shoot whichever way the
Blue men came at us. That's what we call a good field
of fire, Tom, you know. If'n only we could get some
guns up on those hills now, I thought, the Blue men'd
be running away like they did two months ago in the
forest. I wish Sorrel was here. I wish Cap-in-His-Eyes
would come a-riding round the corner now, and hitch
Sorrel up and give me a pat and a word. I wanted my
feed and I could have drunk a bucket and more. Only,
we didn't get none, 'cause no one knowed how soon
our generals would be done and wanting us.

Well, at last Marse Robert and the Bald General
came out of the rose garden, still talking together. All I
could tell from looking at them was that Marse Robert
was pressing the Bald General to do something and
the Bald General didn't like it. Marse Robert kept
turning his head and stressing what he was saying
with his hands, and the Bald General kept on jest
a-listening and nodding, saying very little and looking
down at the ground. He warn't like Old Pete; he
warn't argufying back. He put me more in mind of a
horse that's gotten afeared of something in the road—
you know, a pile of sacks, maybe, or a milk churn—
and jest don't want to go on past it.

A minute or two later we was riding away, back
to the ridge where we'd talked to Old Pete. Headquarters had been fixed up in a little house jest below the
ridge and overlooking the town. I remember the stable
had plenty of rats—Joker said he figured you could
walk on 'em—but I was too tired to take much notice.
Soon as he'd fed and watered us, Dave lay down to
sleep in the hay, jest like that. I'd come to know what
that meant. Orders must 'a been given for a mighty
early start next morning.

XV

WELL, IT turned out an early start, all right—
one of the shortest nights I can remember.
The whole of headquarters was up and astir
in the dark, a good while before first light. I'd been
half-hoping Marse Robert might be riding Lucy—after
all, the day before had been hard 'nuff for me—but
'twarn't to be. I knowed then he must be expecting to
come under fire. Lucy's a good horse and I've always
got on well with her, but she never really got used to
the bangs, you know—not surprising, 'cause she
hadn't been given to Marse Robert for that in the first
place. She'd been given him to ride when he couldn't
use his hands, all on 'count of me a throwing him
down that day. Anyway, I found myself saddled up
again and I recall the sun was jest rising when me and
Marse Robert came back up that ridge.

Marse Robert turned me around, and then he sat
still a long time, looking out acrost the plain below. I
never liked that open country, Tom, you know; I
mean, all that country up beyond the big river we'd
crossed over. 'Twarn't proper country, like where we'd
come from—not like the river country where we'd so
often beat the Blue men afore now. There was fewer
trees, and too much of it was open and flat. What's
more, the grass was different and there was too much
sky. That morning the sky was clear from one horizon

to t'other—clear blue, but sort of purple along the rim. I could tell 'twas going to be a real scorching day. I s'posed the battle was to be fought down on the plain; but if 'twas, there warn't ary a Blue man to be seed yet.

I could soon tell there was something bothering Marse Robert. His seat warn't easy and natural, his hands was taut on the reins and he kept looking round like he was waiting for someone who hadn't come. Our headquarters majors was with us, and after a while he sent Major Venable off towards the town—to talk to the Bald General, I reckoned.

Then up come Old Pete, and right off I could tell, without asking Hero, that he was in a real bad mood. As the two of 'em came up, Hero must 'a done something he didn't like, 'cause he spoke sharp to him and jerked on his bit. That turned Hero sulky and he didn't even answer back my nicker, so I jest held still and waited to see what would happen next.

Old Pete started straight in talking to Marse Robert in a voice which would certainly have upset me if'n he'd been talking to me from the saddle. But Marse Robert, he jest listened, polite and undisturbed as usual. Once't or twice't I felt him shake his head, and 'nother time I felt his hand close into a fist on the reins. I began to feel angry myself. All I could tell was there was something Marse Robert felt we ought to be doing—something important—and Old Pete didn't want to do it.

After a while, Marse Robert dismounted. Dave came up and took my bridle, and Marse Robert left Old Pete and began walking up and down in the trees. By this time more of our generals had arrived. Red Shirt was there—'twas his fellas that we'd come up on in the fight the day before, of course, when we'd ridden towards the sound of the guns. Then the young Texas general rode up, and he went straight over to

talk to Marse Robert. I remember Marse Robert pointing out over the plain and I heared him say something
'bout we must beat those people or else they'd beat us.
But after that Old Pete spoke to the Texas general
where Marse Robert couldn't hear, and 'far as I could
understand he was saying he didn't want to attack—or
not yet anyways.

After a bit the Fat General with the big black
beard come up, and Marse Robert talked to him, too. I
could see he was telling him what he wanted done,
but then all of a sudden Old Pete broke in on what the
Fat General was answering, and said, "No, sir. No, sir,
I don't want that—" or something of the kind. Marse
Robert jest said real quiet, "No, General. I want it jest
there, please," and pointed.

If ever I seed a man all riled up, 'twas Old Pete
jest then. I don't think the Fat General knowed what
to make of it at all. After a bit more talk he jest saluted
and went off—to get his fellas ready for the battle, I
s'pose.

There was a real bad feel to things, and the way it
'peared to me, the day had started all wrong. Soon
after that we rode away, Marse Robert and me, back
to the town. I'd never knowed no time before when
Marse Robert had 'peared so strung-up. That battle in
the snow, when we'd stood all day by the guns on the
hill, he'd felt to me like a big rock in a field, with the
Blue men breaking theirselves to pieces on it over an'
over. Even when the gun blowed up right next to us,
he hadn't moved a muscle. Now he seemed edgy—not
hisself at all—riding here and there, not stopping anywhere for long, fidgeting in the saddle and asking
questions of 'most everyone we met. I decided Old
Pete must have upset him bad.

When we reached town, the Bald General warn't
anywheres around, but we found one of his commanders, who took us to a house with a sort of a little

tower atop it, and Marse Robert went up there to have
him a look-see. Well, I didn't need to go up no tower
to see that now those two hills out beyond the town
was jest stiff with Blue men. Sure 'nuff, we hadn't
managed to put ary guns or fellas up there. By the
time Marse Robert came down, the Bald General had
rode up. They got to talking and I seed Marse Robert
pointing up at the hills. He said something 'bout the
enemy being in a good position, and I figured he was
real disappointed the Bald General hadn't done more
since last night.

We started back with Colonel Long, but Marse
Robert said very little on the way. He seemed to be
listening all the time—listening for something that
didn't come. I know now what it must 'a been; he was
hoping to hear Old Pete's guns starting the battle. He
felt we shouldn't be waiting about. I remember we
rode close to a gun position, and Marse Robert spoke
sharp to their officer for not limbering up his guns and
getting 'em forward. The officer told Marse Robert
he'd made a mistake; he warn't one o' them as was
meant to go—he belonged to Red Shirt. Marse Robert
said he was sorry, civil as you please, and then he
asked, "Do you know where Longstreet is?" I've never
knowed him sound so impatient, not before or since.
Soon after that, he even started leading one bunch of
our fellas forward hisself.

Well, in the end we did find Old Pete, but he still
hadn't started his attack. While him and Marse Robert
was dismounted and talking, I told Hero straight out
that I reckoned it warn't right to disregard Marse Robert's orders thataway. All he said was "Oh, go to the
slaughterhouse, Traveller. What do you know about
it?"

"What do any of us know about it?" I said. "I
know who's s'posed to be commanding this here
Army."

"We'll attack when we're good and ready," snaps Hero, and after that he wouldn't say no more at all.

Well, I'd jest as soon not tell you, Tom, 'bout the rest of that day. What it come to was that what was meant to happen didn't. Marse Robert and me kept a-riding up and down our lines. The fellas was all laying up in the trees and brush along the ridge, and the sun got hotter and hotter till every horse and man was jest 'bout half-crazy with thirst. We left Old Pete for a while, but later we jined up with him again while he was leading some of his fellas down the slope and forward towards t'other ridge—the one the Blue men had got theirselves settled atop of. The soldiers was jest a-pouring with sweat and all those boots was kicking up a power of dust, real thick. 'Twas as much as a horse could do to catch a breath of air, and this was 'bout four hours after the middle of the day, too.

This time Marse Robert and me didn't go forward with the attack. He turned me back up the ridge and we went off to find Red Shirt. He dismounted, I remember, and for a while he was talking to Red Shirt and Colonel Long and some more; but most of the time he spent jest a-sitting there on an old tree stump, a-listening to our guns firing down below. And do you know, Tom—you're not going to believe this—from somewhere way off by the town, I could hear one of our bands playing—playing away real lively? True.

I never did jest rightly understand the rest of that day myself. There was fighting sure 'nuff, but 'twas all too far off for me and t'other horses up on the ridge to take in anything much, 'cepting for the battle smoke and the guns and the yelling. Still, one thing was for sure. Marse Robert and me, we never went forward, like we had in the swamps the year before, or like the day after Cap-in-His-Eyes marched away into the forest. So I guessed that our fellas out there couldn't be driving the Blue men like we generally did. 'Nother thing that seemed out of ordinary was there was so few horsemen coming and going where we was at. Marse Robert only sent one horseman out all that afternoon, and 'far as I can remember only one came to headquarters.

What I think now, after all this time, is that our fellas could surely have beat the Blue men good and proper, but the trouble was we didn't all attack together. I remember Joker saying something like that the same evening. "They're not doing what Marse Robert meant 'em to do," he says to me. "It's all got out of joint—different lots coming different times, and all the Blue men got to do is sit up there and hold their ground."

By the late evening Marse Robert was in one of his silent, pondering moods. "What's the trouble?" I asked Leopard—that was Major Venable's horse. "We're not beat, that's for sure." "No," said Leopard, "but Marse Robert was hoping to beat *them*, and the trouble is they're still sitting up there where they was this morning."

'Twas dark now, and sultry and airless, too; the night seemed real close and oppressive. There was still some muskets firing, but no more guns. After a while the moon came up, out beyond the enemy's ridge, and the whippoorwills began calling among the trees, setting out for hunting. Marse Robert—yes, Tom, he did —he found the time to come and talk to me and Dave while I was being rubbed down and fed and watered. He was fondling me around the neck and stroking my nose, like he often did; and then, jest as Dave had gone off to fill a bucket (or half-fill it, 'cause there warn't all that much water to go round), "Oh, Traveller," he says, so quiet that only I could hear him. "Oh, Traveller, we can still beat them. We've won a lot of ground, and the men are in good heart. We *can* beat them, Traveller! Tomorrow we'll beat them!" Then

Dave come back and Marse Robert began talking to him 'bout what he thought might be a little strain in one of my fetlocks. He'd be needing me next day, he said. Dave told him he figured I'd be fine.

I couldn't honestly have told anyone I was feeling fine when Dave saddled me up again after a few hours' rest that felt like half a feed of thin hay. T'other headquarters horses looked as rough as I did. I remember one of them, a mare called Ivy, actually stumbling over the stable threshold and falling on her knees. Dave led me on over to where Marse Robert was waiting. He looked tired, too. I was beginning to wonder how much longer anyone, horse or man, could go on like this. And yet if I'd only knowed, we'd hardly started.

'Twarn't a still morning, like the day before. There was a bit of wind and a light haze, with blowing clouds dimming the stars. I could smell 'nother hot day coming, though. There was plenty of gunfire already, 'way off in the direction of the town. Soon's he'd mounted me, Marse Robert rode off t'other way, 'long the ridge, to see Old Pete.

Old Pete was jest as full of talk and argument as he'd been the day before, but though Marse Robert listened as patient as ever, all he had to say, near as I could understand, was that our fellas was going to attack the way he wanted.

They rode up and down together for quite a while, looking out acrost to where the Blue men was— too far for me to make out anything much at all. Old Pete seemed sort of aloof and glum, but Marse Robert, he kept stopping every now and then to talk to little groups of soldiers, or to ask some officer a question or look at a gun position. Once't he told a young gunnery officer to get hisself back from out in front, where the Blue men might hit him. I couldn't help wondering

whether he was remembering the Little General and
poor Chieftain that day last fall.

Three times that morning we rode the whole
length of our lines along the ridge. The sun had gotten
high before we was done; there warn't a cloud in the
sky and it seemed hotter'n ever. 'Course, up there
there warn't a creek in sight, nor any water at all that I
could smell.

All the time, our guns was being pulled forward
ahead of the infantry. I remember seeing two of them
huge white Percherons that we'd commandeered,
a-hauling and a-straining on a gun to heave it out of a
dry rut. A hundred yards or so further on, a limber
driver with the sun in his eyes cussed at Marse Robert
and told him to get out the way 'fore he ran him
down. We jest rode on and Marse Robert kind of
hunched hisself over so the man wouldn't see who he
was. All the guns that hadn't already come down the
day before was dragged down off the ridge and sited
'longside a road running 'tween our fellas and the Blue
men. Marse Robert and me rode all along them. You
jest can't imagine, Tom, how many there was. My
withers! I thought; if'n that outfit's going to start firing
together, I jest hope I'll be able to stand steady.

The gunners all seemed easy and full o' jokes, but
that was more'n could be said for most of their horses,
waiting behind the caissons. A lot of 'em looked
starved—ribs stickin' out, coats all rough and staring.
"It's all right for *you*," says one of them to me. "You
don't even know what a counter-barrage is, do you?
How many of us do you think'll be left by tonight?" I
didn't answer him. I never used to answer mules or
artillery horses. What could I have said, anyway?

'Twas the real burning middle of the day when
Marse Robert and me and the rest of headquarters
stood waiting on the forward edge of the ridge for the
guns to commence to firing. Red Shirt and Old Pete

was sitting together with Marse Robert on a log for a while, but then they got up and went different ways. Marse Robert and me, we rode a little ways down the slope. Behind us, a lot of our fellas was laying down under the trees, waiting. You could smell them in the heat, and I could smell they was afeared, too. I remember seeing two-three fellas making their way back of the bushes to drop their pants.

'Twas still for quite a while. Then, from down along the road, come a single gun, and then another. That must 'a been a signal, 'cause a few moments later there followed a noise 'nuff to make you wonder whether the earth was going to smash to bits. The ground was all a-shaking, and I seed several horses bolt and whole groups a-rarin' and having to be held in hard. Men laying side by side couldn't even shout to each other. I've heared guns in my time, Tom, but never a barrage like that. They was all a-firing at once't —what's called salvos, you know. And 'twarn't more'n a minute or so before the Blue men's guns be gan firing back. You could see the flashes and hear the bangs from t'other ridge. I'd say they must have had guns firing all along for a good two mile, near as I could tell. Very soon the smoke and dust blotted out everything. 'Twas like being shut up in the dark with a cloth over your head. All that reached me from outside was the feel of Marse Robert's hands, and Marse Robert's voice saying, "Easy, Traveller—easy, now, boy!" You seemed to be choking on that gun smell, 'twas so thick in the air. You couldn't see the sun nor hardly the sky—only great streams of black smoke a-floating high up, like clouds. Every now and then a shell'd hit one of the ammunition chests 'longside our guns, and there'd come a huge roar, and fellas screaming so I reckon the Blue men theirselves could have heared them over on t'other ridge. Sometimes the shells landed in among our infantry laying under the trees. More'n once't I seed the stretcher-bearers carrying off some poor lad crying and clutching hisself and bleeding all over the ground.

I don't know how long it went on. After what seemed a long time our guns stopped firing, and a minute or two later the enemy guns died down, too. And that was when I suddenly caught sight of General Ringlets, that I didn't recollect to have seed since that day when him and Romeo crossed the river with me and Marse Robert, and we met the ladies with the flowers.

General Ringlets was still riding Romeo, and I could see that though Romeo was doing all he could to keep steady under the fire, he warn't far off from panicking. Some of it, though, was coming to him from Ringlets hisself. Ringlets was dressed jest as smart as he had been at the river, and he was smiling and saluting other officers here and there as though he hadn't a care in the world. But even from where I was, I could tell he was feeling near as bad as the artillery horses. His breathing alone would be 'nuff to signal that much to any horse that had him on its back, and so far as I knowed, this was Romeo's first battle. I felt sorry for him.

Ringlets pulled him in and held him steady while he looked along the lines of his fellas laying down in back of the guns. Then he drew his sword and shouted to them to form line and go forward. They was Virginians, Tom—fellas from round these here parts where we are now. I remember their commanders riding out in front of the lines to lead them. One of 'em was on a big black horse I'd seed once't or twice't before— 'never knowed his name. Another—a white-haired old chap—stuck his hat on the point of his sword and called up his fellas in a voice that carried like a bugle. The soldiers was shouting "Virginia! Virginia!" And as they come out into the open they formed ranks as neat as if it had been for Marse Robert on a parade ground. Soon's they got clear of the trees, all the regiments formed into a single, great line. You could see the red-and-blue cloths going in front, and the officers marching on foot with their companies. I was thinking I wouldn't like to be the Blue men on t'other end of that lot. But I remember thinking, too, they had an awful long way to go acrost the open ground 'fore they could commence to fighting.

Marse Robert was sat real still and steady, watching as the line went off into the distance. Once't, I remember, he pointed and said something to Major Taylor 'bout how many of the fellas had bandages on their heads or their arms—fellas that had been wounded, but warn't going to let that make no difference. I'd never seed so many cloths on sticks goin' forward together before. Behind the whole line came Ringlets and his staff. Once't or twice't I seed young Romeo jib and falter, and I hoped for his sake he'd come through it all right and do hisself credit. I wouldn't have liked his job.

They went on, Tom; they went on quite steady over that dry, sun-baked ground for two—maybe three hundred yards. And then the Blue men's guns opened up again. I'd thought our guns was s'posed to have blowed theirs to bits, but 'twas plain 'nuff now that they hadn't. 'Twas terrible to hear the shells explode and see the smoke blot out whole parts of the line, and then great gaps where our fellas had been. There was men struggling on the ground, only you couldn't hear 'em screaming, 'cause of the guns. It put me in mind of the battle in the snow, only then it had been the Blue men, not ours, who'd come shoulder to shoulder up the slope into Red Shirt's guns.

Soon what was left of our fellas had got a long ways off—too far for me to be able to see what was going on. I could tell they must 'a met the Blue men by now, 'cause there was musketry crackling, and I could hear the Yell, and see the flashes ''way off acrost the field.

'Twas all smoke and noise and confusion, a long ways off. I never have rightly knowed jest what happened. I was expecting Marse Robert and headquarters to go forward any moment, but we didn't. I seed a riderless horse with a great gash in his shoulder come plunging back out of the smoke, and I seed plenty of wounded men crawling 'long the ground—only, some of them didn't crawl far.

And then at last—after what seemed a terrible long time—Marse Robert and me, we did ride forward. Our men was beginning to come back—some by theirselves and some in little sort of broken-up groups. A lot was wounded. They came limping and staggering through the line of our guns, trying to get to the trees behind, where they'd started from. And 'twas while this was going on that me and Marse Robert went out to meet 'em. Old Pete was with us, and Major Taylor and quite a few more. Marse Robert put me into a walk, and we was going from one bunch to 'nother. Marse Robert was encouraging them and cheering them up. "It'll all come right in the end," he kept saying. "It'll all come right. We want all good and true men jest now." Some of them was so badly hurt or so tuckered out that they jest staggered on past as if they couldn't hear, but there was a chance of others was mighty glad to see him, and any number who stopped to cheer. "It's Marse Robert!" calls out one young fella to his mates, who was carrying a wounded man 'tween 'them. They all came a-crowding round me—I could smell the blood—and one of 'em kept saying, "We ain't whupped, General! We ain't no ways whupped! Those Blue fellas have had 'nuff to keep 'em quiet for a long while, no danger!"

'Twarn't only the soldiers Marse Robert had time

to spare for, neither. I'll tell you something, Tom, that I've never forgotten—never will. In the middle of all our riding 'bout among the men and talking to 'em, there suddenly come some sort of a commotion, 'way off in the distance. Marse Robert tells one of the gunnery officers who happened to be nearby to ride off and find out what 'twas. Well, as it happened, I knowed this officer's horse—I'd been picketed with him more'n once't since the spring. He was a nice, easygoing gray called Misty, and he'd always been close friends with the artillery general's horse, Buckthorn. They'd been paired all the way on the march up, and I'd often seed them together. They was standing together now, while Misty's master went acrost to mount him and get on with what Marse Robert wanted done. Well, as I've told you, Tom, horses set a heap of store by friendship. Take a horse away from his friend and he's likely to feel it bad. And now here was Misty being unhitched and taken away from Buckthorn almost by force, at a time when every horse and man had been strained to the limit. You could see he didn't like it at all, but there was no time for his master to be bothering 'bout that. He jumped up and spurred him to get going. But Misty warn't minded jest then to be all that obedient. He simply wouldn't go, so this officer began beating him with a stick. 'Soon's Marse Robert seed that, he called out, "Don't whip him, Captain! Don't whip him! I've got jest sech another foolish horse myself, and whipping does no good!"

Well, maybe I am a foolish horse. I've always knowed I warn't a genius like Skylark, but jest the same, I don't figure Marse Robert and me would've been together all these years if'n that was what he really thought of me, do you? He was certainly right 'bout whipping does no good. He's never had no need to take a whip or a spur to me, not one time since the day we met.

Then General Ringlets came up to us on Romeo, who was all in a lather of sweat and rolling his eyes white. Marse Robert hurried acrost to meet him. "General Pickett," he says, "please get your division behind this hill and be ready to meet the enemy if they come."

Ringlets was looking jest 'bout frantic, almost like he was going to cry. I can't remember ever to have seed any commander look worse. When he answered, 'twas in a kind of sob. "General Lee," he said, "I have no division now. They're all dead"—or something like that.

"This has been my fight, General Pickett," replies Marse Robert. "The blame's all mine." And then, near as I could understand, he said something 'bout Ringlets' Virginians being the greatest soldiers he'd ever seed.

There was all sorts of people, soldiers and officers, crowding round us, and Marse Robert says again that 'twas all his fault and they'd done everything that brave soldiers could do. And jest then he seed some stretcher-bearers coming; so he walked me over to them to see who 'twas.

It was one of Ringlets' commanders. I knowed him by sight. He'd been hit terrible—the blood was soaking the stretcher—and he looked real bad to me. Marse Robert took his hand and said he hoped he'd be all right, but the commander said he reckoned he was finished. He asked Marse Robert to tell everyone how well his soldiers had fought, but after that he couldn't go on talking, and they took him away.

It's all real confused, Tom, the way I recall that bad time. Marse Robert was speaking to everyone he could—soldiers, officers, ambulance men—to cheer 'em up. But I'll tell you another thing I ain't forgotten.

We come to a place where some Blue prisoners was a-waiting by the road. 'Course, as you'd s'pose, no one had much time to spare for 'em jest then. One of them had been wounded, and he was laying stretched out on the grass. As we was going by, this fella began yelling out something like "Hurrah for the Union! Hurrah for the Union!" I knowed he meant his own fellas. Marse Robert pulls me up, dismounts, walks acrost to this soldier and takes his hand. "My son," he says, "I hope you'll soon be well."

'Far as I could make out, we must 'a given the Blue men a hiding, 'cause we stayed where we was all that night and all the next morning, and they never dared to up and attack us. But it hadn't been a good 'nuff hiding to make 'em skedaddle, like they had in the forest. The trouble was always the same. However many Blue men we killed or captured, they always had plenty more—and plenty more guns and horses, too.

★

XVI

THAT NIGHT—the last night of the battle, as it turned out—I thought I'd surely be given a rest now. I'd been more or less in steady action for three days. But come to that, so had a lot of fellas, and Marse Robert had everything in the world to be seeing to. He stayed a good while talking with the gunnery general behind the ridge—soon as it got dark, he was going to have to get our guns out from the road at the bottom—and then we went back to headquarters. As I understood it, now we'd hammered the enemy, they wouldn't be giving us no more trouble for quite a while—I guess it must 'a been as much as they could do to stay where they was—and our job was to get the Army back home acrost that there river—the flower ladies' river. We had to find food, apart from anything else; and we had a power of wounded.

After dark, Marse Robert rode me back 'long the ridge to talk to Red Shirt. They warn't finished till real late—well into the middle of the night—and I remember how we came back—jest me and Marse Robert—all through the camps in the moonlight. I was going at a walk—I couldn't have done nothing more. I was so tired I hardly knowed where I was putting my hooves. Now and then we'd be challenged by some sentry who 'peared as exhausted as we was. The mess of battle was lying all round: everything from ammunition

boxes and spent shells to dead bodies—yes, and
wounded, too. I jest stumbled along best I could and
Marse Robert as good as left me to find my own way.
Once't I thought I heared an owl in the trees nearby,
but 'twas a wounded man piping out, sort of high and
thin, for water. And there *was* some wounded, too,
Tom, I'll tell you. Every ditch, every furrow, every old
shed and barn was crammed with wounded—wherever they'd crawled. But the dead horses, they was
still laying in the open, with their legs sticking up stiff
and white balloons blowed out of their mouths and
rumps.

When we got to headquarters, everyone was
asleep 'cept Dave and the sentry and one of our cavalry generals who'd been waiting up. Marse Robert
couldn't hardly get hisself off'n my back. He had to
struggle down. Fin'lly he kind of half-fell off and
stood leaning agin me to get his breath. The cavalryman said, "General, this has been a hard day on you."

"Yes," answers Marse Robert, "it's been a sad, sad
day for us." But then, after a minute, he speaks up
louder. "I never saw troops fight braver'n Pickett's did
today"—or some sech. I was so tired I couldn't rightly
take it in; but then he said, "And we'd have held the
position—"

Dave had come up to take my bridle, and jest as
we was turning away Marse Robert broke out, real
loud, "Too bad! Oh, too bad!" Dave led me away
quick. I guess he wanted to get to sleep.

You'd have 'spected the enemy might try to attack
us the next morning—I think Marse Robert was
'specting it—but they didn't, so we was left undisturbed to get ready to move. I didn't see much of what
was going on, 'cause Marse Robert was riding first
Lucy and then Ajax. 'Twas jest as well, 'cause I
couldn't have done no more. I was afeared of even the
chance of more gunfire—I guess jest that alone would

'a been 'nuff to finish me—but there warn't none. The lines stayed entirely silent.

But there was almost worse'n gunfire to come. 'Bout the middle of the day it begun to rain like you can't hardly imagine. It came down in sheets—torrents —with a howling wind that blowed it right through you. Pretty soon everything and everybody was wringing wet from head to foot, and as cold as the wind. After an hour or two the whole place was deep in mud as a pigsty. Everyone was cussing, everyone slipping, wagons jest about down to the hub and men pushing till they slid and fell their length, horses over the fetlocks—what was the use of whupping 'em, poor beasts? They nigh on whupped their ribs raw, some of 'em—and no one could see further'n the wagon in front.

The roads—well, you couldn't tell what was meant to *be* a road, 'ceptin' for the fellas laid out beside it, and them you didn't know which was dead from the day before and which was jest all in. Half of 'em looked more mud than clothes. I seed wagon wheels go over some of 'em.

Marse Robert sent the wagons full of wounded first. He'd called for me again by that time, and we stood in the open a long while a-watching the ambulances go by. I'd guess most of those men was dying. You could hear them inside, rolling and pitching around like tent poles. Mostly they warn't cryin' like men—more like cats a-courtin'—kinda high, wailing and thin. We seed mules go down in the mud and lay there on their sides. One pair went over together an' turned the wagon over behind 'em, and that nearly sank in the mud, wounded and all.

It came on the darkest night you ever seed. Jest here and there we had some pine torches burning, but most of 'em went out in the rain. Some of the teamsters was leading a mule with one hand and holding on to the wagon in front with t'other.

'Twas well after the middle of the night before the last of the Army was able to leave the battlefield. A lot of our wagons was lost for good, and as for the march—well, near as I'm any judge, it took us all night and half the next day to go 'bout ten miles. And it never stopped raining—not once't all that next day and night. We bivouacked, but 'twas so cold and wretched we was glad to get on again. 'Twas awful bad—bad as could be—but the further we got away, and on through the mountains, the quicker we was able to go, or so it 'peared to me. I don't recall whereabouts I was on the march; there was that much confusion and rain, I couldn't even have told you whether I was still with headquarters or not. Marse Robert took Lucy and didn't call for me again till we'd been going more'n two days. 'Twas fine and sunny again by then, and I remember the roofs, and the leaves and grass glittering and sparkling as we rode down to take a look at the river.

I remembered that river like it'd been when we'd forded it with Ringlets and Old Pete and met the ladies. This warn't the same place as where we'd crossed, but wherever we was now, upstream or down, it didn't seem the same river neither. 'Twas 'nuff to scare you—a great brown, rolling flood, lapping over the banks and frothing white all along the shore. The banks was slippery and treacherous and several of us horses pulled hard back from them.

"It's the Blue men," muttered Joker. "Pissing in it upstream—thousands of 'em, standing in rows."

There couldn't be no notion of fording that. I know we'd had a pontoon bridge somewhere in them parts, but later in the day I heared from one of the cavalry horses that it had been swept away.

All the same, as the sun went on shining and the

enemy—who was round somewhere—still didn't dare attack us, I got to feeling that the whole Army, horse and man, was still in good heart. Well, we was real tough, Tom, you know. Our bands began playing, and fellas was a-joking and skylarking. We didn't feel so bad. After all, the Blue men was plumb scared of us; we'd hit 'em real hard, and now we was on our way home. Our only trouble was the one that never seemed to leave us—shortage of food. Forage was awful scarce, and even good old Dave didn't seem able to find any. Us horses was living on grass and standing corn. I remember one day me and Joker and some more of the headquarters horses was turned loose in a field of grain. I ate it real slow; I warn't goin' to get the colic, like Richmond had. But 'fore we was done, we'd jest about ate it bare to the stubble.

We stayed several days camping on the banks of the river, waiting for it to go down so we could get acrost. I heared tell from my cavalry friend, next time he came to headquarters with a message, that the enemy had tried to attack our outposts once't or twice't, but only kind of half-hearted. Jest the same, I could tell Marse Robert was jumpy—well, 'much as he ever was. 'Course, we was ready to fight if we had to, but he didn't want to fight with our backs up agin a river. He knowed the Blue men had a chance more fellas than we did, and even if they didn't cotton to our bay'nets, we didn't want to stick around any longer'n what we had to.

Well, in the end what we did was our fellas went out and tore up railroads, tore down old barns and sheds, cut down trees, got together a passel of old boats—anything at all we could make use of—laid down an approach track on the bank and made a bridge. And when 'twas done, it sure was a swaying, crazy sort of affair—I wondered whether it would hold up as long as it was going to take the Army to cross.

The Bald General and his 'uns—so his horse told me one day when he come to headquarters—they'd been told to ford higher upstream, where 'parently the water was lower. But even without 'em, I didn't figure that bridge—if'n you could call it a bridge—was a-going to last out. Yeah, and it might likely get shelled, too. That did cross my mind. Marse Robert's, too, I 'spect.

We was set to cross at night, so natcherly, the afternoon before, it commenced to raining again—yeah, heavy. By nightfall everything was soaking wet, all the ground was half-flooded, but we still went ahead. We couldn't afford to wait no longer, you see.

Now I'm one horse that can surely tell you something 'bout this here crossing, Tom, 'cause if you'll believe me, Marse Robert and me was there the whole night in the rain and dark, watching as the Army tottered and shuffled and seesawed acrost that bridge. The rain kept on right till morning. Like I said, we'd made a new track down to the end of the bridge on our side, but the wagons—which was the first to cross —cut so deep into the mud that they kept stalling on the slope, and then two-three of our guns stalled, too. The only standing points anyone could pull on 'em from was deep in mud—some of it near up to men's knees—and getting worse all the time. There was only three-four pine torches for light, and they kept a-dimming and sizzling in the rain. I seed a wagon full of wounded come down, miss the end of the bridge and go straight into the water. 'Twas a swift current, too, and deep. I thought they sure was goners, but every man round rushed down there and somehow they was got out and the wagon was righted and shoved back onto the bridge.

On the bank, at the approach, they'd laid lines of willow poles to stop the wheels cutting into the mud, but the ground underneath was so wet and soggy that most of them bent to cracking, or else they'd slip to one side far 'nuff to spring up and catch a horse's hoof and throw him down.

Getting the wagons acrost took all night. Hours went by while Old Pete's men stood in the rain, waiting till it come their turn. And still Marse Robert sat there where everyone could see us both—'much as anyone could see anything. Now and then he'd walk me forward through the mud to speak to an officer or cheer up a bunch of the men. I don't believe anyone could have guessed he was tired—not to look at him or talk to him. The only one who knowed that was me; I could feel him on my back. There was times I thought he was likely to fall, he was so wore out. He only let up once't the whole night, and that was jest for a short while when he went to his tent.

When morning finally came, we'd jest got the last of the wagon train over. I don't know why the bridge hadn't busted. Marse Robert left Old Pete where we'd been and led me acrost the bridge. That was as frightening as anything I've ever done in my life. If I hadn't had Marse Robert leading me I couldn't never have done it at all. As you might s'pose, when we got t'other side we found a considerable mess, but at least it was daylight, and pretty soon Old Pete's men was a-crossing in tolerable good order.

I knowed Marse Robert had never 'spected an attack at any time more'n he did now, with the Army half one side and half t'other. I recollect he sent a messenger back to Red Shirt to tell him to bring his fellas on as fast as he could. But there warn't no attack. As Red Shirt's last lot came over, with the bridge swaying one way and t'other and the current lashing and dragging at it, I felt Marse Robert give a huge sigh of relief. Jine-the-Cavalry was with us (even Skylark warn't his usual jaunty self that morning), and he disappeared somewhere and come back with a cup of hot coffee.

Marse Robert fairly gulped it down and told Jine-the-Cavalry he'd never tasted anything so good in his whole life.

All the same, Tom, I wouldn't like you to start thinking that the ruckus that night—all the hours and hours of it—knocked any least bit o' the stuffing out of Marse Robert or changed him at all from hisself. All that night, when the Blue men might have attacked us at any moment, he was jest the same old Marse Robert. And everyone believed the crossing was going ahead real fine, 'cause there we was, him and me, watching every single minute of it and as good as saying so, jest by being there and acting the way we did. But 'twarn't only that, even. 'Twas—'twas—well, I'll tell you 'bout something else I recollect—one of the things Marse Robert did that night.

Before we crossed the river—while we was watching the wagons onto the bridge—every now and then Marse Robert would tell some officer to ride off to one place or 'nother to see how things was going elsewhere, and come back and let him know. 'Twas usually one of the four majors, or it might be Colonel Long or some sech. Well, 'bout the middle of the night he sent Major Venable off on one of these here errands. I got a notion 'twas to see how the Bald General was getting on up at his ford. Anyway, when Major Venable come back he was real feisty. He was talking pretty near at the top of his voice and saying how everything where he'd been was 'bout as bad as it could be. So then Marse Robert, he jest gave him back as good. He said he ought to be 'shamed of hisself to speak like that 'bout senior officers, loud 'nuff for all the soldiers and teamsters round about to overhear him and likely get downhearted from it. 'Fact, he scolded him good and proper. Now, you see, Major Venable was older'n the other three majors and he had quite a feeling—so it always struck me—of his own dignity and his position on Marse Robert's staff. You could see he didn't like this telling-off at all. But he took it without a word; he jest saluted and rode off, all covered in rain and mud. I remember his horse, Leopard, splashing me as he turned in the great puddle we was all a-standing in.

Well, later on that night, while Marse Robert was dismounting to go into his tent for a little rest, he told Perry to ask the major to come and see him. The major came, and I guess Marse Robert was hoping he'd be feeling better 'bout it. But when he come out of the tent I could see—anyone could see—that he was still all in a huff. What with everything that was going on, I thought well, if'n he was going to give Marse Robert a hard time on top of all the rest, it was jest too bad. Anyways, as I told you, we crossed the river ourselves soon after, and by dawn we was on t'other bank, watching Old Pete's men come over. By this time there warn't no one at headquarters warn't jest 'bout ready to keel over—including me. Several did. I seed a soldier holding Leopard's bridle, and then, not far off, I seed Major Venable laid down in the mud, sound asleep, and the rain fair belting down on him. A minute or two later Marse Robert seed him, too. He got off'n my back, went acrost to where the major was laying, took off his own poncho and covered him with it. Then he come back and mounted up again.

I don't know what happened when the major woke up—we warn't there—but next day, when he came to report to Marse Robert again, you could see that they was back on good terms sure 'nuff. I guess he must 'a felt pretty small. Well, he wouldn't forget it in a hurry, would he? I haven't, no ways.

I reckon that coming back from the battlefield, and then the river crossing, was 'bout the hardest march I ever made. And yet we-all come through it— them that did, I mean. A day or two later we was back

on old ground I remembered well, and feeling fine—
if'n only there'd been something near 'nuff to eat. We
warn't no ways demoralized, Tom. We was the
grandest Army ever.

Talking of things Marse Robert did 'long 'bout
that time, I'll tell you something else while it's on my
mind. 'Twas on a hot day's march after we'd crossed
the river. The sun was jest scorching and our fellas
was going by pretty wearily—a long column, kicking
up a lot of dust and everyone suffering from the heat.
Marse Robert and Old Pete and some of the staff had
stopped off in a little grove jest above the road, where
there was a spring of water to go with the feed. I was
hitched up with Joker and Leopard and one or two
more, tossing my head and swishing at the durned
flies, when I seed one of the soldiers leave the ranks
and come acrost towards Marse Robert. He was a
handy-looking fella, too, strong and well set-up, and
he was a-pouring with sweat—'twas running off him
reg'lar like rain, poor man.

He made straight for where Marse Robert was sitting on the grass. He came right past my nose. Someone tried to stop him, but Marse Robert said no, let
him come. So then this here soldier comes up and
salutes, all covered in dust like he was, 'ceptin' where
the sweat had made streaks down his face and neck.
Marse Robert asks him what he wants. "I don't want
much, General," says the man, "but it's powerful wet
marching this weather and I can't see for the water in
my eyes. I came aside to get a rag or somethin' to wipe
the sweat off of me."

Marse Robert takes out his own handkerchief.
"Will this do?" he says.

"Oh, my Lordy, that indeed!" cries the fella.

"Well, then, take it with you," says Marse Robert,
"and get back quick into ranks. No straggling this

march, you know, my man." 'Wonder whether he's still got it?

Things like that was always liable to be goin' on anywhere we was around. I'll tell you something real funny that happened the very day after we'd crossed the river. 'Twas misty weather, and for some reason I don't jest remember now, me and Marse Robert had gone forward on our own, a ways off from the rest of headquarters, and we was walking easy on the grass right 'longside part of an artillery battery on the move. As we rounded a turn in the road, we came on a wagon unhitched, shafts down, standing on the verge —no mules, no teamster. Marse Robert, he looks around, and there was an old fella out in the field alongside, t'other side of the drawbars. He must 'a took them down hisself. He'd unhitched his pair of mules, but he had them by the halter reins, and he was letting 'em feed on the grass—mighty fine grass it smelt, too, in the damp of that mist.

"My man," calls out Marse Robert, "I like that. I'm glad to see you taking sech good care of your mules. Fine mules they are, too! What's their names?"

You could see the old fella was real pleased, but he'd plainly got no notion of who we was. He says the mules are called Dragon and Logan. "And Dragon," he says, "he's rayther the better of the two, maybe."

"Well," says Marse Robert, "I'm glad to see you're keepin' 'em in hand with the lines and not letting them spoil the farmer's property. I wish all our mule-drivers was as careful! But if'n I was you, I wouldn't stay here too long. There are some gentlemen in blue back here on the road a little way, and—"

"What's that?" shouts out the old fella. "What's that you say? Lord, I ain't a-takin' no chances! Them infernal Yankees ain't never gittin' my mules! Come on, Dragon, Logan! We-all's gittin' out of here!"

Well, he was jest hitching 'em up again when up rides Major Taylor and Colonel Marshall and the rest of the headquarters staff, and Marse Robert, he starts in a-giving out orders and saying what he wanted done. You should jest 'a seed that old teamster's face when he realized who he'd been talking to! As for me, I never used to talk to mules, but Marse Robert, he'd talk to anyone.

Directly we'd got back into our own country, we was able to settle down and rest a spell. Oh, yeah, we had about two months, 'far as I remember, of peace and quiet. 'Long 'bout that time Marse Robert held two big reviews. Reviews? What's reviews? Well, that's what we call it, Tom, when all the soldiers gets trim and cleaned up, and then they-all line up in their different companies, with the bands a-playing and all the red-and-blue cloths flying; and then Marse Robert and me, we ride all round, regiment by regiment, and the different generals salute him and ride along with him a piece, and Marse Robert tells 'em they're doing jest fine; and then finally him and me, we take up our place, somewheres up a little bit high, where everyone can see, and they-all march past and Marse Robert salutes them as they go by. Oh, it's something to see, I'll tell you, is a big review.

The second of these here reviews was of the whole of Red Shirt's men—thousands of 'em. There was a whole crowd of fine ladies with bonnets and parasols had come to watch, and all the country people from miles around, some of 'em in carts and on horses, and others jest a-walkin'.

I felt real proud that day. I'd been groomed real special—I was a-shining like the moon—and Marse Robert was in full uniform, with his sash and sword, a brand-new pair of gauntlets and a new hat. The soldiers was drawn up by regiments, muskets and

bay'nets all clean and glittering in the sun, and the
different cloths—colors, as they call 'em—standing
straight out in the breeze. When everything was
ready, Red Shirt and his staff officers rode up to us and
saluted, and then him and Marse Robert set out to
gallop right around the front and rear of the whole
durned outfit.

'Twas a long way to go—'bout nine mile altogether, I'd figure—and I thought, Well, if'n we don't
get on, we ain't going to be done 'fore it's dark, or near
'nuff. Marse Robert evidently reckoned the same,
'cause when I started off at a long lope, he never
checked me nor reined me in. As we passed each
bunch, he jest kept a-lookin' straight at the soldiers.
So I set a good, fast pace and kept it up. After a bit I
realized that we mostly seemed to be leaving other
horses and officers behind. One of Red Shirt's generals
—General Mahone, I think 'twas—was riding a biggish, spirited black called Brigand, that I'd met several
times in action and on the marches.

"Wind and rain, Traveller!" gasps Brigand as we
went on acrost the front of General Mahone's bunch,
"can't you let up a piece? You've busted three staff
officers' horses already."

"Marse Robert's happy 'nuff, if you are," I answered, and jest put myself a few more paces ahead.
"This ain't the only division we got to see today."

During the second half of that ride, the officers
along with us gradually became fewer and fewer. One
by one pretty well all of 'em dropped out, and finally
Red Shirt hisself left me and Marse Robert to arrive at
the reviewing stand by ourselves and rein up where
we was going to take the salute. I could feel Marse
Robert's blood pumping strong—partly with the ride, I
reckon, and partly with pride in his men. As he raised
his hat and saluted, there was a regular storm of cheering and applause from all the folks around, and then

the regiments marched past at the quickstep. Me, I
didn't even feel winded. I stood there tossing my head
and breathing quite calm and steady. I felt that the
best soldier around that day had the best horse under
him, and he'd been so kind as to 'low me to prove it. I
only wished Skylark had been there—yeah, and Hero,
too. But if'n I recall rightly, they'd sent Old Pete and
his 'uns off somewheres else jest 'bout that time, although they came back later.

In fact, we did see some more action during that
fall and right on into the early part of the winter. But
'truth was, the Blue men had pretty well had 'nuff for
the time being and they'd gotten what you'd call leery.
What I chiefly recollect 'bout that time is my notion
that Marse Robert was beginning to feel older and to
get tired more easy. There was something not entirely
right 'bout the feel of him in the saddle. Jest the same,
he seemed to be driving hisself to do as much as he'd
always done since we'd been together. I felt fine myself, but I was glad for his sake when the winter was
fin'lly come and the Army moved into log-hut camps
along that river I'd gotten to know so well.

But you know, Tom, they was gloomy places,
them winter camps. There was never 'nuff to do, that
was the way I felt. And there was a power of sickness
'mong the men. We'd ride to a camp, and as we came
near I could often smell if'n there was sickness in it.
The main trouble was the everlasting shortage of food,
and there the horses and mules suffered worse'n the
men. They starved. And then in cold weather the
men'd be freezing and shivering. They hadn't 'nuff
warm clothes for sticking around doing little or nothing in a frost. They hadn't even boots, a lot of 'em.

Gosh sakes! It's better to be laying down full of a
good feed, ain't it, in a clean, dry stable in summer,
than letting yourself live through times like that

again? I'm going to have a drink and drop off to sleep.
You jump up in the crib, Tom, and settle down. I guess
them dad-burn rats'll be glad to forget 'bout you for a
while.

★

XVII

EARLY MAY, 1864. The Confederacy is undone and its cause doomed. Irreplaceable losses in numbers—which were always inferior—not only of men but also of horses; shortage of boots, clothing and ammunition; lack of means to replace worn-out artillery and small arms; near-starvation, owing to a grossly defective commissariat, itself dependent upon the economy of a ruined country—these make up the hopeless prospect. Yet there is no will to capitulate. On the contrary, the Army of Northern Virginia still believe themselves superior to the enemy.

The hope, when it existed, was that the North, though certainly unconquerable by force of arms, would become weary of continual casualties and the strain of the war, and rather than continue to oppose the indomitable South would desist and agree to a negotiated peace. That this has not taken place—that the North still matches the South in determination—is due in large part to the political skill and pertinacity of a single man, President Abraham Lincoln. If there is one imponderable that has tipped the balance towards continuation of the war until the Confederacy is overthrown, it is the will of the President. Never wavering from his conviction that the Union must at all costs be preserved, Lincoln, patient, resolute and adroit, is proving himself an adversary more formidable than any of the Federal generals. Rather less than two months ago, in March, 1864, he appointed General Ulysses S. Grant to the command of the Union armies.

Grant himself is commanding in the field the re-organized Army of the Potomac, now increased in numbers to a dire 140,000. His scheme for defeating the Confederacy can be expressed in one word: attrition. If the Federals lose ten men for every Confederate soldier killed or otherwise put out of action, this, maintains Grant, is no more than they can afford. The defiance of the South is to be broken by sheer force of numbers. With this bloody horseman of the apocalypse is to ride another—Famine. All fertile land, all crops, fruit trees, pasture, barns, byres and holdings will be laid waste by the advancing Union forces; all sheep, cattle and pigs seized. During April, 1864, before Grant's offensive has yet begun, Lee has written to President Davis, "I cannot see how we can operate with our present supplies." Yet far greater privation, both for soldiers and civilians, is to follow. Grant's design is to hammer continuously against the enemy and his resources until by sheer carnage and devastation he is forced into submission. Lee's troops are acknowledged an army of hard and experienced veterans, an instrument sharpened to a perfect edge. "You turn its flanks—well, its flanks are made to be turned. All that we reckon as gained is loss of life inflicted."

It is no longer practicable for the Army of Northern Virginia to pursue Lee's earlier strategy of offensive maneuver at a distance from Richmond, or to constrain the enemy to conform to his movements. In 1863, at the close of the Gettysburg campaign, he formally offered his resignation to President Davis, but this was unhesitatingly refused. Lee himself is a man of straightforward, unaffected and somewhat uncompromising character, adhering above all to a simple concept of duty. "Private and public life," he once wrote, "are subject to the same rules; and truth and manliness will carry you through the world much better than 'policy,' or 'tact,' or 'expediency,' or any other word that was ever devised to conceal a deviation from a straight line." General Lee, though as a soldier he must now foresee the outcome, will continue to carry out his appointed duty.

This spirit, by one means and another—not least the force of example, for the captain of this ruined band is much among the men—has infused the entire army of about 64,000 that now faces Grant across the Rapidan. Officers and men have a strong will to continue to fight—with barely the means, it would seem. Under Lee's command they have indeed been forged into soldiers: resourceful, adept and habituated to war to a degree seldom if ever paralleled. The formidability of this army has increased in proportion to their hardships.

"The retreat of a great general," said Carl von Clausewitz, "should resemble that of a wounded lion." The May leaves are green on the dense oak, hazel and brush of the wilderness—that wilderness where Jackson was mortally wounded and the battle of Chancellorsville was won; the redbud is over and the flowers of spring are in bloom. A wilderness, trackless and in places almost impassable, with visibility often down to a few yards, is a good place for a wounded lion; a good place for a general who knows his artillery inferior to the enemy's; a good place for those determined to cost the enemy very dear.

Hey, there, Tom. Come on in! Nights turning sharper, ain't they, these last few days? Soon be midwinter. For goodness' sakes, what you got there? That's no rat! Oh, a chipmunk? It's dead, ain't it? You killed it? Poor little fella, I don't see how a chipmunk's going to do us no harm in stables. You've been out prowling in the woods, I guess, han't you? He was a bit slow with the cold and you natcherly grabbed him. I wonder he was out at all. 'Nother day or two and he'd have found hisself a hidey-hole and been asleep for the winter. Well, now you've brung him in I guess you'd better settle down and eat him.

We was out in the woods, too, s'afternoon, Marse
Robert and me. 'Twas the old road to the Baths we
was riding along, as usual, although these days we seldom go all that far. Marse Robert—well, he don't 'pear
to like riding as far as he used to, and he gets tired
quicker. Not surprisin', is it, after all him and me have
done together? Come to that, I don't know that I always feel all that much of a colt myself, though I can
still go. I don't know whether I'd want to do one of
them night marches again, though, through the wind
and rain. Stopping, starting, uncertainty, confusion—
they're the things take it out of you.

What was it I started telling you? Oh, 'bout s'afternoon. Well, you know, part of that road to the
Baths goes through a pretty thick stretch of woods,
and we was right in the middle of this when we come
up on a real plain-looking old fella riding a ways
ahead of us. His horse gave me a nice, friendly nicker
and I answered back. Then, when we got close, he
said, "You're Traveller, ain't you? I seed you often,
back in the old Army days."

Well, 'course, in them days Marse Robert and me
was used to seein' more horses'n there's stars in a
night sky, so I jest nuzzled him friendly-like and said I
was glad to meet up with him again. But meanwhile
his master, who anyone could have told for an old
soldier, reined in and said, "General Lee, I'm powerful
glad to see you, and I feel like cheering you."

Marse Robert evidently didn't recognize him personally, but I remembered him all right, even if I
didn't his horse. I recollected Marse Robert speaking
to him and three-four others that night on the river-
bank in the rain, telling 'em the crossing was going
fine and 'twas all thanks to fellas like them. Anyway,
now he said he was real glad to see him, same as he
was always glad to see any of his old soldiers, but he
figured there'd be no sense in cheering, seeing as how

jest the two of them was alone in these here woods. But that didn't stop the old soldier none. He offs with his hat jest the same and waves it over his head, shouting, "Hurrah for General Lee! Hurrah for General Lee!"

'Warn't much Marse Robert could do, 'ceptin' to salute him and ride on. And that's what we did. But for a considerable time after, we went on hearing the fella behind us, yelling "Hurrah for General Lee!" till we was a ways off down the road.

Let's see, I 'member I was telling you, last time you spent the night in here, 'bout the life in camp that winter after we crossed back over the river in the night. But I been thinking since then, I don't reckon I really said 'nuff, Tom, to make you realize jest how hard life was for the Army horses and mules during them months. As I remember it, the corn and hay got less and less till a lot of us was down to eating straw and glad to get even that. I'll tell you this: me, myself, I sometimes used to gnaw the bark off'n trees when I was out exercising with Dave—*and* he didn't stop me —or when I thought Marse Robert was too busy talking to people to notice. And I know both Lucy and Ajax done the same. Ajax told me that one day, when he was hitched up outside some cottage, he ate a tidy piece off'n the hedge, although, bein' winter, 'twas pretty well all sticks and no leaves. I seed Joker, one day, eat a poke he seed a-laying on the ground— maybe it had some crumbs in it.

And we never seemed to get ary fresh horses sent to us. Skylark told me one time that Jine-the-Cavalry had gotten fair desperate for horses, and that a lot o' his men, who'd once been so proud and particular, was ready to ride 'most anything on four legs if only they could get it. But you see, Tom, an Army's horses are more, much more'n its cavalry. You gotta have wagons; you gotta be able to shift the guns. I thought I noticed, towards the end of that winter, that we had fewer guns. I could have been wrong, of course, but if I was right, it must 'a been on 'count of we had fewer horses to pull 'em.

I know Marse Robert felt the strain something terrible. Actually, I knowed it better'n anyone, 'cause although he never showed it when he was talking to the men, he often used to talk to me when we was out alone together. "Oh, Traveller," he said to me once't, when we'd stopped at a creek for me to have a drink, "it's too much—it's too much for one man!" I wanted to tell him I *knowed* we was going to beat the enemy; that I'd knowed it ever since the day when we'd won the battle in the forest, and the fellas brung that passel of Blue men up to him and said they'd surrendered. But I had to admit to myself that I'd never realized how hard 'twas going to be to finish the job.

Well, the spring came at last, and warmer weather with it. I remember how one day Marse Robert and me rode a matter of ten mile or thereabouts to review Old Pete's lot. Old Pete had been away from us all the winter, but now he'd brung his fellas back, they certainly left Marse Robert and me with no doubts they was glad to see us again. After the review, when they'd broken ranks, hundreds of 'em came a-crowding round us. They was laughing and cheering and laying their hands on me and on the stirrups and Marse Robert's boots—anything of ours that they could touch. I remember thinking, I'll lay the Blue men don't feel like this 'bout their generals. Marse Robert, he was taking all the stretched-out hands he could reach, and saying, "Bless you, my men; bless you; thank you!" Even Old Pete seemed kind of—well, stirred, and 'twarn't like him to show that sort of feeling, I'll tell you. I didn't get no real chance to talk to Hero—only a few moments—but I got the notion that they'd been having what you'd call an adventurous time.

'Twas only a day or two after that review that we went up the mountain again—that Clark's Mountain, with the signal station on it, that I well remembered going up two summers before, when we'd watched the Blue men on the move down below us. They was there again—I could see their tents, far off—and Marse Robert spent a long time looking at them and talking with the headquarters officers. So I guessed we'd be after 'em soon 'nuff, for sure.

I was right, too. 'Twas actually two days later when our Army set out. I knowed the road well 'nuff; 'twas the road that led into the wilderness—them same tangled-up woods where we'd beat the Blue men to pieces. Marse Robert and me was going in front, 'long with Red Shirt and two-three of his commanders. 'Twas clear, sunny weather—jest like it had been the year before—and I was feeling fine. It's funny; you do sometimes, even when you know there's going to be a battle. I think this time it may have been 'cause there was no gunfire. That always worries horses, y'know. I only wished Little Sorrel and Cap-in-His-Eyes had been with us. I still missed Sorrel—missed him all the time.

We didn't go far that first day—maybe twelve mile. But any horse could tell we was looking for the enemy. 'Course, I was an old soldier by now—older'n most in the length of time I'd been with Marse Robert —and I knowed all the signs. Horsemen kept galloping up from out the woods in front, talking to Marse Robert and pointing this way and that. Marse Robert'd ask them questions, sort of sharp and serious, and talk to Red Shirt, and then like as not he'd send one of the majors off to carry a message somewheres else. 'Twas clear 'nuff the enemy was blundering around in them

woods—our woods—and we was going to catch 'em in
there.

All the same, we didn't catch 'em that day. We
came to a little village I remembered—we'd been there
in some fighting during the winter, and real cold it
was, too—and there we camped for the night all 'mong
the trees. 'Twas pretty late at night—I hadn't been
unsaddled till late; I s'pose 'cause Marse Robert reckoned he might be off again—and Joker and me and one
or two more was making the most of 'bout half a feed
of corn each, when I seed a cavalryman ride in and
dismount from a horse I knowed. 'Twas Dancer, and
he was picketed right by us.

We asked him what was the news. He told us
Jine-the-Cavalry and his 'uns was out a fair way
ahead in the Wilderness, and they'd been keeping
close to the enemy and watching 'em on the march.

"They crossed the river," said Dancer, "and now
they're trying to go straight down through these here
woods and out t'other side. General Stuart's idea is
that we ought to attack 'em soon as we can, while
they're all snarled up among the trees."

"Haven't they got a road?" I asked.

"It's precious little use to them," says Dancer.
"There's thousands of 'em—men and wagons—all
bunched up together. My hooves, though, they've got
some cavalry! Great, sleek horses—you can smell the
oats in 'em half a mile off!"

Well, seemed like Jine-the-Cavalry's news ap-
pealed to Marse Robert a whole heap. When we set off
at dawn next morning, he was real cheerful. Jine-the-
Cavalry hisself had ridden back out of the forest, and
him and Red Shirt set out with Marse Robert, straight
'long the road into the thick of the wilderness.

Now I know you go out into the woods round
here quite a bit, Tom, prowlin' around and hunting—
poor little chipmunks, and squirrels, too, I reckon. But

all the same I'd best try and give you some idea of
what this here Wilderness was like, 'cause it sure
warn't like no other battlefield I'd ever been on—not
even like the one the year before, when Cap-in-His-
Eyes and Sorrel had gone for good. This place where
we was advancing was mostly pine and oak, each in
big, wide patches, with a whole lot of underbrush.
There was great thickets of brush—places where men
couldn't hardly force their way, let alone see through
or get guns or horses through. Fellas could split up
from others and lose 'em in less'n a minute and have a
job to find 'em again. Soldiers usually fight in lines,
you know, but here there was no more chance of
fighting in lines than what there was of plowing. And
at night—well, at night you might as well have been
blindfolded, like I've once't or twice't seed done to
nervous horses to lead 'em past something they was
afeared of. Often, the men didn't know which way
they was s'posed to be facing for to fight. I figure a lot
of 'em shot fellas on their own side, and so did the
enemy, too. I heared tell afterwards of men going out a
few yards to get water and finding they'd landed
theirselves in enemy hands. And 'course there was
snakes and poison ivy and all manner of things, and a
man in the dark could poke his eye out on a pointed
stick. This was the place where Marse Robert figured
we could give the enemy a licking. In fact, I've never
felt him so eager for battle.

     We didn't have to look for it long, neither. We'd
set out in the same direction as the day before, and
passed a place where we'd entrenched and fought during the winter. We was going along a road not much
wider'n a cow path, but each side of it was trees thick
as hay in a crib, with jest little bitty clearings here and
there. The horsemen had been coming and going all
morning, and it must 'a been 'bout midday, I s'pose,
when we-all heared heavy firing up in the woods

ahead. Marse Robert acted like he usually did—lit out
and rode ahead, and Red Shirt and Jine-the-Cavalry
with him. But we never come on no fighting, not in
two-three hours.

We'd turned off the track, I remember, into a
clearing and up a little nothin' of a hill with trees,
where I guess Marse Robert thought he might be able
to see anything there was to see without being spotted
hisself. Him and the others had dismounted and they
was all a-talking together, when all of a sudden a
whole line of Blue men come out from among the
pines, only jest a bit of a ways ahead and below us.
They was there maybe a minute before they disappeared again, but 'twas 'nuff to show we'd gotten real
close to the fighting we'd been looking for.

Marse Robert had hardly had time to give some
orders to Red Shirt when a terrible racket broke out
from ahead of us—firing, yelling—yeah, and a gun or
two. The trees was so thick none of us couldn't see
nothing, but 'twas plain that this was what they call
an attack in force.

That attack went on all the rest of the afternoon.
Me and Marse Robert was going best as we could
'mong the trees, moving troops, giving orders and
hearing reports. Those people couldn't shift us, and
they must 'a lost a chance of men a-trying. It had
come on dark 'fore the firing finally stopped. I'd had
no water—we'd been too busy—and I still remember
stopping off by a little creek for one of the best drinks
I've ever had. While I had my head down, a courier
come up to us, but he had to wait. Marse Robert
wouldn't let him interrupt my drink. I figured I'd
earned it right 'nuff, so I jest took my time.

That night—well, Tom, you never seed sech a
mess in all your born days. We rode around to speak to
as many officers and men as we could, but the truth
was that both sides was jest 'bout lost astray—the fel-

las hardly knowed up from down. And in them tangles the enemy might be anywheres. Even to make a noise in the dark, jest a-pushing through the brush, might be 'nuff to make some fella loose off at you. We pretty soon gave it up and came back. Headquarters warn't hardly no distance at all behind the line that was being held by Red Shirt's bunch. You could hear the enemy out there in the dark, plain as plain.

'Twas the usual disturbed night—messengers all the time. I don't reckon Marse Robert got any sleep at all. I know I didn't. I felt sure the enemy was fixing to attack again as soon as it was light. And so they did, and they was closer even than I'd figured—right in among the trees out jest ahead.

Well, I thought, Red Shirt's fellas'll hold them; they always do. And if'n we need 'em, Marse Robert'll be ordering up some more men. But after a while I began to feel kind of shaky—well, real scared, to tell you the truth. Our fellas had been fighting off attacks all the day before, and they was real tuckered out. For all I knowed, the Blue men might have sent up a fresh lot during the night. But one thing was clear: fellas was straggling back and breaking away from the front, and there come more and more of 'em all the time. They was jest wore out; they couldn't take no more. 'Struck me we was well on the way to gettin' ourselves licked.

Marse Robert, he seed all this same's I did. He jest stopped to give some orders to Marse Taylor and then he rode me out from headquarters into the road, right in the middle of our fellas that was doing the sneaking off. Pretty soon he spotted their commander.

"General McGowan!" he hollers. "Is this your splendid brigade running like a flock of geese?"

The general tells him they ain't no ways beat. They jest needed a place to form up so's they could fight again.

Another general—General Wilcox, 'twas—rode up to us. Marse Robert told him to go and fetch Old Pete, and he went off like a flash.

We came back into the headquarters field, where there was a whole row of our guns lined up. By this time I was real frightened—yes, Tom, I was. You could see the Blue men—masses of 'em—plain as plain on the edge of the woods ahead, not more'n two hundred yards off. I'd never in my life been so close to Blue foot soldiers before, 'ceptin' for prisoners. I could foresee anything happening—half of headquarters shot, Marse Robert took prisoner—anything at all.

Then our guns blasted off, right beside me. Well, you can't never think 'bout nothing when the guns are firing and the ground's shaking. It's as much as any good horse can do jest to stand still. There was sech a mess as you never seed—officers yelling, soldiers crowding every which way and the battle-smoke so thick 'twas 'nuff to choke you and nothing to be made out at all.

Suddenly, in the middle of all this, I caught a glimpse of a crowd of soldiers running towards us from behind, a-waving their muskets. They come right up to the guns, which was still firing.

"Who are you, my boys?" yells Marse Robert.

Who are you, indeed, I thought. Don't he know? I could have told him who they was. There was only one bunch like that in the Army.

"Texas boys!" answers one of 'em. "Texas boys!"

Marse Robert offs with his hat and waves it over his head.

"Hurrah for Texas!" he yells. "Hurrah for Texas!"

Then there we was, him and me, moving round and forming them Texas fellas into line of battle. As soon as he seed they was ready, Marse Robert rode me to the left of the line and out in front.

"Forward, men!" he shouts. "I'll lead you myself!"

Snakes alive! Like thunder you will! I thought. Marse Robert personally leading a charge agin the Blue men? I'd never figured on this. 'Course, I'm an awful coward, Tom, you know. Gunfire I'd more or less got used to—'much as I ever did—but leading a charge? I wonder who offers the biggest mark, I thought. The General's horse, I guess. Well, here we go!

But matters was took out of our control—yeah, they was took out of Marse Robert's own control. "No! No!" the Texas fellas all began yelling. "No! Go back, General Lee, go back!"

Marse Robert, he took not a blind bit of notice. I could feel, where he sat, that he'd somehow changed. 'Twas like he was in a trance. He was jest fixing on nothing 'cept leading them fellas straight into the heart of the Blue men and licking 'em, and nothing was going to stop him.

"Go back, General Lee!" they yelled. A whole bunch of 'em stopped and turned round towards him. "We won't go on unless you go back!"

'Twas like Marse Robert couldn't hear one word they was saying. He kept jest looking straight ahead at the enemy. The young Texas general hisself tried to stop him—no good. Then a big sergeant came up and grabbed my bridle. But even that didn't stop Marse Robert urging me forward, a-dragging the fella along with him. By this time I'd caught his mood—I always did, of course. I wanted to do what he wanted. I wanted us to lead the attack.

'Twas Major Venable that finally stopped us. He pulled his horse 'longside and yelled into Marse Robert's ear to tell him Old Pete had come up, and hadn't he any orders to give him?

Marse Robert reined me in and sort of slowly came out of his trance. He was still scowling at the Blue men, but he let Major Venable take my bridle.

Then he waved his hat again to the Texans, and forward they went and back we came. Sure 'nuff, there was Old Pete sitting on Hero, a-waiting for us.

"You ought to go further back behind the lines, General," says Old Pete. And that was all he did say.

In the past, I'd often felt mean 'bout Old Pete at one time and another, but right now I felt I really liked him for a good, sensible fella.

Marse Robert asked him to get his men deployed to attack the enemy. You wouldn't have thought any soldiers could extend into line of battle in that place. 'Twas all undergrowth and low branches, and lots of parts men couldn't even see the enemy till they'd jest 'bout run spang into 'em. A plenty of the scrub runners and saplings had been knocked over by bullets, so that they was leaning into each other thick as hedges. In other places, 'twas all chinkapin branches, right down to the ground. There was no question of a horse getting through that, and 'course this meant messengers couldn't report like they usually did. The guns couldn't be used, neither. This here fighting had to be foot soldiers on their own.

It went on all morning. Marse Robert was forever trying to get to one place and another—often jest so that our soldiers could see him, or so it struck me at the time. But you know, I couldn't hardly pick my way, Tom, even though Marse Robert mostly left it to me entirely. And worse'n that, I often found myself stepping on dead men and sometimes on the wounded, too—they was laying that thick, Blue men and ours all mixed up.

Well, never mind for that. I'll tell you 'bout something different that happened that morning. 'Far as I could make out, Old Pete's men seemed to have driven the enemy back—leastways, they'd stopped coming on—and things was beginning to get a little calmer, when an officer rode up to us on a horse that looked like he might be going to fold up any moment. He was frothing and panting, and his sides was heaving so he couldn't even give a friendly nicker, let alone tell me what was going on. Marse Robert took this in directly, quick's I did. He spoke sharp to the young officer and told him he ought to treat his horse better. "You should have some feeling for him," he said. "Get off, and rest him." And with that he reached into the saddlebag on my back, took out one of our own biscuits and fed it to this horse. This was with the battle still going on all round us, Tom, you understand.

Pretty soon, 'twas us was doing the attacking and the Blue men was doing the sneaking off—leastways, 'far as anyone could tell in all the mix-up. Marse Robert and me had gone forward to jest behind the front line—if'n you could call it a front line—and he was giving orders for a pile of logs to be moved so our guns could be pulled forward. I could see Old Pete, with his own little group of officers, waving to us and riding off into the trees where the fighting was.

A minute or two later there come a fearful din from over where they'd disappeared. I heared men screaming out, horses neighing. Then a loose horse came galloping back out of the trees, with the stirrups flying. Some fella stopped him quite close to where we was at, and led him right up to us.

"What's happened?" I asked.

All he could tell was that Old Pete had been hit. A few minutes later, one of Old Pete's officers—Colonel Sorrel, I think 'twas—came back to tell Marse Robert. At the time I hardly took it in, 'cause of all the firing and the confusion of the fighting going on all round. Marse Robert didn't try to get forward to wherever Old Pete was; he jest carried on running the battle, and 'twarn't till much later in the day that I larned from a horse called Frigate, that had come with a message from Old Pete's fellas up in front, that he'd been hit real bad and they was afeared he was likely to die. As things turned out, he didn't die—he came back to us later on—but he was away a mighty long while and for all that time I figured he must 'a been killed for sure.

I can't give you any real idea, Tom, of what it was like that night in the dark when the fighting finally stopped. What I remember most is the smell of the burning woods. The smoke was everywhere—you had to breathe it. All us horses was a-snorting and cough- ing, half-choking with it. There was 'nuff water, but scarcely anything to eat. The trees was on fire all round, in front of us and behind as well. Every now and then there'd roar up great, blazing flames higher'n the trees theirselves. There was men out all night, creeping round and doing their best to bring wounded fellas in, but they couldn't hardly get about, a lot of 'em, 'cause the brush and scrub was burning every- where. I guess a lot of our wounded must 'a died in them woods—yeah, burned in the fire.

Next day was quiet. I reckon both our men and the enemy was that much wore out that neither of 'em had the spunk left to do no more fighting. We spent most of that day, Marse Robert and me, riding from one part of the Army to another, while Marse Robert talked to the different commanders—Red Shirt, the Bald General and a lot more. Most of what was hap- pening I couldn't follow, of course, but near as I could get it the Blue men seemed to have had 'nuff. 'Peared there was signs they was a-pulling out, and Marse Robert, he wanted to be after 'em quick and give 'em another whipping.

Everyone in the Army got to know—it went through them trees faster'n the fire—that the enemy was in retreat. You could hear fellas miles off in the woods raising the Yell. Then it drew closer, as though something alive was coming fast through the trees, and swept on down the lines—the lines no one could see—and died away in the distance. At the time, I thought 'twas the start of another attack, but now I reckon the truth was that Marse Robert figured he'd done the Blue men all the harm he could in a place like that, and he jest wanted to follow them out of it before we started in on 'em again. 'Course, he already knowed 'zackly where they meant to go. Marse Robert was that smart, he could always tell what the Blue men was a-going to do 'fore they knowed it theirselves. They might jest as well have sent a fella over to tell him.

Our headquarters didn't march off that night, though. Jest for once't, I remember, us headquarters horses had a peaceful night, and I got a good spell of sleep for a change.

Next morning, when we was being saddled up, Joker asked me whether I'd heared the news. "We'll have no generals left soon," he said.

"You mean 'bout Old Pete being hit?" I asks him.

"That and a lot more," says Joker. "It seems Red Shirt's been took sick, real bad, and he won't be able to go on commanding—not for a good while, anyways. And during this last day or two we've had five or six commanders either killed or wounded bad. You'll have to take over a division yourself, Traveller. That's what it'll come to."

'Twarn't good news, and that was partly why I couldn't feel my spirits rising as me and Marse Robert rode away out of all the smoke and ashes. 'Twas good right 'nuff to get out of that durned smell, but all the same I had a worrisome feeling—it had been growing on me for the past day or two—of being left on my own. You see, Lucy Long had been sent away—sent to the rear—a few days before we marched into the wilderness. I'd been half-expecting it, as a matter of fact. She jest hadn't got the strength and endurance Marse

Robert needed. I reckon that winter he'd more'n once't found she warn't up to all he had to have from a horse—maybe a little unsteady, too; I don't know. Anyway, she'd gone, and that jest left me and good old Ajax, that Marse Robert hardly ever rode. So from then on—unless we got another horse, which we never did—I'd be looking after Marse Robert on my own.

I s'pose we might have gone thirteen or fourteen mile that day 'fore we came up with the fighting in the afternoon. All I really remember 'bout them next days is that the Blue men was trying to shift us from where we'd dug in, and we jest warn't going to be shifted. Marse Robert and me spent a lot of time riding round the woods and fields, telling the fellas where to dig—like I've told you, Marse Robert was always great on digging—and where to set up the walls of crisscross trees they cut down to fight behind. He had them working all night, most of 'em, and all the next day, and by the time they'd done I figured any of those people that tried to get through was going to finish up a tolerable sick lot.

'Fact, they made one or two tries 'fore we'd entirely finished them defenses. I 'specially remember one attack the second evening after we got there, 'cause that was another time when Marse Robert wanted to lead our men into battle hisself, but the other headquarters officers wouldn't 'low him. Finally he gave in. "You must see to it yourselves, then," he said, real stern, and what happened was that Marse Taylor and Major Venable galloped off to get the enemy beat back.

What I want to tell you 'bout, though, Tom, is what happened next morning—'cause that was something real strange. 'Twas one of the strangest things that ever happened all the time me and Marse Robert was together. It come 'bout this way. 'Twas still dark, towards the end of a cold, foggy night, but Marse

Robert was up already—he never seemed to sleep more'n three-four hours—when we-all heard heavy musket fire starting up a good ways off. It could only be an enemy attack. I was saddled up in two shakes and we was off in the first gray light—I couldn't hardly see my way and jest had to stumble along through the tangle and brush best I could.

We hadn't gone far when we began meeting up with our own fellas, a-running back past us! Running back! I couldn't remember seeing the like before—leastways, not like that.

Marse Robert snatched off his hat so's they could recognize him.

"Stop, men, stop!" he shouted. "Form line here!" or something o' that sort.

But they didn't, most of 'em. For all he could say, they jest kept right on past him. He was still trying to rally them when some other officer rode up and started in telling him something urgent. All I could make out from the way they was speaking was that it must be bad news.

Marse Robert reined me in and we turned back through the trees. Thousands of our men was all round now, in the half-dark, pulling on their coats and buckling their belts: officers shouting orders and trying to form up lines in the fog and wet. I jest kept on steady through all the confusion, and fin'lly we pulled up in the center of one of the lines, midway between two different regiments. Marse Robert still kept his hat in his hand, so's everyone could see who he was.

By this time I could hear bullets zipping past, a lot too close for my liking, and when Marse Robert turned my head towards where they was a-coming from, I got to admit I felt fidgety and worse. It 'peared to me that during these last days he'd become determined to lead a charge personally, and if'n it warn't one then 'twas going to be another, until either him or me was shot down. But once't again it turned out to be jest the same old riot on the part of our fellas. The commanding general next to him—General Gordon, I think 'twas—told him he'd got to go back. All the men called out the same, and some of the officers made a little crowd of their horses 'tween me and the enemy. And then, jest like before, first the general and then one of the soldiers caught hold of my reins and jerked my head to the rear. Marse Robert accepted it. He couldn't do nothing else.

As the daylight growed clear there was an awful lot of hard fighting in and out of the piney woods and acrost the fields. What it come down to was that we was holding off the Blue men, but only jest. I'd come to my own opinion that Marse Robert was settled he was going to get hisself into the battle one way or another. He rode me back a ways till we came to another crowd of our fellas resting beside a road. He told 'em to form up and go forward to the fighting, and soon as they was ready he lined up to go with 'em. We hadn't been going long 'fore enemy shells began busting all round us, thicker'n I'd ever knowed them. I seed two horses go down near us, one of them screaming something terrible. Well, I'll admit to you, Tom, I was terrified. Every time a shell burst, there was more men laying on the ground. I began to rear and plunge. I was near'bouts in a panic and I warn't the only one, horse nor man.

All of a sudden it came to me—all in a single moment, and I'll never know how I knowed it—that there was a shell coming straight for me. 'Twas as though I was the shell, and I could feel myself hurtling towards the line of men and our leaders on their horses. And one of them horses was me. I seed myself rear up and almost throw Marse Robert to the ground, and as I did that the shell went past, under my girth, jest a few inches from the stirrup. If'n I hadn't reared, we'd both have been killed for sure. It still makes me feel strange to think of it.

That did it, Tom—that did it fin'lly. Goodness knows how many times during them last few days our fellas had told Marse Robert to go back out of the firing. But now they went pretty well crazy. Some of 'em got 'tween him and the enemy. Others simply fell on my reins and pulled me round. Marse Robert couldn't stop them. He was a-sitting there in the middle of it all, holding onto his hat and trying to argue. As for me, 'twas like a dream; I hardly knowed what was happening or what 'twas I'd done. At last Marse Robert told them that if'n they'd promise to go and lick the Blue men, he'd go back. "Yes! Yes!" they all yelled; so then he reined me in and watched them go dashing off. They must 'a done what they said, too, 'cause as we rode away the shelling stopped.

All that day there was fighting as bad as any we ever went through. I told you how we'd put up thick fences made from cut-down trees. Our men and the enemy was fighting only a few feet apart, on opposite sides of them fences, and there was so many killed that in the end they couldn't hardly get near each other. They say there was trees actually cut down by the thousands of bullets shot into 'em. 'Twarn't till the middle of the night that Marse Robert felt able to give orders that our fellas was to come out of that dreadful place and fall back onto a new line. We lost a terrible lot of men that day.

'Twas some time during the last hours of that fighting in the dark that I was fast asleep on my four feet—I was that much wore out—when a cavalry courier arrived, and pretty well fell off'n his horse in his hurry. Before he'd even been picketed, that horse told me Jine-the-Cavalry had been killed. That was what his man had come to tell Marse Robert.

While Marse Robert was telling the rest of the

headquarters officers, I could see 'twas as much as he could do to get the words out, and soon as he'd told them he jest turned away and went back into his tent. I asked the horse whether Skylark had been hit, but he didn't know. Cap-in-His-Eyes, I thought, Old Pete, and now Jine-the-Cavalry. What we-all going to do now? What's Marse Robert going to do?

I can't imagine what would have happened to us, Tom, if that fighting had gone on the way it did, but next morning it commenced to pouring with rain and it kept it up for several days. There was running streams every few yards and the roads was jest pools of water, deep. Even the Blue men couldn't do no attacking in that, so we got some rest at last.

I remember one thing that happened either that day or the day after. Marse Robert and me was riding along the rear of our lines together with a bunch of headquarters officers and a general or two—I forget jest which. Suddenly the enemy guns began firing and shells started dropping round. I was scared silly, like I always was, although I did my best to keep steady. Then a shell burst close and scattered dirt and fragments all over us. Three-four other horses began to get skittish and a few broke away into a gallop, so that our lot was all over the place. Marse Robert didn't like this at all. "Easy, Traveller, easy!" he said to me real sharp, pulling me in hard and holding me up tight. Soon as he had me steady, he made me go on down the lines at a walk. "Do you want them to think we're afraid?" he said, only 'twas in a low, gentle voice that no one else could hear. Then he told General Pendleton—that was the chief artillery officer—that he warn't going to let me do anything that'd make it seem like we might be nervous under fire where the men could see.

A night or two later we left that place and marched all night—and a fine old mess 'twas in the dark and wet. I don't recall the details after all this time, but what I do remember is that I was the first one in the Army, horse or man, to realize that Marse Robert was beginning to fall ill. It must 'a been all the strain and the wet weather; and then, of course, he'd had no proper sleep for nights on end, and I don't reckon his food was hardly better'n what us horses was getting—and that was poor 'nuff. The Blue men, they was still around—plenty of 'em, jest t'other side of a little river not far off—but there warn't no heavy fighting like there'd been in the woods. The Army kept on the move, and Marse Robert rode in a carriage and stopped off at folks' houses where he could lie down and be looked after. I was either led or ridden.

They was terrible hard times: always on the move, night and day. The strain was telling on everyone, horse and man. I couldn't remember when we'd been so long engaged with the enemy. Must 'a been all of a month now, I said one night to Joker, since that morning when I'd first seed the Blue men come out from the thick trees and we'd started the fighting in the Wilderness.

"Yes," says Joker, "an' the feed gits shorter every day, don't it? You hungry?"

I sure was, and from the look of 'em, I reckoned the whole of headquarters was, from Marse Robert down. I was glad Lucy'd gone; even if she'd been able to bear the shellfire, she'd never have stood up to the short rations. As for the Blue men, they was like dratted mosquitoes. Whenever we killed one, there'd come another two.

I remember a chilly, wet evening and a rain that lasted all night, and then, jest at dawn, we heared the enemy yelling and firing, way out acrost the bog that the whole durned place had turned into. The yelling stretched right away into the distance. You couldn't see nothing—not from headquarters—but 'twas plain 'nuff they must be attacking all along our lines.

It was jest at that moment I realized for the first time where we'd got to. I seed the shape of some trees on the skyline and caught the smell of a swamp down below. And then I remembered the first battle I'd ever been in, two years before and jest this time of year. We was right on the spot. I recollected, too, how Marse Robert had asked the young Texas general whether he could drive the Blue men out o' the swamp, and how he'd said "I'll try"—and done it. I'd been a young horse then, I thought. I'd seed plenty since, and I felt a lot older—yeah, more'n two years older by a deal.

All you could see was the battle-smoke hanging over the fields, and the shells a-falling. After a while I seed some of our wounded stumbling back out of the wet haze, but not that many. There was no general retreat and no confusion. We must be holding the Blue men off, I guessed.

As it happened, Marse Robert and me was entirely alone in the headquarters field, 'cept for Dave. All our staff officers had been sent off to one place and another. The firing seemed to have been going on for hours. I figured it must be gettin' on to midday, near's I could tell. There was no sun, you see, Tom. 'Twas all foggy an' cloudy, the battle-smoke an' the fog all mixed up together. After a while the firing died down and I guessed the enemy must 'a quit.

'Twas only later that I heared from other horses what had happened. Sure 'nuff, the Blue men had attacked like crazy—everywhere, right along our lines. But we'd stood firm and gone on shooting 'em down till at last it seems the ones who was still waiting to attack had simply refused to go on—refused to obey their orders. They'd lost thousands of men inside an hour. 'Seems that was one of the greatest victories we ever won, that day, only I never seed none of it. And

if'n I'd only a-knowed, 'twas to be our last really big
battle. But all I seed at the time was the soaking-wet
fields in the haze, the creek flowing muddy and thick,
and Marse Robert talking to two-three old gentlemen
as warn't no soldiers at all—some sort of old fellas that
had come a-visiting. One of their horses told me
they'd ridden out from the city on purpose to talk to
General Lee.

"And if this is bein' a soldier," says this horse,
ducking and dancing at every bang of a shell and zip
of a bullet, "you can keep it. The quicker me and my
master get back to the city the better. I don't care if'n
you *are* the General's horse. I'd rather go on belongin'
to old Judge Meredith. He's a sensible man—knows
how to keep a horse out of trouble, too."

I was goin' to say something back, but next moment a shell burst 'way acrost the field and this horse
was gone like a rocket, judge and all. He took some
getting back, too. The old judge was fairly wild. I recollect how he said—

Hey, Tom, listen! Ain't that Miss Life a-calling for
you? She'll be wanting to know you're safe and indoors on a sharp night like this. Better run along and
jine Baxter by the fire up yonder. And jest you take
what's left of that chipmunk out o' here, too. That's
the sort of mess that attracts rats, an' you're s'posed to
be here to get rid of 'em.

XVIII

YOU'VE HEARED 'bout Ajax, Tom, have you? It's upset me a powerful lot, I can tell you. Poor old Ajax!—to go and kill hisself now, in a silly way like that, after all we've been through together. 'Course, he wouldn't never have noticed nothing 'bout that sharp prong on the gate latch, Ajax wouldn't. I'd seed it. I've knowed for a long time that that prong was dangerous—sharp as a bay'net. I've always took good care to avoid it.

I warn't around in the field when it happened. Lucy told me. 'Seems Ajax ran hisself right full tilt onto the prong—'warn't even looking where he was going, Lucy said. There was blood all over the place and he was laying dead, right there, in a couple of minutes. Stabbed hisself to the heart. I'll lay Marse Robert's real upset. It's a wonder he'd never noticed the prong hisself.

I can't say Ajax and me was ever real close. You couldn't exactly make a friend out of Ajax. He was kind of a loner—warn't really a sociable horse. But we'd been together so long—oh, yeah, must be all of five years, first on campaign and then here. Marse Robert couldn't never really make much use of Ajax—too tall—but he didn't feel he could get rid of him, 'cause he'd been a gift, so Ajax once told me, from some people back home.

I think poor old Ajax felt it, you know—that he warn't really valued; or at least, that he warn't a lot of use to Marse Robert—though other soldiers rode him, of course. Dave often rode him and he got on well with Dave. And I remember once't Colonel Marshall took him on for quite a few days. He might have worked up a lot of resentment agin me, but he never did. He was a real sober, stolid sort—ready to do what he was told and accept it. I guess he was a kind of a dull fella. I never could get much out of him at all. Never let hisself get bothered by enemy fire, though, nor by short rations nor any of the other hardships we-all went through. He was as good a soldier as any of us. I've often wondered whether he wouldn't have turned out livelier and more chipper if'n it'd jest so happened he'd suited Marse Robert down to the ground. *My* life would have been different then, too. There'd have been him and me. I guess I've always more or less taken Ajax for granted. But I'm going to miss him now, sure 'nuff. We lost so many—horses and men. I didn't figure we had any more to lose after all this time.

Come to think of it, I remember Marse Robert taking Ajax one day, jest after the battle in the wet and mist that I was telling you 'bout—the time the old judge's horse bolted acrost the field. But that was 'cause I was being shod. Marse Robert was always real particular 'bout that, even at times when you'd have thought he'd have been far too busy with the fighting. Shoeing, girths, throatbands—all that kind of thing he'd see to personally. He generally used to fold my blanket hisself. And one thing in particular I always remember: he was a great one for dismounting so's I could get a rest. He dismounted as often as he could—and that was more'n Old Pete did, I noticed. People used to be astonished that I stayed so fresh all day. I'd be fresh after sixteen mile or more. Well, 'twas partly

me—I don't say it warn't. But a lot of it was on 'count
of Marse Robert's habit of dismounting whenever he
could.

'Twas jest after that battle that Marse Robert recovered 'nuff to be able to ride again. He felt the men
must have missed seeing him round, I guess, 'cause
during all the maneuvering that followed that battle
(and my land, warn't it hot weather, too! 'Never been
so thirsty on a day's work), he took particular care to
get out 'mong the men and talk to 'em plenty. I enjoyed it. Thanks to Dave, I was always well groomed
and shining, and the men liked to see me and gather
round. There was no sugar goin'—nobody had none—
but plenty of nose-stroking and praise and all that. I
remember one day, when we was riding past a company that was fallen out beside the road, a fella gets
up, waves his hand to Marse Robert and calls out,
"Howdy do, Dad!" Anyone could see he was gone part
crazy, standing blinkin' there in his old rags in the
sunshine. "Howdy do, my man!" answers Marse Robert right away, gives him a smile and on we went. I
don't reckon Marse Robert recognized the fella, but I
remembered him all right. Marse Robert had spoken to
him that night of the battle in the woods, same night
as Cap-in-His-Eyes was hit; he'd been toting ammunition out of a wagon, 'long with three-four other
soldiers. He hadn't been crazy then. He must have had
'nuff to make him, since. There was beginning to be
more and more like that. 'Twas the short rations and
the hard marches—that and the continual fear. And
besides, you know, Tom, there was sickness everywhere. I didn't feel so good myself sometimes. I found
myself getting confused and didn't always understand
what was going on as clear as I used to. 'Twas like
everyone was living in a kind of daze from the hunger
and the fear.

Another thing comes back to me now. One time

when we was out by ourselves, and Marse Robert'd dismounted to take a quick nap under a tree by the road, I was hitched to a post, jest quietly grazing around. After a while I could hear a marching column coming nearer, making a fair lot of noise—you know, laughing and calling out to one another, 'coutrements clattering and all the rest. Then two or three of the men caught sight of Marse Robert, and word went round quick as lightning. They all went by quiet as a bunch of snails; they jest about tiptoed past where we was, not to interrupt Marse Robert's nap.

Mid-June, 1864. General Grant, having during the previous month repeatedly failed, with more than twice their numbers, to defeat the Army of Northern Virginia in the field and finally suffered a severe reverse at Old Cold Harbor, has broken contact, marched across the peninsula east of Richmond and made use of transport boats to throw his army across the James River to the southern bank. From here he has advanced upon the city of Petersburg, twenty miles south of Richmond, but his assault has been halted by the determined resolution of General Beauregard, with no more than two or three thousand men. General Lee, having reached the city with his army on June 18th, has immediately put in hand the necessary dispositions and works to withstand the siege by superior numbers that is now inevitable. This siege, which will extend to include Richmond, is to last for nine and a half months, until the beginning of April, 1865.

I forget, Tom. I forget sech a lot after all this while. But I do remember, 'bout two weeks or so after that battle we won—'time the judge's horse bolted— how we-all rode into the city in the hot sunshine, with all the people out on the streets, a-waving and a-cheering. Of all the things that come your way when you're a soldier, there's nothing more encouraging than marching into a town and seeing all the women and children turn out to holler for you and treat you like a lot of heroes. They was waiting for our fellas at their gates with food and water and flowers to stick in their caps—yeah, and shaking their hands and kissing them, all sweating and dirty as they was from the march. Every now and then some man would dash out of the column and run up the steps of a house to fling his arms round a lady's neck—you know, his mother or his sister—his wife, maybe. 'Twas plain 'nuff to me that the enemy warn't going to be able to get us out of this here city in a hurry. Maybe this was where we'd finally beat them. I'd always knowed we'd do that.

Well, that was when we started what they call the siege. A siege ain't like a battle, you see, Tom, though there's liable to be battles mixed up with it here and there. A siege is when you and the enemy is faced up opposite each other in lines that stretch for miles— lines of trenches dug in the ground—and there's very little moving and no fighting 'cept for the shells and the musket fire. But that don't come all the time. It breaks out more or less like rain, often jest when you're least expecting it. A siege goes on for months— well, that's what this here siege did, anyways. It went on till I'd more or less forgotten there'd ever been anything else.

During that long spell of hot weather after we'd marched into the city, 'twas back to the digging again, jest like two years before, when Marse Robert and me had first took over command of the Army. Day after day, up and down the lines we went, Marse Robert giving orders for what had to be done—revetting, gun emplacements and all the rest of it. I can see it all now —the dust clouding the air, the flies everywhere, the lines of men stripped to the waist, sweating and cussing as they kept on with the digging in the hot sun. There was one way it warn't like two years before, though. They'd used to grumble then, but now they was crazy to get into the ground as fast as they could, 'cause of the enemy shells that was likely to come over 'most any time, day or night. The enemy, they was digging in, too, and they warn't hardly no distance off. By the time we was done, Tom, there was more'n twenty mile of trenches and pits and holes and banks —what we call earthworks—facing each other, ours and the enemy's.

I can't give you no idea of the dirt and mess and the change in the whole country that that siege made. It plumb tore the whole place to ruins, and that's the truth. The fields, the woods, the hedges, the fences, the barns—everything disappeared under that digging and them trenches. All that was left was jest the bare earth dug up into these great ditches and ridges, with our men a-standin' in them, waiting and watching for the chance to fire at the enemy. They lived like rats. There was trenches behind trenches, and trenches running up to jine other trenches like roads, and deep holes the fellas went down when the enemy shells started coming over. Our guns was sited in pits along the lines, and every so often they'd start firing back. The shells did as much as the digging to turn the whole place—miles an' miles—into one great, broken-up mudflat of bare earth and nothin' else.

Our fellas built up the sides of the trenches with logs and posts, to stop 'em falling in. And out in front they often put sort of crisscross fences made of sharp wooden spikes, to hold up the Blue men if they tried to attack. And then all along the lines, in special places, there was what they call sharpshooters—fellas who jest kept watching all the time for the chance to fire at any Blue man who showed above ground. He only had to show hisself for jest a moment and that'd be 'nuff. 'Course, the enemy had their sharpshooters, too. There was lots of fellas killed that way. 'Twarn't safe to be above ground nohow.

During the first weeks it was hot, with dust everywhere, but after that it commenced to raining. It rained day after day, till everything was mud and all the trenches was flooded. I've seed men standing waist-deep in water, soaked through and no shelter nowhere. There was any amount of sickness. The horses went sick as much as the men. They was wet through, you see—no shelter—and starved. There was plenty of horses simply couldn't pull the guns no more, what with the mud and with being so weak. You should jest have seed some of them trenches, Tom: the bottoms full of stinking water, and worse'n water; old shelters—if'n you could call 'em shelters—made of boards all falling to pieces; piles of rubbish, tangles of tree roots sticking out of the sides; and a bullet waiting for anyone who showed his head over the top. But still the Blue men didn't try no more attacks. They'd larned what they could expect from us, I reckon.

'Most every day Marse Robert and me would ride the whole length of the lines, more'n twenty mile. 'Course, we mostly kept back behind the worst places, but even so 'twas hard going and I was often stumbling and having a hard job to pick my way and guess where to put my hooves down. If there's one thing frightens any horse, it's bad going underfoot. All the same, Marse Robert didn't really have to pay all that much attention to me. We understood each other so well that I always knowed what he wanted and what I had to do.

The lines went right up northward, as far as that other city—the first one I'd ever seed when I came up from the South with Marse Robert. I recognized it soon as we got back there, and the big river where I'd first heared enemy fire. I'll tell you, Tom, 'twas a hard day's journey up there and back, from one city to t'other, over so much broken ground. I don't believe any other horse could have done it—no, not Skylark hisself. When we got back at night, I'd get a rub and a feed and then I'd sleep through enemy shellfire, horses coming and going—anything.

The enemy shells was likely to fall anywhere and any time. Our headquarters was in the yard of a house a little ways outside the city, jest 'longside a river. It belonged to an old lady who was an invalid and couldn't get about much at all. She was real pleased to have Marse Robert and his officers, and did all she could for them. But 'course Marse Robert didn't live in the house; he had the tents put up in the yard, same's he'd always done everywheres else. He'd had the same old tent ever since I'd been with him, and I remember 'twas 'bout this time that he finally agreed that it had got so battered and full of holes he'd have to get another one. The stables was comfortable 'nuff, but you never knowed when the shells'd start coming over. Everyone got used to 'em after a time and jest took no notice, though I can recall one particular night when we was all led out in the pouring rain and taken a fair ways off, on account of they'd begun dropping a little too close.

Another day, when Marse Robert and me was riding out to the lines, we'd come a ways out of town when he stopped to talk to a little girl tending a baby beside a garden gate. An enemy shell fell in the field nearby, but this little girl took no notice of it at all. Marse Robert asked her who she was and whose baby it was, and when she'd told him he told her to go back home and take the baby to a safer place.

We often came under fire, of course, riding up and down the lines. Marse Robert never took no notice on our 'count, but he was quick 'nuff to tell off anyone else, officers or men, if he reckoned they was risking theirselves unnecessarily. I remember one time when he stopped to talk to some of our fellas that had their guns set up in the yard of a house we'd taken over. 'Course, soon's they knowed he was there, all the soldiers come a-crowding round to see him, and talk to him, too, if'n they could get the chance. The Blue men must 'a been able to spot us, 'cause pretty soon their shells started falling close around. Marse Robert told the men to leave him and go to the rear; they warn't to expose theirselves to unnecessary danger. So off they went. I stayed where I'd been hitched, of course, and from where I was I seed Marse Robert walk acrost the yard and bend down. There was a fledgling sparrow had fallen on the ground, and he picked it up and put it back in the nest. When he came back to unhitch me, he patted my neck and muttered something 'bout me being of more value than many sparrows. Well, I thought, I should jest 'bout hope I was; and I reckoned at that rate maybe we could hightail it out of the way of the durned shells. But Marse Robert always took care not to let anyone see we was in any hurry to do that.

There was plenty of fighting all that summer—more'n I can recall now—but the time I 'specially remember is the battle we fought after the big bang—the biggest bang of the lot. I still don't know what made it. 'Twas well on into the night—early morning, in fact—and I was sound asleep at headquarters. When the bang came, 'twas a long ways off, but it fair shook the ground, real heavy: a monstrous great bang! That was no gun made that. I'd never heared the like. All the other horses was awake and real scared with the shaking. We couldn't none of us tell what to make of it, you see. Real soon nearly all of us was saddled up and led out. All the same, 'twas some time before headquarters started into action. I guess Marse Robert was waiting for news of what had happened. When a mounted officer finally reached us, Marse Robert listened to what he had to tell him and then gave out his orders right away.

'Far as I could make out from this officer's horse, the Blue men had somehow or other managed to blow a great hole—kind of a huge pit—right in the middle of our lines on t'other side of the river, 'bout a couple of mile from where we was at. A lot of our men had been killed, and now the enemy was doing their best to fight their way through the gap. I couldn't make it out at all, but anyways I didn't have long to wait around thinking 'bout it, 'cause Marse Robert and me set off right away, entirely by ourselves. Everywhere was soldiers staring and talking and trying to make out what was going on. When we got to Red Shirt's headquarters, we found he'd already left to get his fellas together, so me and Marse Robert followed after him. 'Twas all a jumble and a confusion, but after a while we got out of town into the open, and then we came to a place where we could actually see this here hole the enemy had made. 'Twas as big as the field out here, Tom—bigger, I reckon—and a great mass of thick smoke hanging over it. There was fighting all around—bursting shells and musket fire—but so much confusion that you couldn't tell which was our men and which was the enemy.

There was a young officer with Marse Robert— one of Red Shirt's headquarters people. Marse Robert told him that at all costs the Blue men had got to be stopped and we must go back and hurry our fellas forward. We went back, but the men was already coming up as fast as they could, so Marse Robert rode me off to a house a little ways from where the hole was and waited to see what would happen.

From what I could make out, there must 'a been thousands of Blue men crowded into that there hole, ready to beat us to pieces and go on into the city.

They'd begun to spread out either side, too, along our lines. But by this time our guns had started firing and that was holding 'em up. We was so close to the hole, Marse Robert and me, that we could see the Blue men moving 'bout and getting ready to come on. Suddenly they began jumping down and running forward, and jest at the same moment our fellas advanced to meet them.

Well, you couldn't hardly see what was going on for the smoke and the dirt throwed up by the shellfire. That was as near as I ever come to going wild in a battle, I reckon. If'n I could, I'd have bolted, 'cause Marse Robert had gone up to the top of the house, where he could see best, and there was no one near us horses at all.

The fighting went on a long time, and no one could tell who was winning. Marse Robert never moved from where he was, and I reckoned he meant to stay till either we'd driven the Blue men out or else we hadn't no more soldiers left. 'Twas the middle of the afternoon afore things died down. Big bunches of the enemy had begun to surrender, and the rest had come out of the hole and skedaddled back to their own lines. When Marse Robert finally came down and mounted me again, I could tell at once't that he was wore out. But he was mighty cheered, too, that we'd beat 'em back. He must 'a been real anxious for hours —maybe more anxious than he'd ever been in a battle before. I reckon we'd never come so close to being beat.

We never rode right up to that big hole, Marse Robert and me. But Marse Taylor did, after the fighting, and later on his horse told me 'twas the worst thing he'd ever seed in his life. There was guns and weapons and bodies all laying together, half in and half out of the earth. The whole bottom of the crater, as they called it, was covered with dead men, this horse said. He'd thought he'd got used to bad things, but he hoped he'd never see nothing like that again.

I still don't know jest how the enemy blowed that there crater, but we'd evidently made them give up the idea, 'cause they never tried nothing like it again.

Old Pete came back to the Army in the fall. I was surprised to see him, 'cause I'd figured he must 'a died after being shot in the wilderness battle. But now he 'peared to be jest the same as ever in his spirits, though the wound had left him lookin' awful bad. He sure was a real tough soldier, even if he was given to argufying, and I reckon Marse Robert was glad to see him again.

The winter came on, but still there was no let-up in the siege. Conditions in the trenches was bad as could be, and 'twas plain 'nuff that the men was getting 'most nothing to eat; they all looked mighty puny – jest skin and bones, a lot of 'em. Us horses didn't do no better. Many a time I'd have to make the best of a night in stables with less'n half a feed in my stomach. But 'twas worse for the horses and mules on the lines. There was a plenty died, Tom, I can tell you.

There was mighty little to burn, too. We 'most never seed a fire when we was riding down the lines. All the wood there was had been burned up long ago. The men got real filthy, too, living in them soaking-wet trenches and dugouts. There was no soap, and 'course they couldn't heat no water for washing. I could tell how much it upset Marse Robert to see them in sech a bad way. He'd stop to talk to groups of fellas here and there, and one'd say, "I got no boots, General," or, "I ain't had a meal in two days, General." "Oh, Traveller," he said to me once't, when we was riding away from a bunch of 'em on the lines, "what can I do? Where's it going to end? Jest got to go on, that's all." He was beginning to look grayer hisself and a durned sight older, and often at the end of a day I

could tell from the way he dismounted that he was
wore out.

'Twas a strange life. Sometimes we'd be out all
day on the lines in all sorts o' wind and weather, and
then again we'd ride up to the big city and spend a few
hours at Marse Robert's home with the old lady. Even
in them days she was a cripple: she was in a rolling
chair. She used to do all she could to persuade Marse
Robert to give hisself an easier life. 'Twas her and Major Taylor between them that finally got Marse Robert
to agree, for his own sake, to move headquarters out
of tents and into a house with stables. This house belonged to a man called Mr. Turnbull and 'twas 'bout
two mile outside the city where the Blue men had
blowed the hole in the ground. I felt better when we'd
moved in there. Everyone was more comfortable,
horses and men.

Not that there was any more to eat. People used
to send Marse Robert presents of food, but he'd never
accept them. I heared him tell Colonel Marshall one
day that he wouldn't eat any blamed thing that was
better'n what the men had. As for the horses, I know
'twas a hard business for the Army to keep any cavalry together at all. Every scrap of fodder was gone
and the horses had to be sent miles away, all over the
country, jest to find 'nuff to survive.

Things went on like this for months, till at last the
leaves started to show on the trees again and the
weather took a turn for the better. I was glad to see
the spring coming, 'cause I knowed it would bring on
the time when we'd settle with the Blue men once't
and for all. Oh, sure, I knowed it was going to be a
hard 'nuff job, but even I didn't foresee what it would
cost us or what a desperate business 'twas going to
turn out.

XIX

LATE MARCH, 1865. The tattered, starving Army of
Northern Virginia, reduced to some 50,000 effectives and those irreplaceable, with no lack of
men ailing from prolonged exposure to mud and rain,
of men carrying in their pockets letters from wives or
parents telling of conditions at home grown desperate
on account of their long absence, continues to hold
forty miles of half-flooded earthworks against the
overwhelming numbers of General Grant. With the
irretrievable loss of the Shenandoah Valley in early
March, General Sheridan's cavalry have perforce become free—spreading destruction on their way—to
join the Union forces besieging Richmond and Petersburg. The Confederate troops are so thin on the
ground and so short of ammunition that if it were not
for the dread with which their past fighting power has
filled the hearts of the enemy, the line would long ago
have been broken. General Lee, whose courage and
endurance continue to inspire his men as no other
general's since Alexander, has far too much military
discernment to be under any delusion. Both his men
and his horses are worn out and he has no reserves
whatever. With the ending of winter, either the breaking of his line or the turning of his flank—most probably, he thinks, the southern, Petersburg flank—is inevitable. "You must not be surprised if calamity befalls
us," he wrote in early February to the Secretary of
War. His advice that he should withdraw the army

westward into mountain terrain, where it could subsist
indefinitely as a fighting force, having been rejected by
President Davis with the insistence that at all costs
Richmond must be held to the last, what can he do but
put his trust in God, set a daily example of staunch-
ness and valor to officers and men and await what his
young aide, Colonel Taylor, has termed "the dread
contingency"?

My goodness, Tom, I never 'spected anything like this,
did you? 'Course, I'd seed they was building a new
house for Marse Robert, but I never dreamt part of it
was going to be this big new stable for me. I can't get
over it! Marse Robert led me in hisself s'afternoon and
made sure everything was jest the way it ought to be.
Ain't it mighty fine? Not a draft in the place, and
Marse Robert's quarters right 'longside! I've never
been so well stabled in all my born days, and all I can
say is I hope Marse Robert feels the same. Do you
know what he said when he brung me in here this
evening? He said it was going to be real fine to be
under the same roof with his old friend. 'Going to
make a lot of difference to both of us, these new quarters are, 'cause the truth is we're neither of us as young
as we was and we can both do with some extra com-
fort. Why don't you settle down there in the straw
and make yourself at home? This is a sight better'n
them lines I was telling you 'bout—the lines we was
holding opposite the Blue men in the siege, with next
to nothing to eat and shells likely to start dropping
any time of the day or night. Yes, we've certainly seed
some hard times, me and Marse Robert, so maybe
we're entitled to feel we've earned a home even as
good as this 'un.

I promised to tell you, didn't I, 'bout our very last
campaign, after the siege ended? Well, an' that sure *was*
a bad time—'bout the worst I can remember, but the

way it finally ended was jest 'bout the most surprising thing that happened in all the years me and Marse Robert's been together. You see, Marse Robert had decided—I knowed he had—that by this time we'd all done more'n 'nuff of this here fighting, and that now the spring was coming we had to finish those people off once and for all. Yeah, but that warn't so easy done —no, not even by Marse Robert hisself. You see, first of all 'twas a question of picking the best place— where to go about it. That's what us soldiers call strategy, you know, Tom—picking the right time and place to fight. Well, you've done it yourself, han't you? And that spring we had to try a whole lot of times, and a whole lot of places, looking for the right one.

I remember—oh, yeah, I remember this all right— being woke up in the pitch dark at that there Turnbull headquarters of ours and being saddled up by Dave. What the heck's coming now, I thought; some shenanigans, I'll lay. Well, if'n I'm not used to that by now I don't know a horse in the Army that is. I could make out Marse Robert standing outside the door, all dressed and ready, with Marse Taylor and a lot more. I was led up, he mounted me and off we rode in the dark.

We didn't go all that far, though; we went jest acrost to a hill behind our lines, where another of our commanders, General Gordon, was stood waiting for Marse Robert. Down in front of us the trenches was crowded with our fellas, getting ready to attack. I could feel it. Before an attack, you see, Tom, there's always something—well, real uneasy—in the air, and the horses can feel it as much as the men. But this was the most silent thing I'd ever knowed. 'Twas all along of doing it at night, I guess; the Blue men didn't know what we was up to and we didn't want 'em to find out.

Then, away off in the dark, some fella fired a gun, and that was the signal for our men to advance. There was plenty of yelling and firing started up then all right, but me and Marse Robert, we jest stood and waited where we was at. As it growed light, you could make out the fighting, way out at a kind of fort on the Blue men's line, but as Marse Robert still didn't move, I figured it couldn't be going too well. I could feel as much, too, from the look of the officers coming back to report to Marse Robert, and the way they spoke. We stayed where we was about four hours, I guess, till finally Marse Robert, he give the order to stop the fighting and come back. But my land! Tom, coming back, there was a power of our poor fellas knocked over by musket fire. The Blue men had brung up reinforcements, you see, and they was jest too many for us. Oh, yeah, they was fine and dandy as long as we was going t'other way. 'Parently this was one time when we hadn't been able to beat 'em like we usually did.

So that was the first time. Natcherly, Marse Robert was disappointed and I could tell, like I always could, that he felt sad and upset. I remember how we rode back, him and me, almost by ourselves, and how we met young Marse Rob and Marse Rooney coming to meet us. Soon as he seed them, he smiled and showed how glad he was. He did his best to act like there was nothing gone wrong; thanked them for coming so quick, and said he was sorry to have to tell them their cavalry wouldn't be needed after all. It didn't fool Marse Rob's horse none, though. "My stars, Traveller!" he says to me when we was side by side. "What the heck's gone wrong?" I told him I reckoned our attack must 'a failed. "Oh, well," he says, "then I guess we shan't have to be killed jest yet, shall we?"

There warn't very long to wait till the second time. Best as I can recall, it come 'bout four days later, and it happened a good way to the west, outside the city. 'Twas a real nasty morning, pouring with rain, and Marse Robert rode me out—I remember the mud over my fetlocks; jiminy, how I hate deep mud!—to meet General Ringlets. 'Course, I couldn't understand all they said to each other, but 'fore Marse Robert and me rode back to headquarters, I'd got it that General Ringlets had been ordered to attack those people. So this'll be it, I thought. Ringlets'll hammer them to bits, like he did with his charge that time in the big battle up north.

All the same, Marse Robert didn't seem in a very good humor. I couldn't tell why; but 'course, he always knowed everything, and maybe he'd already figured it out that we might not be able to finish the Blue men off this time—'cause the way things turned out, we didn't.

Next morning it was still raining, and out we went, Marse Robert and me—I remember how hungry I was, and wondering whether Marse Robert felt the same; there was never more'n half of nothing to eat, you know, Tom—to see how Ringlets was getting on. There was a whole chance of fighting going on up ahead, but I couldn't make things out all that clearly. We didn't meet Ringlets, but Marse Robert told some of the other generals they was to go on and attack. He was jest finishing the talking when our fellas started in on their own account—that's how keen they was! This time we *did* go forward, Marse Robert and me, 'cause we could see the Blue men dashing away like crazy acrost a little creek. We came up to the creek and I remember we come on a whole crowd of enemy prisoners there. Marse Robert walks me over to 'em. There was one officer bleeding something terrible; he couldn't hardly stand. "Are you badly wounded, Major?" asks Marse Robert. "Yes, sir," answers the major, "I figure I am." "Oh, I'm sorry. I *am* sorry, Major," says Marse Robert. Then he turns to the fellas in charge of the prisoners and says, "Be sure and take good care of

him, gentlemen." It reminded me of that time after the
battle up north, when that other enemy fella had been
shouting out, "Hurrah for the Union!"

'Twarn't long after that when General Eppa came
riding back to us out of the fighting. You remember,
Tom, don't you, I told you 'bout General Eppa, and
how me and Marse Robert rode along with him and
Ringlets one of the days when we was marching up
north to the big river? I told you how his horse, Sovereign, said he'd got a notion we might get beat and I
told him he was talking hogwash.

General Eppa was riding this same Sovereign
now. They came up to us looking like they'd both
been dragged through a hedge backwards. Sovereign
was limping, and bleeding plenty from a great, ragged
gash 'long his flank. General Eppa's scabbard was bent
almost double and he had three separate bullet holes
through his jacket.

"Thunder and lightning, Traveller," says Sovereign, "we've had a time, I'll tell you! There's 'nuff Blue
men out there to start a town, and you'd think the air
was made of bullets. We're lucky to be alive. Our fellas are going to have to retreat—nothin' else for it."

What with the way things was going, Marse Robert warn't in a very good temper, and he spoke sharp
to General Eppa. "I wish you'd sew those places up,"
he says, pointing to the bullet holes. "I don't like to
see them."

Well, natcherly, that annoyed General Eppa, after
all he'd jest been through. 'Course, he couldn't talk
back to Marse Robert, but all the same he found
something to say. "General Lee," he answered, "allow
me to go back home and see my wife and I will have
them sewed up."

Well, come down to it, Marse Robert had always
liked Eppa, and this tickled him. "The idea," he says,

"the *idea* of talking about going to see wives! It's perfectly ridiculous, sir."

I can't remember jest how we finished up, that day. But that was the second time, and it hadn't worked out any better'n the first.

But there was worse to come, if'n only I knowed. Let me see, it warn't that night—no, 'twas the night after—when heavy enemy firing and shelling started up in the dark. Marse Robert was in bed at headquarters, and Old Pete and Red Shirt was there talking to him. All us horses was wide awake, of course—you couldn't be nothing else. All of a sudden Marse Robert and the others came hurrying out of the house and stood around trying to make out what was going on. 'Twas still awful dark and no one could see much, but after a minute Red Shirt said something to Marse Robert and went dashing for his horse. I knowed his horse well, of course. He was the same one he'd had all along—old Champ. Champ was even more of a veteran 'n what I was. He'd been with Red Shirt longer'n I'd been with Marse Robert, carried him through 'nuff bangs and bullets for fifty horses and never seemed no different any time you met him, day or night—always very easy and friendly in his ways. I'd always cottoned to him and respected him. As Red Shirt mounted, I gave him a quick, friendly nicker, and jest at the same moment I heared Major Venable call out to Red Shirt to take care and not go risking hisself. Then they was gone. Red Shirt was off to jine his men.

By this time you could see a bit more, and as Dave was saddling me up I could make out soldiers—long lines of 'em—way off acrost the fields in the distance. I had a horrible feeling they must be those people. Marse Robert hadn't even been dressed when all the trouble started, but didn't take him long. He came out in full uniform and wearing his sword, mounted me and off we went, out into those fields.

Well, they was Blue men, all right—a whole passel. You could see 'em coming on quite steady, and
nothing at all to stop 'em, 'far as I could see. I wondered what in tarnation we was a-goin' to do, but
Marse Robert, he jest sat there watching them and
talking quietly to Major Venable and some of the others was with us.

Suddenly a little bunch of officers came galloping
back to us. They was Red Shirt's people. Champ was
in the middle of 'em, but Red Shirt warn't riding him.
The soldier riding him was a fella called Sergeant
Tucker. This Sergeant Tucker was well knowed for a
real wildcat. He was Red Shirt's special man, who always stuck right 'longside him in any fighting, to do
what he wanted. Champ had told me more'n once't
that Tucker was one fella who didn't give a damn for
nothing and was always ready to eat twenty Blue men
before breakfast. 'Peared that one time, when he'd
wanted a new horse, he'd jest rode out and shot a Blue
cavalryman, helped hisself and rode back. Leastways,
so Champ told me.

"Champ!" I said as they came up to us. "Champ!
For land's sake, what's happened? Where's Red
Shirt?"

"Red Shirt's dead," said Champ. I could see now
that for once't he was shook up real bad.

"Can't be!" I said. "What d'you mean?"

"Red Shirt and Tucker—he was on Merlin—jest
the two of us—we was riding ahead alone," says
Champ. "We come up with two of the enemy, and Red
Shirt calls out to them to surrender. They fired at us.
They hit Red Shirt—killed him stone dead, right there
on my back. His body fell out o' the saddle. When
Tucker seed what had happened, he come 'longside
and grabbed my bridle. He pulled both of us—me and
Merlin—round and got us away. But then he got off
Merlin and left him loose. He rode me back."

Sergeant Tucker had evidently been telling Marse Robert the same thing. I'd never knowed Marse Robert to cry before—although I think maybe he did that time when they told him Jine-the-Cavalry had been killed. Anyway, he shed tears now. I could feel him sob where he was a-sitting.

I was thinking, Where's it going to end? How much more do we have to pay to beat those people? Cap-in-His-Eyes, Jine-the-Cavalry and now Red Shirt. Vot-you-voz, too—he'd been wounded real bad and out of it ever since the summer before; I'd heared that much from Skylark. It had been Old Pete, too, near as a touch; he'd never be like he was. I don't mind telling you, Tom, I felt shook up bad. General Red Shirt—it didn't seem possible he could be shot dead in the saddle like any soldier out on patrol!

Well, the Blue men was still a-coming on, and a minute or two later one of their shells went straight through our headquarters house. By this time we'd got our guns up and all round outside it, blazing away, and this was holding 'em up considerable. Marse Robert—well, you could tell he was real angry now. He simply wouldn't move from where we was at. The house caught fire, burning like a haystack, and enemy bullets began falling all round us; but still Marse Robert wouldn't quit. He waited there, and he stuck there till the last moment. In the end he had to put me into a gallop so we could get away. He very soon pulled up, though. Marse Robert didn't no ways care for running from the Blue men—he never did. He was still sitting looking back at 'em when a shell burst only a few feet behind us. It killed one of the headquarters horses—a nice old gelding called Crockett; I'd knowed him a long time. I was actually spattered with his blood, poor fella. Marse Robert turned me again, but even then he still waited a few moments, looking back over his shoulder. I could hear him actually growling, he was that mad. I believe if'n he'd had his way he'd have turned me round and charged those people by hisself. But of course he was the General, warn't he? He had to be thinking of the Army. So we come out of it, and back among our own fellas.

"This is a bad business, Colonel," says Marse Robert to one of them. "The line's been stretched till it's broken."

All morning the fighting went on something desperate. Marse Robert rode me back only as far as a bit of a hump standing up above a creek, and there he dismounted and stood looking out at what was happening to our fellas. Him an' me, we was under sech heavy fire ourselves we might jest as well have been out there with 'em. I was 'specting to be blowed to bits any minute, like Crockett. Time and again horsemen'd come up to us. They was asking—beseeching Marse Robert—for reinforcements; I could tell that. Marse Robert has to tell 'em he ain't got none. I remember at last he says to some officer, real sharp, "I've received that message several times, and I've no troops to send!" The colonel, he jest salutes and says, "I can't help it, General, how often you've heared it, I've got to give you General Longstreet's message." So then Marse Robert tells him he's sorry he spoke sharp; but jest the same he hadn't got no more fellas—nary a one.

Well, we held 'em off, Tom, though to this day I don't know how. I got sort of confused with all the bangs and the men and horses falling all around, but I recollect that in the afternoon me and Marse Robert come back out of it, and he rode me off to some house a little ways outside town. He'd got his plans, had Marse Robert—I knowed that—and he meant to spend the evening giving 'em out to our generals and the rest.

So that was the third time that hadn't worked. And 'twas that same night that our Army marched out of the city to find a better place to beat the Blue men.

And I'll tell you, Tom, that looking around at what there was to be seed, I was honestly beginning to wonder whether we *would* find it. I mean, all our cavalry was close as dammit to exhaustion, and as for the guns—well, a lot of the carriages was dropping to pieces and being dragged along by wore-out old horses in rotten harness. I should have knowed better, shouldn't I? Fancy the likes of me doubting Marse Robert! Still, I figure you'd have had your own doubts if you'd 'a been there.

Our fellas marched real quiet out of the city, I guess so as not to let those people know we was going. Marse Robert rode me by one of the bridges acrost the river and drew up where the road forked. I soon got the general idea, 'cause I recognized a lot o' the horses —yeah, and some of the soldiers, too. Old Pete and his 'uns was to go by one road and General Gordon's outfit by the other—so they wouldn't foul each other up, you see. Marse Robert and me, we waited there dead silent while they went by—no drums, no orders, no cussin'—they could have been ghosts in the dark; jest the wagons creaking and the Blue men's guns way off in the distance. One lot after another—I knowed 'em all—and the state they was in, Tom, it would have upset even you; rags an' mud, skin an' bones. Some of the horses nickered to me—they all knowed me, you see—but I kept quiet, 'cording to orders. When they'd all of them gone by, and not before, me and Marse Robert came on with headquarters.

By the time it got light, the Army was well out of town. The fellas was resting 'long the roadsides, and 'course Marse Robert and me was going round as usual, talking to them and cheering them up. They was in good spirits, mostly—glad to get out of them miserable trenches, I reckon, and be marching off somewhere, even if they didn't know where. I figured the whole idea was real smart of Marse Robert. Now, you see, Tom, the Blue men would have to leave their own trenches and come out where we could fight them good and proper and give 'em a real hammering.

Jest the same, the roads was awful muddy, and 'course our Army using 'em didn't make things no better. I seed plenty of fellas caked in mud to the knees, and you simply couldn't tell whether they had any boots or not. Evidently we warn't getting on fast 'nuff, and I could tell this was worrying Marse Robert. Although the enemy didn't seem to be anywheres round this morning, he plainly wanted us to press on— maybe so's we could catch them when they warn't expecting us; I couldn't say. All the same, he hadn't the heart to speak sharp to them poor fellas scrabbling and crawling through the mud, although two-three times he stopped to tell drivers to have more patience with their mules. I never had much time for mules, Tom, as I've told you, but I felt real sorry for 'em now. They jest warn't in no state to shift the loads, and that was all 'twas to it. The drivers had to call on any fellas that was around to come and push.

All the same, 'bout midday something happened which showed me Marse Robert still knowed we had the Blue men halfway up a tree. Him and Old Pete and some more of headquarters felt easy 'nuff to stop off for dinner at a fine, smart house. 'Twas jest like old times. We-all left the column and rode 'bout a mile through the woods, and there was this real handsome place—white pillars, gardens, ladies and gentlemen walkin' about and talking, darkies serving drinks and standing by to take the horses—after all we'd been through during the last months 'twas like a dream. Marse Robert hadn't slept all night, of course, but jest the same he offs with his hat and shakes hands like he was real fresh and we had nothing to do 'cept enjoy ourselves.

A darky led me off to a fine, clean stable and I

found myself 'longside a pretty young mare, name of
Emerald. This Emerald was in lovely condition, full of
energy, coat groomed and shining like a meadow on a
summer morning. I could tell she didn't cotton much
to me. She didn't know nothing 'bout the fighting—
nothing at all—I don't think she even knowed there
was any fighting. She figured I must be some old courier horse dropped by with the mail, or something of
that. When I asked her how she'd avoided being took
for the Army she didn't even know what I was talking
'bout. But after a while, from her talk, I caught on that
the house belonged to a big local fella, Judge Cox, and
she was his wife's horse. That was how she'd been
able to dodge the column. I couldn't dislike her, and
anyway the darky stableman groomed me a real treat
and gave me the best feed I'd had in months. I felt
ready to bust.

But all too soon the time came to go on. I was led
back round to the front and Marse Robert came out,
talking with a pretty young lady and smelling like
he'd had a real good meal for a change. I guess we all
felt in better spirits. The young lady, she petted me,
stroked my nose and said she'd heared so much 'bout
the famous Traveller. Marse Robert told her I was
worth as much to him as two regiments, and a lot
more nonsense o' that sort. They was funning around
for quite a few minutes 'fore we finally rode off
through the woods and back to the column of march.

After the judge's house, and being with that Emerald, you could see a lot plainer what we must look
like to anyone as hadn't seed us before: the broke-up
lines of tattered fellas limping through the mud, and
the starving teams, lot of 'em collapsing as they tried
to pull the rickety, broke-down wagons. There was
stragglers, too, plenty of 'em, all the way back 'long
the road. We looked a real bunch of drifters, Tom, an'

that's no more'n the truth. Rags and bones a-marching by packs.

That night we crossed another river—that's to say, the Army did. You never seed sech a turmoil in all your life. There was too many at the one bridge, and all the roadway and the fields and banks was crammed up with soldiers and guns and horses waiting to get acrost. They was all night crossing. Me and Marse Robert waited, going from one place to another, talking to as many fellas as we could, cheering folks up. The Blue men had found out by this time what we-all was up to—leastways, I reckon they had, 'cause every now and then I could hear firing away in the distance.

I guess it must 'a been 'bout two hours after sunrise 'fore me and Marse Robert crossed that bridge. I remember a young officer riding up to report to Marse Robert. As he was speaking, Marse Robert looks him up and down and then he says, "Did those people surprise you this morning?" The young fella 'pears kinda throwed for a loop, but he answers no, certainly not. Marse Robert says that by the look of him they must have. He points at his boots, one trouser leg in and t'other out. The lad felt 'shamed—you could see that. He never said 'nother word—jest saluted and turned his horse to ride off. Marse Robert calls him back and tells him, kind as you like, that it's important he should take care and steer clear of anything that might make our fellas think the Blue men had scared him. He had to set an example.

Well, the Army went a-marching on. Marse Robert and me, we was along with Old Pete. It felt like old times, 'ceptin' I warn't the only one could have eaten his own harness. Jest the same, everyone seemed in real fighting spirits. There was plenty of laughing and joking—singing, too. I knowed it was 'cause we was on our way to beat the Blue men once't and for all. 'Fact, I couldn't help wondering how those people had

ever s'posed it would be any good trying to beat
Marse Robert. The whole idea was jest plain crazy.

I can't recollect everything after all this time, but
I'll tell you something, Tom, that I certainly do remember—something that happened that same evening. By this time the enemy cavalry had started feeling round us—kind of hanging 'bout and watching for
a chance; only they seemed a-scairt of us. Old Pete
kept trying to get at 'em, but 'peared like he couldn't
make it, and after a while Marse Robert took me out
to have a look around for hisself. I trotted a ways
down the road towards the firing, and then, jest as we
came up to where our cavalry was engaged, a passel of
Blue men came galloping towards us. 'Course, our fellas went straight for 'em and Marse Robert, he natcherly jined in, 'cause this time there warn't nobody to
stop him. The Blue men, they went riding off real fast
—knowed what was good for 'em—'ceptin' for one
fella, who come dashing straight on towards us. Four
or five of our men was jest going to fire when Marse
Robert, in his deep voice, calls out, "Don't shoot!
Don't shoot!" Someone caught the Blue man's bridle
and stopped him. He was wounded bad and hadn't
been able to control his horse, but Marse Robert had
been the only one to see it.

I had a good rest that night. Headquarters was
pitched in a big yard outside a house. 'Twas quiet,
with plenty of trees and grass. Us horses was tethered
there and left to graze. That raised my spirits quite
some, but by morning it had commenced to rain and
come on a real nasty day.

April 5, 1865. General Lee's intention in leaving the
lines at Richmond and Petersburg has been to march
westward, join General Johnston in North Carolina
and engage the Union forces under Sherman. To
achieve this, however, he must outstrip pursuit by

General Grant. After a forced march of some forty
miles, including a confused and stressful night crossing of the Appomattox River, the famished army has
reached Amelia Court House to find that the food expected to be delivered by railroad has not arrived. Efforts to commandeer provisions in the surrounding
countryside have wasted a vital day and produced almost nothing. The army is now literally starving. During the early afternoon, General Lee, riding southward
with Longstreet, has come upon the enemy strongly
entrenched across his intended line of march to Dan-
ville. For his exhausted troops to attack is out of the
question. The only possible course is a further night
march to Farmville, some twenty-five miles west. It is
not long before signs of disintegration begin to appear.

There was some mighty tired horses when we set
out that night, and I have to say that I hadn't exactly
been counting on another night march myself. Still, I
thought, it'll be worth it to finish those people off.
Anyway, I'm the General's horse. I've got to set an
example.

Well, you know, Tom, any night march is bound
to be full of stops and confusions and no one knowing
rightly what's going on—and goodness knows I've
been in 'nuff of 'em—but this was one to beat the
band. First of all, 'twas a real mean little track. I seed
that much 'fore it got dark. And I guess more men and
animals must 'a gone over it that one night than all its
other nights put together. Pretty soon it was a mass of
mud, full of soldiers and wagons jammed spang together like flies on a dead mule. Somewhere up ahead
of where me and Marse Robert was, the enemy's cavalry had made a sudden attack and the road was
blocked with smashed-up wagons. We had to wait I
dunno how long 'fore the way was cleared and things
got sorted out.

Some time later, Marse Robert had stopped off for

supper at a gentleman's house, and I was having a bit of a feed myself, when a courier came dashing up. I guessed something else must 'a gone wrong, and I warn't mistaken neither. Marse Robert came straight out and we set off up the road. We hadn't gone more'n a mile or two 'fore we came up with the trouble, right by a little creek. Our guns had been too heavy for the bridge—if'n you could call it a bridge. 'Twas jest smashed to matchsticks. Marse Robert stuck around a considerable time, till he was satisfied the engineers had got down to fixing it, and then on we went, him and me, in and out through the biggest mess you can imagine: foundered horses, lost soldiers; false alarms and shouting in the dark; fellas so jumpy they was ready to loose off at anything—and me with not the least idea what was under my hooves from one moment t' the next. Marse Robert, he was jest like the moon on a windy night—the only calm thing in the whole durned welter. His hands, his voice—they was all that kept me steady. Else I'd have bolted. Lot of horses did.

As it growed light, what was puzzling me—although I was that tuckered out I was nigh on past being puzzled 'bout anything—was that 'parently we was fighting a battle while both armies was on the march. Usually, Tom, you see, when you fight a battle, at least one side's standing where they mean to stay put. Well, I thought, Marse Robert's up to all the tricks; I guess he's trying some new sort of plan to catch up with the Blue men and beat 'em while they're trying to get away. But foals and mares! don't it jest 'bout take it out of you? I felt ready to fall down, and I don't quit easy, Tom, you know.

'Twas jest at that moment, while we was stood still, that I suddenly noticed a horse almost under my hooves—a horse laying abandoned in the ditch. There was nothing so very remarkable in that—there was horses a-laying in ditches all along the road. But then I recognized him—and at the same moment he recognized me. 'Twas Ruffian, the sorrel that had been my very first friend when we was colts together, back in the big meadow where we was foaled and Jim trained me. He was laying there in the mud, his sides heaving and ragged strips of harness still sticking to him where he'd been cut loose.

"Jeff," he gasped, best as he could. "Jeff Davis, is that you?"

'Course, I'd forgotten that name—I hadn't been called Jeff Davis for years. I dropped my nose down towards his.

"Ruffian!" I said. "What's happened? Where's your man?"

"I couldn't—couldn't pull the gun no more, Jeff," he said. "They cut me loose and left me. I figure I'm on the way out."

" 'Course you're not," I said. "You're going to be all right." But looking at him, I couldn't believe it.

"I'm glad to have seed you again, Jeff," he said. He was panting for air. "Them was good days with Jim and Andy, warn't they?"

Marse Robert had been holding me steady all this time. Do you know, I'm sure that somehow or other he'd guessed we knowed each other? No other man would have seed as much—and at sech a time as that, too—but *he* did.

After a few seconds he looked all round us and called to a couple of teamsters who'd pulled off the track to fix a shifted load. They came over and saluted.

"This horse here," says Marse Robert, pointing to Ruffian, "he only needs some care and attention to put him right. He's jest exhausted. Get him out of that ditch and see to him."

"Sure will, General," says one of them, and right away they set about heaving Ruffian out o' the mud.

Jest then an officer comes up at the gallop. Marse Robert hears him out; then he says, "Very well, Captain. Tell him I'm coming right away." The captain rides off again. Marse Robert turned my head into the road and we was gone. Horses forever saying goodbye.

Now you know, Tom, don't you, why I was so happy to meet Ruffian that morning in the hills two years back, when me and Marse Robert and the family was staying at that there big place, The White? That was the first I knowed that he'd survived. I hope he's still doing fine. No reason why he shouldn't be, I reckon. *You* are, ain't you? And I sure am.

When it came full daylight, we stopped off a while at a little village where Old Pete's lot was marching in. I got a rest and some grazing while Marse Robert talked a long while with Old Pete. Then we set out—jest Marse Robert and me; I can't remember that we took any escort at all—to ride round and have a look at the neighboring country. Personally, I didn't like the look of it—real bad ground, I figured. For a start, 'twas all wild hills. Some of 'em was close above the creek below, kinda dropping down near'bouts sheer, while others was stood further back. The bottom, what I could see looking down at it, was swampy. There warn't hardly no tracks and they was shocking bad. From the hills down to the creek the going was mostly steep—nasty for guns and wagons—for soldiers, too, come to that. And second of all, everywhere was these thick, piney woods, so you couldn't see far in any direction. I couldn't make out jest what Marse Robert meant to happen. I couldn't see where the Blue men could be planning to take up a defensive position, or how we might be aimin' to attack them in that rolling country. Still, I knowed Marse Robert must have it all figured out, jest like he always did.

'Twas getting on to afternoon when he rode me along a ridge until we was right spang above a big river, jest where the creek ran into it, and there we jined up with a bunch of our cavalry. They warn't engaged with the enemy; they was jest stood a-waiting. But we could see fighting going on now all right, 'way over on t'other side of the creek. Marse Robert dismounted, held me by the bridle and stood a while, taking a good, long look.

"What do you figure those are?" he asks a young officer, pointing into the distance. "Sheep?"

"No, General," says the officer. "Those are enemy wagons."

I could tell Marse Robert didn't like this at all. He remounted at once't and we set off back the way we'd come. Near the little village we'd left, the first soldiers we met up with was General Mahone and his 'uns. Marse Robert rode up and spoke to him. Then we turned back together, 'long the ridge, with his fellas following us.

I knowed General Mahone's horse, of course—a stallion name of Brigand. You could see he'd had quite a time. He was all in a lather and 'peared jumpy and nervous. Once't, when some reflection caught him in the eye, he shied and the general had to pull him up short. You could hear the guns going hard now, over t'other side of the ridge, and 'twas plain 'nuff there must be heavy fighting over there. 'Twarn't the same fighting we'd seed earlier, though—'twas much nearer. We hadn't gone back as far as the mouth of the creek.

"I don't like this at all, Traveller," says Brigand when, he'd collected hisself together. "I reckon we're in trouble, don't you?"

"I'm blest if I know," I answered. "I thought we-all was aimin' to attack and start a battle, but now I'm not so sure."

"I figure *they're* the ones have started this here battle," says Brigand, "and I don't figure it's going any too well, neither."

"Ah, come on, when have we ever been beat?" I asked him.

"You're a good goer, Traveller," he says. "None better in the Army. But you're real thick in the head—you always was that."

Before I could answer, we came out 'long the top of the ridge. You could see straight down into the creek and right acrost the valley. And there, Tom—there was a sight I'd never seed but the once't afore. 'Twas our fellas—our fellas *running away*! Heaps and heaps of 'em, all mixed up, no muskets, no cloths on sticks, no wagons—jest an every-which-way mob on the run, coming out o' the woods. And behind them was the Blue men—a whole power of 'em, all advancing in good order.

Marse Robert pulls up short, staring. "My God!" he cries. "Has the Army been dissolved?"

What's the good of asking me? I thought. There was a horrible few moments' silence. Then General Mahone says, "No, General, here are troops ready to do their duty."

Marse Robert had only let hisself go jest for an instant. He was his old self again right quick.

"General Mahone," he says quietly, "will you please keep those people back?"

General Mahone put Brigand into a gallop and off they went to get his fellas into line of battle. And straightaway Marse Robert and me, we was going lickety-split down that hill—fast as you could on a slope like that. Somewhere 'long the way Marse Robert grabbed up one of our cloths on a stick—the old red and blue. Then he reined me in and held it up. "Steady, Traveller, steady!" I stood like a rock, right in the way of the fellas was doin' the running. Actually, some of 'em was limping and some was wounded, but

they was all a-going one way. A whole bunch went
right on past us—took no notice of us at all. Then
someone shouts out, "It's Marse Robert! It's Uncle
Robert!" And a crowd started a-gathering round us.

Marse Robert begun calling out to them, telling
them they was better'n all the Blue men in the world,
that they was his best fellas, who'd never let him
down, and all things like that. He told 'em General
Mahone and his lot was right there to back them up;
they must form up again and turn round to stop the
Blue men. That was something, I'll tell you, Tom, to
see them poor men—shredded jackets, grimy-black
faces; bleeding, a lot of 'em—cheering as we rode
'mong them and calling out to Marse Robert to lead
them back hisself agin the enemy. Thank goodness he
didn't, though. Down below I could see even more
Blue men now, coming out o' the woods, and there
was a whole lot too many for my liking.

Soon General Mahone comes back and takes the
red-and-blue cloth from Marse Robert. Marse Robert
left the reins loose on my neck and stayed where we
was at, looking out acrost the valley. There was still a
passel of our fellas coming back, but Marse Robert left
them now to form under their own officers. After a
while he said to General Mahone, like he always used
to, "Well, General, what ought we to do?" They talked
for a time and then Marse Robert called for Major
Talcott, who was jest nearby.

" 'Hope you're enjoying yourself, Traveller," says
Joker as he came up. He hisself looked near beat—
made me hope I didn't look the same.

"I ain't complaining," I said.

"That's what I've always liked about you, Traveller," replied Joker. "You've always got sech a real turn
for enjoying yourself. I believe if'n they filled your
nose bag with gravel you'd set to and fair tear into it."

'Truth was I was feeling so dismal I couldn't think

of nothing to answer back with. I could guess what must 'a happened. Some of our generals had set out to fight the Blue men on their own, without Marse Robert to tell 'em what to do. How else could we have been beat like that? This was the fourth time we'd set out to finish the Blue men and still hadn't done it. 'Course, I still knowed we would; it was jest that it was turning out to be so much harder'n I'd ever 'spected. 'Twas costing so much, and I warn't the only one, horse or man, ready to keel over. Marse Robert hisself was ready to drop in his tracks. I could feel he was; and sure 'nuff, jest a little while later, once't it was plain that those people didn't care for the notion of attacking us where we was stood ready for 'em on the ridge, he dismounted again and lay stretched out flat on the ground.

'Twas getting pretty dark when we fin'lly rode back to Old Pete's outfit, where we'd been that morning. I couldn't believe it when we formed up to set out for another night march, but set out we did. We went 'bout ten mile, Tom, if'n you can credit it, till we came to a little town; and there I was stabled for what was left of the night, while Marse Robert slept in some gentleman's house. 'Course, I was saddled up again at first light. That was always the way 'twas.

April 7, 1865. The previous day's action—known as Sayler's Creek, where Federal troops attacked in strength the worn-out and attenuated Confederate column of march, cut it in two and destroyed virtually the entire forces of Generals Ewell and Anderson, as well as a division of cavalry—is to prove fatal. General Lee has lost in all some 8,000 men, and now has left, under Longstreet, Gordon and Fitz Lee, a force of about 12,000 infantry and 3,000 cavalry, though this is melting gradually hour by hour, since many men have nothing left to give. The tiny force, opposed to 80,000 well-equipped Federal troops, has reached Farmville, where some, though not all, have been issued with rations. Since there is still a realistic possibility of joining General Johnston, Lee orders the march to continue. The army crosses the Appomattox to the north bank (which the Federals have already gained downstream), burns the bridges and once more turns westward.

First thing after he'd left the house where we'd slept, Marse Robert walks me acrost the road, hitches me to the rail of another house and walks up to the door. While I was stood waiting there, a dog came acrost the garden and we kinda fell into conversation. "We're awful poor now, you know," says this dog to me. "There's only my mistress and one or two darkies left on the place. The master—he was a soldier, like your master—he went away to the fighting and I heared he'd been killed—oh, more'n two years ago now. Mistress, she cried and cried for days. Somewhere up north 'twas, near as I can understand."

We went on talking, and after a bit I guessed, from what this dog was able to tell me, that his master must 'a been a pretty high-up cavalry officer and he'd been killed round about the same time as I hurt Marse Robert's hands.

Jest then Marse Robert came out, and the lady with him. She was crying. "I'm sorry I haven't time to stay longer," says Marse Robert, "but I couldn't pass without stopping to pay my respects." The lady did her best to stop crying. She blessed him for his kindness and petted me for a few moments while he unhitched me and got in the saddle. She was still a-standing at the gate while we rode away.

A lot of the fellas we passed now was staggering 'long like they was dead to the world. I figure some of 'em was asleep on their feet. Jest the same, I somehow felt it was going to be a lucky day for us, and that was how it turned out. It was a *great* day!

We started by crossing the river—a real big 'un, Tom, 'twas—on a bridge longer'n you'd believe. 'Twas longer'n the entire high street here in town. A whole chance of our fellas had got over t'other side already, and 'far as I could understand Marse Robert wanted everyone over quick as possible. There was two bridges—a railroad bridge and another—close together, and soon's he could Marse Robert had them both set afire, to stop the Blue men coming over behind us.

All the same, some of them *had* got acrost—don't ask me how. I often think the Blue men used to come out o' the ground, like maggots. I mean, even if you *could* stop one lot of maggots crossing a river, there'd only be another lot hatch out t'other side, wouldn't there? Anyway, there they was—cavalry, doing their best to smash up Old Pete's wagons along the road.

At the time they attacked, Marse Robert was dismounted and resting, with his back agin a tree, and I was snatching a few mouthfuls of grass. Soon's we heared the shooting, Marse Robert got up and rode me forward, with all the fellas cheering as we went past.

I seed the fight, Tom—I seed the whole thing. Our cavalry—our poor, tired-out cavalry—they smashed those people all to bits, so they ended up a-running for their lives. They was as glad to get away as chipmunks from a bobcat. In fact, a whole lot of 'em didn't get away at all; they was took prisoner. Their general hisself was took prisoner—I seed him brung in. You never knowed sech a brilliant action in all your born days. 'Twas one of our greatest ever.

"That'll stop 'em farting in our oats for a while," says Joker as the last of them disappeared through the bushes.

"If we *had* any oats," I said. "I've forgotten what they taste like."

"You can't taste dream oats," said Joker. "You don't reckon it's all a dream, do you? Only I've been asleep for about two days now, Traveller, haven't you?"

He 'peared ready to fall down, but that was how everyone felt. Jest at that very moment I seed a cavalry horse ahead of us collapse and roll over, with his man right there on his back.

And still we was beating the Blue men, all day. That same afternoon they tried to attack us again—infantry, this time—and General Mahone gave 'em another good licking. Marse Robert and me was right there, Marse Robert telling our fellas, like he always did, what grand soldiers they was and how each one of 'em was worth ten Blue men any day.

Later that afternoon, I remember, he rode me out to the edge of a hill, and we was stood near a bunch of our guns that was firing jest as fast as they could go. 'Course, I'd long ago larned to stand steady by the guns—I wish you could hear 'em, Tom; that'd be a real education for you—but I confess I didn't enjoy it. The enemy counterfire was heavy all round, but Marse Robert warn't taking a blind bit of notice—he was jest sat there watching the front and our shells bursting 'mong the enemy. That takes some doing, you know.

Well, while we was there, up comes an officer to bring Marse Robert a message, and he reached us riding 'long the side of the hill facing the enemy. Yeah, and warn't his horse happy, too? I felt real sorry for that poor animal, standing there a-trembling all over while the young officer was making his report to Marse Robert.

When he'd finished speaking, Marse Robert started in on him sharp—told him he'd come 'long the wrong side of the hill, and he'd acted bad in exposing hisself unnecessarily to enemy fire. The officer replied that he'd be 'shamed to shelter hisself when his general was sitting there in full view of those people.

"It's my duty to be here, sir!" answers Marse Robert, real blunt. "I have to see what's going on. Go back the way I told you!"

"Thank goodness for that!" mutters his horse as his master salutes and sets off without another word. "Rather you than me, Traveller!"

I don't remember a lot more 'bout that night. But I *can* recall thinking that if'n we didn't finish the Blue men soon, I reckoned we was going to have a job to do it at all. A lot of the fellas hardly looked like soldiers no more—no muskets, no knapsacks, clothes all in shreds and covered in mud, eyes jest sunk in and mouths a-hanging open. There was plenty a-laying there on the ground that couldn't be shook to their feet. There was broke-down wagons that hadn't even been pulled off the road before they was abandoned and set fire to. There was horses and mules in the mud that had struggled to get out till they couldn't struggle no longer, nostrils bunged up with mud, jest staring up at you as you went by. You never seed the like.

But jest the same, next morning—'twas bright sunshine, too—we was still a-marching, and the Blue men was still plenty scairt of us, that was plain 'nuff. They was holding right off.

That was the quietest day we'd had since we left the city. There warn't no attacks. We marched on best as we could. Come evening, our headquarters was pitched 'longside Old Pete's lot, nice and snug in a clearing in some thick woods. It came on a fine, moonlit night. We hadn't ary tents nor tables nor anything —they'd all got lost somewhere 'long the road—and Marse Robert and the rest, they sat theirselves down round a fire on the ground.

Suddenly the guns began, 'way off in front. I

knowed they was ours. I knowed it must be the beginning of an attack—I could sense it; and I warn't wrong,
neither—though I reckoned the actual fighting probably wouldn't start till next morning.

Any whichway you looked, there was a red glow
all acrost the sky. I knowed it must come from our
own campfires. I'd seed the same thing before on campaign, of course, more'n once't, but never stretching so
wide. There must 'a been an awful lot of fires. I
knowed that could only mean that Marse Robert had
concentrated his reinforcements—that means got more
fellas up, you know, Tom—for this here big battle.
They'd be cooking whatever food they'd brung with
'em and preparing for the attack tomorrow. That was
how we always done it.

From where I was picketed I seed General Gordon
come up to jine Marse Robert; and then General Fitz
Lee, our cavalry commander—him that was son of
Marse Robert's brother, so his horse once't told me.

That last meeting of our generals—for it *was* the
last meeting, though I didn't know it at the time—I
can rightly see it now: Marse Robert standing by the
fire, Old Pete sitting on a log smoking his pipe, and
General Gordon and General Fitz Lee settled nice and
comfortable on a blanket on the ground. Marse Robert
began talking quiet, like he always did, telling them
the way he seed things. I couldn't understand what he
was saying, of course, but sure 'nuff the bit I knowed
so well warn't long in coming. "Well, gentlemen, what
ought we to do?"

Natchrally, Marse Robert had got it all worked
out already—our big attack—same as he always had.
He gave out his orders and made sure they was understood; then the generals rode away, all 'ceptin' Old
Pete, who bedded down where he was, with his head
on his saddle.

I was afeared, like I always was afore a battle, but

I felt kinda excited and lively, too. I'd picked up the tense feeling that always built up at these times. The campfires making the clouds smolder and then, after a while, the distant hum and murmur of fellas on the move. I thought of Little Sorrel and Cap-in-His-Eyes riding away into the woods that morning two years before, and of Jine-the-Cavalry dashing up on Sky-lark, in the battle in the forest, to report to Marse Robert. *I'm* like them, I thought. I reckon I've earned the right now to feel that *I'm* like them. We was friends, we was comrades. Maybe—who knows?—one day people may talk about me and Marse Robert same's they will 'bout Little Sorrel and Cap-in-His-Eyes.

Before he went to sleep, Marse Robert came over and stroked me and spoke to me. He looked carefully at my hooves, too, and ran his hand 'long my back. Marse Robert was never too tired or busy to remember 'bout me. But this time I somehow felt he was more'n usually kind—more'n usually anxious that I should be jest right. "Tomorrow is in thy keeping, Lord God," he said, and then, "Good night, old friend." I thought, Well, I'll do my durnedest for him, starving or not.

In the middle of the night I heared a bunch of our men marching 'long the road close by. Somehow, I don't know why, I figured they must be Texans. I wondered whether there might be any chickens around, roostin' mighty high. I remembered how the Texans had told Marse Robert, in the wilderness, they'd drive back the Blue men on their own if'n only he'd go back. They'd done it, too. The Blue men had never liked feeling there was Texans around. They warn't going to like it no better tomorrow.

Not long after, the headquarters officers was up and dressing by the light of the fire. Marse Robert, he dressed hisself up to the nines—best uniform, red silk sash, smartest sword—the lot. He meant business for sure. When we set off, the guns was beginning again, up ahead.

'Twarn't far we had to go to the front. Our fellas —our poor, ragged fellas—had started the attack already. There was plenty of musket fire, but even though he rode me up onto the highest ground he could find we couldn't see a single thing, Marse Robert and me, on 'count of the early morning fog covering everything all over.

We waited round a considerable while, listening to the sound of the battle up ahead. Finally, Major Venable came riding back to report. I asked his horse how things was going, but Leopard had always been a durned fool—if Brigand thought *I* was stupid, he should have knowed Leopard—and he hadn't no real idea.

Well, I could always put one thing and 'nother together as well as any horse, and I could tell, from the kind of solemn way Marse Robert replied to Major Venable, that this must be important news all right. Once't, while they was a-talking, Marse Robert broke out with a kind of a burst, like he couldn't hardly control his feelings—something 'bout "I've only to ride down the lines . . ." He was real stirred, no question of that, but still I didn't know rightly what to make of it. Only, I reckoned something strange was going on—something altogether outside my experience—something that'd never happened afore now.

Pretty soon Old Pete rode up, and Marse Robert seemed to be telling him whatever 'twas he'd heared from Major Venable. General Mahone was round, too, I remember. They was all as solemn as could be, and I could jest sense a kind of—well, I'd guess you'd say a kind of graveness in all the officers and soldiers who was there with us on that little hill as the fog began lifting. General Alexander arrived, him that was chief of the guns, and Marse Robert dismounted and talked to him for quite a time, walking up and down.

After a while Marse Robert mounted again and we rode off along the road with Marse Taylor and Colonel Marshall. Sergeant Tucker, he was there, too, riding Champ, that he'd kept hisself ever since Red Shirt was killed.

'Twas now I began to feel real puzzled, 'cause when we came up to our front line, where our fellas had set up a barricade of logs acrost the road, they shifted it, and we went straight on through. I couldn't form no idea what we was s'posed to be doing, but it all 'peared to be in order, 'cause Marse Robert hisself was in charge, and the fellas gave us a cheer as we went past. There was only the four of us. In front went Champ, with Sergeant Tucker carrying a white cloth on a stick. I couldn't understand why it warn't the old red-and-blue, but I s'posed there must be some special reason. The whole business was so durned queer anyways that by this time I don't think I'd have been surprised at anything he was carrying. Then came Major Taylor and Colonel Marshall, and then me and Marse Robert a bit behind. We've never done nothing like this before, I kept a-thinking to myself. For goodness' sake, what's it all about?

Pretty soon we spotted some Blue men a ways off. And would you believe it? Colonel Marshall rode off and began *talking* to them! There warn't one of 'em even looked like he was going to shoot, but jest then I heared the bangs start up again. And those, Tom— though o' course I never guessed it at the time—those was the very last bangs I was ever to hear from that day to this.

Jest at that moment an officer I knowed by sight— one of Old Pete's staff officers, a man with only one arm—came dashing towards us on his horse from round the bend in the road behind. And I've never,

before or since, seed a horse rode so desperate hard as
that. She was a real beautiful mare, and she was going
sech a lick that she went on a considerable ways past
us before she could be pulled up at all. Poor thing, she
looked half-dead as they turned and come back to us. I
reckon it may very likely have injured her for life.

Marse Robert, who was always real considerate
for horses, as I've often told you, he shouts out to the
officer, good and strong, that he shouldn't never have
ridden his mare that way. And 'twas while the officer
was replying to Marse Robert that it suddenly came
over me what must 'a happened—why he'd ridden his
mare that way and what his news must be. There *could*
be only one reason. The Blue men had finally quit!
That was why we was out 'tween the lines with no one
firing at us! We'd done it! The Blue men was beat!
Marse Robert had knowed it, of course, but now
they'd sent, theirselves, to say so, and this officer had
brung Marse Robert the message! *That* was what the
white cloth on a stick was for—to show we knowed
we'd won. And sure 'nuff, there was Colonel Marshall
up ahead, telling some of 'em what they had to do.

For a start I couldn't rightly take it in. I felt dazed.
As we stood there, I could see more of those people—
quite a crowd—a-coming up the road. I guess they
must 'a wanted to be took prisoner, but Marse Robert,
he wouldn't have nothing to do with 'em. He jest
turned and rode me back, quite slow and easy, to
where Old Pete was waiting with our fellas on the line
of battle.

Well, 'course, after all this time I don't remember
all the details, Tom, and you wouldn't want to be
hearing 'em anyways. But I do remember Marse Robert hitching me up in an orchard a little ways back,
and then laying down hisself to take a rest on a pile of
fence rails. He must 'a felt jest like I did, I reckon—
kind of dumbfounded with what had happened.

After a while Major Talcott and Joker came up to where we was at.

"Ain't this jolly, Traveller?" says Joker when he was hitched beside me. "'Won't be nothing to do, will there? We'll have to go and pull cabs in the big city."

"I'd never thought of that!" I said. "You mean the Army'll be disbanded? Oh, I'm going to miss you, Joker! I really am."

"You want to thank your stars the Blue men missed you," said Joker.

Jest then Major Talcott came back for him, and off they went to organize a ring of soldiers round the orchard so Marse Robert and me could have some peace and quiet. Only you see, Tom, the big news seemed to be spreading fast and there was all sorts of fellas hanging around who evidently wanted to come and talk to Marse Robert 'bout it. But natcherly he didn't want to be disturbed. We was going to have work to do later on.

There warn't no noise, no commotion at all. News like this was plainly beyond all cheering. Me, I felt sort of subdued. After a while a Blue man—an officer —came riding up—everyone let him alone—with one of our fellas 'longside him to make sure he didn't get up to no tricks. Old Pete asked Marse Robert should he kick his arse—at least, I think that's what he must 'a said—but Marse Robert, he says no, he'll hear whatever it is he wants to tell him. And so he did, and I have to say that the man spoke and acted civil 'nuff.

So then we set off again, Tom, jest three of us this time—Colonel Marshall, Sergeant Tucker and Marse Robert. I couldn't imagine where we was a-going to; but not to no fighting, that was plain 'nuff. This Blue fella, he rode 'long with us. I talked a while with his horse on the way and he seemed a nice 'nuff animal. He told me he hadn't been long with the Army, 'didn't understand much 'bout it at all, but if'n it really was finished, like I said, he hisself would be only too glad.

Colonel Marshall, he'd gone on up ahead. We came to a stream, and soon as I smelt the water I realized I was as thirsty as a whole pack of mules after a day's march. Now would you credit it, Tom? At a time like this, when we was off to larn those people their manners and he had everything else in the world to be thinking 'bout, Marse Robert drew rein and waited till I'd drunk all I wanted. Yes, he did. After that we went on.

We came to a house—jest an ordinary house, like plenty of others, with a flight of steps, some pillars and a verandah with a balcony above. Marse Robert dismounted in the yard and walked up the steps, while Tucker took me and Champ off round the side. He found a place in the shade and settled hisself there, 'long with the two of us and Colonel Marshall's horse, Mercury. Everything was quite quiet and peaceful— 'twas a fine afternoon—and soon I'd near'bouts forgot what we was there for. A good horse never has no problem loafing, you know.

After some considerable time we heared a whole bunch of horsemen coming. They was all Blue men— you could smell that as they came close. The officers must 'a dismounted in front of the house, 'cause the soldiers—some of 'em—led the horses round to where we was at. I noticed that Tucker didn't talk to the soldiers, so I took my lead from him, and didn't set out to talk to the horses neither. There was one black horse, I remember, pulled up 'longside me; he told me his name was Cincinnati. He acted quite easy and sociable—you couldn't dislike him. I acted the same, which was what I felt Marse Robert would want. But pretty soon his soldier led him off a ways, so we was left by ourselves again. We was free to graze, and I remember the dratted flies was a nuisance. 'Twas coming on to summer, you see.

I reckon we was a-waiting round till pretty well halfway through the afternoon—quite a while—but still Marse Robert hadn't come out. I know what he's doing, I thought. He's giving them Blue men a real good piece of his mind. And I sure know one thing he *ain't* saying, this time. "Well, gentlemen, what ought we to do?"

'Twas well past the heat of the day, and me and Champ was stood head to tail, a-swishing away, when at last I heared Marse Robert's voice, from round the front, calling, "Orderly! Orderly!" I didn't recognize it for a moment—he sounded kinda gruff and a bit choky. I guess he must 'a been pretty tired after taking all that time to tell those Blue generals 'zackly what he thought of 'em. Tucker answered him quick as a flash, though. He led me round to the foot of the steps and put on my bridle. Marse Robert hisself drew my forelock out from under the browband, parted it and smoothed it down, so I looked as smart as I ought to. It reminded me of the young fella who'd left one of his trouser legs outside his boot. We warn't goin' to have none of that, not riding away from those people. Then Marse Robert mounted up, and Tucker and Colonel Marshall, too.

Jest at that moment one of the Blue men—somehow I got the feeling he must be an important fella—walked down the steps from the porch, stopped in his tracks and took off his hat to Marse Robert. As we set off, there was a whole chance of Blue men standing all around, and every single one of 'em took off his hat. And I should durned well think so, too! I thought. That'll be something for 'em all to remember when they get home. 'Twas the proudest moment of my life, Tom—and of Marse Robert's, too, I'm sure 'nuff.

I couldn't help wondering—and I've often won-

dered since—jest what Marse Robert could have been
saying to those people for all that time. But I guess he
told 'em straight out that if'n they didn't pack up and
go home right away we'd be 'bliged to set to and blow
'em all into the middle of next winter, jest like we had
in the snow and jest like we had in the forest; and
they'd better get that and get it good. It took so long, I
s'pose, 'cause they must 'a been trying to persuade
him to alter some of the particulars and let 'em down
easy. I've often imagined in my mind, since then,
those Blue men sitting there, in that house, and dick-
ering with Marse Robert, realizing their big mistake
and that this was the reckoning come round at last;
and Marse Robert jest sat there, kind and quiet like he
always was, telling 'em firmly that things had got to be
jest like he said. Well, the job was done good and
proper, that's for sure. When he came out, they hadn't
'nother word to say, an' that I seed for myself.

We rode along nice and steady, me and Marse
Robert in front this time, and came up the hillside,
through our pickets and back into our lines. Marse
Robert plainly warn't fixing to be high an' mighty
'bout what he'd done—that warn't never his way. I
could feel him sitting upright, not moving in the saddle, looking straight ahead and determined to avoid a
lot of fuss. Me, I jest kept going, like he wanted.

But 'course our fellas, they warn't going to let us
get away with that. They commenced to cheering.
They cheered considerable—jest like they had after
the battle in the woods, two years before. Then they
broke ranks and come a-crowding round us. I tried to
go on—that was what Marse Robert wanted—but
they pressed round hard, shouting "General! General!"
and grabbing at us from all sides.

Marse Robert took off his hat, and I tried some
gentle pushing and shoving, but no way. I had to give
it up—the road was jammed solid. Marse Robert

reined me in and began talking to the fellas. I managed to get some of it. "Men, I have done the best I could for you. . . . You will all go home. . . ."

At that, some of the fellas actually began crying for joy. Others seemed sort of dazed and bewildered. I remember one soldier shouting "Blow, Gabriel, blow!" and throwing his musket down on the ground. "Blow" means "go away," "go home," Tom, you know. Gabriel must 'a been his buddy, I s'pose. People was catching a-holt of Marse Robert's hands, his coat, his boots—anything at all. Those who couldn't do that grabbed at me, stroked my nose, patted my neck and my flanks. We was jest surrounded. I can smell them now. They smelt what you'd call pungent.

You'll reckon I must 'a been thinking how fine it all was—that this was the grand reward for all them hours hungry in the mud and snow, all them nights on the march, all those bullets zipping past your ears and shells bursting round your hooves. But 'tell you the truth, Tom, all I was thinking at the time was I could do with a feed and a rest. I'd had as much as I could take. I'd knowed since the morning that we'd won, and now I was suffering a kind of a letdown. I felt ready to fair go to pieces.

We came back to the orchard at last. Marse Robert dismounted and commenced to walking up and down under the trees. He didn't show it, but I guess he must 'a been in such high cotton he couldn't keep still. I was roped nearby, so I jest put in some more grazing. Pretty soon, little groups of Blue men began coming up and speaking mighty polite to the headquarters majors—'far as I could make out, begging to be 'lowed to pay their respects to Marse Robert. Marse Robert, though, he wouldn't have nothing to do with 'em— what did they 'spect, the durned fools? He simply drew hisself up and glared at them. Some of 'em had the impudence to come up close and take off their hats. Marse Robert jest touched the rim of his hat back. 'Course, he warn't going to lower hisself to cuss at them. He jest wanted to get rid of 'em quick as he could. I don't know, maybe they wanted to make sure he knowed they'd hollered 'nuff after the licking they'd had. Anyways, they was politely showed off.

Jest the same, they did do some good, those people. They carried out the orders Marse Robert must 'a given that they was to hand us over an elegant sufficiency of their own rations. The rations arrived by the wagonload, and you should jest have seed those people handing them out to our fellas, polite and mannerly as you please! There was even some laughing and joking 'tween 'em! Looking at 'em, I thought, That's the difference between our outfit and theirs. We'd been ready to give all we had—to starve, to go sleepless for days, to march without boots, to lie in rags in the rain. The Blue men, they looked like they'd jest walked out of some fine lady's house after a dinner party. Call those people soldiers? I thought. No wonder they've been beat.

It was nigh on sunset when Marse Robert bridled me up hisself and rode about a mile back to headquarters. All the way, as we went, there was folks rushing from each side of the road—two solid walls of our fellas, cheering and yelling. That Yell—I couldn't believe I was hearing it for the last time. I did my best to live up to the occasion—to do Marse Robert credit, like I reckoned I always had. I kept tossing my head, looking to one side and t'other and picking up my hooves like we was on full-dress parade. The fellas was shouting, "Bless you! Bless you, General Lee!" And I even heared that special word they'd called out two years before, when the woods was on fire—"Surrendered, General! Surrendered!"

When   we   reached   headquarters—someone seemed to have found our tents by now—even Marse

Robert couldn't entirely keep from tears. 'Course, 'twas the relief and the reaction. He spoke to as many of the fellas as he could, shook hands with 'em and all that, but in the end he finally took off his hat one last time and went into his tent. Good old Dave led me away for the biggest feed of oats I'd had in months— they was Blue oats, I guess—'much as I could eat and more.

I slept pretty sound that night, Tom, I can tell you. But not as sound as we'll sleep now, in this dry straw, under a roof; 'cause before morning it commenced to rain, and by first light the rain was falling steady. Still, never mind 'bout that for now. Let's go to sleep. 'Nother time I'll tell you how we came away, and how we finally fetched up here.

XX

DID LUCY Long tell you 'bout her accident yesterday, Tom? She didn't? I'm surprised. It could 'a been pretty bad. She's lucky it was no worse, and 'far as I can make out, it's entirely due to Marse Robert that it warn't. She could have choked to death.

You know that little carriage, don't you, that the old lady has for going out on fine afternoons? Marse Robert got it 'specially, a while back. Sure, I figured it was a good idea, but I figured too that I'd be durned if'n I was going to pull it. 'Course, I'd do anything for Marse Robert—anything within reason, I mean, like shells, bullets, starving, forty mile a day—but a horse in my position, he jest can't be seed out in public doing work the like o' that. 'Twas bad 'nuff having to go through town 'longside that old Frisky. Marse Robert evidently feels the same, 'cause I've never been called upon to go in shafts. If I had, I guess I'd have been 'bliged to object, but fortunately the situation's never arisen. No, pulling the old lady out in the little carriage has always been a job for Lucy.

Well, seems that yesterday, when Lucy was harnessed up for the afternoon outing, she could feel right away that her collar was way too tight. Personally, I'd have showed my feelings, but of course Lucy's a gentle, docile kind of creature, and she told me she reckoned she'd jest put up with it. Marse Robert was driving, as usual, but this time he warn't carrying the old lady. 'Seems it was Marse Rooney's wife and the baby. Marse Robert didn't notice nothing wrong with Lucy's collar—and that ain't like him, you know. I've often told you how he's always paid attention to every last little thing 'bout us—shoes, harness and all the rest—even under fire. It only goes to show—I've been feeling it for a while now—that he's not altogether in top shape.

Anyhow, off they went to call on some friends in town, and Lucy told me that while she was waiting round, the collar seemed less uncomfortable. But then, coming back—up that stiff slope round to the front of the house—it suddenly caught her—choked her—and she stumbled and passed right out. When she came to, she was a-laying in the road with Marse Robert kneeling beside her. He'd got the collar off and was calling hisself all manner of fool for not spotting the trouble earlier. He kept stroking her and telling her he felt real 'shamed of hisself after all she'd done for him. She was right 'nuff in a while, but it left her shaky and glad to be back in stables. 'Course, Lucy never was what you'd really call a sturdy mare—nice, quiet horse was what Jine-the-Cavalry was after for Marse Robert —but jest the same I don't blame her over this. Must 'a been a nasty shock.

It's strange, though, that Marse Robert *didn't* spot it earlier. I always spot things 'bout *him* earlier'n any of the human beings he has to do with. You recollect I told you how he was took sick a while before our great victory in the forest; how Perry made him go to bed and then they was 'bliged to move him out of camp for a time? Well, right now he strikes me as having the beginnings of something like that there all over again. He's older, of course; he *feels* older, I mean. I can tell it from the way he rides. He finds my old buck-trot

harder'n he used to, and he seems to get tired quicker.
Jest the same, I know he still feels closer to me than he
does to anyone else. When we get out together on one
of these fine fall afternoons, it always perks his spirits
up and after a while he's a different man. I wish we
could light out on another good, long trip together—
you know, for several days, like in the past—but I
guess there must be too much to do, what with him
having to command the country an' all.

I never did finish telling you, did I, how we came
away from that last camp and what happened after the
Blue men quit? Well, I jest recall one thing and another. For instance, the morning after their surrender,
when every one of us, man and horse, was feeling the
better for a few good feeds, one of our officers comes
riding up to Marse Robert's headquarters to bring him
a message. His horse was tethered near me, so I asked
him what was doing.

"Why," says this horse, "it seems the enemy's
commander in chief's ridden over to pay his respects
to Marse Robert. 'Course, he's been stopped on our
picket lines and told to cool his heels till Marse Robert's been informed and decided whether he can be
bothered to see him or not."

He'd hardly told me this when out comes Marse
Robert in a great hurry, has me saddled up and off we
go real quick. 'Way I seed it, Marse Robert wanted to
act generous and be polite to this here Blue general.
We finally came up with him waiting on a little hill
between the lines. Both generals raised their hats,
shook hands and started in talking. No doubt the fella
had come to get some further orders from Marse Robert, 'cause they was talking a goodish while—maybe
as long as it takes to groom a horse. That black horse—
that Cincinnati—he was there, but we didn't hardly
converse none. Not that I was out to show any ill-

feeling, any more'n Marse Robert was; 'twas jest that we warn't hitched near 'nuff each other.

Marse Robert and me was on our way back to camp when we met another Blue general, with some of his officers, and he offs with his hat to Marse Robert, too, real respectful, and says him howdy.

Marse Robert shook hands with 'em all, real grave and dignified, and then we-all rode back to our headquarters together. As we came past our boys, they commenced to cheering, like they always did. The Blue general, he had the impudence to tell his orderly to unroll one of their cloths on a stick—the one with stripes on. One of our fellas shouts out, "Damn your old rag! We-all are cheering General Lee!" The Blue general, I figure he looked pretty small, but jest the same Marse Robert invited him into his tent for a talk and to make sure he understood his orders. They parted quite friendly. Yeah, I thought, you're civil 'nuff now you're licked. But you know, Tom, I don't think Marse Robert felt bitter towards him at all. He was polite and kind to him, like he always was to everyone—humans and animals, too.

'Twas two days later, if'n I remember rightly, that we lit out for home. All our fellas and horses was setting out to home, this way and that, south, east and west. There was jest Colonel Marshall and Marse Taylor with me and Marse Robert, and another officer, who was sick, in an ambulance. The Blue men gave us a mounted guard of honor to 'company us 'long the road out of camp a good ways.

'Twas a four-day trip, taking it easy, back to the big city. We camped one night, but t'other two we stopped off at gentlemen's homes. There warn't a great deal happened. One day I cast a shoe, but that was soon put right. Marse Robert seed to it that I had feeds of oats—and mighty good they was, too. 'Twas raining heavy, I remember, the afternoon we finally rode into the city, and I was plenty muddy—tired, too, and showing it, I 'spect. The place looked pretty knocked-about, and you could see and smell there'd been a lot of burning. Still, I thought, that's not surprising after all the fighting. Marse Robert'll soon change all that, now he's in full command. And in fact I did spot quite a passel of Blue men around. They'd evidently been brung in to start cleaning up the mess they'd made and get down to putting things to rights.

We can't have looked all that smart, you know, Tom, what with the campaign we'd jest fought, the rain and the mud and the journey, and our rickety old wagons coming 'long behind. But that didn't stop whole crowds of people turning out to cheer us. If'n you'll believe it, even some of the Blue men was jining in the cheering. Knowed what was good for 'em, I reckon.

We came to the house they'd got ready for Marse Robert. There was people a-crowding all round, cheering and crying, and he shook hands and spoke to as many of 'em as he could. Finally he went indoors and I went off to stables.

Well, after that I got a real good rest, Tom. I can't tell you how 'greeable it was after all we'd been through—no more bugles, no more night marches, no more bangs to drive you crazy; easy exercise and plenty to eat. Marse Robert, he had a good rest, too. For quite some days, in fact, he didn't leave the house at all. But I guess that now he knowed he was going to become commander of the country—soon's everything was ready, that is—he had a whole lot to be thinking 'bout. Well, 'stands to reason, don't it?

When I was taken out for exercise, I noticed there was often a Blue man standing sentry outside the front door. Yeah, I thought, good idea—let one of *them* stand about in the wind and rain, 'stead of our fellas. That really gave me satisfaction.

Then, one day—I s'pose it must 'a been 'bout a month later, or maybe a little more—Marse Robert had me saddled up and off we hightailed, jest us two and no one with us, acrost town and out into the country. And would you believe it, Tom, we rode past that same village where I'd been in my very first battle three years before, and then right by the diggings where we fought those people the previous year? It all seemed so strange—the empty trenches, the silence, the greenness—you know? It felt—it *smelt*—like another place, but I remembered it all right. So did Marse Robert; he showed that. Well, 'course, it's bound to make him feel sad, I thought, but leastways we don't have to feel 'twas for nothing. If I could talk, I'd tell him that—I'd remind him of all that them poor men and horses made happen.

Anyways, we soon left it behind. I wondered where we could be going—somehow it didn't feel like more soldiering; and it warn't. Turned out we was off for a holiday at a country house—nice old-fashioned kind of a place 'twas; belonged to one of our artillery officers. Soon's I seed him, I remembered him well.

Gee, Tom, that was fine, that holiday! When we arrived, they didn't 'pear to be 'specting Marse Robert, but jest the same they was delighted to see him, same as people are everywhere.

"And of course Traveller's going to have a holiday," he said. "He's earned it more'n anyone. Traveller's going to have hisself a *real* holiday!"

Right off he turned me loose on the lawn. The midsummer grass was long and jest prime, more'n 'nuff for a whole power of horses. I ate it right down short. Marse Robert, he says no more corn for me—I'd had 'nuff of that, campaigning. He'd sit comfortable in the shade and watch me enjoy myself. I used to roll in that grass, Tom. I very soon picked out my favorite rolling places. You know, I'd almost forgotten 'bout

rolling. I didn't realize, till I had it back, how much I'd
missed it. Soldier horses don't get much chance to roll
at leisure, let alone settle on favorite places. But on
this holiday I made a proper job of it. I'd start by
sniffing the ground and pawing at it. Then I'd put my
nose to it and shake my tail. Then I'd go down fore-
quarters first and rub my withers well into the grass.
After that I'd lie on my back, squirm about and scratch
the top of my head and neck—yeah, and my tail, too.
In my best place there was a nice rock to scratch your
rump on as well. Get up, shake myself all over and
back to grazing. Think of it! I could take as long as I
liked over a roll and do it as often as I pleased! And
Marse Robert sat there watching, jest as happy as I felt
myself!

We visited quite a few houses round about. Very
light work. Plenty of friendly horses. Still, like all
good things, that holiday came to an end, and back we
rode to the city.

Somehow, though, I got the feeling that Marse
Robert didn't want to command the country and do all
his judging and deciding and palavering from a headquarters in the city. I guess he had a problem. He
wanted to live in a nice, quiet, countrified place, but of
course it had to be somewheres he could have all his
advisers and headquarters people round him, too. He
wanted to combine his commanding with some peace
and quiet. He needed to be out of the way of the people forever cheering and yelling and shaking hands;
and of course now he could have it a whole lot more
comfortable than them old tents. We warn't going
fighting no more—never again.

We tried this place and that. Nigh on a month
after the holiday I've jest told you about, Marse Custis
rode me 'bout thirty mile out of the city. Marse Robert, the old lady and the rest, they came along on the
boat. First of all we was a-visiting with a lady. Then

we-all lived a while in a little wooden cottage, an' that really *was* out in the country. I enjoyed it; Marse Robert and me used to ride round the neighborhood plenty. I thought at the time that he was looking out on his own 'count for the right place to take up this commanding business. But if only I'd knowed, all that was being took care of.

'Twas early fall, five years ago now, when Marse Robert and me lit out on our journey to come here. We was four days altogether on the road. 'Reckon we might have done twenty-five or thirty mile each day— jest the two of us. We took it easy; the weather was real sultry and the flies was jest as tiresome as usual. We stopped off at gentlemen's homes along the way. 'Twas the third day when we rode up high into the mountains—these mountains, Tom—and next afternoon we rode down into town here.

'Twas jest like Marse Robert—the way he arrived where he was going to take up command. No show, no fuss. But of course we was expected people recognized him right away. There was some of our old soldiers happened to be in the street at the time, and they welcomed him jest the way you'd reckon they would.

I remember for the first few days we lodged out at the Baths. Wonder how often we've ridden out there since? That was while they was finishing getting everything ready for him here, you see.

Some of his counselors and advisers nowadays are men who used to be our Army officers. For instance, one's the chief of the guns, General Pendleton. I often see him around. I wonder what he does now there ain't no guns?

Marse Robert—well, 'course, Tom, you know yourself how busy he is all the time, talking and advising and giving out the orders. Commanding a whole country—gosh sakes! It must be an even bigger job than commanding the Army—'ceptin' there's no enemy to mess us around, of course. Important folks come to see him, and sometimes he has to go away, too, on 'count of this here commanding—often for a good while. I never know when he's coming back. Well, I 'spect there's still some Blue men left in back parts who need a good talking to now and then, to keep 'em in line. But I always know the time'll come when he's back and we're off again, jest the two of us, for a good, long ride through the fall woods, with the red and yellow leaves dropping; or maybe the spring woods, when the groundhogs are out and you can smell the new greenery. Not a commander, not a great general's campaigning horse; jest a couple of friends who've seed a lot together and understand each other through and through.

I often think I must be the luckiest horse alive. Sure, I've seed some rough times—there's no denying that. Oh, I've seed terrible things, Tom, and no one can say I ain't seed hardships, too. But for near nine years I've had the greatest General in the world for a master, and if'n there's anyone, horse or man, who's served him better, I'd like to know who 'tis.

I've only one regret, even though it's maybe kind of a fool one. I often wish we'd managed to get to that War place, Jim and me—that there War we started out for, you know. I've been to The White, sure 'nuff, and that was a real fine place. But I never did get to the War, on 'count of I was handed over to Captain Joe and the major in them there mountains full of rain. I guess maybe it's stupid of me to have any regrets at all, considerin' how lucky I've been, but in my imagination I can jest see that War—all green grass and oats and friends—horses from whom you never have to part. I'd like to have seed it, jest once't, but of course I wouldn't stay. No Marse Robert—no, I wouldn't like that.

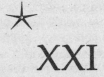

XXI

COME IN, Tom, come in! I'm real glad to see you. I'll be glad of some company. Settle yourself down. It's a sharpish night, ain't it? Soon be winter now. Leaves have turned—started falling, too.

Can you kindly listen to me for a while? I need to talk. 'Truth is, I'm puzzled. I'm a mighty puzzled horse. It's being without Marse Robert, really. 'Course, I'm used to him going off on these here commanding trips. He's been away a heap this last spring and summer. Must be a deal of commanding to be done, all up and down the country. All spring he was away and then again best part of a month during the hot weather. But when he came back, 'bout a month ago, I was 'specting he'd be settled in for the fall and the winter. Yeah, I was really looking forward to plenty of good rides over the hills and all round and 'bout—even if'n they usually are shorter nowadays.

We was doing pretty well for that till a short while back. But of course the heavy rain and the flooding round town has been all agin getting out for riding. The whole town's been surrounded by floodwaters. That's what's kept him out of the saddle, for sure.

Well, but 'tell you the truth, I can't for the life of me make out whether he's here'bouts or not. He ain't been down to the stable—not for days—and that ain't like him, you know, without he's away on this commanding business. Perhaps he *has* had to make another trip—only somehow it jest don't feel like it usually does when he's not here to home.

Another thing: I'm seriously wondering whether we-all may not be going off on another campaign soon. Yeah, a real campaign! You could see things that way. And do you know, Tom, I reckon I wouldn't altogether mind if we was? Well, 'course I don't want to do forty mile a day in the mud and live on half-rations —'don't know whether I could do it no more, anyway. And yet—well, to hear the bangs again, to see horses and fellas I'd remember from the soldiering days—I guess this last day or two's kind of stirred up my memories. If'n Marse Robert's going, then *I'm* going— I'm sure 'nuff of that. He'd never dream of campaigning without me. If those people are up to their mean tricks again, then he's going to need me right 'nuff.

This last couple of days, you see, it's kind of 'peared like we was getting ready for 'nother campaign. Well, it does and yet it don't. Some ways it don't feel jest 'zackly right. But—well, I can't make it out, and that's the truth. No more can't Lucy. We was talking 'bout it in the field only s'afternoon.

It all started yesterday—early afternoon. I was in here as usual, hoping the rain had finally let up and maybe Marse Robert would be coming 'long for one of our rides. Like I told you, I've been missing 'em. And then in come the stableman, Isaiah, 'long with two other fellas. I called to mind the smell of them two right away, but I didn't recognize them directly, 'cause they warn't dressed like soldiers. But then I recollected who they was. They'd been in our Army sure 'nuff. One of 'em I didn't recall—not where I'd seed him, I mean—although I knowed he must 'a been one of our soldiers. But t'other I could mind: he was one of General Ringlets' men. I remembered Marse Robert speak-

ing to him after the attack that bad afternoon in the
big battle up north—when we was down among the
fellas coming back out of it, and cheering them up.

One of these fellas says to t'other, "For gosh
sakes, ain't he gone real white!" T'other one didn't say
nothing. They both jest stood staring at me a while,
and then they commenced to stroking me and talking
to me like they was real happy to see me again. But
the queer thing was I could tell they was feeling sad,
too. There was something awful downhearted 'bout
how they talked and the way they set about their
business. Well, you know, Tom, soldiers generally
laugh and joke, and sometimes cuss too. But there was
none o' that. These fellas conducted theirselves what
you'd call mighty solemn.

They put on my bridle and saddled me up, and
then they covered the saddle and bridle all over with
black cloth. I've never knowed that to be done before,
and I'll be durned if I can tell what manner of use it
was, neither. Still, 'twarn't uncomfortable and didn't
make no difference that I could tell. Then they led me
outside. I reckoned either Marse Robert—or someone
—would be going to ride me, but it didn't turn out
that way. Truth to tell, 'twas altogether different from
anything I've ever knowed round these here parts or
anywheres else.

Outside Marse Robert's house was a whole crowd
of folks. They was all mighty quiet, and that was
queer for a start, don't you reckon? The fella in charge
seemed to be Captain White. You know him, Tom,
don't you? He lives around here: talks to Marse Robert, advises him, helps him with the business of commanding and all that. He's always been a great friend
of the family—went with us on that trip to The White
a year or two back—the trip when I met Ruffian again
up in the hills. Well, he was getting all these folks
formed up in a kind of line, pretty much as though we

was going soldiering again. In fact, the ones up front *was* soldiers, in uniform, lined up real military-looking. They couldn't have looked more serious if'n we was going off to do some fighting. For a while I thought we was; only then I seed they hadn't ary muskets or bayonets, so I figured that whatever 'twas going to be, it warn't no battle.

Directly behind the soldiers was a kind of a long cart, all glass, with a box in it. They warn't fixing to put me in the shafts, though—the horses was already hitched. I'd never seed them horses before, and I didn't get a chance to talk to 'em, 'cause my two old soldiers led me straight round behind the cart and held me there steady. I hadn't nothing to do. Back of me was this great, long line of people. Some I knowed and some I didn't: friends and helpers of Marse Robert, fellas I'd seed round the place, people from downtown, quite a few rough fellas who looked like they'd been our soldiers. And a heap of ladies, too—a lot of 'em crying. 'Tell you the truth, Tom, I felt real confused. I couldn't make it out at all. To begin with, I was stamping my hooves and jerking my head around, but the two old soldiers calmed me down, stroking me and talking quiet, and pretty soon I steadied down.

Well, after a bit we-all moved off, but we didn't go that far. We jest went a ways up the road and through the grounds, from Marse Robert's house as far as that house with the pointed tower on it—you know, the one nobody lives in, where they sometimes have meetings and singing and the rest of it. There was fellas walking alongside this glass cart in front of me—spaced out regular all around it—and they got together and lifted the box out and carried it in. Most of the people went in after them, but I didn't hear ary singing nor anything of that. I jest stood around some more, and then my old soldiers brung me back here.

Well, then, this morning they did it all again, only

this time there was a whole lot more to it—more people, further to go and it took a lot longer. I was led
along behind that there cart jest like before, only this
time there was nothing inside. They had a band for
music, jest like the old Army days, and there was—
Oh, you heared them, did you, Tom? 'Scared you silly,
did it? Well, now you know what the guns sound like.
Sure, I guess them bangs *are* 'nuff to scare you silly till
you've got used to them. Yes, those was guns right
'nuff, Tom—firing steady—but I couldn't make out
where the fighting could be. 'Twas somewhere real
close, though. Those guns was right here in town. I
was 'specting to see Marse Robert any moment, or
maybe Old Pete, but they warn't around. Marse Taylor was there, though, and Major Venable and a whole
crowd of our officers and soldiers. Smelt pretty much
the same as the Army always used to, only cleaner.
But they warn't dressed like soldiers, and 'sides there
was a whole passel of ladies as well—Miss Life and
Miss Agnes I seed, and a lot more—friends of Marse
Robert as well as strangers.

There warn't no cloths on sticks, though, nor
none of that. Everything 'peared to be black—black
clothes, black ribbons, all the houses hung with black,
and I had this black stuff hung all over my saddle and
bridle again. We set off real ceremonious and marched
all round town, with the music playing, bells ringing
and guns banging. Whatever 'twas all 'bout, I could
tell it was something mighty serious and grand. The
whole town was out, and crowds of people—strangers
—had come in from out of town, too. 'Twas a real nice
morning, and I kept hoping it might end with a ride
out into the country, but all I got was this here slow
walking along behind the long cart.

'Twarn't a good column of march. It didn't feel
right at all. In fact, it was real terrible. I sure hoped the
Blue men warn't nowhere around to start an attack. It

all felt mighty chancy to me. Marse Robert warn't with us, we hadn't no cavalry that I could see, and our soldiers hadn't ary muskets. It's like I've always told you, Tom: if Marse Robert ain't there to see to it, none of 'em can't never get nothing right by theirselves. 'Twas a real mess, and we was lucky not to be attacked.

When we finally got back again to the pointed tower house, there was a huge crowd of people stood there, and not a musket or a horse between the lot of 'em! No one raised a cheer or a yell and no one gave ary orders. Some of 'em went inside and some stayed outside. Talk 'bout disorder! Me, I stood quiet and steady 'nuff, but I was jest wishing I could see Joker again, or any of the old headquarters horses. I felt real perplexed with all this soldiering that warn't soldiering, and in the end I was glad 'nuff, I can tell you, when I was led back here and things 'parently finished without no trouble. Blest if'n I know what it can all have been 'bout.

'Course, you and me—well, all of us animals, really—we can't always understand what human beings are up to, can we? I sometimes wonder whether *they* do. I guess all this carrying-on must 'a made some sort of sense, but I'll tell you, I'll feel a whole lot happier when Marse Robert gets back and things start being properly managed again. I mean, imagine having ladies round when there's guns a-firing! Did you ever hear of anything the likes of that? Well, I guess you wouldn't know, Tom, not being a soldier, but you can take it from me that that's blame nonsense for a start. And then, marching all round town as slow as that—no cavalry, no wagons, no ambulances—and ending up by coming back to the same place. I reckon it's lucky for us Marse Robert put those people down good and proper when he did—finished their tricks once't and for all. Else they'd surely have taken advantage of us today.

I'll tell you, I can't wait for Marse Robert to come back. The floods are pretty well down now, I reckon. It's turning out a nice fall—sunny days—good for riding. Yeah, I tell you what he'll do. He'll come in, maybe saddle me up hisself, see to the girth and that— you know I've often told you how considerate and particular he is—and then off we'll go through the woods. "General Lee, I feel mighty like cheering you!" Oh, that was dead funny, that old fella all alone up in the woods! Or maybe we'll go off on the trail for three-four days, like we have before. Now that really would be something!

Say, Tom, I'll tell you what. You jump up there on the manger—that's right!—and act like you was Marse Robert. It's early morning on campaign. You look all round camp to see that everything's been tidied up and fixed right for starting off. And I'm waiting here, saddled up, with Joker and the others. That's it—fine! Now you turn around this way, and what do you say? You don't remember? I'll tell you. You say, "Strike the tent!"